The False Knight

Harry Walker

To anybody who feels like they haven't got a voice, find your voice and share it. You'll make the world a brighter place.

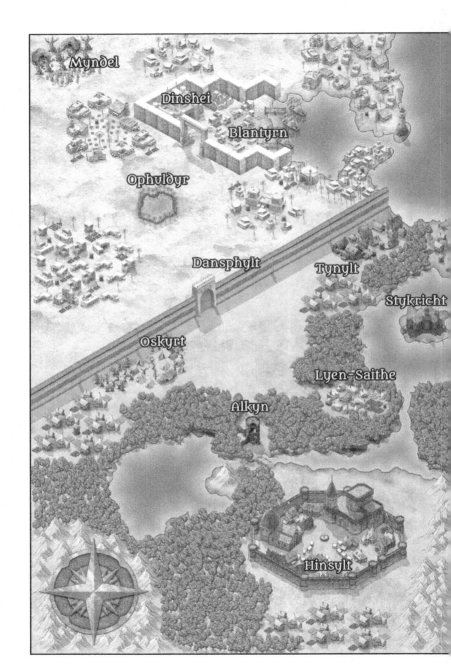

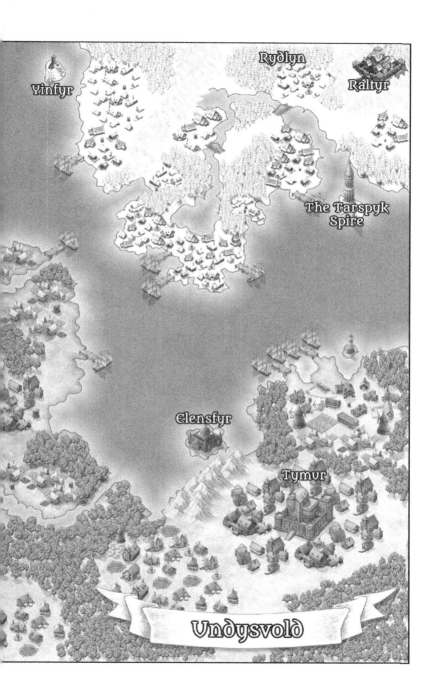

Yinfyr

Rydlyn

Raltyr

The Tarspyk
Spire

Elensfyr

Tymvr

Undysvold

A Scrap of Faith

The False Knight had spent the last five hard years alone on the road with just a scrap of faith to keep him going. Blynkiln often questioned if that scrap of faith was misplaced. Yet, here he was, still standing and somehow still struggling on, with nothing but that little scrap of probably misplaced faith to keep him alive.

He was exhausted, practically dragging his sore legs along. He didn't know how much longer he could go on living like this, if he was being honest with himself.

To make everything worse, and to beat that little scrap of faith out of him altogether, he stood just a few strides from the base of an enormous shadow. Blynkiln had to crane his neck up at the grey-eyed man casting the shadow, since he was about seven feet tall.

He cleared his throat as the wind whistled around him. A soft rain pattered down on his head and shoulders, covering the tall grass with shining beads of water. Water wouldn't be the only thing covering these blades of grass soon, no doubt.

"I mean no trouble," The False Knight stated. "I'm just looking to cross that bridge behind you."

The enormous man rested all of his weight on the hilt of his greatsword, the point of the blade stabbing into the ground.

"You are trouble itself, False Knight, a stain on the honour of true knights," the man replied.

Of course I am, Blynkiln thought. His reputation wasn't the greatest, not after what he'd done five years ago.

Blynkiln tried to seek a peaceful resolution. Maybe he was trying to spare his already aching body, or maybe he was trying to save this man's life.

"I had no choice. If I didn't kill them, they would've killed me. Besides, it was half a decade ago. Move on and let me pass through," The False Knight said, keeping his tone flat and void of emotion.

His enemy stood unmoving, unwavering. The bottom of his grey surcoat flapped in the wind as the rain bounced off the top of his greathelm.

"Half a decade ago, three centuries ago, it makes little difference. You cut down a dozen faithful knights, and for what? To save your own worthless neck?"

Blynkiln couldn't say that this great big bastard was lying, but the words stung all the same. It seemed that this giant of a man was set on killing him. So, The False Knight wearily unsheathed his sword, knowing this conflict had only one end. The one where he'd cross that bridge covered in sweat, likely blood, too, feeling even more tired and sore.

"Put up your sword, I'm done talking to you," Blynkiln said, his voice cold and heartless.

His enemy rolled his muscular shoulders and stretched his neck out left and right as if he came here to spar rather than to face his death.

There's a simple joy in killing arrogant shitheads like him.

"So be it. People will tell tales of Talfyn the Tall, the slayer of The False Knight, for generations," the enormous man growled.

Talfyn's legs were as thick as tree trunks, but not very well protected. Other than that, he wore a greathelm and light chain armour.

He'll have good reach and power, no doubt, I won't be able to match it. Big doesn't always mean slow, but the chances are, he won't be faster than me.

Blynkiln weighed Talfyn up, eyes narrowed, with his hands wrapped tightly around the grip of his sword. He'd put this sword to work for years. It was a gift from the very woman he searched for, the only woman he'd ever loved, and the one he'd been forced to separate from five years ago.

The narrow blade of his sword glinted as he angled it, ready to attack. The steel caught the light of the slowly emerging sun, highlighting the sharpness of the blade. It had been crafted by the Dwarven forgers up in the North-East, near where he'd grown up, and it had never lost its edge or shine in all that time.

After a moment of circling each other from a distance, they both shuffled closer. With a sharp exhale, Talfyn swung first, not wasting any more time. Blynkiln stepped around the attempted blow.

Keep sharp, lad, eyes front, Fuldyn's voice reminded him, her lessons always with him.

He took a swing for himself once he'd stepped around Talfyn, aiming to cut him across the leg. The giant of a man had seen it coming and blocked the swing with ease.

The False Knight leapt back and returned to circling his opponent, playing it safe for now.

Talfyn wielded the greatsword as if it had no weight. He released a flurry of slashes, forcing Blynkiln to knock the powerful swings aside with his own narrow-bladed sword.

Talfyn had more speed than Blynkiln had anticipated. Two of the slashes came close to making him bleed or worse. He swept each blow aside, the vibrations from the contact running down his hand and arm as he gritted his teeth and tried to hold as much ground as he could, keeping himself steady.

Talfyn lunged forwards, close to catching Blynkiln out, but thankfully not close enough. He ducked under the lunge.

As he spun up and around, a harsh blow crashed against the back of his head. He stumbled and wobbled a few steps before regaining his balance.

Blynkiln couldn't allow himself to lose any more ground despite the rattling and banging in his head. He redirected Talfyn's endless attacks, swatting the greatsword aside. Every time steel met steel, the vibrations clawed down his entire body, never letting him catch a breath.

He kept the woman he loved in his mind, he kept the last five years in his mind and he kept his training in his mind. He wouldn't lose. He couldn't lose. He had to keep the search going, he had to keep that single scrap of faith burning away within him. Otherwise, what was the point of it all?

He gritted his teeth and stamped his foot down among the tall grass. *Be a right stubborn bastard and stand firm. Take their ground, don't give them yours.*

Talfyn swung. Rather than redirecting it, Blynkiln leapt forward, taking the enormous man by surprise as he stared in disbelief at the narrow-bladed sword holding its own against the monstrous greatsword he wielded.

The swords met in a violent, savage embrace, as steel scraped along steel, the both of them shaking from the effort. Blynkiln clamped his jaw shut tight, until his teeth were about ready to shatter. He dug his feet into the ground, a terrible ache running through his arms, legs, and head.

With some effort, a lance of pain and a loud shrieking of steel, The False Knight ripped his sword down Talfyn's and barged into the giant of a man with all the force and strength he had, letting free a long-held breath.

Blynkiln knew better than to overstep now. Instead, he welcomed Talfyn's charge with open arms. Not literally, of course.

Talfyn panted away whilst Blynkiln readied himself, lightening the weight on his feet, ready to catch his opponent out. The giant of a man sprung at him, faster than ever, and Blynkiln leapt out the way, spinning around and dragging his sword across the backs of Talfyn's legs, or where he hoped they'd be.

A howl of pain and a scream of anguish rang out into the morning air as blood spurted from the deep gashes across Talfyn's legs. He fell to his knees, now facing Blynkiln.

As The False Knight prepared to finish him off, standing close to his mortally wounded enemy, a lance of cold and sharp pain shot up his side. Using the hilt of his sword, he hit Talfyn under his greathelm in answer, letting out a cry of his own.

Talfyn's greathelm spun into the air until it met the cold ground with a dull thud, leaving the man's ugly slab of a face laid bare. A great river-like scar ran down it.

Blynkiln watched Talfyn's face grow paler as the enormous man whispered, "May my brother avenge me, if I have not already. Curse you, False Knight."

He flopped over into the tall grass, a pool of blood forming around his legs, seeping into the cold ground.

Blynkiln reached for the source of the pain and wrapped his hand around the grip of a knife that had been plunged deep into his side. He winced and grunted, cursing to himself. He hadn't paid attention to Talfyn's hands among all the rain-beaded, blood-covered grass.

Blynkiln swayed like a thin branch caught in the middle of a raging storm, growing faint until he tumbled to the ground, dizzy and disorientated.

The world spun around him for a few moments as he stared up at the grey sky, the sun barely visible through the darkening clouds. The trees surrounding the area were blown left and right, the crumpled leaves rattling on their branches.

Blynkiln kept a hold of the knife, not daring to take it out. With each stab of pain, he grimaced. Pain like this was familiar to him by now but joining it this time was the fading of that final scrap of faith as he feared that this would be where he'd meet his end, lost in the tall grass, a few strides away from the body of his final enemy.

5

As despair threatened to swallow him whole, the wind whispered in his ears and the voice of his gods came to him, offering some hope where little could be found.

He forced himself to his feet, nearly slipping over as he did. He hunched over, keeping as tight a hold of that knife as ever. After a few deep breaths and pained gasps, he found the strength in him to move.

He shook his pounding head and stumbled over to Talfyn's sack-like corpse.

At least he's dead, then. I suppose that's something.

The False Knight leaned over the body, gritting his teeth as the wound in his side burned. He tore at the grey surcoat and wrapped the fabric around the hilt of the knife, tying it off. The pain came in unbearable waves that near enough doubled him right over.

He stumbled off through the tall grass, droplets of blood leaking out his side as he went. The rain eased off but the wind kept on. Blynkiln didn't slow his steps as he struggled over towards the forest, ignoring the bridge that led to the walled city of Hinsylt, his original destination.

He wanted to rest by an ancient tree, and meet his death head-on, where the whispers of the wind were loudest. That was his wish, right then, since he couldn't die at the side of the woman he loved.

The world's a shit place sometimes, alright. Some luck, minding my own business and doing no harm, only to get stabbed by someone I've never even heard of. Typical. Talfyn the Tall, what kind of name is that anyway? Theatrical arsehole.

He ranted away to himself as he went, finally making it to the treeline and taking a deep breath. The trees sheltered him, the moss-covered boulders and stones kept him company. He slumped down against the wide trunk of what he reckoned to be the oldest tree in the forest.

His inevitable death had been put off for too long. If he really thought about it, what did he have to live for? The distant hope and dream of reunion? *Don't be a dolt, that'd never happen. Well, it certainly won't be happening now, will it?*

He rested the back of his head against the trunk.

Part of him meeting his death pleased him, if he was being honest. After all, his life had been filled with nothing but misery for five hard years, falling asleep each night with little hope in him and waking up in much the same sorry state.

A bird chirped to his right, and as he looked at it he spotted a dirt road not too far away. *I could go... try and find someone. But... what's the point?*

A single tear rolled down his cheek as he stared at that road, hoping that some cart or wagon would come rolling along, kicking up a load of dirt, mud and shit. Did he want that, though, or did he just want to die in peace right here, right now? He thought about tearing the knife out and making the process a lot quicker and a lot easier, for a moment, then he thought better of it.

He didn't deserve saving, not really, not after what he'd done to survive. *I was there, I had it all. Then it vanished and I killed them. Twelve faithful knights, just like Talfyn said. Thirteen, now he's dead. I cut through them all without remorse. I had to, didn't I? For the chance of seeing her again.*

As he was about ready to be embraced by the cold arms of death, or the warm arms, depending on how you looked at these things, the whispering of the wind was replaced by a joyful whistling. As he looked back at the dirt road, a cart came rolling down the way. The woman steering it was whistling a pleasant tune.

In a moment of total madness and amidst all of that despair, that scrap of faith seemed worth holding onto once again. He dragged himself up the tree's thick trunk, leaving a streak or two of blood up the rough bark.

Maybe I'm in the gods' favour today, after all. Fuck the pains and sorrows of living, why give up? Why not push on? I can't give up, not now, after all this time. I won't do it, he told himself, gritting his teeth and groaning as he stumbled through the woods.

"Stop a minute, someone's out there!" a cheerful voice called out, the voice of a young man.

"Be careful, might be they're dangerous! Wait a minute for your mother. Bloody hell, I said wait, lad!" a woman's voice this time.

The young man came running up to Blynkiln and had him over his shoulder just as the woman made it over, red-faced and wary. Her bright green eyes were just like her son's.

The False Knight, breathless and in crippling pain, managed to say, "My lucky day today. I mean you no harm." He took a few deep breaths. "Just need a spot of help... as you can see. Please. If you don't mind."

The words hurt as they poured out, or was it the knife in his side that made everything hurt, or maybe his pounding head?

"You're in a right state. We don't live far from here, just in a small village called Lyen-Saithe. We'll load you up and get you to our healer, ok?" the kind woman replied.

Blynkiln managed a pained nod and was helped over to the back of the cart by the boy and his mother.

The journey to the village was a blur, a short blur. Blynkiln fell in and out of consciousness with memories of snow-ridden courtyards, the clashing of sparring swords, but mostly of the woman he loved and the fear of never seeing her again. The memories faded and the pain dulled as he slipped into a temporary darkness.

He woke a few times, heard the same voices now joined by another. This one belonged to an older man. Blynkiln tried to speak, tried to say something, but no words came out. A firm hand patted him on the shoulder and a calming voice whispered something to him. Before he could work out what it said, he drifted off to sleep.

When he woke, he let out a pained sigh and sat upright, raising a tender hand to the back of his head. A soft cloth of sorts was wrapped around it. He winced and rubbed his eyes, looking down at his stomach where a strange tingling sensation came from. It wasn't hunger, sickness or even pain. *Makes a change.*

Aside from the bandages across his body, which were layered at the side where he could've sworn a dagger once lived, he was the cleanest he'd been for years. Clean of any dried blood, grease, sweat and dirt.

The table he sat on was smooth to the touch as he ran his hands along the piece of furniture that had served as an operating table for him.

As he was about to stand up, someone appeared before him. A man, a white-haired man with a full white beard. His eyes were a deep blue, pitched against a pale face with a few wrinkles around the forehead and at the corners of his eyes. He had an angular nose, was of average height and build, but had the broadest shoulders Blynkiln had ever seen.

"Ah, you're up! Excellent!" The healer's voice was gentle but sounded worn by the trials of a long life.

"Well, I expect you've got a dull pain in your head and a strange sensation in your tummy. Least you aren't dead though, eh, I suppose that's a minor relief! Or, praps not, depends on your circumstance, doesn't it?" he paused for a moment. "Sorry, sorry, just an old man's babbling. I do apologise."

"You've nothing to apologise for, it looks like I've got you to thank for me still being here. Then again, and like you say, might be that isn't such a good thing," The False Knight replied, rubbing his eyes once again.

"You needn't thank me, just doing my work as any capable soul would, or so I hope. Best get yourself thanking

Aedlyn and her lad, Ofryth, if you really feel like it. Not sure you'd be here if not for them."

Blynkiln nodded and yawned.

"So, I'll say I hate to pry, though that isn't entirely true..." the humble healer paused for a moment, frowning out his window. "Never really is true when someone says they hate to pry. They just say it to be polite, don't they? A pleasantry, I believe it's called. Yes, anyway, where was I? That's right, I don't hate to pry. I would, in fact, very much like to know what you were getting up to. Quite a wound you had there, and uncommon round these parts."

The False Knight took a moment, weighing what to say in response. *Honesty is likely best, I suppose.*

"I was trying to get to Hinsylt by crossing the bridge at Alkyn, but someone blocked my path and wouldn't budge, so I had to move him myself."

The healer gave a few curious nods of his head as he listened.

"Well, seems as though you were the victor, even if you didn't come off too well yourself! You young sort always trying to prove something. Ofryth, Aedlyn's lad, he's always trying to impress not just his mother but the rest of the village." He raised his eyes to the sky and tutted.

"Bloody youths. I was no different back when I was a young lad, though. You get the point, I'm waffling again aren't I?"

"Aye, not like I can take off though, is it?" The False Knight responded. He hadn't put enough humour in his tone after the words had passed from his lips. *Perhaps a bit harsh, I don't mind all that much really.*

The older man let out a chuckle. "Enough of me rabbiting on, what's your name?"

"Blynkiln, more commonly known as 'The False Knight' much to my misery. And you?" he responded, shifting his head to track the random movements of his saviour.

Maybe I shouldn't have said that...

10

"Oh, is that right? Praps I should've left you to bleed out since you're such a dishonourable soul," the old man stated, his tone as cold as ice.

An uncomfortable silence stretched out as they both stared at each other, the healer's face dark, his eyes no longer as bright as they had been.

"Ah ha ah, I fooled you there didn't I!" the old man bellowed, the walls of his house nearly collapsing.

Relief washed over Blynkiln.

"Your face was a picture! Oh god, oh god," the humble healer said, wiping a tear from his eye before he shook his head and cleared his throat.

"Anyway, that's enough of that nonsense. Forgive me. I'm Merek, Lyen-Saithe's healer. Pleasure to make your acquaintance, Blynkiln."

The False Knight noticed a shift in tone as Merek ended his statement. He sounded more sincere and more genuine than he had done before.

Some time passed and the moon took the place of the sun as owls hooted amidst the darkness, the stars twinkling high in the sky. Merek had no problem with Blynkiln staying in his home. He'd healed him and practically ordered him to stay in the house for the time being, to recover as needed, for as long as he needed.

That night, The False Knight settled down in the spare bed and closed his eyes. His thoughts dwelled on his gratefulness to the people that had saved him, that single scrap of faith he'd kept with him all this time, and above all else, his faith in the promise he'd made to the woman that he loved. They would be reunited, one day, they *had* to be.

Journeys

She woke up slumped against a sandstone wall, her head spinning from the day spent drinking and gambling. Darkness covered the streets and the air was as fresh as it could be in the North-West of Undysvold.

Henfylt rose to her feet, placing a hand against the same wall that had just been acting as her mattress. She then came to the realisation that she'd been expected by the King before sundown, yet the paved streets of Blantyrn were showered with bright rays of moonlight.

Shit. Late again, she thought.

Despite being a professional mercenary with a half-decent reputation about her, Henfylt had trouble keeping track of time. The sodding stuff always seemed to be running away from her. Added to her troubles with time, her memory often let her down, too. Only if she'd spent the day drinking.

After standing still for a moment to regain her balance, Henfylt took her hand off the smooth wall and tried to remember why she was here in Blantyrn. She shoved her fist against her forehead and rubbed her knuckles against the thing as if that'd make her remember everything.

Soon enough, the pieces slotted back in place and she started to amble towards the great fortress of Dinshei. It wasn't her own desire that brought her to the North-West, after all, it was just another job. *How dull.*

Henfylt had never viewed her profession as boring or particularly purposeful, she only worked as and when she fancied a change of pace to her life. Having the coin to live, as helpful as the stuff was, didn't have to be earned as a mercenary. Henfylt, more often than not, made enough by gambling at the tables. She liked to think she was quite good at it by now.

As she made her way, unrushed, through the pristine streets of Blantyrn in the general direction of the fortress, Henfylt found peace in the briskness of the night. It had a somewhat soothing nature to it as the breeze never turned into a violent, howling wind that whipped its surroundings into nothing short of a frenzy like it did in the South-West of Undysvold, her home.

The North-West, far warmer during the day with its thick and humid air, made her skin crawl. At night, though, everything became cooler and more calming. Tolerable, that was the best word for it.

As she gained her bearings, Henfylt remembered how odd the message from the King of Dinshei had been. It came when she gambled in one of the many taverns in Hinsylt, the largest city in Undysvold. All that Henfylt remembered being told was that King Slyvard of Dinshei had asked for her, fancying her for a job. It must've been of some interest, otherwise why would she have come all the way here? She certainly didn't come to admire the view of the sand. For the life of her, no matter how firmly she rubbed her knuckles against her forehead, the reason for her interest in this job never leapt out at her. She shook her head and cursed.

The streets were wide and spotlessly clean. Many lanterns gave a warm light to the streets, adding to the general calming ambience of the city.

Much of Blantyrn was taken up by housing, though a number of well-placed inns and taverns also found their place in the port city. A few shops, too. All of the houses were made of the smooth sandstone found in the North-West, paired with the expensive natural white wood, wynluk, which came from the North-East of Undysvold where snow never stopped falling.

Henfylt increased her pace and no doubt would've knocked into anyone who happened down the same street as her, if there was anyone to knock into. Not a soul wandered the wonderful city. *How late is it?*

Many little lanterns hung from walls and sat on barrels of fresh water, lighting the way. Everywhere she looked there were sources of light, beacons amidst the shadows of the enveloping night.

It wasn't long before she found herself at the open gates that led into the fortress of Dinshei. The gates were elegant but strong. The enormous things towered over her. She must've looked tiny down here, as she stared up at the sparkling gates, watching the stars twinkle high in the sky.

"You must be Henfylt, the mercenary. Slyvard is expecting you," a soldier stated.

There was just the one soldier, no other armed guards were in sight.

"That's me. He's not... sleeping?" Henfylt asked.

"Not yet. You'll find him in his study. Once you enter the courtyard, go straight ahead through the door and follow the stairs on the right up as far as they go," the guard replied.

They trust people too much round these parts. No escort?

The mercenary did as she was told for the most part, though she did wander around the beautiful courtyard which had a fountain at its centre. There were a few benches around the yard and a number of neatly trimmed hedges, too. As she peered into the spiralling water that tumbled into the fountain's base, the delicate reflections of the stars stared back. She ran her hand through the cool water and watched the reflections ripple.

After seeing the charming plainness of the courtyard, and wiping her wet hand on her shirt, Henfylt went up the stairs to the highest level and entered the study.

A few candles lit the basic room which smelled of old scrolls, texts and tomes. King Slyvard sat at a wynluk desk, writing a letter as Henfylt walked over to him.

In the corner of the room, by the large desk and a small window, an enormous greatsword leant against the wall. It had a long, thick blade sheathed in a bland leather scabbard. The crossguard of the weapon had been crafted using wynluk wood and the hilt looked both durable and strong. It was reinforced by a strange material, most likely some blend of the rare ores that the King had used to make the North-West so well off.

The leather-wrapped grip of the greatsword had grown black in parts from excessive use and a rather modest golden piece formed in the shape of a diamond acted as the sword's pommel. It wasn't a shiny gold, more of a dull and worn colour that suited the greatsword's sense of character well.

Henfylt respected that this King was a fighter. Most rulers never seemed to get stuck in very much. They often just sent their soldiers at the enemy and sat at the back twiddling their thumbs.

"Ah, Henfylt, sit down if you would like to," the King said as he scratched his quill away at the piece of paper on his desk.

"I'll stand if it's all the same," she replied.

"As you see fit. I take it your journey here was easy enough?" King Slyvard asked.

He signed off his letter, then raised an ink-stained hand to his mouth to release a muffled cough.

"Uneventful, boring and long. Easy enough. What's this job you've got for me?" Henfylt asked. Generally, she despised small talk, always wanting to get straight to business.

The King placed his quill next to the finished letter, clasped his hands together and leaned back in his wooden chair.

"It is a personal matter that concerns my plans for the future of Undysvold in its entirety. As you have spent a day experiencing the life of Blantyrn, you will have no doubt noticed how everyone lives here in great comfort. When you venture South or dare to explore the North-East, however, this life of comfort fades. The farmers toil their fields and work harder than most, yet they remain poor in the South whilst it is those that do nothing who reap the rewards. The North-East isn't much better. They seem to grow more isolated and reliant on trade with each passing day. All they can produce and export is their famed wynluk wood, nothing more. Yet here we all thrive. Nobody is poor and without a home and the people of the North-West still purchase items of luxury whilst maintaining their wealth. I do what I can from my seat here in Dinshei to help those seemingly beyond my reach, I truly do. Then it dawned on me, why shouldn't I do something more about it all? I cannot openly overstep the borders we laid down a number of years ago, naturally. But perhaps I can wield my influence in other ways."

Henfylt chose this pause to take a seat. It seemed she might be here a while.

"You mean sabotage?" the mercenary asked, sharply.

"In essence it is sabotage, but I would press the claim that inaction against injustice of such a wide nature is, in itself, a violation of what separates us from the most villainous in our ranks," the King of Dinshei answered, scratching at his broad forehead.

Henfylt replied, "True, so long as you're in a position where you can act."

King Slyvard nodded in accord and went on, "I want you to find two people, Henfylt. I don't know where they are specifically, though I know neither dwell here in the North-West. The first person I wish you to find is the daughter of

Queen Meurd. I have it on good authority that she is alive and somewhere in the South-West having been sighted near Alkyn. She was always said to be a friend to the common folk of the South when she was growing up, they all miss her terribly. I wish for her to take Meurd's place because of that. My sources say that she has unmistakable bright green eyes and long brown hair, just like her mother."

The King paused for a few moments, giving Henfylt a chance to process what she'd just been told.

"The second is a woman named Adelyka. She was the ruler of Raltyr in the North-East prior to Rancylt taking over. She had her region faring well which of course changed when she fled after all of that business with her lover. I want you to find her so that she may once again be the ruler of Raltyr after we deal with Queen Rancylt. I don't know where she is at present, but I do have resources that could help you to locate her, if it is your wish to use them."

The King looked at Henfylt as if to ensure that the mercenary was paying full attention. He then continued, "This conquest of mine is not about seizing power for myself. Though admittedly, should we succeed, Undysvold would have rulers chosen by myself and to my benefit. My purpose here is to give ordinary people the chance to flourish. You see, I have spent the entirety of my twenty-two years as a king improving the lives of those that live here in the North-West to great avail, thankfully. Now, I must help those of a greater need outside of my own jurisdiction. So, will you help me in this matter?"

He'd finally finished and Henfylt took a moment to think, looking at the King of Dinshei as she did. His brown hair reached the bottom of his neck in thick waves. He had a trimmed beard and sunken eyes that were deep green in colour. He didn't wear a crown or any expensive jewellery, and his shirt was grey and patternless. Henfylt put a small amount of trust in him, then, even though this plan of his must've had more to it than he'd let on.

The mercenary pushed her chair out and stood up, still feeling somewhat disoriented.

After the short pause, she answered the King's question. "I'll do what I can. The daughter of Meurd should be easy enough, but Adelyka will obviously be harder to find."

King Slyvard rose to his feet.

"Your attempt is all I can ask. After finding the two of them, and getting them here safely, I may have need of your skills again should you wish to assist me further. There's a pouch of coin over there, take it and the other half will be yours after completion," he said, pointing towards a small shelf in the corner of the dimly lit room which featured a potted plant with a sizable bag at its side.

Henfylt wasn't the sort to bow. Slyvard didn't seem the kind of ruler who wanted to be bowed to, either. She simply took her bag of coin and turned to leave. Before she could, however, the burning desire to ask one last question gripped her.

"Why me?" Henfylt asked.

"From what I hear, you are the best. You have helped a number of your fellow mercenaries with their own jobs in the past. Comradery isn't something we see all too often these days, but I want this job to be done by someone with a positive reputation. Someone with a heart, someone who cares. From my understanding, you stand out from the rest for those reasons. I rarely misjudge people," Slyvard answered.

With that, she was satisfied. So, she left with a nod and a smile on her face.

Of course, she had to think about the next frustration. Travel. The journey from Blantyrn to Dansphylt, the enormous wall that separated the North-West from the South, wasn't the most appealing.

Regardless, she had to make her way there and deal with the misery of trekking through the endless grains of sand with nothing to keep her company but the strength of the sun.

How am I supposed to keep myself sane for near enough a week of travelling through this shit? She asked herself, having wandered through the courtyard and the elegant gate.

She sighed in irritation and shook her head, thinking it best to start the journey as soon as possible, through a chunk of the night whilst the temperature was cooler and more bearable.

*

A few days of joyless travel passed, leaving Henfylt fed up of the sand, the heat and all things North-Western. She marched on through the days regardless, drinking plenty of water to ward off any hallucinations that came with marching through this region of Undysvold.

Having passed Ophuldyr, an oasis that marked about halfway between Blantyrn and Dansphylt, the next few days went on much like the last, all full of more tiresome travelling.

The mercenary would set off at dawn and not settle until sunset came. Thankfully, she only had to spend one more night out in the open, the other found Henfylt embraced by silk sheets, where her thoughts dwelled on her need for a new dagger as she drifted off to sleep. She'd always liked knives. They were useful things, handy for getting out of those particularly messy scraps she often found herself in, and they were honest, too. Steel was always honest.

After those days of relentless journeying, the mercenary arrived at Dansphylt. The wall that acted as a border spanned much further than the eye could see, towering above its surroundings.

A wide road led to the first enormous gate and a great many carts were being taken along this route. They each contained different wares, likely all being sent to the South in order to fulfil the trade agreements between Slyvard's region and Meurd's.

The road leading up to the great border from the South, on her way to see the King of Dinshei, had been shoddy and rough. The state of the road had led to a delay in her passing through, as several carts lost wheels along the way. For this current part of the journey, however, she doubted there'd be any problems. The North-West, after all, had a pristine stretch of road leading to its side of the wall.

The closer she came to Dansphylt itself, the more sentries could be counted by their glinting armour and spear tips. Looking up at the border, now closer to it, Henfylt realised just how massive the thing was, all smooth and stern, unbending and unbreaking. A gigantic sheet of stone, metal and wood. For how many years it had stood, Henfylt couldn't say.

This side of the wall had been tidied up using sandstone to fit in with the climate and general feel of the North-West. The South side had been much like its path, muddy and dark. *That's just the South all over. Well, the Western side specifically.*

She stood in the ever-expanding queue for passage to the South. At the end of the line, there was an elderly man sitting behind a dark, wooden desk on a cushioned chair. Before Henfylt could get to him, though, she had to stand about waiting in this queue for who knew how long? That was the trouble with queues, the bloody things.

Henfylt thought about her straightforward plan. She'd head straight for Alkyn over the coming days, hopefully finding some lead or other to keep her at it. If she found nothing, she'd head over the bridge and make her way to her home, the Mercenaries Guildhall, in Hinsylt. In the city, and with some help, maybe she'd get some answers that way.

Eventually, the queue shuffled on enough for the elderly man to call her up.

"What is your name, your profession and your purpose in travelling South?" he inquired, not wasting any time.

"Henfylt, a mercenary, travelling South for a job given to me by King Slyvard of Dinshei," she replied.

The elderly man's ink-stained fingers left smudges across the thin paper he scribbled some details onto. He didn't look up until he'd finished. When his beady eyes settled on her, he nodded and lifted the lid of a small wooden box that was full of used paper, placing the message he'd just written in with all the others before snapping the lid shut.

"You are cleared for passage, on your way," he said.

Seeing no reason to disagree with him, Henfylt strode on, following the narrowing path as the last grains of sand trickled away and blades of grass shot up in their place, leading to the first of three massive gates. The three gates inside the border were all made of darkened iron mixed with other durable metals, the mercenary assumed.

Henfylt shivered as she made her way through the first gate of Dansphylt, guarded by many soldiers. The guards stood tall and short, female and male. They were all dressed head to toe in heavy plate armour, gripping fierce halberds in their hands and wearing a shortsword at each of their hips. They stood motionless in the enormous corridor-like space that led to the exit at the other side.

There were many large beams that spanned the entire width of the passage that led through to the South of Undysvold. Like the hall of a great lord, a few seats and benches were spread around the place, a couple of hearths, too, to keep the soldiers from freezing in the night.

In a roundabout way, the interior of Dansphylt made Henfylt think of her home. That was a proper building, an old and warm one. The Guildhall of Hinsylt was a large, relaxed place which hadn't changed a bit since the days before her time, or so Henfylt had been told.

She thought back fondly to the first time she entered the Guildhall. Green flags with silver accents and decorations covered its large brick walls. The flags were a deep green, dark but not so dark as to not stand out against the rest of the space. The silver swirls that added some flair to the flowing green banners helped give the Guildhall a sense of uniqueness and homeliness. Shields and swords hung up in the spaces between the banners to add further distinction to the large hall. Better than all of that was the enormous hearth that had more comfortable seating placed around it. The sense of relief that had washed over her when she entered the Guildhall for the first time, the relief at the place being *her* home, came flooding back to her. The hearth had welcomed her as had all of the other mercenaries who were present. They knew she was an initiate just by appearance alone.

The Guildhall had a feeling of history about it since the tables were all weathered, the stools and chairs all worn by the tales of time, but still comfortable. The floor, of course, had been made using thick oak wood as well. It was as it should've been, a place crafted with heart and love. The balance struck perfectly between being practical and homely. Even the floor creaked under her weight, a sign some would take for an aged floor in need of replacing, but one she took for the sound of home.

The greatest feature of the Guildhall was its custom of keeping the hearth blazing at all times. Food cooked away in the gigantic pot that sat above the hungry flames, making sure it stayed nice and warm. The mercenaries could help themselves to food and drink. It wasn't a tightly run establishment, far from it. It functioned as a proper family would, unlike some of the other guilds known to operate in Undysvold, like 'The Den'.

Henfylt looked forward to getting home, to seeing her family and chatting over warm food and a roaring fire. She wanted that more than anything as she strolled through the cold of Dansphylt. To be back home with the thunderous rain and howling wind outside, whilst sitting by the comfort of her hearth with a large cup of ale in her hand and Gylphur, her closest friend and the mercenary blacksmith, at her side. She'd smell the birch wood as it cracked and burned, she'd smell the well-seasoned pot of warm food as it sizzled away, and she'd taste the fine ale. First though, she had to get this job done.

Admittedly, Dansphylt's hall had no flags or banners, no shields or swords, no pot of food cooking over a hearth quite like that of the Guildhall, but the memories came to her all the same. Her Guildhall, after all, held such an important place in her heart.

Before long, she'd reached the other side of the border and the trees were being whipped violently by the strong wind whilst rain soaked her and the poor souls who were queuing to enter Dansphylt to head North. Henfylt put the desert behind her and pressed on through the conditions she loved so very much.

To Alkyn now, not so far but not close enough to make it without a night's rest. Travelling light has its issues, this clothing won't keep me warm enough either. Best go to Tynylt first, it's the closest village and I'll get there by nightfall easily. Take a slight detour, it's for the best. Alkyn will wait a day, I'm sure.

With her sudden change of plan, instead of trudging through the rain South, she turned her gaze to her left and followed the road which forked in a few directions. At the crossroads where the signpost stood, Henfylt made sure she hadn't lost her wits and was going the right way. Sure enough, a sign pointing left indicated 'Tynylt'.

The path leading to the village wasn't too long. Besides, what could be so bad about enduring a few hours of South-Western weather?

Henfylt got her answer soon enough, as the forceful wind and the aggressive rain never let up. She was used to being layered up when heading out around these parts or enjoying the sound of the wind and the rain from the warmth of a roaring fire with a reliable roof over her head.

Regardless, Henfylt didn't slow her pace. She kept a smile on her face as she looked up at a sky full of dark, menacing clouds which cast gloomy shadows down onto the world. At least she wasn't back in the sodding desert.

As darkness began to sweep across Undysvold, the warm light cast by many lanterns chased the shadows away from Tynylt. The mercenary shivered as the constant rainfall set into her thin clothes. She reckoned there'd be a merchant about who'd be able to sort something more practical for her, but that was tomorrow's work. Maybe she'd even get that dagger she was after.

The village welcomed her with open arms, or near enough. The houses were made of wood with brick chimneys, the roofs most likely thatched, though Henfylt found it a challenge to see the material used on the top of the houses since it was so dark. A few patches of land for growing vegetables were scattered about the place, as well as some fenced-off areas for animals.

A shadow sat off not so far away, with distant clamour, raised voices and cheerful singing coming from it, floating in the cold air from the centre of the village. Henfylt knew exactly what that meant: ale.

She approached the inn, opening the oak door which had seen better days. It creaked and groaned, then thudded shut behind her. Even though she was drenched head to toe and the door had made a racket as she rattled the stubborn old thing open, nobody stared at her.

A small fire was burning away opposite her, surrounded by stone and safely away from any wood. It was hardly like the hearth at her Guildhall. Henfylt was used to great roaring flames which warmed an enormous hall, leaving no corner damp or cold. She shrugged her shoulders. *Fire's fire, it heats all the same.*

The mercenary strolled across to the portly innkeeper who smiled as Henfylt approached.

"Welcome, welcome. Rare to see a new face come by. I'm Kynfor, pleased to meet you," he said.

"I'm Henfylt. Well met, Kynfor." She returned a smile and crossed her arms.

Kynfor went on, "Weather's been rough today, I see you've experienced as much. I'll get you some food and a drink, if you like. In the meantime, pull yourself a chair in front of the fire. Get yourself warmed through."

His cheeks were bright red and flushed, his light brown hair was thinning, and his warm green eyes were cast against pale skin.

"Won't catch me complaining about this weather after the week I've spent up in the North-West. Won't do much good for the crops though. I'll have whatever's easiest and quickest, paired with the best ale you've got on offer. You don't happen to have any rooms spare for the night do you?" Henfylt replied, her hands on the wooden bar top.

"Been busy up there lately, I heard, bunch of carts always up and down that bloody road. No wonder it's in such a state. You get yourself sat down by that fire and I'll bring you over some grub and a tankard of ale. As for a room, I have a couple free, so take your pick. There's one looking over toward the lake or one without any view if that's your preference," Kynfor replied.

Henfylt reached for the bag of coin to pay Kynfor, but he waved a hand. "Pay me in the morning. For now, get yourself warm. You look as though you need it."

The mercenary smiled at him and nodded.

Henfylt picked a reasonably comfortable chair and dragged it over to the fire. The heat warmed her through a little, and the dancing flames, which had nearly finished charring the wood to nothing, offered some entertainment whilst she listened to those around her.

A couple were arguing about the state of the South. One of them defended Queen Meurd and said, "Nobody would do better than her, she's trying her best. She's the kind of leader I want in charge if we're ever going to war again."

The other objected, "No, no. Load of shite that is, her best ain't nowhere close to good enough. There's no bloody need for war, anyway. Besides, it's not even like she fights with her own men and women. She's one of them like Ynfleyd was what sits at the back and lets 'em all die."

How dull.

Henfylt was about to focus in on the chatter of another group, when she noticed a figure in the far corner who wore a red and black robe and had their hood up.

The mercenary thought it seemed a bit odd that someone would wear a hood indoors. It didn't seem so odd once she made the connection with the red and black striped robe. Whoever this person was, they were a Tarspyk. She'd read about them when she went to Elensfyr, the Great Library, a few years ago. She'd never met one of these Tarspyks before, though.

The mercenary abandoned the heat of the fire in favour of the hooded figure's company. Her curiosity outmatched her want for warmth.

As she came closer to the Tarspyk, she noticed the robed figure was male. Amidst the darkness of the inn, she struggled to see, even though there were a few lamps and candles about the place.

The robed man sat at a small, round table. Henfylt thought it telling that this mysterious Tarspyk chose to sit specifically in the darkest corner of 'The Forlorn Fox', right in the shadows. Where this would cause concern and perhaps caution for some, it caused nothing of the sort for Henfylt.

It wasn't until the mercenary pulled a stool to the round table that the cloaked figure looked at her from the shadow of his hood.

"Conversations were dull and you caught my eye. Never seen one of you Tarspyk lot in person, but I recognised those robes," she said, pointing a finger at them. The red and black stripes told her this one could manipulate fire.

The Tarspyk pulled his hood back. He was dark-skinned, like Henfylt, but his skin was slightly more bold in its tone. His flame red hair reached the bottom of his neck in waves, tumbling down and streaked with black. The dark red found a way to shine even in the low light, whilst the black streaks weren't overpowering or too subtle. The Tarspyk's goatee complemented a thick, flicked moustache that matched the colour of his hair.

"Most conversations are terribly dull. We Tarspyk are few in number, it is true. You are Henfylt, if I am not mistaken?" he asked, crossing his arms.

"Have we met?" Henfylt replied.

"No, I would have remembered that encounter, I'm sure. They don't call me 'The Observer' for nothing. My name is Jynheln, though few people know it and those that do tend not to use it."

The Tarspyk, Jynheln, had a deep but very calm and soothing voice. He spoke with great clarity and precision, hardly the sort to rush a sentence.

"Whose service are you in?" Henfylt asked, sharply.

"I keep my own council. I'm not one to pledge to another soul. Though, I do like some people more than others."

Jynheln shuffled in his seat and leaned back as far as his rigid chair would allow.

"I hear you Tarspyks are sharp and wise. You have to be, otherwise you wouldn't be able to learn and use your magic, right?" the mercenary asked.

"I wouldn't say we are wise. I certainly wouldn't call myself wise, for wisdom and intelligence are quite different. It is true, we do have to have some intellect, but wisdom is learned through experience and trial. Intellect can be natural and sharpened by reading a book. Wisdom is far rarer, far more important in this age. Wouldn't you agree?" Jynheln replied, leaning forwards as he spoke in hushed tones.

"I don't disagree, that much is true. You're humble for someone of your capabilities. I heard you can be quite up your own arses," Henfylt said.

"Well yes, most of us are. That's why I am not at The Tarspyk Spire poring over theory and learning useless skills. I prefer to be out in the world, meeting people such as yourself. Most of those who share my... talents are dullards really, they know how to remember things and understand things but put them among the common woman or man and they know next to nothing, yet they think themselves above all others." Jynheln's tone was almost playful.

The mercenary found it hard to disagree with the Tarspyk once again.

He spoke once more, "I listen to people and I watch them. Not in a strange, predatory way, but out of curiosity and with the aim of learning. You see, people fall into three categories in my experience. There are those who think they are better than all around them, there are those who *know* that they are better than all around them, and there are those who simply live. Not one person truly believes themselves to be worth less than another soul. They may say it for sympathy but they never truly believe it. I simply live and observe, the third category is the one you fit into as well, if I'm not mistaken."

The mercenary tilted her head to one side, "What makes you say that?"

"The way you walked over here with no reservations. If you thought you were better than me, you wouldn't have approached out of the fear of being proved wrong. If you *knew* you were better than me, you wouldn't have bothered to even think about who I was or what I was doing here. Everyone else in this room thinks they are better than the rest. Only Kynfor, the innkeeper, shares a space with us. He has a good heart and he is a humble man who spends his nights serving these folk who stroll in with their noses turned up at the sight of him. It's a shame really, the way we behave, don't you think?" Jynheln replied.

"I see why they call you 'The Observer', Jynheln," the mercenary stated.

Over by the bar, Kynfor had Henfylt's plate of food in his hands, casting his warm eyes around the room to try and find her.

"I must go and eat now, take care," she said, eliciting a slight nod from Jynheln who then shrunk back into the shadows, pulling his hood back up without another word.

Kynfor handed Henfylt her plate and ale when she sat down by the fire again. He offered up a knife too, but the mercenary refused.

The heat from the fire warmed her through, and the meat, so tender and flavoursome, put an end to her stomach's grumbling. She took a long gulp of ale and savoured the taste of it.

It wasn't long before Henfylt looked over to the small round table Jynheln had been sitting at. He'd disappeared and was nowhere to be seen. It hardly surprised the mercenary. Jynheln seemed the sort to melt away into the shadows.

It didn't take Henfylt long to finish her food for the evening. She went over to Kynfor to claim the room with the view for the night. It was a cosy space, not enormous but not cramped either, and decorated in a simple and pleasant way.

The mercenary had warmed up, her thin clothing had dried and she undid her belt which held her sheathed longsword on her left hip. She threw the belt to the ground at the left side of the bed and slipped under the sheets. Henfylt usually fell asleep in a few minutes, but on this wet and stormy night she fell right into a deep, long slumber the second her head hit the pillow.

No, No, That Wouldn't Do

The mercenary groaned and yawned. The thought of moving wasn't very appealing. She rubbed her eyes and brushed a few strands of her long, black hair out of her face before clambering out of the bed and opening the shutter.

Kynfor hadn't lied to her about the view from the room. He'd said it overlooked the lake, but he'd forgotten to mention how it also overlooked a few houses that had plumes of smoke puffing out of their chimneys.

Henfylt breathed in the crisp South-Western air as she stuck her head out the window. The land was in its recovery period after the violent wind and torrential rain of the evening just gone. There really was nothing quite like the day after a vicious storm, where everything had time to settle but the ground remained damp, the grass windswept and more scruffy than usual.

Henfylt's wild black hair blew in the breeze as she untangled what had been matted. She scanned over the landscape, making out Stykricht at the centre of the distant lake. From this far away, the enormous building was little more than a dot.

The Ruler's Conference must be coming up soon, Henfylt thought. She couldn't see Slyvard as the sort to ever go to such a pretentious place as Stykricht, but it was tradition for the three rulers of Undysvold to meet there once a year. *Trade agreements and other boring policy renewals. How dull.*

The mercenary put her belt and shoes on and smoothed the thick sheets out, placing the pillow back onto the bed once she was done. She swung the door open and left the room in as good a state as she'd found it, heading down the creaking stairs.

"Ah, you're up. I take it the room was suitable, seems you had a nice long kip," Kynfor said, smiling.

"Out like a candle in the howling wind. Just what I needed," Henfylt replied, returning a warm smile to the innkeeper.

"I don't s'pose you have someone selling warmer clothes around here, do you?" she asked, crossing her arms.

"You should find Roldyr. I think she arrived a few days back and won't leave till her wares are all taken up. She should have something for you. Her prices are fair and she's true, you won't be swindled, that's for sure," Kynfor answered, his belly bouncing as he chuckled. His face was bright red, just like it had been last night.

"Thank you, you've been very kind. Here's the coin for the food and ale last night, the room too." She tossed seven black coins on the bar top from her large pouch.

"It's five altogether. The room isn't worth five alone," Kynfor said, his eyes flashing with honesty.

"Times are tough, keep the extra," Henfylt replied.

She turned to leave and a few words of thanks rang out behind her as she opened the door.

A mixture of wet grass and mud squelched under Henfylt's shoes as she set off down a slippery path. A few people had steam rising from the little cups in their hands as they sat out chatting with their neighbours. *Even with the*

31

problems of the South, these people still seem happy enough amongst themselves.

Children were running around near some battered trees not so far away. Most of them were covered head to toe in mud, their hair decorated with a mixture of yellow, orange and brown leaves.

A blonde-haired girl sat away from everyone else, reading a tattered book. Why Henfylt went over to her, she couldn't say. There was something about the girl that separated her from everyone in the village. Her hair, for one, being blonde rather than dark. But there was something else. Maybe she reminded Henfylt of herself when she was growing up. Whatever the reason, she approached the girl who peered over her book at the sound of the brittle leaves crunching under Henfylt's feet.

"What are you reading, if you don't mind me asking?" the mercenary asked.

The blonde girls' eyes were blue and a sense of sorrow filled Henfylt as she crouched down at a level with the sitting girl.

"It's a book about Sphyltyr, the greatest warrior that ever lived," the girl replied.

Henfylt's heart melted as the cover of the book matched the one she'd read in her youth. The cover depicted a man of average height with broad shoulders and fairly long, blond hair flapping in a soft wind. He had a trimmed beard and wore only light armour. His longsword had plain and simple features with no fancy decorations, apart from a pink and red leafed tree that marked its sheath. He stood protecting a tree with the same pink and red leaves falling from it. That was the strangest part of the cover, it always had been. *Why a tree? Why a pink and red leafed tree?* She'd never understood its significance and still didn't as she stared at the cover as a grown woman.

"I read this same book when I was your age, probably slightly older actually. He was my hero growing up," Henfylt stated.

The blue-eyed girl looked as if she was about to speak, then she stopped herself.

"What were you going to say? You've nothing to fear from me," the mercenary said, sitting opposite the girl.

The girl found her confidence and asked, "It's a good book, but surely it's fiction?"

Henfylt answered, "He was real. I didn't think so at first, either. But I went to the Great Library a few years back and they have all sorts of books and scrolls in there. He's mentioned in his share of them. They all say he was a good fighter, a great fighter. The best. I always wanted to meet him when I was younger, but everyone said he was dead. He'd have to have been living for a hundred years or more if he was still alive today. So, I stopped holding out much hope of ever meeting him."

The girl laughed and the mercenary smiled.

After a moment, the girl looked at Henfylt's sword and asked, "Did he inspire you to become a...?"

"A mercenary," Henfylt answered, and the girl nodded. "Aye, he did. Without growing up on those stories I wouldn't have bothered. I wish I was as good as he was though, with a sword, I mean."

There were a few more reasons for her becoming a mercenary, of course, but she didn't want to waste this girl's time by telling her about Irys. If she started on about her mentor, the pair of them would've been here all bloody day.

"How did you go about becoming a mercenary?" the girl, who looked a good few years over a decade old, asked.

The mercenary thought about that for a quiet moment. It was Irys who found her on the streets of Hinsylt, alone and orphaned, like many who lived on that same street. Henfylt didn't want to revisit those times too desperately, though, so she settled for easing any concerns the girl might've had instead.

"Well, if you're worried about strength and height, don't be. You're fairly tall for your age and you'll only grow and get stronger. No reason why you can't become one, too. If you wanted to, of course."

The girl seemed to listen carefully to Henfylt's words before responding. "I suppose I don't know how strong I am, not really. The others are the ones that do the pushing, I've just never risen to it. I have thought about it, though, often enough."

Those words made Henfylt's stomach sink. The same used to happen to her when she was a similar age, younger, maybe. She noticed the mud on the girl's knee. It looked as if she'd wiped some mud off her face, too.

"You know those others you mentioned, do they give you a lot of grief?" Henfylt asked, in a soft tone.

The girl nodded. "It isn't so bad, Kynfor keeps an eye out for me. He runs the inn." She pointed to 'The Forlorn Fox'. "He tries to look after me. He's the only person who's ever bothered to try, but he's got a lot on. Running an inn isn't easy."

Hardly a surprise that Kynfor looks out for her.

"You can trust Kynfor. He seems like a good man, an honest man. You know that better than me, no doubt. He wouldn't mind you talking to him, if you ever needed to. What do the others tease you about, if you don't mind me asking?"

Tears formed in the girl's eyes. Henfylt rested a supportive hand on her shoulder.

"I'm an orphan, never met either of my parents. I just got left here, unwanted I suppose," the girl answered, fiddling with the chain of a necklace she wore. It was in the shape of a triangle, the single point angled down at the floor.

A tear rolled down her cheek and Henfylt winced. "It's not something they should laugh about. What's your name?"

The girl wiped a few tears away. "Typhylt."

"It's good to meet you, Typhylt. I'm Henfylt."

The mercenary hugged Typhylt hard until the girl stopped sniffling. *I feel bad leaving her like this, but they're young and I can't do anything about it, even though I'd like to. Well, she could stay with me whilst I'm here in Tynylt. That'd just make it harder to say goodbye. No, no, that wouldn't do.*

Henfylt stood up and looked at Typhylt, unsure about the conflict within herself. She couldn't bring Typhylt with her, they barely knew each other. Equally, she couldn't leave her here in such a vulnerable state. She sighed to herself. *Fine.*

"Come with me, if you like, to Roldyr. I don't know where she'll be so you could show me the way. I need new clothes, thicker clothes that'll keep the chill off my back," Henfylt said, after an awkward delay.

Typhylt looked up at Henfylt and nodded. A smile formed across her red, dirt-stained face.

"She's not far, just down the way. I'll lead," Typhylt said, and the mercenary followed.

The path was as muddy further down as it had been closer to the inn, if not more so. Typhylt seemed to be no stranger to the slippery mud as she made her way down the path with speed, never losing her footing. The mercenary struggled to match the speed as her thin, treadless shoes lost grip and she found she'd got two left legs all of a sudden. *Good job I'm not at a masquerade.*

"You're quick on your feet, far less clumsy than me," the mercenary stated, once she'd made it safely to the bottom of the path.

Her trousers were flecked with strings of mud, but Typhylt only had mud on her shoes. *She's agile. With some direction and training she could be something impressive, I reckon. No, no, that wouldn't do.*

In the lower village smoke plumed from the chimneys of all the houses. Most of the villagers were cooking meat over their fires. The scents of sizzling sausages and cooked bacon drifted through the crisp air, making Henfylt's stomach grumble.

Typhylt pointed towards a large wooden stall with a tall woman standing behind a counter. "That's Roldyr," she said.

As Henfylt was about to thank her, footsteps squelched in the mud behind them. The mercenary turned around. A few people similar to Typhylt in age started whispering among themselves.

One of the girls called out, "Looks like Typh the orphan has an actual mother now."

The other three laughed and Henfylt gritted her teeth.

Typhylt's jaw set itself more firmly, her face went red. With embarrassment or rage, Henfylt couldn't tell. Either way, she wasn't sure what to do, so she rested a supportive hand on Typhylt's shoulder. She'd never been in this position before, where the need to protect someone of Typhylt's age burned within her.

The one girl approached, set on tormenting Typhylt more. Before the mercenary had to do anything, Typhylt leapt out of her reach and a loud crunching rang out as her fist connected with the other girl's nose once, then twice. As the girl toppled to the floor, blood streaming down her face, Typhylt hit her again. The others watched in silent horror, eyes wide and faces pale.

Typhylt leapt up off the ground and turned to Henfylt who nodded and smiled. "Good of you to leave off. It's not about going overboard, it's about protecting yourself without being too violent."

Typhylt's shaking hands were dashed with blood. Henfylt passed her a rag she kept in her pocket, usually used to clean her sword with. The girl nodded in thanks and wiped her hands on the piece of cloth until most of the blood was gone or at least smudged.

Meanwhile, the girl on the floor cried at the sight of the blood that covered her hands and stained her shirt. Her friends all sprinted off when Typhylt glared at them. Soon enough, the one with the likely broken nose ran off too.

"You alright?" Henfylt asked.

"I think so," Typhylt answered, looking down at the blood-specked rag she held in her hands.

"Here, let me have a look at them," Henfylt said, nodding at the girl's hands.

Typhylt offered them up, hesitantly. The mercenary took the girl's hands in hers, turning them over to look at her knuckles. She pressed her thumbs against them gently. Typhylt winced.

"You should be fine. Might be a light bit of bruising, but it shouldn't be too bad." She released Typhylt's hands and smiled at her.

"I've never hit anybody before, not like that," Typhylt said.

"Well, you did the right thing, and you didn't take it too far," Henfylt replied. "Now you know you've got some real strength in you after all."

She hit with some force and her technique wasn't bad either. Perhaps she would come with me. No, no, that wouldn't do.

Typhylt smiled at that. It was the first time since their recent meeting that her deep blue eyes glinted with genuine happiness.

"Roldyr?" Typhylt asked, after a moment.

"Roldyr," Henfylt answered, with a nod, and off the two of them went.

The merchant was a little further down the path, and by the time they got to her stall, it became obvious that Roldyr had witnessed Typhylt's victory.

"Taught her a convincing enough lesson, didn't you?" the merchant asked, grinning.

"She did," Henfylt said, her tone full of pride.

Typhylt smiled.

"Right, to business. What is it you want from me? I've got no swords, axes or spears. Only the two daggers you see there." Roldyr pointed to her left. "I don't have any armour either, but I do have some clothes if you need. Oh, and I have some provisions for the road."

Roldyr had a sharply featured face. Her nose was small, her thick eyebrows arched up a little, and her cheeks were slender. *I'm getting distracted,* Henfylt thought.

The mercenary cleared her throat, a rising heat in her cheeks. "One of those daggers'll do me fine and whatever warm clothes you've got too, so long as they fit well enough. Got any boots?"

"The daggers are the exact same but sold as a set. I won't let them go separately, sorry. I have boots, gloves as well," the attractive merchant stated.

I should give Typhylt the spare dagger, shouldn't I? To say goodbye. Or, I could see if she wants to come with me and teach her how to use it properly? No, no, that wouldn't do.

"I'll take the set then," the mercenary decided.

Roldyr nodded, moving the two sheathed daggers to the centre of the counter.

"For clothes, I can offer you these. They ought to fit," she said, lifting a hefty bundle of gear onto the counter, eyeing Henfylt up to judge her size and build.

The merchant spread the clothes across the table so that Henfylt could see what she'd be buying. As soon as the mercenary laid eyes on the bundle of gear, she was ready to grab it all and give the whole bag full of coin over to Roldyr. *It's not like I'm short on coin, thanks to Slyvard.*

The set included a chainmail shirt, fitted trousers, boots, gloves and even a belt that had room for a dagger as well as a sword. Each bit of gear, minus the belt, was fleece-lined and green and black in colour. Henfylt ran her hands along the clothing, surprised at the thickness of it all. Even more surprised by the lack of any loose threads or signs of damage.

She turned to Typhylt and asked, "What do you think?"

The girl weighed her words as she crossed her arms. "It all looks good. It'll keep you warm and the green will suit you."

"Well, I'll have it all then. The daggers too. Dare I ask the price?" Henfylt asked Roldyr, after nodding to Typhylt.

The merchant didn't bother lining the truth with honey. She blurted out, "Hundred and fifty should cover it."

Not half bad, Kynfor was right. I'm not the one being swindled here. The mercenary didn't let surprise fill her face as she shifted the gear to the side, nodded, and grabbed her bag of coin to pour out what was needed. They made high-pitched clinking sounds as they scurried into each other along the counter, rolling and wobbling until they fell flat.

"This'll all do nicely, I'm sure. Thank you," the mercenary said, once the counting had been done.

"Not a bother, farewell," Roldyr replied, scooping the coins up.

Henfylt nodded and smiled, then turned away to stop her mind from wandering again. She clutched the clothes and handed the two daggers to Typhylt.

"Mind taking these for now?" she asked, as she passed the twin blades to the girl.

Typhylt shook her head, smiling as she held onto the weapons.

"So, where are we going now?" the blonde-haired girl asked. "Where are *you* going now, I mean?" she corrected herself.

Henfylt let a smile cross her face, knowing that Typhylt would see.

"I have to head off to Alkyn. It's where someone I'm looking for was last seen near, apparently. First, though, I need a wash. I'll set off later this afternoon," she replied.

Typhylt lowered her head. *I can't take you with me just like that. Well, perhaps I could. No, no, that wouldn't do.*

"We'll head back to the inn if you fancy coming with me," Henfylt said, cursing herself for being such a pushover. It really wasn't the end of the world. In fact, she enjoyed the company.

At that, the girl's ears pricked up and her head rose once more.

The afternoon was cold and fresh, the sky bright and cloudless. Walking back to the inn didn't take long. Henfylt welcomed the heat and Kynfor's warm smile. She asked about the chances of a bath, and Kynfor got it all sorted for her.

Henfylt asked Typhylt to stay with Kynfor and not wander off. The girl, of course, listened. Kynfor always had a good story or two to tell, according to Typhylt, so she had no problems with chatting to him for any length of time.

Henfylt shut the door to the small room and after throwing her thin rags to the side, climbed into the spacious tub. The temperature of the water soothed her sore legs and the steam relaxed her like nothing else in the world could.

Henfylt let out a sigh of deep relief. She'd finally got new clothes and could press on to Alkyn in her own time. The question of Typhylt still remained, though. *There is no question. She can't come with me. Well, maybe she could. Kynfor might be fine with it. Not that he has a real say in the matter, anyway. Maybe he'd support it? No, no, that wouldn't do.*

It wasn't long before the water had cooled and she started shivering thanks to a draught. Henfylt clambered out of the tub with a weary sigh and started pulling on her new gear once she'd dried herself off. Her smallclothes came first, then the fitted fleece-lined trousers, followed by the fleece-lined chainmail shirt. Lastly, she dragged the fur-lined boots on, buckled her new belt and tucked the gloves into a pocket since she didn't need them indoors. She slid her longsword back into the sheath at her left side and placed her new dagger in the sheath at her right side. She let her long, black hair flow loose and free.

By the time she'd made it into the main room, Kynfor was in the middle of a deep conversation with Typhylt. The two of them looked at Henfylt when a floorboard creaked under her weight.

"You'll be warmer in that," Typhylt said, pointing at the mercenary's new gear.

Kynfor nodded and asked, "Do you need anything before you set off, a meal or some ale? Provisions for the journey?"

Henfylt shook her head. "That won't be necessary, thank you Kynfor. I'd best set off and be on my way now." A note of sadness crept into her voice as she spoke.

I may as well suggest it. She'd make for good company and I can keep her safe, maybe even teach her to fight properly. No, no, that wouldn't do.

Before she could turn to leave, or find the courage to suggest anything, Typhylt spoke. "Take me with you. I'm not entirely useless. I don't think I am, anyway."

"You want to come? Kynfor, are you alright with that?" Henfylt asked, grinning.

The innkeeper chuckled and answered straight away, with an enormous smile on his large red face. A hint of sadness lay in his honest green eyes. "Of course! She has an adventurer's spirit and she isn't useless. Far from it. You'd keep her safe. More so than I can. She's bright too, so very bright and sharp." He raised his eyes and tutted at himself. Henfylt got the feeling that they'd been discussing this whilst she'd been in the bath.

"Well, do you have anything you want to bring with you? I can't promise we won't get into trouble along the way, but I think we should be fine on the whole," Henfylt asked.

"I'll get you both some food to pack even if you don't think you need it, free of charge," Kynfor said as he strolled through to a room across the way.

"I don't need anything else, not really, and I don't mind trouble," the girl answered.

"You need warmer clothes since we won't be sleeping in comfy beds most of the time, usually on hard ground instead," Henfylt replied.

Thankfully, as Kynfor came back through with some provisions, he also brought a bundle of clothes with him.

"These might be good for you to wear, Typhylt," he said as he handed them to her.

"They're clean and warm, with a fur cloak at the bottom that shouldn't be too long. I kept them from when I was your age in the hopes that I could give them to... well, they'll serve you well."

He meant to keep them for a child of his own.

Typhylt, with watery eyes, gave Kynfor a long hug and said, "I'll wear it with pride. Thank you for looking after me for so long, I won't forget it. You really don't mind me going?"

The innkeeper refused to let any tears roll down his face, but it looked as if he struggled. "I don't mind at all. I'll miss you terribly, but this will be good for you. You be strong now as you always have been. Come back here whenever you want to, only if you'd like to, of course. You've a good heart and a sharp mind, keep it that way and do as Henfylt says if you're ever in any trouble."

"I'll miss you too, and I'll be sure to come back to see you plenty," Typhylt replied.

Henfylt found it a struggle to go through with this after seeing Kynfor and Typhylt in such a way, but Kynfor thought it best and Henfylt had grown to care for Typhylt over such a short period of time.

The girl ran off to get changed into her new clothes, but soon enough, she returned in her travelling gear, the dull silver necklace still hanging around her neck, all beaten and worn.

The clothes fit Typhylt well. The sleeves of the grey shirt were a bit short but they'd do. At least the trousers were a decent fit, and the cloak, with its fur all ruffled, would serve to keep her warm. At the hip, Henfylt spied a small, empty sheath.

"Here, take this and put it in that sheath at your side," the mercenary said, handing the spare dagger to Typhylt. "It'll serve you well, I'm sure. It's a fine piece of steel. I can show you how to use it properly when we get on the road, if you like."

"Thank you, Henfylt," the girl responded, smiling up at the mercenary.

"Thank you for the provisions, Kynfor. For your kindness, too. We'll come back when this job is done, I promise," the mercenary announced as she placed a hand on Typhylt's shoulder. The girl said goodbye once again and Kynfor waved a hand as they both left 'The Forlorn Fox'.

Following the Trail

The journey to Alkyn took a couple of days. The skies were overcast for most of it, but thankfully there were no storms. They weren't bothered by much rain, only a light drizzle that came and went. In the afternoons, the wind got quite sharp and cold, but Henfylt's new clothes kept her warm and comfortable.

After two nights and three full days of travel, the mercenary spotted the dark outline of Alkyn, struggling to pick it out despite the near-full moon offering its best light. Her and Typhylt had pressed on after sundown so they could use the tower as shelter for the night.

"So, why *exactly* are we here?" Typhylt asked.

"Well, my job was from the King of Dinshei, as you know. He said that the daughter of Queen Meurd was spotted around Alkyn recently. So, I thought we may as well come here first and see if there are any traces of, well, anything," Henfylt answered.

"She was last seen here when he sent you to find her? That would be more than a week ago?" the girl asked, half inquisitively, half mockingly in tone.

Henfylt nudged Typhylt and answered back, "You have a point, it does seem foolish. Did Kynfor ever tell you how sarcastic you can sound sometimes?"

They both laughed as the girl nodded.

"See, the problem is he really gave me nothing to go on other than what she looks like, roughly. Her eyes are bright green and her hair's long and brown. That's it. I do wonder why I took the job, but without it I wouldn't have a trusty companion to keep my wits about me. You know what I told you about rulers?" Henfylt asked.

"You said there's a difference between a ruler and a leader. A ruler rules to maintain their own power and influence, but a leader leads to give power and influence to those who couldn't get it otherwise."

Henfylt smiled. "Exactly. We call the three people who govern Undysvold rulers. Two of them *are* rulers, but King Slyvard struck me as something of a leader. So, he gave me nothing to go on but I don't mind because I genuinely believe his cause is just and true."

As they drew closer to the tower, Typhylt stated, "It doesn't look as strong as you said it used to. It is tall though."

Henfylt nodded in agreement and replied, "I s'pose that's what time can do to a thing."

Alkyn had a daunting quality to it as it towered above the trees in the surrounding area. It had certainly lost some of its strength since the days of the Civil War, when it was a famed outpost, going some twenty-odd years back. Henfylt placed her gloved hand on one of the many loose, moss-covered bricks of the tower. Once she let go, the brick fell into the grass with a thud.

"Must just be around this corner here," the mercenary said as she glanced back at the girl who nodded in return.

There was some kind of entrance to the ruined tower, but it wasn't a large wooden door or even a small one. The entrance was more of a hole. A big hole admittedly, but a hole nonetheless.

"Well, here we go. It'll do for the night," Henfylt announced.

As she went to climb through the gap, Typhylt asked, "What's that over there?"

Henfylt turned around and took a few quick steps towards Typhylt, her hand hovering over the hilt of her sword as she followed Typhylt's pointing finger to a large shape lying in the distance.

"Stay by my side. We'll go and have a look," the mercenary said, keeping Typhylt close behind her.

The nearer they got to their target, the more squashed the grass was. A chunk of the blades were chopped short and swept over to one side. As Henfylt took her next step, it sounded as if she stood on metal rather than the usual firm ground.

Behind her, Typhylt reached down and grabbed at something. Henfylt stepped to the left and the girl used both hands to lift a greatsword off the ground.

"It's heavy," Typhylt stated, letting the slab of thick steel rest on the floor whilst she held onto the grip. She then passed it to Henfylt.

"Well, something happened here then. Recent, too," the mercenary said, weighing the greatsword in her hands.

Typhylt looked at Henfylt, her head tilted to one side. The mercenary dropped the sword and took a few steps towards the enormous shape. It was the body of a man, an enormous man that was the size of a tree.

"Well, we know who the sword belonged to. You alright with blood?" she asked Typhylt, who nodded sternly.

"Feel free to come closer, then," Henfylt said, crouching down at the side of the corpse.

The girl took two large steps forward to stand at Henfylt's side once more. The mercenary looked up at Typhylt. The girl's face didn't change much, she simply frowned and raised a hand to her chin in thought.

The corpse stretched a good seven feet, by Henfylt's reckoning. Chain armour covered his upper body, heavy stuff by the look of it. There was a tear in the dark grey surcoat he'd been wearing when he died. She assumed this man had been on patrol. For who, she couldn't say, but he had the look of a Southerner about him. Whoever he was, he had legs as thick as tree trunks and arms to match. *Not many people this size, that's for sure. Evidently put up a good fight what with all the ground that's been trodden down.*

"I've found what must be his helmet!" Typhylt called out, holding a greathelm in her hands.

"Well spotted. Got keen eyes, haven't you?" Henfylt replied.

Typhylt nodded and smiled, heading back over to Henfylt and the body. She placed the greathelm at the side of the corpse.

"See this?" the mercenary said as she pointed to both deep cuts across the lower legs of the corpse. "Our killer's clever. He's seen the size of this poor sod and decided to take advantage where he can. Look at his legs, see how poorly protected they are?"

Typhylt nodded and replied, "So, they went for his legs because his armour, like yours, protected his upper body but his legs were left more exposed?"

Henfylt stood up and said, "Exactly right. He probably didn't fancy any restrictions about his legs, or the added weight. Paid the price for it, though. Wasn't quick enough on his feet."

"This too," Henfylt stated, pointing to the tear in the surcoat. "If this has been torn, what do you think it's been torn for exactly?"

"If the person who killed him was injured then they'd try to stop the bleeding with whatever they could," Typhylt answered.

"Spot on," Henfylt replied, patting the girl on the shoulder.

The large, lifeless man had likely been a corpse for most of the day. Whoever he was, he had an unsettling look about him. Perhaps being dead made him look unfriendly, but a crooked nose and a big old scar across a cheek never won anybody a beauty contest.

"There's nothing we can do. I say we rest here for the night inside the tower. Then tomorrow we see if there's a trail to follow. It's just strange to see a body out here. I think it's worth investigating. Could be something serious. The job can wait another day, or maybe this is somehow tied to it?" Henfylt asked, turning to look at Typhylt.

"It could be, I suppose. Either way, it seems like a good idea to get some sleep and start fresh tomorrow," Typhylt answered.

Henfylt always thought it was right to ask Typhylt what she thought the pair of them should do, even though the girl agreed with whatever she said all the time anyway.

Henfylt helped Typhylt up through the gap in the tower onto a large slab that had come loose. Once inside, Henfylt glanced in all directions, taking in the scratched wood and crumbling stone.

"Well, it's not great but it'll do," Henfylt said.

"It's quite eerie but it feels safe enough to me," Typhylt replied, shrugging her shoulders.

The stairs were tucked away in the corner, clinging to the walls of the round tower, spiralling up to the very top. The gnarled and worn wooden floor was covered in a thick layer of dust and dirt, with old footprints stamped into the muddiest sections. Soot surrounded the few empty sconces on the walls.

"I think we'll be able to light a fire up top. There's supposedly always wood up there to be burned," Henfylt called out as she pointed at the stairs. "Won't have as much cover but it's cold down here, anyway. Best to head up, I think," she finished, with a glance over at the girl who nodded in return.

Henfylt tested her weight on the stairs to make sure the pair of them wouldn't fall to their deaths halfway up. She looked back at Typhylt, not wanting the girl to slip. "You go first if you like, but don't go running up the stairs. I'll be just behind you."

Typhylt led the way with confidence and care.

A breeze hung in the air as they reached the top. A pile of old wood sat to the right, covered with a bulky blanket, a campfire straight ahead. It wasn't lit, but there were smaller sticks stacked at the side with some candles, too. Those were also covered, protected from any rain. *Bit of a gamble, but thankfully it paid off.*

Before long, the flames were roaring, providing some warmth against the cold night air as they both laid out their thin blankets to prepare for sleep.

Typhylt settled down at Henfylt's side, the pair of them watching the flames flicker and listening to the wood crack as they spoke about anything that came to mind, sharing a laugh over a meal of dried meat and water.

With the stars twinkling overhead and the moon casting gentle beams of light down on them, Typhylt fell asleep slumped against Henfylt's shoulder.

With happiness and a sense of purpose filling her, the mercenary soon closed her eyes and let her mind drift freely.

*

Henfylt opened her eyes to the sight of a few thin clouds hanging in the otherwise blue sky. Birds chirped away all around her as she blinked a few times and looked to her right where Typhylt still lay sleeping.

The girl's hair was a mess, her blonde strands were layered across the mercenary's shoulder. How she was comfortable, Henfylt couldn't say. But, she was, so whilst Henfylt wanted to get going, she stopped herself from moving and settled for lying still, staring up at the sky with a smile on her face.

Eventually, Typhylt stretched. She rubbed her eyes and yawned.

"Slept well I take it?" Henfylt asked.

"I was undisturbed and warm, so all in all, a good sleep," the girl replied, yawning again.

"Good," the mercenary stated.

Her stomach grumbled, then Typhylt's did too.

"Right, best get some food sorted," Henfylt said.

Once they finished, they set off down the stairs, climbing back out of the gap in the wall. Henfylt forged the path ahead, sweeping the taller blades of grass to the side. Typhylt followed and the two remained silent, but the silence was far from awkward.

There was no trail over by the damaged bridge that led to Hinsylt, so Henfylt kept her focus on the evidence, as she'd been taught to. Chunks of grass were strewn across the battleground. It was a struggle to pinpoint anything worth following, but the mercenary's trained eyes soon locked onto some dried blood that had spattered against a few disturbed blades of grass.

Henfylt glanced at Typhylt, who stood at her side. "Well, at least we have the start of a trail. We'd best see where it leads."

The girl nodded in response, keen to get a move on.

There were sections of the grass that had been bent sideways and squashed, suggesting that the killer had struggled and stumbled all over the place.

They followed the evidence, leading them through a dense forest, specifically to one tree which was a bit odd. There was a dirt road not so far away. The road, if it could be called that, hadn't been maintained well at all. It was full of bumps and holes which didn't surprise Henfylt a bit. The roads of the South, particularly on the Western side, were known to be in a right state.

Torn branches and uncoordinated footprints dashed the ground along the way. Interestingly, there was more than just a set belonging to one person.

Once they reached the road, the trail seemed to disappear. Henfylt stood for a moment, unsure of where to go next. *No obvious signs of anything, really. No blood, dry or otherwise. Just cart tracks from the trading paths. Unless?*

Typhylt called out, interrupting the mercenary's train of thought. "There were carts that went through here, I think. Look at the marks on the road. Could it be that they got help?" the girl asked.

Henfylt smiled to herself before replying, "Makes sense that whoever got wounded would look for help out on this road. It goes off to Dansphylt here, but the other way seems more likely, heading to some village, perhaps."

Typhylt ran over to the mercenary. "Best get a move on then," she said, to which Henfylt agreed.

They moved faster since the hunt for subtle clues had ended. The state of the road grew worse because it sat so far away from the palace, 'Tymur', which was situated in the South-East. Queen Meurd had never given much of a shit for the folk that lived far away from her.

Well before noon, Henfylt and Typhylt reached the end of the trail, arriving at a tiny village. The houses acted as the centre of the village, whilst animals were fenced in areas around its edges. Further out, people were working in the fields full of crops.

Typhylt exchanged a glance with the mercenary as a man with a bandage wrapped around his head came stumbling out of one of the houses, lowering himself down onto a step outside the door, taking a sip from a steaming cup.

"He's got to be our killer," Henfylt said, looking at Typhylt.

Common Ground

Blynkiln was sitting on a step outside Merek's house as he stared up at the sky. All there was to remind him of his near-death experience was a dull aching in his side.

He let out a quiet sigh and took a long slurp from the steaming cup in his hands. The drink had a smooth texture and a bitter taste.

As he was about to enjoy another peaceful sip of his drink, the wooden door next to him swung open with a loud creak. Merek stumbled out and Blynkiln leapt to his feet as fast as he could, wincing from the flash of pain that lashed up his side. A blur of black and white stormed past him.

"Ah, bugger!" Merek shouted as he struggled to find his balance.

"Are you alright?" Blynkiln asked, resting a hand on his stitched wound.

"It's nothing, just the village cat trying to kill me again! Happens most mornings these days. It pops its head in to see what I've been eating and if there's anything left for it to nab," Merek answered.

"Ah, that explains it," Blynkiln replied, taking another slurp of the bitter drink. The pain faded back down to its familiar dull ache. "Just the one cat that patrols the village, then?"

Standing opposite him, Merek answered, "It is, it is. No more round here so I do my best to keep the little devil content. Doesn't stop it from tripping me up all the time, though!" He chuckled to himself as he finished.

A brief silence stretched between them and Blynkiln thought it was as good an opportunity as any to get to know more about the man who'd saved his life.

"So, what's your story? Have you always been out here?" he asked.

"I've been here a while, but I've been all over really. That's the benefit of making it to this age. I may be a little wrinkly and whatnot, but age can't take away where I've been and what I've seen." Merek broke off, taking in the horizon with his deep blue eyes. Then, he carried on, "My mind is still as sharp as it ever was. Well, at least I think it is!"

Merek's tone changed as he bolted on the last bit of his speech with humour.

"What's the best place you've been to?" Blynkiln asked.

"Oooh, tricky question that is. Elensfyr's a cracking place, great architecture and full of these wondrously thick tomes. Oh, and scrolls aplenty. It's the sensations you get as you sit down and have a read through rare texts. The smell of it all too, ancient manuscripts written before even my time. I've gone off on one again, haven't I?" Merek's eyes rolled up to the sky as he tutted to himself.

"No, not at all. I asked and you answered. I've never been to Elensfyr before, but I'd like to go. Might be a bit of a challenge these days, though," Blynkiln replied.

"Tell you what, I'll pack you in a barrel, nick off with Aedlyn's cart and deliver you there so you might have a chance!" Merek exclaimed.

The False Knight laughed for the first time in five years. He soon made himself stop when he forced himself to remember the situation he was in.

"I'll go sometime if I can ever clear my name," Blynkiln replied, after a moment.

I'll go with you, when I find you. We'll go together, he thought, keeping the woman he loved in his mind.

Merek put a firm, supportive hand on Blynkiln's shoulder. "Look, you don't deserve what's been thrown your way. I've seen much in my time, some good and some not so good. Where there's happiness and joy there tends to be the fear of losing it. Where there's sadness and despair people don't bother looking for hope, they just want it to find them as if by magic. We need hope just as we need food in our bellies. I may be an old fool with a wasted dream, but what is life without a dream? I'd sooner live with the fool's hope rather than the realist's curse."

"You make a fine point. You should be a philosopher, Merek," Blynkiln replied.

"Haven't got the patience of a philosopher," Merek stated, smiling.

The False Knight allowed himself a brief smile before speaking once more. "I believe I'm at that stage where I've nearly lost all hope. It's been so long that it's become my nature. All I need is a sign, that's all. A sign from my gods."

Merek weighed Blynkiln's words for a quiet moment. "Who knows? Maybe your sign is coming, maybe it will arrive sooner than you think. In some ways, you remind me of an old friend. A very old friend. He struggled with many things but he was a good man, until envy got the better of him. There's no emotion or feeling that causes more trouble than envy."

"I'll keep that in mind. But why envy?" The False Knight asked.

"Why envy? Look at King Inshelt and Queen Ynfleyd. He was envious of Tynuks for the power they had, the same power which he thought he deserved. The lengths he went to in order to take that power for himself, well, they were frightening indeed. Ynfleyd was no better, a queen heralded as a hero in most books, but if you find the right ones, you'll learn that she too was just as envious as her sworn enemy. They call it genocide, her 'Tynuk Hunts'. A whole race of people wiped out because of her envy and insecurity. They might call you 'The False Knight', Blynkiln, but trust me, you're far from the worst to have walked these lands," Merek answered. His eyes flashed with all kinds of emotions as he spoke.

He then turned to go inside, leaving Blynkiln frowning into the fresh air.

A voice called out behind him, "Back on your feet already? How do you do it, Merek?"

Merek spun around and grinned, "It's a secret. If I told you, I'd have to kill you!"

His tone had changed once more, gone from matching the tone of someone speaking over the corpse of a loved one, to the tone of a joke cracked in a tavern.

"Come on in and have a chat if you aren't too busy," Merek said.

Aedlyn followed Merek and Blynkiln inside.

Merek pulled a few chairs out from his table and moved over to his own seat, sitting at the table's head.

Blynkiln took a seat and looked at Aedlyn. She had long brown hair and unnaturally bright green eyes set against pale skin, though not as pale as Merek's. Where the features of his face were generally soft, aside from his sharp, angular nose, hers were harsh.

"Thank you, Aedlyn, for bringing me here in your cart. I know for a fact I wouldn't be here if you and your lad hadn't helped me," Blynkiln said.

"I'd hope anybody would do the same, but nothing's so certain these days. You seem to be healing quickly, which I'm glad to see," the brown-haired woman replied.

Merek's glance shifted around the room as he drummed his fingers on the table. "He's made of tough stuff, this one, I tell you," he stated, with his usual chuckle at the end.

Blynkiln thought about whether he should mention why he was healing so quickly. *Better not actually, best to wait before prattling on about that sort of thing.*

"So, Aedlyn, where's Ofryth?" Merek asked, breaking the silence.

The green-eyed woman crossed her arms and shuffled more upright in her chair. "He's just with Wylf, learning about who knows what. Could be history, or warfare. Maybe something altogether different. You know how he is, likes to jump about but gets the job done."

"I've known Wylf for years, Blynkiln. He's younger than me but he knows all sorts of random stuff. Some of it's useful, other bits... not so much. That's part of learning, I suppose. Who taught you how to fight, if you don't mind me asking?" Merek replied.

"I grew up in Raltyr. Not sure how I got there, mind, but I suppose it doesn't matter all that much now," he paused, noticing a curious glance from Aedlyn.

"Anyway, my teacher was a woman named Fuldyn. She was firm but fair and taught me all I needed to know and more. I had a lot of time for her."

Enough detail, stop talking. The truth was, Fuldyn was more like a mother to him than a teacher, and he missed her every day.

"With a sword like that, you must be good," Aedlyn stated as she pointed at Blynkiln's narrow-bladed sword which was leaning against the wall. "Can't be easy fighting with such a thin blade."

Blynkiln didn't want to brag about the sword being the product of Yinfyr's famed forgers. He settled for replying, "It's stronger than you'd think, in fairness. I've found it more than a match for all other blades."

His thoughts turned to the day he received the gift. He'd always used an ordinary longsword when training at Raltyr. He remembered the snow fondly, how it would fall and fall with no end in sight.

Fuldyn made training a challenge. She always aimed to put him on his arse at least three times over whenever they sparred. He'd be bruised afterwards, but that didn't matter to him, as long as he'd learned something new.

After an assassination attempt on the Queen of Raltyr, he received the sword as a formal gift. They'd been in the forest a distance away from the fortress when bandits attacked. Blynkiln fought alongside Fuldyn. After the fight, he'd buried her. It wasn't the happiest of memories, but he'd saved the life of Queen Phenyrt, which did him no harm.

The False Knight's thoughts were interrupted by a knocking at the door. The boy, Ofryth, walked in. He had the same brown hair and green eyes as his mother.

"What were you learning today, then?" Ofryth's mother asked as she pulled a chair out for him.

"We started off discussing Hinsylt and how it's changed because of trade over time, but then we ended up talking about the Civil War again, like always. That was more interesting, but he always ends up teaching me about that Civil War and how it started after Queen Ynfleyd's 'mysterious' assassination. He can't stop himself from mentioning it. Every single lesson. It isn't boring, but I've heard the same story five times now about how he was overlooking the area around Alkyn because he was scouting for the independent forces, against the loyalists. I could probably tell you how long each blade of grass was, the way he goes on about it."

Aedlyn and Merek laughed, Blynkiln smiled.

"You seem better than when I last saw you. How are you feeling?" Ofryth asked him.

"I'm doing well, I think. I have all of you to thank for that," The False Knight answered.

"So, might I ask what you were doing wanting to get to Hinsylt of all places?" Merek asked.

Blynkiln didn't think it was worth dodging the truth. "I'm looking for someone. I've been looking for her for half a decade or so and I figured that with the tournament coming up, it was best to go there in the hope of hearing something. Anything."

After he'd finished, a silence hung over the room.

Merek spoke first, "I believe I know who you're looking for. Am I right in thinking this is all to do with that business when you had to flee Raltyr some five years ago? That's how you got your unfortunate title, isn't it?"

Aedlyn's eyes widened. Ofryth's chair creaked as he leaned in.

"Aye, it is. Most people just assume I decided to kill twelve people for no reason," Blynkiln said, angrily.

"I'd heard rumours, but it did seem odd to me that you fled just as Adelyka mysteriously disappeared. You both grew up at Raltyr, where she ruled after her mother, Queen Phenyrt, passed away. I'd guess that it's Adelyka you're looking for and that the two of you are bound."

Blynkiln sighed and leaned back in his chair. "At least someone knows what happened, I suppose that counts for something."

Aedlyn and Ofryth were still and silent, eyes flitting between Blynkiln himself and Merek.

"Most people in my field would try their hand at saving anyone who needed it. I only save those worth it. My guess would be that those twelve soldiers you cut down were blocking your path to freedom. You and Adelyka must've planned to meet back up and you couldn't risk getting captured. So, it's only natural that if you're good with a sword you'd lay them all to rest. The problem is, people heard you'd killed twelve people and they never thought *why* you might have done it. They never do, never have. Nothing's changed. It's always been about, and will always be about, not using your mind and instead just nodding in agreement with whatever you hear first."

Finally, someone who understands.

Merek, Aedlyn and Ofryth exchanged glances, then they nodded in answer to some unspoken question. The False Knight got the feeling that a rehearsed request or a practised speech was coming next.

Aedlyn confirmed Blynkiln's suspicions as she leant forwards and cleared her throat. "There's something of a... situation at the minute. We're thinking we might have to leave here for a while, if it's as bad as we think. Maybe, if you wouldn't mind, we could come with you and help you find Adelyka before we settle somewhere else?"

Blynkiln frowned. "What's the situation?"

Aedlyn raised her eyebrows at Merek.

"The other week, when I was out gathering herbs and doing other boring stuff, I saw a hooded figure among the trees. It was only a quick glance I got, but it was enough to see the red and black Tarspyk robes they wore. You know, the people who can manipulate the elements and all that nonsense," Merek broke off, tutted and raised his eyes to the sky. "Anyway, the Tarspyks stick to their spire and leave the rest of us well alone. So, what was one doing alone and so far away from home? Here of all places?"

He leaned back in his chair and nodded to Aedlyn, as if encouraging her.

She took a deep breath. "Well, there's nothing here that anybody would want. Apart from something my mother, Queen Meurd, would be interested in."

"I see now. The bright green eyes were a bit of a giveaway, come to think of it. She wants you back, but why?" Blynkiln asked.

"I don't know. To see her grandson, to control him as she tried to control me? Either way, we're assuming the Tarspyk Merek saw is one of her spies. She always had close ties to the Tarspyks, and I doubt that's changed even after all these years I've been away. Why else would one of them be down here? That's the situation, and that's why we need to leave," Aedlyn answered. "I'm not risking us being found by her, taken to her."

"I've got no issues with causing Meurd trouble. Truth is, I don't like her one bit," Blynkiln stated.

"Few people do like her, and those that do must also suffer," Aedlyn said, in a voice as cold as the snows in the North-East.

I wonder what happened between her and Meurd?

"So, what do you say?" Ofryth asked.

Blynkiln took a long few moments to think this through, to make sure this was the best thing to do, or at least the right thing to do given his own situation. He had nothing else on his plate, no leads, little hope. Maybe the company would do him good? Maybe these three good people would make the process of finding Adelyka faster? Maybe not, but what did he have to lose?

"I'll travel with you," he decided. "But I won't lie to you all. I can't and won't prioritise this over my own troubles. I wish I could, but if it's a straight choice between Adelyka and you, there's no contest. Adelyka is my focus, always."

Blynkiln wasn't about to set off on a journey with these people without giving them the full truth, even if that truth was a ruthless one. He had to be honest with them. He owed his saviours that much.

"I wouldn't even ask you to put us before Adelyka. It's evident how much she means to you, and you've not long met us. It would be unreasonable to ask that much of you," Aedlyn said, warmly.

"There's somewhere we should pass through on our way to Hinsylt. I have an old friend, a very old friend called Yuneld. He lives in a mountain not far from Hinsylt. Blynkiln, I think you might benefit from it, too. Yuneld's brother, Yunylt, is the lead forger at the Yinfyr forge. As you will no doubt be aware, Adelyka had a close connection to the Dwarven forgers since she was young. It might be that they know something about Adelyka that we don't. What do you say to it?" Merek asked.

Hope? Perhaps it is a sign. Doubt it, but I have fuck all else to go on.

"Seems smart to me. We meet Yuneld to see what he knows, if anything, then decide what happens next," The False Knight answered.

With that agreed, the four of them left the house. Aedlyn and Ofryth went off to sort out some supplies for the journey.

Merek strolled at Blynkiln's side, looking at the floor then at Blynkiln as he scratched his beard and cleared his throat, as if he was building up to saying something.

"What is it, Merek?" The False Knight asked.

"I knew your parents," he blurted out.

Blynkiln's eyes shot up to meet Merek's. His jaw went slack. "They were good people, terrible what happened. I told Aedlyn she could trust you. I told her that because I trusted your parents, and I know I can trust you. But, since Aedlyn and Ofryth are out of earshot, I'll speak more plainly."

The two of them walked along the village path. Trees rustled in the wind and Blynkiln's skin crawled with the sensation that he was being watched. He shook his head and turned his attention back to Merek.

"I know why you're healing so fast because I knew your parents. I helped them during the Tynuk Hunts when they were being pursued. I didn't say earlier because I didn't know if you wanted something like that to be put in open play," he said.

Blynkiln nodded, waiting for more.

"It was a long while ago when the call was made by Ynfleyd, to hunt and kill all Tynuk people because of their blood. The funny thing is that many Tynuks actually helped that vile queen in her war. So did some Tynukei, those who had weakened Tynuk blood in their veins. Regardless of the

Harry Walker

help they offered, once they helped her win the war against the dreaded Inshelt, she decreed that they should all be hunted down and killed. You have the blood of your mother in your veins, Blynkiln. She was a reasonably powerful Tynukei, which explains your quicker healing and so on. Anyway, we hid for some time in the North-East out of harm's way for a good few years until we were found. You were three and your parents asked me to take you to Raltyr whilst they were set upon. You were their priority, so I did as they wished. I was of half a mind to keep you myself and teach you what I knew, but they asked for you to be taken to Raltyr. Safer to be brought up as a warrior than by a superstitious old fool, I suppose. Anyway, that's how you ended up at Raltyr. That's how I knew I could trust you with Aedlyn's situation."

Merek took a deep breath and sighed.

"I didn't know any of that. Maybe my gods put me on this path so that I'd find out. Perhaps there is hope. Thank you, Merek, for your honesty and kindness. At least you tried to do something in the face of injustice. So few do," Blynkiln said as he patted Merek on one of his broad shoulders.

As they picked up the pace, heading for Aedlyn's house, two figures approached them. One was average in height but looked strong. She had wild dark hair and dark skin to match. The other, strolling at her side, was a blonde-haired girl with pale skin.

"We've been following the trail you left. I wasn't sure we'd ever bloody well catch up to you," the dark-haired woman said, staring at Blynkiln. Her hand dangled close to the hilt of her sword.

"What can we do for you two on this fine morning?" Merek asked.

"Nothing much, just came for a chat really," she answered, before turning her gaze to Blynkiln. "Nice bit of work you did on that big bastard back at Alkyn. I'm Henfylt, by the way, and this is Typhylt."

She placed a hand on her companion's shoulder. The blonde-haired girl smiled at Blynkiln and Merek. They exchanged a glance, Merek shrugged his broad shoulders.

"Well met. Let's head in somewhere warm and get a few drinks so we might have that chat you're looking for, Henfylt," Blynkiln said.

Allies

As they followed the two men along the village path, Henfylt whispered, "Look, Typh. What do you reckon to these two?"

One of them, the killer, was probably a few years younger than Henfylt. He had messy blond hair, icy blue eyes and a lean frame. He was slightly hunched over as he walked, probably thanks to some wound he'd got from the man he'd killed. The other, an older man with white hair and a white beard, had some of the broadest shoulders Henfylt had ever seen. He carried his stockier frame in an energetic way that made Henfylt struggle to settle on an age.

"I think the older man is nice, I don't know why but he just seems kind. The younger one is a bit intimidating but I don't think he means to be," Typhylt replied.

The mercenary nodded.

"So, what are your names, if you don't mind me asking?" Henfylt said, as they approached the small tavern's door.

"I'm Merek, this one here's Blynkiln. Truth be told he is a little intimidating, Typhylt. It's something about him. Might be his hair and the state it's in, could be a bird's nest for all I know," the older man replied, chuckling heartily.

Typhylt went red-faced, evidently hoping she hadn't been heard. Henfylt laughed and Blynkiln shook his head, with the trace of a smile on his face.

Once they were at the door, Merek swung it open and led them all in. The tavern was cosy but not as nice as 'The Forlorn Fox'. The whole space smelled as if it'd been here for centuries. The creaking of the gnarled and weathered floorboards suggested the same.

Merek spoke to the owner, a stout woman, at the counter. "Just my usual for all of us, if you don't mind. Maybe not for the youngest though, eh Gladys, got to be responsible and all that I suppose."

"I'll have whatever you all have," Typhylt said.

Henfylt smiled to herself.

Merek looked at the girl, then at Gladys. "Whatever the general says, wouldn't want to be in trouble with her," he stated, humorously.

They'd all been given the same dark coloured drink. They wandered over to the largest square table and took their seats, the mercenary's chair wobbling and groaning as she sat in it.

"So, I saw that you got into a nasty scrap back at Alkyn. You seem to be doing alright now though," Henfylt said.

Blynkiln took a long gulp of his drink before he answered her. "It wasn't an easy fight, I tell you. What were you two doing around there anyway?" he asked.

May as well be honest, not like these two will do much with anything I tell them.

"We're looking for Queen Meurd's daughter. She was seen near Alkyn a few weeks back, or so I'm told. It's a job from King Slyvard, you see. He wants us to find her and someone else. He has this plan which... Nevermind," Henfylt stopped herself from going on. Blynkiln's icy blue eyes somehow grew colder, like a freezing mist caught in a glass globe.

"Feel free to tell us both what his grand plan is. The suspense is killing me," Merek said. His bushy white eyebrows angled with intrigue.

"It's no big secret that Meurd and Rancylt are fools, is it? I mean, you look at the roads down here and the state of the North-East, hardly how it is in the North-West. Slyvard wants them out and Meurd's daughter in. He also wants a previous queen, called Adelyka, back ruling the snows. Being honest, it sounds fine to me, so long as Meurd's daughter and this Adelyka are competent and actually give a shit about the folk they lead."

"Adelyka's a fine leader, the North-East was in safe hands when she ruled. Her plans would've worked if it wasn't for..." Blynkiln broke off. He seemed familiar with Adelyka, somehow.

"You know her? Any idea where we might find her?" Typhylt asked, looking at Henfylt and raising an eyebrow.

Blynkiln looked at Merek and moved his head to the side as if he was asking a question. Merek nodded, and Blynkiln leant forwards.

"I've probably been too open with the both of you already, but maybe we can help you and you can help us," he said. His shoulders dropped as he uncrossed his arms.

Typhylt leaned in, Henfylt did too. Merek leaned backwards and took long gulp after long gulp of his drink until it had all gone and a thick froth was stuck to his lips. He wiped his mouth with the back of his hand and sighed, as if settling in for a story being told next to the heat of a roaring fire.

"You're looking for Meurd's daughter and we're both looking for Adelyka. Good news for you, this is where Meurd's daughter lives. We can introduce you to her later if you like." Blynkiln paused for a moment, taking a sip from his tankard.

There's luck and then there's luck. This can't be some coincidence, surely.

Henfylt drank from her own tankard, enjoying the bitterness of the beer.

"Maybe we could work together to find Adelyka. I'm guessing, like me, you've got nothing to go on. But, thankfully, Merek's got an idea. He's got a friend who might know where she is. I doubt it'll come to anything much, but who knows."

The rest of the conversation in the tavern took a while. Henfylt couldn't stop thinking that maybe there really was some divine force that controlled the world and everyone living in it. It was just so strange that something like this could happen by chance alone. *Quit thinking like that. Coincidence, that's all this is.*

Soon enough, they left the tavern and got back on the village path, strolling along in silence. Henfylt needed the quiet so she could wrap her head around what was going on. *Meurd's daughter must be the brown-haired woman that left earlier, before Merek and Blynkiln did. She's also got a son. Maybe that's why she left Tymur.*

"Henfylt, isn't it a little bit strange that we all met. I don't believe in fate or anything like that, but is something happening that we don't know about?" Typhylt asked.

"I think you might be right. I can't help but think Slyvard has something to do with this, or... someone else, maybe?" Henfylt responded. She didn't like the thought that she was being manipulated.

"But, surely if he knew anything he would have told you, or he wouldn't have needed you to help him in the first place?" Typhylt asked.

"You might be right there, too. I did think he was hiding something, but what that is or was I can't say I know," the mercenary answered.

Henfylt stopped and put both of her hands on Typhylt's shoulders. "You know, if it all gets too much and you're not happy at any point, let me know and I'll abandon the job. I'm not short of coin."

Typhylt's eyes widened. Henfylt frowned, wondering how she'd become so glad of this girl's company so quickly.

"Without this job, I'd never have met you. Also, I'm interested to find out more about... well, all of this," Typhylt said.

"You're sure?" Henfylt asked.

"I am," Typhylt answered.

"Well, we'd best get back to it, then," Henfylt replied.

They shared a smile, and the mercenary patted Typhylt on the shoulder before they caught up to Blynkiln and Merek.

Henfylt took in the sights of the small village, the smell of burning wood and the freshness of the cool air. Thanks to her fleece-lined gear, she hardly felt the chill at all.

Just up ahead, Merek knocked on a door. Once it opened, Henfylt had no doubt that this was Meurd's daughter. She had long brown hair and bright green eyes, her skin was pale and she was a similar height to Henfylt.

She welcomed Henfylt and Typhylt just as she welcomed Merek and Blynkiln, inviting them all in with a warm smile on her face that lit up her already bright eyes.

"Aedlyn, this is Henfylt, and this is Typhylt," Merek said, once he'd shut the door behind them. "They're our new recruits, and fine recruits I reckon they'll make."

"Nice to meet you both," Aedlyn said, smiling at Henfylt, then at Typhylt.

"Pleasure's all mine," Henfylt replied, smiling back at Aedlyn.

Typhylt added, "You have a lovely home."

Aedlyn thanked Typhylt and said, "Please, sit down if you'd like to."

Typhylt was right. It was a small but cosy place. Potted plants, one or two small paintings, and some little sculptures decorated the room. A few panels separated two sections at the back of the house and a square table took up the centre of the main room.

Whilst Henfylt took a seat over by a tall and narrow bookcase, Aedlyn introduced her and Typhylt to her son, Ofryth. He also had bright green eyes and brown hair, though his hair was short.

Before long, Typhylt and Ofryth started chatting away, awkwardly at first, but Typhylt soon uncrossed her arms and started laughing with Ofryth whose posture became less stiff as the conversation went on. Henfylt reckoned Ofryth was a similar age to Typhylt, but he was quite tall for such an age.

Aedlyn laid some plates of food out on the square table in the centre of the room. Piles of beef, pork and chicken took up two full plates, carrots and other vegetables covered a single plate, and a large board of bread and cheese was set down in the centre of it all.

Henfylt's stomach grumbled. She didn't want to seem rude but still made the first move after nodding her head at Aedlyn to thank her. Everyone else stacked their plates and began filling their stomachs.

Once they'd finished eating, chatting and laughing, they all found a place to stand or sit and the real conversation began.

They told her and Typhylt what their plan was, before turning to stare at Henfylt, expecting words to pour out of her mouth like gravy from a jug. So, she told them all she knew about Slyvard's scheme, how he wanted Meurd and Rancylt replaced with Aedlyn and Adelyka. Once she finished, everyone was silent.

"Well, if that's everything, may as well get what you need and set off sharpish so we get to Yuneld's before dark," Blynkiln said, breaking the silence.

"Let's get a move on then. Blynkiln, come with me to get your sword and I'll bring a few things of my own, too. We'll meet by the sign at the side of the road," Merek announced. With that, it was decided.

Henfylt and Typhylt had nothing to fetch, so Merek said that the pair of them could come to his house and wait. The mercenary hung back whilst Typhylt ran on to join Merek. Blynkiln strolled at Henfylt's side.

"I thought I'd best thank you for your help. I know it's Slyvard you're helping really, but by doing this you're giving me the chance to see Adelyka again. That's a priceless gift," he said, after a moment.

"Well, you owe me now which is never a bad thing." Henfylt replied, chuckling. "In truth, it might've been Slyvard who sent me to do this job, but he's not the only reason I'm still here. I only met Typh not that long ago, you know. She's given me a purpose. Before meeting her, I had no idea what I was doing, not really. I have friends at the Guildhall, I've been living a fine enough life, but I've had no purpose for such a long time that I forgot what the stuff felt like. This job isn't like most. This is purposeful and it affects people's lives. Properly affects lives, like yours and Aedlyn's. Ofryth's too, even Merek's. So, I'm not here just for Slyvard. Yes, I admire him, but seeing how you all live and, in your case, suffer, I'm thinking why shouldn't I do something purposeful for once? I've been lucky because of this job to meet Typh, but you haven't had any luck in five years from what you've said."

"Seems to me we aren't so different. I'm glad you've found something that you didn't know you were looking for," Blynkiln replied.

There was an understanding that passed between them, then. An understanding that made Henfylt even more set on her course to see this job through, especially since Typhylt was happy with the situation.

Soon enough, they made it to Merek's house. It had the same layout and style as Aedlyn's, but with more space and an extra room. Henfylt took the opportunity to sit down again. After all, she knew she'd be walking for the rest of the afternoon.

Typhylt sat in a chair by the table whilst Merek went through into the other room to gather some supplies for the journey. Blynkiln, meanwhile, reached down by the spare bed and buckled his sword belt around his travelling gear. Henfylt assumed that Merek had given Blynkiln some clean clothes since the clothes he wore were so loosely fitted.

"Interesting sword. Why so narrow, if you don't mind me asking?" Henfylt said, her gaze on Blynkiln's sheathed sword.

"It was a gift from Adelyka after I saved her mother's life years ago. It's served me ever since. It's surprisingly strong. Here, try it," Blynkiln replied. He handed the sword to her after he pulled it out of its worn sheath.

Henfylt looked around to make sure she wouldn't damage anything and began to swing the blade through the air in soft, slow motions. She soon realised this must've been made by the Dwarven forgers up at Yinfyr. Their weapons were the stuff of legends, and Blynkiln's sword was balanced perfectly, light in its weight but with an impossibly sharp edge.

As Henfylt was swinging the narrow-bladed sword about, twirling it around in her hands, Merek strolled out of his room and started laughing. "Careful not to break anything, else you'll pay with your life! Only joking, you can smash the entire house down for all I care, to be honest. I won't be back anytime soon!"

The room lit up with smiles and laughter. Henfylt passed the thin sword back to Blynkiln, though it was a struggle to let such a fine thing go. Merek let them all know it was time to head off, as soon as they were all ready. He slung a medium-sized bag, made of old leather, over his shoulder and reached for a large object wrapped in cloth that he'd laid down by the door a moment ago.

Merek took one last look around his home, as they all set off to leave. "Glad to be rid of you in all honesty. Damned thing had me bored for decades," he said.

As the four of them went outside, they were met by a fierce wind and a light drizzle. Orange, yellow and brown leaves were being whipped up in a frenzy, so were the branches of the large, thick trees that surrounded the small village.

Henfylt no longer felt the need to check on Typhylt as often as she had done when they first met. She knew that Typhylt would be there at her side. It was an instinct she could trust. Whilst Typhylt wasn't an adult, she had an independence about her, a cleverness too. As the days since they met had passed, Henfylt learned more about who Typhylt was, just as she assumed Typhylt did about her. What she didn't know, however, was the significance of the necklace that Typhylt wore and sometimes twisted between her fingers. It had to mean something, but Henfylt didn't think it was right to ask just yet.

When they reached the battered old sign, Merek stopped and they waited for Aedlyn and Ofryth to arrive. Darker clouds gathered overhead, casting gloomy shadows down on Lyen-Saithe. As the rain started lashing down and the sharp wind became more aggressive, Aedlyn and Ofryth turned up and the group set off. If they waited for this to pass, they'd have to stay another night in the village, and nobody fancied that. So, off they went.

The harsh conditions lasted a few hours before the sky opened up again and the sun attempted to dry what had been soaked. They stopped for a short while to eat and drink, but soon carried on their way. Typhylt walked alongside Ofryth, the pair getting to know each other. Henfylt spent some time with Aedlyn, who she found to be an interesting and kind woman, whilst Merek and Blynkiln chatted away as they led the line up top.

After another hour of journeying, Merek joined Henfylt and spoke to her about Blynkiln. She learned that some people knew Blynkiln by the title 'The False Knight'. Merek shared that Adelyka went missing just after Blynkiln had to flee Raltyr when he'd been discovered to have Tynuk blood in his veins, of the weaker variety. It made sense of how he'd healed so quickly. The mercenary also learned that Merek knew Blynkiln's parents and helped him survive by taking him to Raltyr at a young age. The only thing that confused Henfylt was why Merek decided to tell her, specifically, all of this. She thought it best to ask him.

"I'm telling you because I need another perspective on the situation. Blynkiln warned me, Aedlyn and Ofryth that his priority is Adelyka, which makes sense. He does seem to be warming up to the idea of helping Ofryth and Aedlyn, though. Anyway, for so long I've committed myself entirely to keeping Aedlyn and Ofryth safe. Only now, the child of my closest... my good friends, has returned and also needs help. I'm asking you for advice because an outside perspective can help with such things," Merek answered.

This makes sense of why he seems so close to Blynkiln, even though he just met him a day ago. Or so I thought.

"S'pose I'd say why can't you do both? All our purposes are nicely lined up. Well, it's probably more likely that they've been aligned that way, but still. Aedlyn and Ofryth are on board with Slyvard's plot, the same plot that means we need to find Adelyka who Blynkiln is also looking for. We all aim for the same thing, really," Henfylt replied.

"I see what you're saying. Though I'd argue that we don't all aim for the same thing. I think Blynkiln has lost hope for so long that the very thought of being reunited with Adelyka is all that's driving him on. Problematically for him, Adelyka is wanted for ruling the North-East by Slyvard, as you told us. What if Adelyka chooses Blynkiln over leadership? Who takes the place of Rancylt then? It leads me to think about Slyvard's true motive. As you say, what if we've been manipulated into meeting this way? What if we're all on strings? What's the one thing that's connecting us all together right now?" Merek asked.

"The hunt for Adelyka," Typhylt answered, coming out of nowhere.

"When did you get here, Typh?" Henfylt asked, impressed that she hadn't heard the girl before she spoke.

"I've been listening for a while, sorry. I've been thinking, what if the man you saw in the red and black robes was actually sent by Slyvard and not Meurd. Surely her soldiers would have found Aedlyn by now. Maybe the hooded man was placed exactly at the right time so that it would force you into leaving when we arrived. Maybe he was put there as a catalyst to get us all moving. You met him in 'The Forlorn Fox' didn't you, Henfylt?"

The mercenary nodded, "I think you're right again, Typh. I hadn't thought of it that way. I thought Jynheln was suspicious, but I never associated him with Slyvard. When Merek told us about seeing a Tarspyk near Lyen-Saithe, I thought he must've been Meurd's spy."

"For all my years of experience and my supposed 'wisdom', which isn't really wisdom at all, I just use a lot of words to make myself sound clever sometimes, I couldn't see another perspective on this Tarspyk. Maybe I didn't want to, I don't know. Well, Typhylt, you are bright. Very bright indeed. Never stop sharpening that mind of yours," Merek said.

"I won't, I promise," Typhylt responded.

Nobody spoke a word for a share of the journey. Henfylt carried on walking, deep in thought, assuming the others were doing the same. They passed by forests and dirt paths as the rays of daylight grew weaker and then began to fade altogether as the sun sank below the mountains in the distance. All that remained was a blaze of pink and orange, a hint of red glowing at the mountain's peak.

Aedlyn, Ofryth and Blynkiln all chatted quietly in the background, but Henfylt, Typhylt and Merek stayed quiet. The revelation didn't change anything, it just meant that there'd been no need to leave Lyen-Saithe in such a hurry. Aedlyn and Ofryth already seemed keen find Adelyka so that they might then go with Henfylt to Dinshei, so there was no real problem.

"Not far now, probably half an hour or so till we get there," Merek said.

The sun, fully covered by the towering mountains, offered a low light, a gentle ambience. It didn't take long for darkness to sweep over the South of Undysvold. The group dragged their feet, plodding ever-closer to their destination.

Henfylt's clothes, whilst doing their best to keep her warm, were soaked, and her ears and nose were numb from the chill wind. She wanted to be sitting in front of a raging fire with a plate of food on her lap and a strong beer at her side. She wanted to rest her head on a soft pillow and drift off to a restful sleep.

They'd marched across the bridge by Alkyn, as if heading to Hinsylt. Instead of carrying on around the city's walls, they went off into a clutch of trees and ended up near the base of a smaller, more isolated mountain.

"Any of you hear that?" Blynkiln asked.

Henfylt couldn't hear anything other than the whistling of the wind and Blynkiln's voice.

"What is it?" Ofryth asked.

Blynkiln shrugged his shoulders. "I don't know, but I can hear something. Follow me," he said.

Henfylt and the rest followed Blynkiln's lead, stomping over some tall grass and a few damp tree stumps. Soon enough, a thudding came from nearby and a small light flickered in the vast blackness of the night.

A short but thickset figure was raising an axe above his head, the steel glinting as it caught in the light of a lantern. The figure, who Henfylt judged to be a Dwarf by his stature, brought the axe down rapidly, splitting a log in two.

"What? Ye just gonna stand there are ye?" the wood-cutter asked. His accent was thick, not unpleasant or sharp though.

He put down the axe and turned to the group.

"Where there's Merek there's trouble! You lot better scarper fast, this old bugger's a right deviant!" the Dwarf announced, chuckling at the end of his sentence.

"They're already familiar with my trouble making, I tell you. This is Yuneld, everybody. He's an old friend," Merek replied as he trudged over and embraced him. They shared a few whispered words and friendly slaps on the back.

"Ah, let's get inside. Can't have guests out in the cold. What would me mother think of me?! Come on, come on. I'll lead the way. Merek, to the back wi'ya. Keep everyone on the path, eh? Before we go, who are you fine folks? What are your names?" Yuneld asked.

He had hair as black as ink and thick stubble that was similarly dark.

Without any delay, the mercenary stretched out a hand. "Henfylt, nice to meet you."

Yuneld laughed and said, "Come here, we aren't doing handshakes."

He gave Henfylt a bone-crushing hug, slapping her on the back a few times.

Yuneld went around the entire group, embracing them all one by one. Then he came to the front, lantern in hand, and set off leading everyone up the winding mountain path. Henfylt wasn't sure what the Dwarf's home would be like, whether it would be homely or all stone and steel. Either way, she was happy to be getting out of the cold.

The moon was full and the trees shook the remnants of rain off themselves as they were beaten by the howling wind. Tired footsteps marched along the winding path as they followed Yuneld up to his home in the mountain.

Dwarven Hospitality

T he night had been a shit one. By the time Blynkiln and his new companions reached the door to Yuneld's home, they'd all struggled up the steep path that led to it. The track went up and around, sharply left and right, until Blynkiln thought he was about to collapse from the effort. Without Yuneld's guidance along the way, they'd all have tumbled down the mountainside.

When the friendly Dwarf opened the heavy wood and stone door to his home, Blynkiln's jaw dropped. Thick, high-quality wood had been used for the flooring. Heavy furs were laid over the dark wood, making the space all homely. The walls were a mixture of hand-made wooden panels and the natural stone of the mountain itself, with great broad beams of old wood spanning the length of the ceiling to support the whole structure. The smell of burning wood rushed at him once the door had been closed, the cold air of the night shut out. To his right, a large fire chucked out some much-needed warmth that went right through his bones.

"So, do ye fancy some food?" Yuneld asked, looking around at Blynkiln and the others.

"Might be a good idea. Come on then folks, let's get sat down," Merek answered, with an appreciative nod to his friend.

"Actually, never mind. You're all piss wet through. Go and get yourselves into some clean, warm clothes first," Yuneld said, before anybody could move. "If ye follow the corridor, you'll get to a section where it opens up into a kind of fan. Pick any of the rooms and have a look in the drawers for some clean clothes. Something will fit ye, I'm sure. Bring your damp clothes back so they can be dried out by the fire, too."

The False Knight thanked Yuneld for his hospitality. The others did the same, then they all set off down the corridor. He was hardly surprised by the good treatment from Yuneld. Blynkiln had always been interested in Dwarven culture and how it differed from Human culture. For Dwarves, hospitality was an important thing. If a Dwarf didn't welcome their guests respectfully and with honour, then they were no true Dwarf. It just wasn't in their nature.

On the way down the corridor, Henfylt raced Typhylt to a room that they both liked. The blonde-haired girl won and Henfylt laughed as she tripped over her own two feet and went flying into a wall by the door. Typhylt checked to see if she was alright before laughing with the mercenary. Blynkiln grinned to himself before walking into one of the rooms.

An enormous bed covered much of the floor space. Its thick, dark wooden frame was complemented by rich, dark red bedding. A huge bookcase spanned the entire length of one of the walls, packed full of books with colourful spines.

Soon enough, Blynkiln spotted the drawers that were overflowing with clothes of all colours. He picked a dark red shirt which had a low collar and no detailing or patterns on it, thick black trousers, and a pair of black, fur-lined slippers. He unsheathed his sword and placed it by the bed, taking the sword belt with his old damp clothes to be put by the fire to dry.

The False Knight wandered out of the room to return to the hall where he found Yuneld stretching out a rack close to the fire. It wasn't long before everyone else had finished. They all put their damp clothes and belts over the rack and Yuneld took them into the next room for some food.

A few lights of a soft, almost orange colour, dangled over the great big table that filled most of the room. Plates of cooked meats and steaming vegetables, little jugs of gravy and a fair few big jugs filled to the brim with beer were spread out over the table. Two of the jugs were full of golden lager and the other three overflowed with ale.

"Please, tuck in," Yuneld said once they'd all sat down.

Henfylt and Merek went straight for the ale, filling their tankards up before they even looked at what else covered the table. Yuneld had a jug all to himself, but that didn't surprise Blynkiln. Dwarves had a reputation for drinking heavily. At least they could handle it better than Humans. Everyone else piled up their plates and poured on the gravy. Blynkiln helped himself to some of that crisp, golden lager. He needed a top up almost straight away, despite hoping he'd managed to show some restraint.

Once everyone had finished, Aedlyn spoke. "Thank you, Yuneld. All of us appreciate everything you've done for us tonight. Let us do the cleaning up for you since you've done far beyond enough for us."

"No, no, it's a kind offer but you're all tired and it'll wait. Get yourselves to bed and have a good rest. It can be sorted tomorrow. Whichever room ye went in, have the same one for the night, or for however long ye fancy staying," Yuneld replied, graciously.

"Don't argue with him folks, you'll lose that bout, I promise. You're a generous host, Yuneld, always have been. A very generous host indeed," Merek rested a hand on the Dwarf's shoulder before he stood up and everyone else followed him out, thanking Yuneld once again as they left one by one.

Blynkiln's legs were sore and he yawned a few times as he dragged his feet down the corridor. After he'd said goodnight to everyone, he went into the room with the dark red bedding, took his slippers off and climbed into the comfortable bed. For the first time in a long miserable while, Blynkiln went to sleep with a slight smile on his face.

He woke up as the sun rose. Blynkiln's rest had been undisturbed and heavy.

His wound was now painless, so he took the bandages off, expecting to be left with a scar. But, there was no sign that he'd ever been stabbed, nothing at all. He frowned, wiping at his bleary eyes, and still saw no scarring. Wondering how that could be, he pulled his clothes on and strolled down the corridor until he reached the hall and swung the door open. He wanted to see the sunrise, to feel close to Adelyka, as he did every morning.

Sitting by the door of Yuneld's home on a large, flat stone, he looked out over the horizon. The beaten landscape of the South of Undysvold stretched out before him. Wild, rough and harsh on the eye, Blynkiln felt at peace. He preferred the deep snows of the North-East, of course, where the sun set the bright white snow off glittering and sparkling. That was his home.

Even so, there was something to be said for the fresh and clear mountain air. The scenery, too. The heavy rain and powerful wind that always came during the night made this region of Undysvold shine when morning came. The leaves of the trees sparkled as the morning sun caught them with its glare, the coating of rainwater making them shimmer.

The solid wood and stone door shifted open. Yuneld wandered out and greeted Blynkiln.

The Dwarf had hair as black as the North-Eastern sea and green eyes that seemed to sparkle with warmth. He reached up to Blynkiln's chest in height, had muscular arms and weighty shoulders.

"Morning, morning. I brought ye a hot drink," Yuneld said as he handed a steaming cup to The False Knight.

Blynkiln took a quick sip, not wanting to burn his tongue. It wasn't as bitter as the brew Merek had given him the previous morning. This drink had a stronger sweetener in it which made it go down easier. The steam warmed his face as he took another sip with less caution, taking in the earthy scent of the brew.

Blynkiln held the cup in both hands, warming them through before he looked at Yuneld and said, "It does the trick, that. Very nice. What is it?"

The Dwarf took a long sip from his own cup. "It's a new recipe I've been working on. I call it 'Woody'!"

"Well, like I say, it's good," Blynkiln replied, smiling at Yuneld as he spoke.

"The name's a bit dull, perhaps, but it tells ye what it is. Have another sip and tell me what ye taste," Yuneld said.

Blynkiln focused his senses as he took a longer sip. "It's earthy, there's a nutty flavour. Some vanilla, too. There's a good balance of bitterness and sweetness in there, a slight spice too, I think."

"Good, good! Ye have a fine sense for picking out flavours! I'm impressed. The spice was the bit I thought ye might've missed since it's so subtle. Well, there ye have it! My true calling. Not smithing or crafting in the traditional sense. I'm built for creating recipes for hot drinks," Yuneld replied, chuckling after he'd finished speaking.

Blynkiln sensed some sarcasm in the Dwarf's voice.

"You still craft. You craft things that people take for granted. I hadn't had a good warm drink for a long time before yesterday. But this," Blynkiln said as he pointed at the cup in his right hand. "This is even better. A warm drink can put you right when nothing much else will. Remember that."

Yuneld smiled and thanked Blynkiln for his kind words. "I'll leave ye to it. Come in when you're ready, but there's no rush. I get it. Sometimes it all gets too much and ye just need a moment to yourself."

Once Yuneld had closed the door behind him, Blynkiln returned to admiring the view.

Before they were forced to split, he and Adelyka had agreed to watch the sunrise each morning from wherever they were as a loose form of connection. He'd never missed a sunrise, not in half a decade.

Five years away from civilisation had given him time to think about who he was and who he wanted to be. He'd once been asked that by Fuldyn, many years ago. He didn't know the answer then, and he wasn't so sure he knew it now. But, as he stared out across the land, he realised that there could be happiness in his life. Whilst a part of his soul had been ripped away and thrown to the wolves when he and Adelyka had been forced to part, perhaps there were other things worth carrying on for.

He doubted he'd be truly happy until he was back with her, if he ever got there, since the bond they shared was so sacred. But, some of the weight that had burdened his aching shoulders for so many years lifted itself, then, and the world seemed a slightly brighter place.

He finished his drink, closed his eyes and prayed to himself in silence. Before he could finish, however, the door swung open and the blonde-haired girl, Typhylt, appeared.

"Sorry, I didn't know you were out here," she said, with respect in her voice.

"There's nothing to be sorry for. Sit, if you like. I'd offer you some of Yuneld's new drink, but it's all gone. I do apologise," The False Knight replied.

Typhylt had thick blonde hair and blue eyes that were bright with a need for adventure. Her face was neither harshly featured like Aedlyn's or softly featured like Merek's. *She seems familiar but I don't know how, why or where from.* Was it the more defined cheekbones, or just her general energy? It didn't really matter either way.

"Don't apologise, I interrupted you. Were you praying?" the girl asked.

"I was, but I don't take prayer as seriously as some do. Are you... spiritual in any way, if you don't mind me asking?" he replied.

Typhylt took a moment before answering, twisting a dull silver chain that hung around her neck between her fingers. "I don't believe but I don't not believe, really. That doesn't make sense, does it?"

"It makes perfect sense," Blynkiln replied, after a moment. "Who's to say you should have all the answers? I don't. Just because I believe doesn't mean you should, that's the beauty of believing. It should never be forced on anybody, otherwise, it isn't true belief. If you've been threatened or promised to be rewarded for following a set of ideas, that isn't belief. Not in my eyes, anyway. Belief, I think, has to be an active choice we make. A decision that only one person can make for themself if it feels right for them. If you don't want to believe, then you shouldn't. If you do want to believe, then you should."

"What advice would you give me on finding out if I want to believe or not?" Typhylt asked, keeping her eyes on Blynkiln.

"I'd say you'll get an answer to that when you're ready. Some people never feel the desire to believe, others believe from the day they can first understand what believing in a thing means. Either way, it's best to never listen to anybody else about certain things. Religion or belief in some system, whatever it is. Always make those choices by yourself. People place too much care on listening to other people rather than themselves. I guess that'd be my advice, if it's any help," The False Knight answered.

"It is helpful. Thank you," Typhylt replied. "I suppose I'd never given it much thought. Not because I'm ignorant. Well, I don't think I'm ignorant, anyway."

"You're far from ignorant," Blynkiln said. "I've met my share of ignorant people, and you're certainly not one of them."

Typhylt smiled at him and embraced him, catching him off-guard.

"Thank you," she said.

Blynkiln awkwardly patted her on the back. He hadn't been hugged in a very long time.

"Anytime," he said as she let go and walked back inside.

He frowned once the door closed behind her. *Henfylt's lucky to have found her. She's clever and kind. Two things I wish more people were. Anyway, time to head in, get warm and see what Yuneld knows about Adelyka. If anything.*

Once inside, the warmth hit Blynkiln as it had done the night before. He passed through the room with the great big table sitting in its centre. It was as clean as it had been before they all ate and drank the previous night.

Typhylt and Ofryth were having a conversation by the hearth that took up most of one of the walls in the big room. They acknowledged him, and once he'd greeted them, he went on through another passage which led to a crossroads of sorts. There were three paths. One went straight ahead, one left and one right. The False Knight went right, following the small corridor and entering the room ahead of him.

A roaring fire sat pride of place against the wall opposite the door, inviting him in with its warm glow. It had a shiny silver guard in front of it and furs laid down all over the floor. There were a few comfortable looking chairs in the room, each with detailed etchings set into the dark wood they were crafted from. The room smelled oddly of home.

Blynkiln heard a quiet grumble and found Henfylt lying in a heap on the floor behind a sofa.

"Are you ok?" he asked, assuming she had a bad head.

"Mmh," Henfylt replied, sitting upright and raising a hand to her temple. "I'm fine, I think. What are you doing here?" she asked, her dark brown eyes meeting Blynkiln's gaze.

"I came to have a look about, see what else was in this place. Didn't think I'd find you here. Have you been here all night?" Blynkiln asked, offering a hand to the mercenary in case she wanted help getting up. She took his hand, thanking him as he dragged her up.

"I don't know. I didn't drink much at all, I don't think," Henfylt said as she stumbled around. She plonked herself down on the sofa, and Blynkiln joined her.

"I've remembered now. We drank quite a lot more than I first thought, actually. I was playing card games with Merek, I think," Henfylt stated, after a moment.

"I see. You both followed all of us to the rooms, though, didn't you?" Blynkiln asked.

"We did... then we went back for more beer," the mercenary answered.

The False Knight laughed. "Well, at least you had fun."

The mercenary fell asleep after a few minutes.

Blynkiln, convinced she wasn't going to chuck up her last meal and all the beer she'd got through last night, found a dark blue blanket draped over an armchair. He cast it over Henfylt and left the room.

Wandering back into the main room, he strolled over to Typhylt and Ofryth who were still chatting away by the fire.

"Sorry to interrupt, but for now I'd stay out of the room through that way and on the right because Henfylt's asleep and she's got a bad head," Blynkiln said as he pointed to the passage he'd just walked through.

"She did drink a lot last night," Typhylt replied, with a smile on her face.

Evidently, Blynkiln thought. Something about the glint in Typhylt's eyes told him that she'd joined in with the card games.

He said farewell, smiling as he went, and returned to the room he'd claimed last night. Nothing would be done until Yuneld or Merek gathered everyone together. So, rather than getting impatient, Blynkiln retreated to the peace of his own mind. It was a place he visited often enough. It had served as his only companion over the last five troublesome years.

In the early days, he'd been more cautious. Off the back of killing a dozen knights, he sort of had to be that way. As time went on, however, he risked the odd trip into small villages that were far out of the way to get a decent meal. Then, he pushed for towns, on the days when he wasn't so anxious. He didn't want to risk being caught stealing, so first he spent the money Adelyka had given him on the night she broke him out of the cell. Of course, the problem with coin is, it disappears quicker than you think. By the time a year had passed and he'd had enough of eating wild animals, he headed to a town and risked stealing.

He broke most of the ideals of knighthood in those five wretched years. He'd murdered his comrades, stolen from those he was meant to protect, and worst of all, he knew that he was responsible for Adelyka's disappearance and he had no way of knowing what had happened to her over their period apart.

He'd found some comfort in the thought of reunion, perhaps that was what had kept him alive for so long. Even so, he'd let himself down. For years. He'd let her down, too, and that stung all the more. Stumbling through the woods had been one of the few good things that had happened to The False Knight in such a long time. Ironically, he had to get stabbed in order for his luck to change. *Doesn't fill me with the greatest confidence.*

After a short while of reflection, Blynkiln's stomach grumbled, so he went to find Yuneld. Impatience had a way of winning, more often than not.

He strolled through the house until he found his way back to the part where three small corridors went off in different directions. He went left, hearing the distant sound of muffled voices. He stopped outside the door and listened in.

"I wouldn't know. I haven't been there in a bit. It's been a few years," said the first voice. It sounded like Yuneld's.

"Do you not keep in contact with him?" asked the second voice. It sounded like Merek's.

"How would I? Send him bloody letters asking if he's seen her anywhere? Ye ought to imagine what'd happen if those letters were intercepted."

They must be talking about Adelyka, surely. The forge, too.

"You have a point, but still. You really haven't spoken, seen or heard from your brother in a few years? At all. How many years? I know the pair of you haven't always seen eye to eye, but I really just need you to think, really think. Anything could help, even the most seemingly useless piece of information. Please, Yuneld," Merek pleaded.

"All I know is that two years ago, there or thereabouts, Adelyka was at the forge."

The False Knight burst in. Merek and Yuneld stared at him in silence.

"How was she? Did you see her? What exactly happened when you found out, were you there or did you just hear she was there?" Blynkiln asked, anxiously.

Yuneld raised his hand to his brow. "I went there to see Yunylt, my brother. The forge too. I hadn't been for a while, another couple of years, but this time I chipped up and I saw her there."

Blynkiln's face softened.

"She was in good health. She used to visit with her mother, Phenyrt, when she was young, ye see, so she liked

87

the forge plenty. Anyway, I saw her and she was fine. Slightly distant as if something wasn't right, but she seemed as strong as ever. Fierce too. I see now that it was you she'd been trying to get back to. Yunylt told me that she'd been all over the place, once it was safe, to try to find someone. Always plotting her next trip out with his help," Yuneld said.

She was looking for me, of course. Risking it for me, just as I have been for her.

"Did she tell you anything of where she would go or what she might do?" Merek asked.

"It all seemed fine. I'm assuming she used the forge as a place to stay in between her journeys looking for Blynkiln here. That's why I'm not sure we'll see her there if we do go. Might be she's on another trip out to find ye, Blynkiln, I don't know. The only other thing I know is that the ruler of the North-East does a formal inspection of the forge every three years to check it's functional and worth sending resources to. Ye know how these things are. So, she won't have wanted to be hanging around when that happened because they check thoroughly, and Yunylt's a bloody terrible liar," Yuneld answered. He lowered his head as he finished speaking.

"When was the inspection? Two years ago?" Blynkiln asked.

"About a year and a half ago or so, give or take. They skipped the one before because that wasn't long after Adelyka had fled and Rancylt took over. So, Rancylt thought we'd be fine for a while longer while the dust settled. I had no idea till Merek told me this morning after we spoke that ye and Adelyka were, or are, together. I'm sorry I didn't speak up sooner," Yuneld stated.

Blynkiln placed a hand on the Dwarf's shoulder. "How would you have known? It's not your fault. Either way, this information is a big help. I have something to hang onto now. We have a lead."

Blynkiln, Merek and Yuneld thought it best to gather everyone together for some food and a conversation about their next destination. The False Knight allowed a sense of hopefulness to fill him. He didn't take such a feeling for granted.

Strengthening Bonds

Henfylt yawned and sighed as she opened her eyes. Somehow, a blanket had been laid over her and she was lying down on a comfy sofa.

She stretched wildly and yawned once more before stumbling over to the mantelpiece. The varnished surface was smooth to the touch as she ran her hand along it.

The fire calmed her, it flickered more like a candle than roared like a blazing hearth. She grabbed a few small logs from the pile at the right of the fireplace and tossed them into the glowing embers. The flames soon tore through the birch wood, giving off a homely smell. She warmed her hands and turned around as the door creaked open.

Typhylt joined Henfylt over by the fire.

"You alright, Typh?" Henfylt asked, crossing her arms.

"Yes, are you?" Typhylt asked back.

"Sore head. Other than that, no complaints," Henfylt answered with a smile on her face.

Typhylt laughed. "I'm not surprised. You and Merek drank most of the beer between yourselves."

"We did. I wonder how he's feeling. I doubt he's ever drank so much, certainly not in a while," she replied, humorously.

Typhylt smiled. "I just wanted to say thank you for last night, for not minding me joining you and Merek."

Henfylt rested a hand on Typhylt's shoulder and smiled back at her. "No need to thank me. We had a right laugh, the three of us. You really are good company, Typh. You're always welcome to join me when you fancy, but never feel like you have to. You're your own person, a person I've got rather fond of having around."

Maybe her spinning head and loose tongue made her speak so freely to the girl. Either way, she didn't regret saying what she'd said.

Typhylt's smile turned to a grin, and the two of them shared a hug. Henfylt's eyes blurred, probably thanks to her foggy head. When she pinched her eyes shut to steady herself, however, tears were clinging to her eyelashes and blurring her sight all the more. She raised a hand and wiped her eyes, then held Typhylt out at arm's length and saw that the girl's eyes were similarly damp.

"I'm glad we met when we did, you know," Henfylt said.

Typhylt nodded. "Me too. You've already taught me plenty. You've given me so much."

"I think you've given me plenty too, Typh. I really do," Henfylt replied, thinking back to how purposeless she'd been back at Blantyrn, before she'd ever met Typhylt.

"We're a right pair, you and me," the mercenary added, after a moment.

Typhylt laughed again. "We are."

As Henfylt lifted her hands from Typhylt's shoulders, the door creaked open once more. It was Aedlyn. She raised a hand to apologise. "Sorry to interrupt, but Yuneld's asked us all to head in for some food and a chat. There's probably no great hurry, though, if you're in the middle of something," she said, leaning against the door frame.

Henfylt and Typhylt exchanged a glance, nodding at each other before following Aedlyn out.

On the way to the dining room, Aedlyn asked, "I heard you've got a sore head from last night, how bad is it?"

"It's not too bad, I've had worse. Thank you though," Henfylt answered, smiling at Aedlyn.

By the time they made it, Yuneld was standing at the head of the large table. Blynkiln had Ofryth at his side and Merek sitting opposite him. Merek's hair was no more scruffy than usual and his eyes shone as brightly as always. Once Henfylt, Typhylt and Aedlyn sat down, Yuneld began with a sigh.

Not a good sign.

"There's good news and bad news, folks. The good news is that Adelyka was last seen by me two years ago at Yinfyr, my brother's forge in the North-East." He cleared his throat. "The bad news is that we can't go straight there."

Henfylt's shoulders dropped, her body slumping in the chair. Typhylt picked at the skin around her fingernails, offering a supportive glance to Blynkiln, who put his head in his hands and exhaled sharply. The usual gleam in Merek's blue eyes faded even when Aedlyn, whose eyebrows lowered themselves, patted him on the arm in consolation. Ofryth placed a hand on Blynkiln's shoulder, offering some words that Henfylt couldn't hear. Blynkiln soon thanked the boy before looking up at the head of the table once more.

"Yuneld, is there any chance you could explain *why* we can't go straight to Yinfyr. I mean, surely that's most likely where she is, as we discussed earlier," Merek said.

"Ye see, it's my brother that runs the forge these days and he isn't actually going to be there at the moment, because he'll be heading to the tournament at Hinsylt. The timing couldn't be worse, really."

Yuneld paused, aggressively rubbing his forehead as he stared into the distance.

"So, he isn't there which means it'll be all locked up with no way in?" Merek asked, with his arms crossed.

Yuneld let out a long sigh. "Exactly right. Rancylt put an end to our 'unnecessary bonuses' which were agreed with

Phenyrt and then Adelyka, when she ruled. They both supported the forge and we were grateful for that. However, Rancylt stopped it which meant we could no longer, legally, receive the ores from the North-West to create our unique weapons. We went behind her back to draft up an arrangement with Slyvard himself, directly. All he asked for in return was that we didn't sell the weapons to Rancylt, but why would we? We didn't want her to know anyway. It was a good deal, a fair deal, so we took it. Yunylt goes to the annual tournament to meet with Slyvard in person and make any necessary changes to this arrangement. He usually tries to sell some of his goods, too, in the buildup, since a tournament's as good as any ground for that."

Yuneld sat down and a brief silence stretched over the table.

"Rancylt was always jealous of Adelyka because the North-Easterners loved her," Aedlyn said. Blynkiln smiled a sad smile, and Aedlyn continued. "So, I suppose she saw you as loyal to Adelyka and didn't want to assist the forge in any way simply for that reason."

"Exactly. She's a right piece of work. Anyway, we must find Yunylt in order to learn when he last saw Adelyka and if she was indeed at the forge when he left. It's impenetrable, so we wouldn't manage breaking into it if she is there. Also, I don't much fancy breaking into my own family's property. And before any of ye ask, no I don't have what we need to get in. The 'key', if it could be called that, is always with Yunylt. Blynkiln, if she is in Yinfyr, she's the safest person in all of Undysvold, trust me," Yuneld replied.

Blynkiln nodded.

A grim silence fell over the table as everyone began to eat some of the food that Yuneld had kindly brought out for them. Safe to say, there was a share less laughter now than there had been last night.

Rancylt must've thought she'd rule the entire continent after her mother was assassinated. Slyvard and everyone else got sick of poor leadership, though, so the Civil War began before she could inherit Ynfleyd's throne. At least we have something to go on, now. It just seems pointless since we follow the thread to one person who then leads us to another. How many more times will we have to go somewhere to see someone who might, just might, know something about it all?

The rest of the early afternoon was spent preparing for the short journey to Hinsylt. The city wasn't far away, so they'd comfortably make it there before sunset.

After everyone disappeared to freshen up, the mercenary asked Typhylt to meet her out front once she was ready. The girl agreed and Henfylt went off to change back into her own gear that she'd bought from Roldyr back in Tynylt. She'd almost forgotten how comfortable and warm it all was, from the softness of the trousers to the well-fitted shirt of chainmail, lined with thick fleece. She grabbed her sword and dagger which had been leaning against the bedside table, sheathing them before leaving. With the familiar weight of her longsword at her hip, she found herself bouncing along the corridor.

As she made her way to the hall with the blazing hearth, she bumped into Aedlyn, nearly knocking her off her feet.

"Shit, sorry, I didn't see you," Henfylt said, steadying Aedlyn with her own hands.

Aedlyn smiled. "No harm done, don't worry about it."

She lifted her hands from Aedlyn's arms and smiled back, apologising once more.

"It's a shame we can't just go straight to Yinfyr," Aedlyn said. "You must be fed up with it all by now, especially since you came all the way from the North-West."

"It's not so bad, but it is getting on my nerves a bit. At least we have something to look into, though. Before I got to Lyen-Saithe and met you lot, I had no idea where to even start," Henfylt replied, leaning against the wall with her arms crossed.

"At least we helped. It's strange how we've all ended up with one goal, in one place, don't you think?" Aedlyn asked.

"There's more to all this than we know, I reckon. I'm sure it's something to do with Slyvard. There's bound to be a reason for everything when he's involved," Henfylt answered.

The mercenary looked into Aedlyn's bright green eyes, getting the impression that she'd experienced a great deal of difficulty in her life. *Likely when she was younger. I wonder why she left her home.*

"So, you met Slyvard? What did you think of him?" Aedlyn asked.

"He was... interesting. It was like I'd met him before even though I knew I hadn't. You know the feeling that I mean, when you just feel comfortable around someone? It wasn't like I'd just met the King of Dinshei at all," Henfylt answered.

"Interesting. I only saw him a few times a long while ago, when my mother used to drag me along to Stykricht. He always seemed so composed, as if he was always calculating something," Aedlyn replied.

"That doesn't surprise me at all," Henfylt said.

"Well, anyway, I'd best let you get on," Aedlyn stated.

"We'll talk again," Henfylt replied, nodding at her.

"I'd like that," Aedlyn said, before offering a smile to Henfylt and heading off down the corridor.

Henfylt left the hall, glad to be forming connections with her new companions, and waited outside for Typhylt.

It was a dreary afternoon and the mercenary took a deep breath to clear her head of any remaining fog from last night's drinking. The sharp, refreshing air rushed through her nose. She could smell a storm brewing. The trees swayed in the steady wind, and dark clouds scurried across the grey sky.

Heading into Hinsylt with the company she'd found herself in was a dangerous thing and probably not the wisest, but it had to be done. Keeping Typhylt safe was the priority, but Aedlyn was her main concern. Perhaps that was just Henfylt being worried for no reason, but Aedlyn's eyes were uniquely bright and her hair was also distinctive, even in the South.

As for Blynkiln, well, it had been five years since he'd killed those twelve knights, or so Henfylt understood it. There was hardly a risk of him being identified by his appearance alone. With Typhylt's hair being blonde as well, the pair of them wouldn't draw too much attention. They'd just be reckoned North-Easterners that had come down here to trade or explore a different part of the world, nothing more. Plenty of folk from up in the snowy mountains came to Hinsylt for a taste of South-Western life.

Before the mercenary could spend any more time thinking about the situation, the door swung open behind her. Henfylt knew what was at stake the second she saw Typhylt strolling out to join her.

What is the Difference Between a Ruler and a Leader?

Every day, when the sun rose and a new day began, Slyvard asked himself what the difference between a ruler and a leader was.

The answer never changed, not in the twenty-two years that he had led the North-West of Undysvold. *Rulers are arrogant, but leaders are ambitious.* It had been his mantra for all of his political life. He wished to remain a leader and to never stray into the common but disconcerting practice of rulership.

The foundation of his desire to lead and not to rule stemmed from his hatred of the ruling powers acting out of self-interest. Of course, he knew it was natural to wish and hope for things that benefitted oneself, but he held the opinion that those who could not put their own people before themselves ought not be in such a position to begin with.

Slyvard stretched until his back cracked, letting out a sigh of relief. He turned to face Qwynlo, his closest friend and greatest advisor.

"Leadership should be second nature to those who are given such a high honour, and yet, why is it that so few rulers

97

try and lead every once in a while? Is that too much to ask for, Qwynlo?" he asked.

"You wouldn't think so, but I believe it is the innate state of the mind of most rulers. A natural disposition, we ought to call it. The problem is, those acting in the name of the self-proclaimed 'greater-good' tend to tire of the good work they are supposed to be doing and prefer to waste everybody's time while reaping the same benefits and rewards for doing next to nothing themselves," Qwynlo replied, pushing his delicate spectacles further up his narrow nose.

"Oh, Qwynlo, whatever would I do without you?" Slyvard asked, in a humorous tone.

"Well, you probably wouldn't still be a king without me. You always mean well, but you occasionally work outside of the strict boundaries of legality. Such as you did against my advice with Yunylt, if you recall," his intelligent friend answered. He always brought up the business with Yunylt and the forge.

"Well, perhaps you're right. Although, seeing Rancylt made a fool of really is quite something, you must admit. It is also-"

Qwynlo interrupted Slyvard. "All part of your plan. I know. It has its reasons, though the chances of you getting discovered are extremely high. And what will happen then?"

"Then, my good friend, we skip the second phase and jump straight to the third," Slyvard answered.

"You really should not ignore an entire phase of a delicately crafted plan. The possibilities for what could-"

Slyvard cut his friend off, rising to his feet and placing a hand on Qwynlo's shoulder.

"I'm sure everything will work out as intended. We've been doing this for a while now and nobody has become even remotely suspicious of us or our plans," Slyvard said, employing a patient tone.

"Very well, I suppose that much is true," Qwynlo replied.

After patting Qwynlo on the shoulder, Slyvard left his cabin. The rocking sensation underneath his feet brought back pleasant memories. Slyvard never enjoyed the annual meeting at Stykricht, but he always looked forward to being at sea each year in order to get there. As a younger man, he had always enjoyed sailing.

Of course, that all changed when he had been elected for leadership. But, it was a sacrifice worth making. He never once regretted it. *Regret is purposeless unless you can truly learn from your mistakes. Sadly, so few of us do learn from our mistakes.*

He wandered onto the deck, admiring the view of the expansive sea as he took a deep breath. The salty sea air filled his lungs. He coughed and placed a hand on his chest. The usual sharp pain bothered him, but he had become accustomed to it over the past few months.

He rested his hands on the railing of the ship and judged that they weren't too far away from Stykricht, now. He could tell as much from how the water had changed. In the North-West, it was a lighter shade of blue and calmer in its movement. Yet, the closer to the South-West one got, the darker the sea became.

I cannot give anything away at Stykricht, especially given the circumstantial changes of late. Rancylt will become suspicious if I seem anything other than my usual self. She knows me too well. She always has done. Meurd isn't such a problem, though. All I have to do is treat her with deep respect, even if she doesn't deserve it.

Slyvard stared at the sea. The sun's reflection in the water rippled as the waves crashed against the sturdy hull of the ship. The strong scent of salt rushed up his nose. It was a smell like no other, so freeing and humbling. He breathed in once again and exhaled in calmness, no cough followed on this occasion.

The sea wasn't as rough as it had been the previous year when he had made the very same voyage. The waves still

99

possessed immense power, but there was a restfulness to their charm. Water brought him peace and time to think, to properly *think*. These days that was a greater gift than ever.

Having stood alone for a while, overlooking the natural beauty of the sea, Slyvard ventured back into the cabin.

It was well-varnished, clean and decorated in a rather simple manner. The wood, light in tone, contrasted with the darkness of the thick beams that ran across the ceiling. The bed was as large as it could be, but Slyvard had sacrificed bed size for a far more valuable feature. In the centre of the cabin, there dwelt a large map that served as a table. The carved map had been coloured by professionals. Slyvard loomed over it, resting his hands on the far edges of the smooth table. His body cast a shadow over the entire continent.

"Is everything alright?" came the ever-inquisitive voice of Qwynlo as he finished signing off his latest letter.

"I'm certain it is. My hope is that they will arrive in Hinsylt late this afternoon. I will be at Stykricht by then. Remember, Qwynlo, you are to head to the front gate where you must wait out of sight for Henfylt to arrive with Aedlyn and Ofryth. Once she does, follow them wherever they go. Jynheln will be there, too, and he will know when to approach them, or when to be seen by them." Slyvard spoke with determination and certainty, two things he had manipulated into serving him rather faithfully over his many years as a leader.

"I am unlikely to forget my role, I'm more concerned about you going off script. We both know what you are like. You have the frustrating tendency of doing that," Qwynlo responded, adjusting the angle at which his little spectacles sat on the edge of his narrow nose.

"You are right, of course. This time there is no room for such spontaneity," Slyvard stated, his tone severe.

He turned his attention back to the map, tracing the path that Rancylt's ship would be taking from the North-East down to Stykricht. The painted details were fine, scaled well and crafted with care.

"I must see Thalyen now, they will need her to find their way back to me, or to go wherever Adelyka might be, if Henfylt has a lead to follow," Slyvard said as he cast his eyes over the map, locating Hinsylt.

He departed without pause or another word, a frustrating tickling manifesting itself within his throat as he stepped back outside.

Slyvard admired the flawless work of the shipbuilders as he strolled to the top deck in search of the captain.

The sails flapped and billowed in the harsh sea wind. He smiled to himself as he thought about how he had turned his long-held passion into both a weapon and a fortification for his people. Knowing that the North-West had the most illustrious naval fleet in Undysvold filled Slyvard with pride. He had the most versatile captains and the finest vessels ready to answer the call. More importantly, he had the love and support of those he served. Slyvard loved his people as much as they loved him. They were the reason for him doing everything that he did, after all.

He ambled up the stairs and saw Thalyen peering through a brass telescope. The captain wore her typical garb: a tattered pair of thick grey trousers, a thin but simple shirt with a leather jacket of questionable quality on top of it, her sturdy but shabby brown boots and the unique, feathered hat that she was rarely seen without. The right side of the hat's brim had been pinned to the crown of the hat and the feather stood proud without needing support. As black as ink, aside from the flamboyant decoration of the purple feather, the hat suited her character.

Slyvard clasped his hands together and allowed them to rest by his stomach. He then remained motionless. After a brief period of blissful silence, the captain lowered her telescope and turned to Slyvard.

"We haven't got too far to go now," she said.

"Excellent. I'm afraid I have another task for you, Thalyen," he replied, speaking softly.

The captain didn't roll her eyes or sigh. In fact, her brown, amber-flecked eyes brightened at the prospect. "Go on, I'm happy to help. Always," she said.

Before he knew her so well, she spoke rarely and often in a quiet manner. Her confidence had grown over the years. Around people she knew well, by any measure.

"I would ask that you take the ship further down South once you have docked near Stykricht and I have left. Qwynlo will tell you where specifically, but I would advise docking as close to Hinsylt as possible. It is still further away than I would like, but it will suffice. The crew, on your orders, will gladly stay with the ship and protect it, so you have nothing to fear on that front. Qwynlo will fill you in on the details of where you're both going after docking, but the key is to get the people that he points out to you onto the ship. Oh, I would advise getting some horses saddled, too, to make the journey from Hinsylt to the ship faster. Five horses should do the trick," Slyvard said.

As he finished speaking, he was overwhelmed by a violent fit of coughing. The pain burst from his chest and spread through his whole body, making him hunch over.

"Are you alright?" Thalyen asked as she placed a hand on his shoulder.

He straightened himself once the coughing fit had passed, regaining his composure. He wiped the back of his hand on his grey shirt, marking it with a faint trail of blood.

"I'm fine, thank you. Listen, Aedlyn was always a good person, and she's been through a lot from what I know. I'm assuming her son is a good person, too. As for Henfylt, well, she is important in her own right. I know I am asking a lot of you, but it really is necessary. I wouldn't ask otherwise, as you well know," he said.

Slyvard raised his eyes to the sky. As clear as the day was, he found himself more confused than he had been in a long time. Among the vast emptiness and beauty, Slyvard spied the threat that loomed ahead of him. He wished for more time, a more complete life. The constant plotting had been tolerable when he was young, for he had the energy. Of late, however, he had been finding himself tiring with greater ease.

At least he knew the positive impact he had on his people over the many years of his fruitful leadership. The constant re-elections told him that much. He had the adoration of an entire region of Undysvold. A region that had once been the poorest of the three, until he had sculpted it into the richest.

"I'll follow Qwynlo's instructions accurately, don't worry. The job will be done. Do you know where I'll be taking them?" the captain asked, crossing her arms.

"I'm afraid not. If everything has occurred as intended, Henfylt should have some idea of where Adelyka might be by now. This is the enjoyable part of any plot, the element of unpredictability. Remember, no plan is ever truly perfect. Anything can happen and the entire thing can be derailed at any moment. Thankfully, I am prepared for such a derailment on the off chance that it does in fact occur. If she has nothing, simply bring them to the North-West, to Blantyrn," Slyvard stated.

He had delivered what he hoped was the final instruction in enacting his long, intricate plot, before the real action started. He knew he could trust Thalyen. Not just because of the help he had given her when she was younger and this ship he had commissioned for her, but also because she was inherently a good person. She had experience but also youth, a few years off thirty, and he had tutored her from thief to seasoned sailor.

Slyvard himself had lived for forty-four years and he knew, deep down, that whatever this illness plaguing him was, it had done him no good. What remained was a king with his mind intact, but a body that had begun to fail him. His mind had never been sharper, his breadth and depth of knowledge never more vast, but his body started to deliver the ultimate punishment. He had to push on regardless. He wasn't an old man, just an ill one. And whilst little can be done about age, a person can rise above illness. There was hope for him yet.

"Thank you, Thalyen," Slyvard said, after a moment.

"Not at all. You gave me a chance to make myself a better person by giving me a purpose years back. Without you then, I wouldn't have anything now," the captain replied.

She smiled and Slyvard turned around to head back to the main deck once he had said farewell.

The world was changing. Slyvard could see it and he had heard it, too. People were growing tired of their suffering under Meurd and Rancylt's rulership. Jynheln had told him of the situation in the South, the angry faces and the divisive mood. He had seen it firsthand. Year upon year it had grown worse. Each time Slyvard arrived in the South for the annual meeting at Stykricht, the atmosphere had deteriorated further.

Meanwhile, his people lived comfortably and in total happiness. It wasn't uncommon for Slyvard to wander the streets of Blantyrn and venture to the settlements that were tucked away in the far corners of his region. He wished to be viewed as any common man, woman or child would be. Slyvard didn't lead for the hope of status and power, he led with the aim of improving the lives of those he served.

The ship rocked under his feet. He kept his balance and carried on his way. The possibility of war had always been present, hanging over him like a black storm cloud, itching away at the back of his mind, always threatening to come to the front of it. Yet, all he could do was hope that warfare could be avoided, and hope that this plan of his would work.

The Walled City of Hinsylt

As the group approached the entrance to Hinsylt, Aedlyn strolled at Blynkiln's side. Henfylt and Typhylt walked with Merek, Ofryth and Yuneld just ahead.

The journey had been easy enough, but the closer they were getting to Adelyka, the more frustrated Blynkiln became. Before he travelled with company, there was little hope to keep him struggling on. In a way, that was easier than what he had now, perhaps too much hope. There wasn't anything to go wrong before, now there was a cost, and it was a damned steep one at that.

Blynkiln tutted to himself as he followed his allies through the heavy gates, the guards at their posts casting suspicious eyes over everyone who entered the walled city.

"Are you familiar with Ghoslyn, the deity my mother worships?" Aedlyn asked once they'd passed through the gate.

"Aye, I am. Some of his worshippers took over for a while, some twenty or so years back, didn't they? Led by… what was his name?" Blynkiln asked.

"Dunisvold," Aedlyn answered.

"Dunisvold," Blynkiln repeated. "He took charge a couple of years after Ynfleyd was assassinated, if my memory serves."

"Spot on," Aedlyn said, with a nod of her head.

"Why were you wondering?" Blynkiln asked.

"Well, because we're in Dunisvold's city now," Aedlyn answered.

Blynkiln's pace slowed as he frowned. "I thought he was exiled to Oskyrt with the rest of them? Well, the ones that weren't killed."

Aedlyn raised her eyebrows as she walked by his side. "He was, at least to begin with. But, soon enough my mother managed to get him some of his influence back. She admired him so much because he told everyone he was Ghoslyn's representative in our material world, like a prophet, almost. She did all she could to keep him alive and in some form of power. And, here we are. Now, he wields his influence as Mayor of Hinsylt."

Blynkiln shook his head in disbelief. "Strange times. I was at Raltyr when the zealots seized power in the South. None of us in the North-East gave it much thought, really. We knew it wouldn't last. I was only young at the time, but I remember it well enough. I wasn't aware of Dunisvold's influence now, though. We'd best be careful whilst we're here."

"You're right, we'll keep our wits about us. What was Raltyr like, if you don't mind me prying?" she asked.

"I miss it, in truth. There were frozen lakes, clear skies and soft winds, loads of snow, obviously. It never rained, it never got very windy, either. I do miss it, but it's the lack of Adelyka's presence that bothers me more. I'd go as far to say I'd live in the desert so long as she was with me, and I despise the idea of living in the North-West. But it would be worth it," The False Knight answered with honesty.

Aedlyn squeezed his shoulder sympathetically. "We'll get you back to her, I promise. No matter what it costs, we'll get it done."

The way she talked gave Blynkiln no choice but to believe her.

"Thank you," he said. "For your help and kindness since we met."

"You needn't thank me, Blynkiln," Aedlyn replied.

After sharing a smile, they continued following the others. Henfylt led them all through the city as the sky darkened. Blynkiln, whilst frustrated by the fact, knew there was no point in looking for Yuneld's brother now. It'd have to wait for tomorrow.

As they continued striding through the winding streets, Blynkiln reckoned Hinsylt had never been so busy. The rich scent of herbs hung in the air at first, then a combination of other strong smells joined it. There was thick smoke, a sweet fragrance that he couldn't place, the scent of meat being cooked, and a horrendous smell that came from the masses that lumbered around the streets, packed in tighter than fish in a fisherman's barrel. The False Knight's nose wrinkled as the sweet fragrance was overpowered by the more grim ones. *Typical, just typical.*

The streets were uneven, the architecture was crude and many people in ragged clothes huddled for warmth by small fire pits all around the edges of the sharp, unrefined paths that wound through row after row of grimy houses, taverns and shops.

Drunks lurched out of the taverns and inns and a few brawls broke out along the way. Each ended with the spilling of both blood and tears. Blynkiln kept an eager hand on the hilt of his sword and a keen eye on Typhylt and Ofryth, noticing that Henfylt did the same.

The False Knight knew that the speed of his reactions would come in handy if anything did happen, but he doubted it would given how many he travelled with. People with anything other than wool in their heads would avoid attacking a decent-sized group. Blynkiln found himself asking just how many people in the world truly had something other than wool up there. The answer he came to didn't fill him with much hope, but he pushed on regardless.

By the time they got closer to the centre of Hinsylt, which was by far the safest place within the city thanks to the greater number of guards patrolling the area, the first signs of sunset glared orange, pink and red, setting the place ablaze.

The group stopped outside a great big building with neat and smooth walls, the lanterns both inside and outside reflecting in its shiny windows.

"We're here. Stay close and hope they have space. It's the safest spot in Hinsylt, so we should be fine. Even so, don't go running off anywhere. Just in case," Henfylt said.

Blynkiln and the rest nodded in agreement, following her lead. The mercenary opened the thick, wooden door with a creak. Written in blue on a sign at the door's side was 'The Sightseer's Shelter'.

Once inside, Blynkiln's eyes widened. Meals were being served, people were chatting and laughing, creating an uplifting atmosphere. The inn smelled sweet but also fresh and clean, which Blynkiln and his nose were certainly happy about. A few candles were lit on each table and two large staircases spiralled up each side of the large hall and met in the middle.

"Welcome, get sat down over here!" a cheerful voice called out from afar. The source of the voice, a Dwarven woman, pointed to a long table that sat tucked away in the corner of the room.

"Ye didn't tell me it was a Dwarven inn!" Yuneld said as he cast his green eyes over at Henfylt who shrugged her shoulders in mocking return.

"I thought it was a nice surprise, s'pose I wasn't wrong," she replied.

"We're in for a right treat, folks!" Yuneld cried out in excitement.

Once they'd strolled over to the table, the Dwarf who welcomed them in came over.

"My name's Ephryn, pleasure to meet you all," she said.

"I had no idea there was a place like this in Hinsylt!" Yuneld exclaimed as he sat down at the head of the table.

"Well, we've been here for a while but a lot of people can't come in, so it's unlikely you'd hear about it from anyone at random," Ephryn responded, pulling a few loose brown hairs back into place. She wore her hair in a bun and had lively, grey eyes, with a thin slit across her right eyebrow.

"It's the Dwarven tricks that keep this place so safe, you see. Nobody who fancies causing a storm of trouble can walk through that door," Henfylt stated, pointing over at the door they walked through. "I'm still not sure how it works, though, especially given how all of you lot got in here," she joked.

Merek chuckled as he so often did and everyone else joined in, including Ephryn.

"I've known this one for a while now. She comes here whenever she's in Hinsylt and she's helped us out before, so you can all eat and drink for free. If you want a room, we only have two available but they're big enough for a few of you in each. Pick between yourselves and have that on the house, too," Ephryn stated after the laughter had died out.

"No, no. It's a generous offer but we can't have *everything* for free. At the very least, let us pay for the rooms," Merek said.

"Very well, but I'll knock a bit off the cost. No further arguments, it's the least I can do. Just come to the desk tomorrow to pay. I'll bring over a jug of ale and you can all have our house special," Ephryn replied.

The False Knight glanced around the cosy hall. A large fire sat against one of the longer walls, roaring away and filling the space with warmth. The floor was soft, carpeted purple and blue. The walls were a rich, dark wood whilst the fireplace was all stone.

Before long, Ephryn returned with plates full of food. A few others assisted her with carrying more plates and jugs so that everyone could eat and drink their share. It was set to be another joyous night, even with the lack of Adelyka's presence.

Regardless of his own guilt, Blynkiln engaged in the feast that had been laid out before them all. He spoke with everyone around the table and shared laughter with each of them, blocking out his sadness. For a time, anyway. He allowed himself a long overdue night of peace and joy.

Blynkiln leaned back and let his mind wander, hearing the quiet mutterings of two people in the hall. He focused his sensitive hearing on the conversation as he took a long slurp of his beer.

"We were given the choice of suffering under Meurd's rule or allying ourselves with Slyvard, so we obviously chose Slyvard. This happened a few weeks back, now. You know how it is with these things, we all want someone else in charge but she's clinging on somehow. Bribery and fear, most like, but we've got a shot now. He's planning something. We were on this ship that got sent off to deliver goods to the North-East, but we were set on by an unmarked vessel. They didn't threaten us, they just started stealing our gear, which was mostly food anyway, since they're struggling up in the snow. They stole it all and told us that it was going to be circulated to their contacts in the North-East so that Rancylt didn't catch wind of what was happening," a middle-aged man said, between swigs of his beer.

"Good, 'bout time someone did somethin' to put this mess right," a middle-aged woman replied.

Interesting, Slyvard's doing more than just leaving this up to Henfylt. Stirring up conflict between Rancylt and Meurd will probably work well, assuming that's his plan. I'm sure of it, Blynkiln thought, before turning his attention from the conversation back to his food and drink.

The beer was flavoursome, the food was filling and Blynkiln bounced off the positive mood of the group he sat with. After a few hours, the room swayed and tilted and he started laughing with the others over the most stupid things. Maybe he deserved this break, since he hadn't had one in such a long time.

In those few hours of sitting around the large table, Blynkiln bonded with his companions more than he had over the whole of the short while he'd known them. They'd all shared some misery and disappointment along the way, but tonight they were sharing genuine joy. In Blynkiln's eyes, there were few greater ways to bond with people than over some tears of laughter.

They all had stories to tell, even Blynkiln did. Whether that was thanks to the beer or the laughter of his friends, he didn't know, but that didn't matter. He spoke about the trouble he and Adelyka used to cause in their youth at Raltyr, and his friends couldn't get enough of the stories, always asking him to tell another. Then, it would be someone else's turn and the table would shake as palms were slapped against it. On and on it went.

As the hours ticked by, the yawning began and the conversation slowed. They were all about ready for some sleep.

When Blynkiln stood up, only a very dull ache in his side reminded him that he'd been stabbed not so long ago. His body had healed at a faster rate than usual. Even with his Tynukei blood, how he healed as quickly as he did remained a mystery to him. Perhaps he'd overestimated the size of the injury and the depth of the wound. Either way, he was glad to be rid of most of the pain.

"We best get our heads down. Don't know about you lot, but I'm bloody shattered!" Merek exclaimed as he let out a long yawn and a subdued belch.

"Before we all go, I just wanted to say thank you. I can't help but feel I've been a mood killer the past few days on the whole, but because of you lot I'm in a far better place now," Blynkiln said.

He received warm smiles and nodded heads, the odd friendly slap of his shoulder, too.

As everyone left to find the rooms that they were going to be sharing, Blynkiln grabbed Aedlyn's attention.

"Is everything ok?" she asked.

"It is, but I overheard a conversation. Apparently Slyvard's been sabotaging the trade between the South and the North-East. Ships have been raided and the food set aside for the North-East has been taken at Slyvard's command. I'm assuming he's trying to cause some upset between Meurd and Rancylt, especially with the annual meeting starting so soon. I'm wondering if you've got any ideas about the fallout? All I can see is the disagreement getting settled and it backfiring if they both work out he was behind it all. I figured since you know more about Meurd and the type of ruler Rancylt is than I do, it might be you could shed some light on what could happen," Blynkiln answered.

Aedlyn took a moment to respond. "Well, it is a gamble. If there's anything to know about Meurd and Rancylt it's that my mother's proud and pious and Rancylt's stubborn and aggressive. Arrogant, too. I'd guess that they wouldn't be able to overlook each other's accusations. Meurd will be accused of not giving the necessary resources to the North-East and Rancylt will accuse Meurd of lying. Once she does that, my mother will be hard to appease. I always knew Slyvard was cunning, but he really has thought this all through. He knows their greatest weaknesses and he's exploiting them. If Rancylt isn't riled up enough, Slyvard knows that she'd figure out what's really happening. That's my only concern, I hope he hasn't underestimated her intelligence."

"I see now, thank you. It did seem a risky strategy, I must admit. I never paid much attention to Rancylt, neither did Adelyka. It wasn't out of a dislike for her, necessarily. She was just one of those people that most people avoided since we all thought she'd probably be like her mother, and we both know how poorly Ynfleyd was thought of," The False Knight replied.

"Not everyone is the same as their parents, to be fair," Aedlyn said.

You fucking dolt, Blynkiln. What were you thinking saying that?

"Shit. I'm sorry, Aedlyn. I didn't mean-"

She raised her hand and smiled. "It's fine, Blynkiln. I know what you meant, and from what I've heard, Rancylt didn't do herself any favours in the eyes of her people. I don't think she had much of a chance, though, not that I ever knew her well."

"I'm sure you're right. She never seemed particularly horrible whenever I saw her. Then again, I generally stayed out of her way," Blynkiln said.

An awkward silence stretched between them as Blynkiln struggled to think of something to say, besides apologising again.

"So, you've known Adelyka for most of your life?" Aedlyn asked after a moment, bailing him out.

"Since I was about three or four. It was fine at first because Ynfleyd ruled the whole of Undysvold, so there was no pressure on Adelyka to become an electable queen until I was about seven and she was eight. We could just spend as much time as we liked running around Raltyr causing trouble. But when her mother was elected Queen of the North-East after the Civil War, it all changed and we had less time together because Adelyka was always being taught how to be electable as a queen in the future, and I was always left to train with Fuldyn. Either way, we didn't let that stop us," Blynkiln answered.

He frowned as he realised he'd spoken freely about Adelyka, feeling no tug of sorrow in his gut, only a happiness at talking about her, as if his words brought her back in front of him somehow.

"Your relationship with Adelyka sounds much like mine with Ofryth's father. Things got in the way, slowed us down, but we never let them stop us. He was a hopeful fool, but I loved him for it," Aedlyn said.

Before Blynkiln could ask anything more about Ofryth's father, Aedlyn cleared her throat. "What was Fuldyn like, as a person, not a fighter?" she asked.

When their eyes met and Blynkiln frowned, Aedlyn was about to speak again. But, Blynkiln had no desire to ask her a question she wasn't comfortable answering, so he spoke before her.

"Fuldyn was like a mother to me. She taught me how to fight, of course, but she also taught me how to think. I mean, really think. About the world and my place in it. She once told me, *'We are who we are, you can't change that just as I can't bake a cake.'* She was the only one who knew about me and Adelyka, yet she kept it quiet even though she served Phenyrt first. She was killed in an assassination attempt on Phenyrt's life when I was seventeen or so. I was given this sword by Adelyka after that, as a gift. She had it made for me by the forgers at Yinfyr."

His voice weakened as he thought about all Fuldyn had done for him. Sometimes he'd find himself recalling scraps of her advice, or remembering certain moments he'd spent with her where he learned something particularly important that he still carried with him to this day.

"I'm sorry, Blynkiln," Aedlyn said. She spoke softly and embraced The False Knight as his vision blurred. He quickly wiped the forming tears away and took a deep breath, composing himself.

"It happens, we all suffer. All that matters in my view is that we learn from the words and actions of those we've lost.

It's the best way to honour the dead, I reckon," he replied. The strength returned to his voice once more.

They were interrupted by Yuneld. "There ye are! Bloody hell, ye had me worried. We need to determine who's in which room because it's all a big drama. I don't like drama, it gives me a sore head! Merek's busy fartin' about nearly knocking vases off the damned tables, it's utter chaos!"

Blynkiln and Aedlyn laughed, Yuneld's brow crumpled up. "It's not a laughin' matter, I tell ye! Come and see the chaos they've all caused!"

The False Knight and Aedlyn followed the usually cheerful Dwarf. He led them up one side of the silver-railed staircase. The stairs didn't creak or groan, they were made of a strong, solid wood.

The top level of The Sightseer's Shelter was even more inviting and impressively built than the lower, though the use of colour remained the same.

He heard the ramblings of his friends just down the way and made his approach.

"Listen, there are two rooms and seven of us, so we split. Three in one and four in the other. Aedlyn and Ofryth together, Henfylt and Typhylt together. So, that leaves me, Merek and Yuneld. What's the layout of the rooms?" Blynkiln asked, raising his voice to be heard over them all.

Merek stumbled out of one of the spare rooms. "Layout. Yes. One big bed and two long chair things. Err, sofas, yes. Sofas." His words were slurred and he struggled to keep his balance as he leaned against the door frame.

"Merek in with Aedlyn and Ofryth, then me and Yuneld in with Henfylt and Typhylt. Does that work for everyone?" Blynkiln asked. The last time he spoke in that captaining voice was when he trained the knights and warriors of Raltyr.

Everyone nodded in agreement and split off into two directions, saying goodnight to each other as they went.

Blynkiln followed Yuneld, Henfylt and Typhylt into one of the rooms. Once again, it was decorated in a similar way to the rest of The Sightseer's Shelter. An enormous bed sat in the centre of the cosy room with its dark wooden frame that matched the walls. The bedding was purple and blue, and a large fluffy rug of the same colours covered the floorboards by the small fire. The two sofas that would serve as Blynkiln and Yuneld's beds for the night sat at a slight angle, either side of the fire, each near a window.

"This is fancy," Typhylt stated as she leapt onto the large bed.

"It'll certainly do for me," Henfylt replied, as she, too, leapt onto the bed.

Yuneld went over to the fire and warmed his hands, rubbing them together and laughing to himself. "This is wonderful! Ye know, Henfylt, we've all got you to thank for this!"

"Well, it's an honestly run place, they're hard to find these days. Most folks are struggling so they have to put the prices up or lower the quality of the service they offer. But here, they stick to what they know and do it right. Seems to me, they get rewarded for it and all," she replied, with a large smile on her face.

"How does the magic work?" Typhylt asked.

"I'm not sure to be honest, it's a good question. All I know for sure is that it does work. Yuneld, do you have any idea?" Henfylt redirected the question.

"It's hard to explain. It's sort of a blend of Tynuk and Tarspyk, ye see," he started.

Blynkiln moved closer, listening carefully.

"So, the Tynuks have a natural magic. It cannot be learned, ye either have it or ye don't. It's in the blood, a thing you're born with. Tarspyk's don't have that, they come by their unique talent through knowledge and hard study. Very few folk are bright enough to learn it, and even fewer, to master it. We Dwarves are similar to both. It is natural, but we can't just use it unless we harness the skill. Does that make sense?"

"Yes, thank you Yuneld," Typhylt replied.

"No problem. You're a heck of a lot brighter than I was even when I was in me sixties, ye know," Yuneld said, chuckling once he'd finished.

Knowing that Dwarves lived for many more years than Humans did little to dull the shock Blynkiln got whenever he looked at Yuneld. The Dwarf had generally smooth skin, aside from a few lines across his forehead, and looked a similar age to Blynkiln. Yet, he'd lived for far longer.

The False Knight strolled over to the crackling fire. Yuneld shifted slightly to give Blynkiln room. The feeling of heat on his palms never grew tiresome, neither did the calming crackling of wood. He closed his eyes for a moment, hearing the quiet chatter of Henfylt and Typhylt at the other side of the room.

"Ye alright, Blynkiln?" Yuneld asked him.

"I'm alright. Better than alright, actually. When did you last see your brother?" he asked Yuneld as he crossed his arms and turned to face him.

"Good, I can't imagine it'll be long now before ye see Adelyka again. When did I last see Yunylt? A few years ago, now. I ought to visit Yinfyr more often, in fairness, but ye know how it is sometimes. I find the distance gives me a clear head. I don't just live alone up in a mountain for no reason," Yuneld replied, planting his hands on his hips.

"I know what you mean, the solitude must be nice. Look, without your involvement, I wouldn't have a clue where to find Adelyka. So, thank you. I'm glad we met, and not just for the knowledge you have of where she might be," Blynkiln responded.

"It's not a problem. I'm glad we met, too. Too few people are willing to help those in need these days. I've been about for a while, as ye know, but there have always been terrible people as there still are and will always be. The thing is, most people have similar values and priorities. Yet, we still keep up the divisions and the arguments for the sake of it. I try where I can. Merek came to me and ye all needed help, so I gave it. There's no need to thank me, it's what everybody should do," Yuneld stated.

"I agree with you there," Henfylt said, jumping into the conversation. "Everyone whines about how difficult their life is even when they have it easy. Plenty of people can't be arsed to help those less fortunate than themselves. I haven't heard you complain once, Blynkiln, but you've hardly had it easy."

"Why don't you complain more?" Typhylt asked, respectfully. "You have more reason to complain than a lot of people."

Blynkiln smiled over at Typhylt and looked back into the flames. "I complain enough to myself, I just don't see the need to weigh down others with my problems. It isn't some noble thought or some rare talent I have for managing my own problems, I promise you that. Of course, I still complain, but I try not to bother people where possible. We all have things that trouble us, we all have our struggles. It's just about taking life as it comes and doing your best with what you've got right in front of you, I reckon. Too many people find it easy to place the blame everywhere but on themselves. I recognise what I do wrong and what I do right and I act accordingly, or try to. I bear the weight of my own problems and I alone should bear the consequences of the actions I take."

"That seems logical to me. Maybe everything would be a little better if everyone thought more like that," Typhylt said.

"I believe it would be, but I don't know if I'm right to believe it," Blynkiln replied.

"Typh, you've quite the mind for philosophy, you know," Henfylt stated as she ruffled Typhylt's hair.

"Keep at the books and you'll be a Tarspyk before we know it!" Yuneld exclaimed.

Blynkiln frowned into the flames, then at Typhylt. Maybe Yuneld was right.

"You don't actually think I could, do you?" Typhylt asked, looking right at Blynkiln.

"I do wonder. I don't know enough about Tarspyk studies to comment, in fairness. But I have heard that they have to be philosophical thinkers with open minds," he answered.

"You are genuinely bright, I don't just say it for no reason," Henfylt stated.

"If ye put your mind to it, ye never know. If it's of interest, of course. We could help if ye wanted us to," Yuneld added.

All eyes rested on Typhylt, she was evidently giving it some thought.

"I'd have to find out more about what it means to be a Tarspyk, of course, and what I would have to be able to know and understand. Maybe it's worth it," she said, shrugging her shoulders.

"It's always worth trying. Worst case is it doesn't work out and ye haven't lost anything other than a bit of time. Never put yourself down and always keep an open mind, ye never know what might come of it," Yuneld replied.

"Spot on, haven't heard a greater truth in a fair while," Henfylt responded.

"Well, I try my best!" Yuneld said, humorously.

Before long, Typhylt was yawning in bursts, then Henfylt started, so the two of them settled in for the night.

Blynkiln and Yuneld were left standing by the dancing flames.

"Ye know, Blynkiln, I'm looking forward to seeing my brother again. It's been too long. Perhaps I need to see him more often," Yuneld whispered.

"What's stopping you?" Blynkiln asked, turning to face his friend.

"The past, differences of opinion and not much else. Just the usual," Yuneld answered.

"Bad disagreements, I take it?" The False Knight asked.

"We were on opposite sides during the war between Inshelt and Ynfleyd. Most of our family died in the conflict, fighting for the same side Yunylt fought for. Of course, I took no joy in their deaths, I loved them, but my opinions on who was a better ruler were different to theirs. It's war, always the same, never different. The problem is, we were both wrong about who we championed, as most misguided buggers are. We should have been fighting for a third party, together, with everyone else in the name of freedom. Instead, we fought for a mad man or a mad woman. The details are irrelevant, I'm waffling on like some old nutter. The point is, we get on well, me and Yunylt, and I think we're past our old quarrels, but I can't know for sure. Are we truly past it?" Yuneld replied.

"I think you'll only know when you see him. Everyone has different opinions on certain topics. You made the choice that you thought was right, so did he. We all make what we reckon to be the right choice when we have to. We only look back on those decisions harshly because that's the beauty of hindsight, the beauty of knowing what comes after. At the time, nobody truly knows what'll happen or when it'll happen," Blynkiln said.

"Thanks, Blynkiln. That's a big help. You're right and I'm glad we spoke. Even with all my years and all I've seen, the greatest fear is my damned brother and what he'll think of me. Anyway, I'm tired and I need some rest. Ye should sleep, too. Thanks, though. I appreciate it," Yuneld stated as he backed away from the glowing embers and the soothing sound of the hissing fire.

The False Knight nodded and smiled at Yuneld, he then yawned and strolled over to the sofa he'd claimed for the night. The temperature of the room was ideal and his sofa wasn't uncomfortable.

It had been an evening of bonding, happiness and hope. All three things were valuable to Blynkiln, and he knew that the bonds he'd formed over the past few days were growing stronger and stronger with time and conversation. As he drifted off into a blissful sleep, he thought that perhaps the strength of these bonds would be the difference between success and failure.

A Familiar Face

After last night's celebrations, Henfylt and the rest had all been more focused and serious in the morning, as they'd followed Yuneld's lead to one of the few academies in Hinsylt, where he thought Yunylt might be.

The blazing fire gave the chamber a restful atmosphere as well as heating the whole space well enough.

A storm had been brewing for a while. Henfylt had caught the scent and feel of it as the humidity increased. When a real storm came, a proper South-Western storm, it was best to keep indoors where possible.

Outside, the wind had grown more ferocious and the heavy rain raged on, pattering down onto the roof and whipping at the windows, giving them a wash, free of charge. The academy was strong and well-built, so there wasn't an immediate fear of the roof being taken right off just yet. Then again, with the power of the wind it wouldn't have surprised her one bit if that did happen.

Henfylt was sitting in a large, cushioned armchair. A smooth, round table stood between her chair and the one opposite her. They were both crafted from mahogany, like the rest of the furniture that filled the richly decorated academy.

Typhylt spent her time looking at the enormous bookcases that lined every single wall of the large room. Henfylt strolled over to chat to her whilst they waited for everyone else to come back from searching the building for Yunylt. They'd had no luck themselves.

"Spoilt for choice here, need a hand looking for anything?" Henfylt asked, resting a hand on Typhylt's shoulder.

"If you don't mind. I'm looking for something that can tell me about the Tarspyks," Typhylt replied, scanning the spines.

"You know, I'm glad you're giving it some thought, Typh. There really is no expectation for you to become a Tarspyk, though. Never feel pressured into doing, well, anything you aren't sure about," Henfylt said.

Typhylt turned to look at her. Her eyes had a spark in them. The same spark that always popped up whenever Henfylt ran Typhylt through some drills to improve her knife-work. They hadn't had a huge amount of time for that since they'd met, but there'd been a few cold afternoons on the way from place to place where they took a short break to get something started.

"I've got you to thank for the thought. I wouldn't have met these people without first meeting you. I know we haven't properly talked about what will happen after all of this is over, but I want to stay with you, if you'll have me, I mean. I don't want to live in Tynylt or go back there unless it's to visit Kynfor. Will you keep me with you?" Typhylt asked.

"It didn't need discussing, Typh. Unless you wanted to go anywhere I wasn't going to let you run off that easily. Come here," Henfylt answered, smiling as she embraced Typhylt. "Now, let's see if we can find something useful for you here."

They both turned their attention to the bookcase. There were a few large, thick books with colourful spines. Most of the tomes were dull browns and washed greys, though, to draw the interest of scholars.

Henfylt scanned each shelf in the vain attempt of finding a book that was full of knowledge of the Tarspyks or even their spire. There was nothing, only the usual scholarly tomes that every academy had in them these days. *They're known to be right secretive bastards, so it was probably always going to be a struggle to find anything about them in a place like this. Elensfyr might have something more useful, though,* Henfylt thought.

The mercenary wandered over to Typhylt. "I've had no luck, Typh. I've got an idea, though, but you'd have to be patient."

"I can be patient. What are you thinking?" Typhylt asked.

"Elensfyr, the Great Library. We'd have to find Adelyka and sort all this mess out first, but straight after we could go there if you wanted to. It's the only place other than The Tarspyk Spire itself where there might be something useful to read, and they wouldn't let us in there unless it was to actually learn their ways. Elensfyr, though, is a different story," Henfylt answered, crossing her arms.

"Well, there's no rush so it makes sense to wait. It's more important we get Blynkiln back with Adelyka, anyway. A distraction won't help with that."

"You're right but keep it in mind and we'll get you where you want to be," Henfylt said.

The two of them went to sit down on the cushioned chairs, back at the circular table. Before long, Merek ambled over to them with his head bowed, his hands holding the leather strap of the cloth-covered thing that rested over his shoulder. Aedlyn, Ofryth and Blynkiln weren't far behind him. Their faces were all glum. That left only Yuneld to make it back to the chamber.

The wind howled outside and the rain hammered down on the walled city of Hinsylt. As the storm went on, thunderous bangs started to crack down on them whilst flashes of lightning lit up the darkening sky.

Finally, Yuneld strolled back into the chamber, alone. After a moment, he looked at them all and said, "Other than the tournament grounds, which nobody with half a brain will be at thanks to the weather, I've no clue where he might be. I'm sorry."

"I see two choices," Henfylt replied. "We either wait in here for however many hours this storm'll rage on for. Or, we leave and carry on. If some of you want to stay, that's fine, but I'm keen to get a move on."

Once she'd finished speaking, her friends all nodded in agreement.

"No reason to delay, then. Let's go," Henfylt stated, and everyone followed.

She assumed that Merek or Yuneld would take the lead, but for whatever reason, everyone looked to her for the answers. *Answers that I don't have. Leadership's never been my strong suit.* But she led them anyway.

They strolled down a corridor which had many paintings decorating its walls. Two older women were having a discussion just up ahead. They were standing under a painting of a pink-leafed tree, the veins in the leaves all dark red. A middle-aged, blond-haired man had a sword by his side as he sat against the white-trunked tree. Sphyltyr, she assumed. The sheath had a tree sharing the same pink and red leaves on it, in the form of a symbol. Whatever the meaning of the piece of art was, she stared at it as she strolled along, struggling to take her eyes away from it as she passed.

The corridor, narrow and long, led to a large room which split off in several sections. Henfylt carried on straight ahead through another door which led into yet another room. The academy was more of a maze than a building.

She stopped abruptly, her gaze fixed onto a robed figure in the distance.

"What's wrong?" Typhylt asked.

"I've just seen someone I recognise," Henfylt answered.

She marched over to the corner of the room. Sitting at a mahogany table, she recognised the red and black robes of Jynheln. His dramatically coloured, wavy hair, too. *What's he doing here?*

The mercenary towered above the Tarspyk. He turned to his right and looked up at her, his deep and clear voice echoing around the chamber as he spoke softly. "Ah, Henfylt. I've just beaten this poor soul at a game. Would you like to play?"

"I'll play," Ofryth said, confidently, before Henfylt could get a word in.

She looked at Ofryth and he smiled at her. The expression on his face told her he had this covered. She stepped back, nodding to the boy, trusting him.

"Are you familiar with the game?" Jynheln asked.

Merek smirked and Aedlyn looked on with a glint of pride in her eyes.

"I am. I've never played in a place like this, though," Ofryth answered.

Jynheln's last opponent rose to his feet, wished Ofryth luck, and strolled off with a miserable sigh. Ofryth took the empty seat.

"If you win, I'll share some valuable information with you. If I win, you will have learned how to play better. A piece of advice before we begin: no matter where you play, play your game and enjoy it," Jynheln said, with an encouraging smile.

The varnished mahogany table had one or two subtle scratches on the surface, but it had been crafted with care and made to shine in any room. It was a perfect square with a large circle set within it. The circle, Henfylt assumed, represented a map of sorts.

Whilst she was totally unfamiliar with the game, she watched on with interest. It seemed to be one of those strategic games, the kind she never had the mind for playing but always wished she had.

This chamber was as vast as all the others in the academy. There were three more tables, purpose-built for playing this game. The rest of the tables that were spaced out around the edges of the room were clearly made for studying.

A grey-bearded man sat alone by a lamp, reading a thick tome with his arms crossed and his brow crumpled in thought. A slim, spectacled man with a narrow nose, brown hair and pale skin sat opposite a bronze-skinned woman who wore a feathered hat. She caught the eye of Henfylt, slender and charming.

There was another student, too, but she had her head stuck in a book and craned her neck in the kind of way that would give her neck pains for the rest of her life if she kept at it. The rest of the seats were empty.

Henfylt turned her attention back to the table in front of her. Ofryth and Jynheln were immersed in their game, paying attention to the pieces on the board and nothing else. Whilst they strategised their next moves and rubbed their foreheads in thought, Henfylt enjoyed the sounds the pieces made as they were placed down with a soft tap. She also enjoyed the sight of Jynheln's puzzled expressions.

The game shortly came to an end. Jynheln conceded, shaking Ofryth's hand and congratulating the boy on his win. The Tarspyk clasped his hands together and lowered them onto the finely crafted mahogany table.

"That was excellent! I've only ever lost once before now to someone who played with a similar style of countering to you. It's a skill I've never mastered, turning a defensive action into such an effective offence. Well played," he said.

"Well played, yourself. It was a good match. Who did you lose to?" Ofryth asked.

"Who else but King Slyvard of Dinshei? I think you could beat him with some practice, you know!" Jynheln exclaimed.

"Anyway, you won, so I will give you some information as promised. The person you seek is currently in the Guildhall. In your Guildhall, Henfylt," the Tarspyk said, his dark eyes settling on her.

Henfylt exchanged a glance with Yuneld. They both frowned.

"How can ye possibly know who we're looking for?" Yuneld asked.

"I'd hate to concern you all, but I've been keeping an eye on you ever since you walked through Hinsylt's mighty gate. I overheard you mentioning Yunylt, so I set off to find him myself before coming here to let you know. It's a long story, one that I would recommend saving for later. The storm outside will only get worse and I think it best we move fast," Jynheln answered as he ran his hands through his shoulder-length hair.

"We? *We* don't even know anything about you," Merek stated.

"I can't argue with that, but we have the problem of Aedlyn," Jynheln replied, speaking quietly and signalling to Aedlyn with a hand. "You look so much like your mother, you really do, despite the years separating you. The guards around this place aren't all loyal to Dunisvold and Meurd, in fact, many of them aren't. But, I imagine quite a few would recognise you. Perhaps the alarm would be raised. Slyvard has a plan, and I'm to help you all find Adelyka or see you to the safety of Blantyrn. We really ought to go now, though, whilst the storm can cover us at least to the ship."

"Ship?" Ofryth asked.

Jynheln nodded. "There's a ship waiting for us, a short distance from the city. Horses nearby, too, to see us there quickly. The only problem is, we may be a few horses short since we weren't expecting quite so many of you. Never fear, we can just double up."

Henfylt looked at Typhylt, then at Blynkiln and the rest. They all looked as confused as she felt. *Some consolation.*

If Jynheln was an enemy, he'd have caused them plenty of trouble by now, surely?

Henfylt sighed, then replied, "I met Jynheln back in Tynylt before I met Typh. I don't know him too well and can't vouch for him necessarily, but he's evidently on Slyvard's side. He didn't come across as a total tosser when I met him, either, so that can only be a positive, right?"

"Thank you for the glowing report, Henfylt," Jynheln muttered, sarcastically.

She continued, "We need to get to Yunylt whilst we know where he is and then on to Yinfyr to see if Adelyka is really there. There'll be spies loitering about the streets around here, spies belonging to both Rancylt and Meurd. Aedlyn has changed from when she was last here, no doubt, but if we got detained by Dunisvold's soldiers... Well, let's not think about that too long. We should move to avoid the risk altogether."

Yuneld nodded in agreement as did Blynkiln and Ofryth. Typhylt, of course, voiced her support for the idea.

Jynheln appealed to Aedlyn. "I am with Slyvard, it was me who spotted you near Alkyn which is how Henfylt knew where to start. I know it means little, but you can trust me. I would've just turned you over to Meurd when I had the chance if I wasn't wanting you to take your mother's place as the ruler of the South, should you wish. That's all I can say in order to convince you. Please. We have to leave. The storm is a curse but also a gift, it means there are fewer guards and people on the street so our chances of encountering trouble are significantly lower than they would be if everyone was out by the tournament grounds. I'll explain everything later, you have my word."

"I'll hold you to that. I think you're right, our best chance is to leave now," Aedlyn replied, her right leg twitching as she looked at Merek for his input.

Merek took a deep breath and nodded in agreement. Jynheln thanked them all and promised he wouldn't betray their trust. With that decided, they all followed Henfylt's lead once again.

As they reached the door to leave the academy, Henfylt turned to the group. "Stay together, we move as fast as we can. I wouldn't want to be out in this for long."

Everyone nodded in acknowledgement, and Henfylt opened the door with a smile on her face. She was leading them to her Guildhall, to her home.

A Chaotic Departure

T he sharp wind and heavy rain assaulted the mercenary as she stepped out into the dark streets of Hinsylt. The dense black clouds cast such murky shadows over the city that Henfylt wondered what time it actually was.

Armoured footsteps clanked nearby as she led the way, occasionally glancing over her shoulder and through the already wet strands of her hair to check that Typhylt and the rest were still following her.

In such a grey, stormy light, Hinsylt's sharp and crooked architecture took on an even more dramatic appearance, sending shivers of nostalgia down Henfylt's spine as she passed the rows of buildings that lined the streets like soldiers with pikes. Having grown up on and around these very streets, the place seemed less of a shithole to her than it probably was.

The shoddily paved floor was slick with a thick layer of water. The large wooden signs that were chained up outside certain shops leapt up and danced in the wind. The metal chains creaked and clunked as they were twisted and twirled to breaking point.

Henfylt made sure that everyone kept up with her as she increased her pace and turned down yet another grey street. Each step became more of a challenge as the wind pushed against her and the rain never stopped falling.

The conditions were horrendous, worse than ever. A few of the taller buildings shielded her from the blows of the savage wind, thankfully. But, with the twisting of the streets, any cover the mercenary received was short-lived.

Henfylt led her friends around the last corner and spotted the outline of her home. It stood as colossal as ever, the solid foundations fending off the storm. It was the only building along the entire street that looked fit enough to deal with a storm like this. Some houses were struggling, some taverns and shops were crying out for help. All the while, the Guildhall stood unyielding. Its turret-like corners reached for the clouds and the grand door didn't so much as creak under the pressure of the fierce wind and rain.

Henfylt led her friends to the door and opened it. The heat rushed at her, the laughter rang in her ears and the smell of beer and cooked meat filled her nose. It was as it had always been, a true welcome. The oak creaked beneath her feet, telling her she was home.

The hearth was enormous, all stone and flame. The weapons and shields hung on the walls in between the flowing dark green flags. Plenty of tables filled the room, each one old and wise to many secrets.

There were old faces and young, the wrinkles of wisdom and experience and the fresh faces of the untried but passionate. Both parties mixed and mingled with each other, sharing smiles and laughter. It was a family in all but blood.

The storm raged on outside, whilst the world within the Guildhall was one of warmth and joy. Henfylt was home.

"Henfylt!" came a shout from the other end of the room. The voice belonged to the Guildhall's blacksmith, Gylphur.

Before she knew it, he'd embraced her and lifted her right off her feet. It was the same bone-crunching hug as always. He lowered her to the floor, grinning wide, his eyes bright.

"Gylphur, you'll be all damp now!" Henfylt exclaimed.

"Ah, as if I care! I've missed you," he replied.

She grinned up at him, patting him on the arm. "I've missed you, too."

"It has been a while. Come on by the fire, this lot will move for you and your friends," Gylphur said, leading Henfylt and her companions over to the hearth. "You'll have to introduce me to them, but get warm first. I'll bring some beer over."

The warmth grew in its intensity the closer they came to the blazing fire. Henfylt greeted some of her brothers and sisters, who all welcomed her with hugs before leaving to let her and her friends warm up. She was home, surrounded by the people she'd shared so much with.

Henfylt admired everyone in the hall for all kinds of different reasons, even the ones she hadn't met who were new.

She understood what it took to become a mercenary in Undysvold. Irys had taught her that much. *Before she upped and left without a word,* Henfylt thought, looking around the room in the hope that her mentor would appear from nowhere. She didn't.

A few guilds operated across the continent. Some were full of good people, others were full of shit ones. The difference between her guild and others was that her lot looked out for their own. She'd helped people with their jobs in the past, and a few people had repaid the favour.

The mercenaries that had chosen the Guildhall had one rival above all others, the lot on the other side of the city, at The Den. They were a strange bunch, all out for themselves and for the coin, the glory. Life was about living, not worshipping coin like it was some all-powerful deity, at least in Henfylt's eyes.

The mercenary turned her attention back to her friends. They were huddled around the hearth, warming themselves through.

"When Gylphur comes back with the beer, I'll ask him if he's seen Yunylt, then we can go from there," she said.

"Good idea, he certainly isn't in this room," Aedlyn replied, as she cast her bright green eyes around the room whilst standing up on the tips of her toes.

Gylphur was on his way back over to them. He had a small cart with him that carried jugs of beer and a fair few tankards, too. "So, Henfylt. Introduce me to your new friends!" he exclaimed.

Henfylt placed her hands on Typhylt's shoulders. "This is Typhylt. Then there's Blynkiln, Merek, Aedlyn, Yuneld, Ofryth and Jynheln." As she announced the names of her companions, she nodded to show which name correlated to which face.

"I'm glad to meet you all. If Henfylt likes you then you are basically family," Gylphur declared, as he smiled at everyone by the fire.

He looked at Henfylt, then at Typhylt. The mercenary nodded and the muscular blacksmith lifted the blonde-haired girl up into the air as he hugged her, then gently placed her back on the floor. Typhylt smiled, slightly red-cheeked.

"Typhylt, a pleasure to meet you. Something tells me you mean a great deal to Henfylt, so you look after her because she may appear tough, and she is, believe me. But, she's as much a lover as she is a fighter, underneath that steely glare of hers. I can trust you to do a good job though, you look strong and brave!" Gylphur said.

Typhylt nodded up at him, not because she was short, but because he was so bloody tall.

Henfylt took Gylphur to one side, after a moment. "Listen, we can't stay long. This is to do with that job from King Slyvard. We need to find Yuneld's brother, so have you seen a Dwarf around here at all?" she asked.

"Yes I have, he's in the other room. Wasn't in a good way when I last saw him. He's had far too much to drink by my reckoning," Gylphur answered.

He paused, darting his warm brown eyes around the room. "It's known that Aedlyn is in Hinsylt, you know. The guards at the gates were getting grilled over letting her in, apparently. They should have detained her, but they didn't know it was her or that she had a son until Dunisvold stuck his nose in late last night. I thought you ought to know, but I'm sure you suspected as much already."

Henfylt's stomach sank.

"We need to move even faster, then. I did wonder about her, but it had been a while since she was last here so I thought we'd manage. Fuck. Help me, would you?" she asked, an unpleasant chill running down her spine.

"Do you even need to ask? Show Yuneld to his brother and gather the rest of them up. There shouldn't be any issues in here, though a few from The Den have tried to sneak in lately. I'll head out and check the street," Gylphur answered.

Henfylt placed a hand on his muscular arm and left with a grateful nod, turning back to her other friends swiftly. Merek was already helping himself to the jug of beer. She interrupted his slurping.

"Yunylt's in the other room, follow me and then we've got to leave. They know you're in Hinsylt, Aedlyn. So, we have to move fast. No questions at the minute please, let's just go and get Yuneld's brother," she said to the group.

Jynheln spoke as they all rose to their feet. "We have to make our way to the gate after we have Yunylt, remember. The horses are waiting for us there, and so is a captain called Thalyen. It is her ship that we're to take you to."

Merek placed the jug of beer back on the cart and wiped his mouth with the back of his hand. "We follow your lead, Jynheln. Keep your wits about you and let's move quickly," he said to the group, with a cold determination, before he nodded to the Tarspyk.

Henfylt led the way from the main hall with the blazing hearth to the steps at the right that led to the quieter room that had its own separate bar. She scanned the room and her gaze landed on a Dwarf slouched over the counter.

"There," Henfylt said as she pointed for Yuneld to see.

"I'll get him. ye all stay here, I won't be a minute," Yuneld replied, striding towards his brother.

Henfylt took a few steps back so that she could see the door to the Guildhall. She waited, hoping Gylphur would come back shortly.

She wiped some sweat off her forehead and tried to steady herself. Typhylt spun the thin chain of her necklace around in her fingers, Blynkiln's leg twitched, Ofryth was looking all about the room and Aedlyn shifted her weight from one foot to the other, never staying still for long. Merek, meanwhile, stood perfectly straight and steady once he'd widened his stance, rolling his broad shoulders back as if preparing for battle.

The door opened and Gylphur's dark figure reappeared.

"Listen up everybody!" his shout boomed around the main hall, bringing everyone's attention to him. "We've one of our own in need and guards are fast approaching! Cover your sister, Henfylt, and her companions, for they need all the help they can get! Fyndor and Pyrclo, come with me to help get them out the back way. The rest of you, tell the guards nothing but distract them however you see fit!"

The other mercenaries cleared a path for Gylphur, Fyndor and Pyrclo as they made their way over to Henfylt and her companions. Once there, Gylphur turned to Typhylt and Ofryth who were standing together.

"You two brave youngsters, maintain your strength and dispel your fears. Everyone here will protect you with their lives, me included. That, I promise you," he said, speaking softly.

Typhylt and Ofryth nodded as Gylphur smiled at them both.

Yuneld soon returned with his brother slumped up against him. "He can hardly move. Why he's so pissed I can't say, but we've got to carry him somehow!"

"I'll take your brother, place him across my shoulders. Aedlyn, wasn't it?" Gylphur said as he looked at the brown-haired woman, placing one of his large, scarred hands gently on her shoulder.

"Yes," she replied, her eyes darting about the room before they settled on him.

"Take my axe, you look able to hold your own! Have faith and remain strong!" he responded, sounding confident and upbeat despite the situation.

"Thank you, Gylphur. For all of this," Aedlyn said as she took the large axe into her hands.

The blacksmith chuckled to himself. "I knew you were capable! You are strong, my axe is very heavy! Is someone ok to lift the Dwarf onto my back?"

Aedlyn gave the axe to Henfylt and helped Blynkiln and Yuneld lift the other Dwarf onto Gylphur's muscular back and shoulders. Once it was done, the mercenary handed the finely crafted axe back to Aedlyn.

"Let's hope all that wood-chopping has come in handy," Aedlyn said, finding a smile among the chaos.

Henfylt clapped her on the arm. "I'm sure it has."

A loud crash came by the main entrance to the Guildhall. "Where is the Queen's daughter and grandson? We've got it on good authority that they are both in here!" came the harsh voice of a city guard.

Without another word or further delay, Henfylt led her friends out the back way. The rain and wind were stronger and more powerful than before. The downpour was intense and the wind pierced Henfylt's ears, numbing them.

She pushed on through the limited visibility. Typhylt rushed at her side. Gylphur wasn't far behind. Somehow, Henfylt's enormous friend managed to keep up with her and Typhylt even with Yunylt across his back.

An unpleasant shiver ran down Henfylt's spine again as her stomach started churning ever so slightly. More sweat gathered on her forehead and clung to her back as her throat tightened and her mouth became drier than the North-Western dunes. She took long, deep breaths, but her heart raced on, beating in her temples as well as her chest.

Henfylt had only ever been in risky situations when she was alone, or with her fellow mercenaries. This time it was different. She was directly responsible for all of those following her, Typhylt among them, and she couldn't let anything happen to the girl. She had to keep going. People were relying on her.

Whilst the fear threatened to drag her under, she locked onto what this fight was for. *Typhylt.* Her drive came from Typhylt. Her purpose was Typhylt. With that thought never leaving her, Henfylt no longer dragged her feet. She kept her concentration and her focus in mind, and she didn't let it slip.

The mercenary glanced back to make sure everyone was still with her. She couldn't see as far back as she would've liked, but she could see Typhylt, Gylphur and Ofryth. She assumed the others weren't far behind the young man.

They were getting closer to the main gate, she could tell as much as they'd passed the sign for 'The Gilded Cloud' which sat a street's length away from their destination.

She turned to her companions and said, "Nearly there now. Horses just beyond the gate, right, Jynheln?"

A distant word came from what must have been the very back of the line. "Yes!"

The mercenary pressed on. There were no sentries at the gate, just a distant figure with a purple feather sticking out of a hat she wore. Henfylt drew her sword in anticipation.

"Wait! This is Thalyen, the captain I told you about!" the Tarspyk exclaimed as he sprinted up to the top of the line with his hands raised.

Henfylt sheathed her sword and sighed in relief. She recognised the hat the closer she came to the captain. *The woman in the academy.*

"The horses are just over here, we have to go!" Thalyen commanded. A few horses neighed in the background.

We made it, just about, Henfylt thought.

"We've got company, I'm afraid. They're from The Den," Fyndor stated as he jogged up the line, his black hair snapping in the wind, soaked from the relentless rain.

Or not.

"Take the horses and go, we'll deal with them!" Gylphur roared.

"No, there are too many of them for you three alone. We'll help you," Blynkiln replied, drawing his narrow-bladed sword.

The message was received quickly enough. Henfylt drew her own sword and the familiar sounds of metal being unsheathed rang out around her.

"With me, Typhylt. Stay close," Henfylt said to the blonde-haired girl.

"Been a while since I've had to use this," Merek said as he took the long, cloth-covered item with the leather straps from his back and unwrapped it enough to bare a sword of dark, heavy steel.

"You've done this before?" Pyrclo asked, in a voice thick with shock.

"I wasn't always this old you know! I did have a life before I became a wrinkly old bugger, you cheeky bastard!" His reply lightened the black mood of the group as they formed an organised arrowhead.

"Fire will help, but if you want great streams of flame, that requires focus and takes a lot of energy to produce on such a scale, so I will use them sparingly and only when necessary," Jynheln said.

"It would be only too easy if ye could just spew fire for an eternity now, wouldn't it?" Yuneld replied, his tone was sarcastic but not unkind as he weighed his two hammers in his hands.

Gylphur lowered Yunylt to the ground and slapped him. He shot up in a hurry and caught wind of the danger of the situation right away.

"Here, 'av this and get ready, ye useless bastard!" Yuneld exclaimed, as he handed his brother one of his hammers.

The enemy encircled Henfylt and her friends, moving slowly and angling their blades in preparation.

"Just hand over the woman and her lad, then we'll leave the rest of you be," a lanky, shabbily dressed man said. His voice was as rough as gravel. He had greyish hair, thick eyebrows and a gaunt, skeletal face.

Blynkiln angled his sword. "No such luck, I'm afraid," he said, in a tone as cold as their enemy's was rough.

"In fact, we'll have you too. I don't much like your tone, boy," the raspy voice came again.

"You're welcome to try," Blynkiln retorted.

His confidence and the lack of fear in his voice filled Henfylt with the hope of a winnable battle.

There was a brief silence. The numbers didn't look good as the enemy closed in on Henfylt's small arrowhead. She breathed deeply and readied herself.

The first blow came, bouncing off Merek's surprisingly strong parry. Blynkiln, rather than wasting time on defence, spun and slashed, blood flicking everywhere as a lifeless sack collapsed to the ground.

One down. Just a few to go...

The enemy came in strength, one after the other, and Henfylt set herself to her work. She caught a blow and returned one, stepping around the odd slash here or there before delivering a final slash or lunge of her own. She was the better warrior in every encounter. Her strikes were faster and stronger, her footwork superior, dominant, even.

Aedlyn brought Gylphur's axe down onto the head of one of the mercenaries in a powerful swing. Spouts of blood shot up as the crunch rang out in the cold, stormy air. Yuneld and Yunylt fought well as a pair, their arcing swings generating all kinds of cracking sounds. Merek swung with strength and speed, decapitating and maiming any who came close to him. Thalyen, the captain, wielded a shortsword and a dagger, claiming her share of lives along the way.

Henfylt glanced back. Jynheln was launching little balls of fire at the more tightly grouped clusters of their enemies. Each ball of flame found a target, often sending up a light showering of sparks that caught one or two others and grew more intense. Flesh seared and the screams of the burning rose in pitch. The Tarspyk clasped his hands together and with gritted teeth generated an ever-growing ball of red and black flame.

"Step back!" he ordered.

Everyone listened and an enormous wave of smoking, swirling fire shot out in front of Jynheln. The red and black robes of the Tarspyk fluttered in the wind.

The flames engulfed those from The Den that didn't move fast enough. Hideous shrieks and guttural screams rang out as the smell of burning flesh drifted through the thick air and entered the mercenary's nose. It wasn't pleasant, but it did the trick well enough.

Jynheln stepped back, his forehead lined with sweat, his limbs shaking as he took deep breaths and widened his stance for a short while before getting back to throwing smaller, more contained balls of fire once more.

Burned corpses littered the ground, but still there were more. Steel met steel and sparks leapt up from nothing. The arrowhead was being broken down as wave upon wave of enemy mercenaries launched themselves at Henfylt and her allies.

Gylphur used his bare fists and raw strength to tackle, subdue and beat those in his path, since he'd given his axe to Aedlyn. He wasn't struggling, though.

Fyndor and Pyrclo held their own, providing cover for Henfylt's close friend as he launched himself into the wall of enemies in an attempt to break it. It worked, delivering a chance for the perfect counter.

Merek was twirling around faster than Henfylt herself could. He dodged blows and cut down his enemies as if they were nothing.

The pair of Dwarves brought their hammers down on the heads and chests of their opponents. The crunching and crashing rang in the mercenary's ears.

Blynkiln, meanwhile, slashed in great rotational swings that protected his body and also hacked the enemies down one by one in front of him.

With every slow swing of the axe Aedlyn wielded, a shriek or scream came up in response.

Everyone did their bit, holding the mass of foes at bay. Thick strings of blood decorated the faces of her friends as much as they did the ground. It was as messy a fight as any.

As things were looking dangerously close to positive, a horn sounded from behind the gate. It wasn't more mercenaries from The Den. It was worse. The city guards began to stream out in full force to bring order back to their city. The grey cloaks, all tattered and worn, flapped about behind them as they charged.

"Get back!" Blynkiln exclaimed, over the clanging of metal. Everyone obeyed the command.

"We have to leave!" came the shout of Jynheln. "The horses are there!"

"He's right, we must," Merek stated as the clanging stopped.

Their enemies retreated as they waited for their allies to get closer. Henfylt checked everyone was accounted for. They were. There wasn't time for further discussion. The attackers came once more, with the soldiers now at their side.

"There aren't enough horses for everyone here, even if we doubled up!" Thalyen shouted.

She was right, there were only five horses.

"You get to the horses. We three will delay them!" Gylphur shouted. Fyndor and Pyrclo nodded in agreement.

"I'm not leaving you," Henfylt replied.

Gylphur looked her in the eyes and grinned. "Ah, Henfylt, but you must go and look after Typhylt. She needs you, and I think you need her, too."

Before she could speak again, and as their enemies were closing in, Jynheln released an even larger burst of scorching fire. It provided enough time for them to turn and run. They had to get to the horses, Henfylt knew as much, but she couldn't just leave Gylphur like this, could she?

"I'll stay behind, too, to buy you lot some time and help these three fine folk where I can," Merek said over the roaring of the flames. "I never much liked horses, anyway, the miserable things give you a sore backside and little else."

"You can't!" Typhylt shouted.

"Listen, we'll manage. You've got to be brave now, all of you have. There's only a few of them! Nothing we can't handle!" Merek responded in his usual humorous tone.

The fire stopped. Jynheln fell to his knees, raising a hand to his sweaty forehead.

"Now go, Henfylt! Please!" Gylphur exclaimed, as the soldiers closed in.

Henfylt slapped him on the arm. "I owe you more than a keg for this."

"Repay me someday. Until then, farewell," he said.

Aedlyn handed Gylphur his axe back, thanking him. Blynkiln went over to Jynheln to help him to his feet. Merek had his sword at the ready and Fyndor and Pyrclo stood firm, by Gylphur's side.

Aedlyn waited for a moment, looking at Merek with tears in her eyes.

"Aedlyn, you have to go. Flee and look after that lad like you always have done. Go!" Merek shouted, as the enemies closed in.

"I love you, Merek, as a daughter loves her father!" Aedlyn shouted back, tears dripping down her face.

"I love you, too. You're a daughter to me, so go and let me do a father's job! I'll be fine!" Merek replied. He smiled, waving his sword out in front of him. "All this, it's light work."

Aedlyn hesitated, but ultimately turned and left just as Merek had asked of her, offering Merek a final loving smile.

These people were Henfylt's friends, her family. But, Gylphur had it right. Typhylt was the priority. She had to be both the first consideration and the last.

As they bolted for the horses, some further ahead than others, the man with the gravelly voice was on Henfylt. She had to parry his attack. The swing came so quickly, out of nothing and from nowhere.

Typhylt was just behind Henfylt as the lanky bastard swung his sword again and again. Each blow was stronger than the last. She spun and whirled, parried and countered as she tried to get the upper hand, or at least get her balance back how she wanted it. It wasn't enough. She tried to defend but his blows didn't weaken, they only grew more fierce and damaging despite how weedy his arms were.

As she stumbled back from another of his blows, he barged into her and knocked her clean off her feet. Typhylt had been left undefended. Any air in the mercenary had been knocked out of her as she met the cold, hard ground.

Typhylt had her knife ready and slashed at her attacker, but the brute knocked it out of her hand and prepared to lunge.

Henfylt couldn't move from the blow that had floored her. She was helpless, gasping for air. The fear took over as she attempted to struggle back to her feet, slipping about in the puddles of slick rainwater and sticky blood.

Gylphur stormed in, his huge figure was unmistakable. He swung his axe to kill the brute but he leapt away before the blow met skin and bone.

Henfylt's head was ringing. She placed a hand on her forehead and attempted to scramble to her feet, but she couldn't quite make it as the pounding grew more intense.

The Guildhall's blacksmith had been shoved and kicked. He attempted to fight back but wasn't fast enough. The sword pierced through Gylphur's stomach, but he let out no cry. Once the blade was yanked out of him, he rose to his feet, unrelenting.

Blood poured from his mouth as he bellowed, "Run Typhylt, run!"

Tears rolled down Typhylt's cheeks as she ran over to help Henfylt up instead of fleeing altogether.

"Run," Henfylt managed to say to the girl as Typhylt grabbed her by the arm and struggled to yank her up.

"Please. Listen to me," she added, staring Typhylt right in her tear-filled eyes.

The girl shook her head.

"I'm not leaving you. Get up," she said, dragging Henfylt to her knees, lending her some strength.

In front of them, Gylphur threw his enormous axe at the lanky bastard, knocking him off-balance slightly. He swung his enormous fist at the grey-haired man, landing one hit on his sharp jaw, before collapsing to the floor and bleeding out among the rain-soaked ground.

The anger boiled inside of Henfylt, the hatred and the sadness too. Gylphur had been there for her since the first day she'd arrived at the Guildhall.

As she struggled to her feet with Typhylt's help, she handed the girl her knife and told her to stay back if she wasn't going to run. Typhylt nodded, setting her jaw.

"Henfylt, Typhylt, go!" Merek commanded from afar. He had four soldiers slashing at him.

The mercenary blocked his words out and let her fury take hold of her as she swung and swung at the man who'd killed Gylphur.

Her swings were weak and uncoordinated, her footwork lousy and unresponsive as rage and grief blinded her. He laughed as he deflected each blow, disarming Henfylt and shoving her to the ground once more. Her sword skittered well out of reach.

As he stepped up to her, he grunted and the lines in his forehead thickened. He held a hand to a knife that had been plunged into his leg.

Typhylt stood behind him, ready to leap back, but he hit her right in the stomach before she could, doubling her over before shoving her out of the way with force.

Rage hardened his features.

Henfylt struggled forward. She had to protect Typhylt. But her enemy limped back to her and brought the weight of his boot crashing down onto her leg. She shrieked as a harsh pain shot along her shin, knee and thigh. The cracking sensation ripped through her entire body, leaving her motionless among the torrential rain and whistling wind.

Her thoughts were stuck on Typhylt and how she had to get her to safety, but as she was, she couldn't move, let alone defend the girl.

She heard Merek's familiar voice as he shouted for help, appearing before Henfylt and taking on the bastard who'd slain Gylphur and hurt Typhylt.

Blynkiln and Yuneld sprinted over, helping Henfylt up and getting a winded Typhylt to her feet, too. All Henfylt could do was cry in pain as they lifted her up.

Her eyes found Typhylt who was staring back at her with a fear so intense in her eyes it made Henfylt feel sick, but at least the girl was alive.

"Take her and don't look back! Go!" Merek commanded as he pressed Gylphur's killer, who was retreating to the safety of his ranks.

Blynkiln and Yuneld carried Henfylt through the onslaught as she worried for Merek and the others. All the while, a thirst for revenge brewed away within her.

Fyndor and Pyrclo cleared a path for them. She could only see Merek surrounded by guards and soldiers, now, but that was all.

She heard the neighing of horses, and soon after felt the galloping strides rattle through her body. She saw nothing, and as the pain became all too unbearable, she became nothing. Her eyes closed as the wind whipped around her and the rain battered down on her head. She fell to darkness and silence.

Developments and Destinations

Slyvard glared over his shoulder at the enormous
entrance to Stykricht. He had wasted days of his life
confined within those thick, suffocating walls of
marble with no escape but the imaginative haven of his own
mind.

Every year it was the same, with Slyvard being forced
into petty disputes. Of course, he enjoyed witnessing Rancylt
and Meurd both lose their tempers at one another whilst he
remained silent where he could, contenting himself by taking
sips from his cup of water. It did, however, become rather
tiresome as the hours ticked by. After all, there was only so
much water one could drink before the cup became empty.

Slyvard coughed three times once he had taken a deep
breath of fresh South-Western air. The metallic taste of
blood lingered at the back of his throat as he clamped his
eyes shut to stop his head from spinning. The wave of
dizziness faded until he could bear to open his heavy eyes,
again.

He had endured the meeting at Stykricht over a lengthy
period, so there hadn't been any way of receiving news about
how his plot had been developing. He hoped that Henfylt had
an idea of where Adelyka might be by now and he would

have prayed, were he a religious man, that Thalyen was on her way anywhere but Dinshei. Because, if they were heading to Dinshei, that meant that they were out of leads.

However, a pit of sorts formed in his stomach as he thought about these things, and Slyvard wasn't one to disregard his instincts. He had to be patient and wait for Qwynlo to come sailing across the shimmering lake to pick him up. Then, he would know all that was needed.

He couldn't fail in this scheme of his, not with things as they were. So many people suffered each day thanks to the incompetence of the rulers of their lands. Problematically, Slyvard himself had grown tired of the endless scheming and of having to fix things all the time. He wanted to be undisturbed and left in peace for a while, before he inevitably succumbed to whatever illness was ailing him.

Perhaps he was being punished for his past crimes. If that was the case, then so be it. He still viewed the vast majority of the decisions he had made over the course of his life to be the correct ones. The cost of any bold choice never mattered, for the benefits that came from taking such action far outweighed what could have come to pass had he not intervened at all. *Regret is purposeless. It is nothing more than a hindrance and an excuse,* Slyvard thought.

The soft white sail fluttered in the wind as a boat appeared in the distance. Slyvard sighed in relief and left the marble step he had been standing on.

As he went over to the small docking area, he had to encourage his legs to move with him rather than against him. Each long stride he took did nothing to loosen his legs up, not even a small amount. He shook his head, holding back the desire to hit his legs until he couldn't feel them anymore. At least that way he wouldn't have to suffer this wretched stiffness any longer.

When he reached the small dock, the wood creaked under his weight. It had grown damp and even started to rot in parts. It still served its purpose well enough.

Qwynlo was seated in the sailboat, the frame of his spectacles glimmering in the sun as they perched at the end of his narrow nose. He didn't look particularly pleased, but he never did.

The boat swayed as Slyvard left the rotting dock, balanced himself, and sat down opposite his greatest advisor and closest friend.

"So, Qwynlo, any developments?" he inquired, as Qwynlo began to steer the boat away.

"Yes, though it isn't entirely positive, I'm afraid. Whilst they obviously have a decent head start, the good news is that we know they are heading to Yinfyr as we speak, thanks to Jynheln's... mental communication to me. The bad news, however, is that the mercenary was badly wounded in an altercation between those searching for Adelyka and some mercenaries from The Den. It seems as though the city guards were involved, too. Quite a few corpses were disposed of," Qwynlo answered, speaking as clinically as he always did.

More dead women and men. It's the way of battle, but another reason why I wish warfare could be avoided.

"I suppose we must be thankful for the fact that they managed to get away. Hopefully Henfylt will recover and we won't be exposed. It is far too early for that," Slyvard replied, looking up at the blue sky, admiring its beauty.

"It is indeed," Qwynlo said, frowning.

"Why the frown?" Slyvard asked.

"Well, there were more people with Henfylt than we anticipated. So, their escape was a close call," Qwynlo answered.

"More people? Who specifically?" Slyvard inquired, his heart skipping a beat.

"Well, I don't know all of their names. There was a man with blond hair, two Dwarves, a girl with blonde hair, an older man, and three mercenaries from the Guildhall."

Slyvard leaned forwards and rested his elbows on his knees. "How did they all get away?"

Qwynlo lowered his gaze. "They didn't all get away. I overheard the gossip of some of the citizens that gathered by the gate once the conflict had ended. Apparently, three mercenaries from the Guildhall were killed, and a number of city guards and mercenaries from The Den were, too."

Slyvard straightened his back and sighed. "This is troubling news, Qwynlo. The rest got away, though? Save only the three mercenaries?"

"Jynheln managed to tell me that one of the horses had only one rider, whilst the rest were full. So, I'm assuming that someone other than the three mercenaries also didn't make it," Qwynlo answered. "But, he was exhausted when he communicated this information to me, so that's all he managed, I'm afraid."

"I suppose it could have been far worse. But it is not a good sign of things to come if they are already encountering trouble. We ought to move fast and reach them at Yinfyr before too much time passes, just to be safe," Slyvard said.

Qwynlo nodded.

As they both fell to silence, the mood rather sombre, Slyvard tried to distract himself from dwelling too heavily on things that were out of his control. That didn't make it easy, though. Few things were easy these days.

On the upside, he would be leaving the South-West today. Heading to the North-East wasn't the most warming notion, though, it had to be said. But at least it would only be a brief change until they could all sail back to Dinshei, where the sun would shine so very warmly on them all, soothing his stiff joints.

The South-West had lost its charm after Slyvard had been here for little more than an hour. Everywhere he had looked there were dark clouds and a depressing greyness. Wherever he listened, there howled a violent wind. All the while, rain dripped on his head and trickled down his neck.

This day was different, much to Slyvard's relief. No rain pestered him and the soft wind that blew through his hair as they sailed across the lake didn't anger him. By all accounts, it was a wonderful day. Well, as wonderful as a day could be in the South-West of Undysvold.

When the lake narrowed into something of a wide river, Slyvard knew that he and Qwynlo weren't far from the little village that harboured their mode of transport back to the North-West.

He sighed in relief.

"Is everything alright?" Qwynlo inquired, pushing his spectacles further up the bridge of his narrow nose.

"I'll be glad to see the back of the South-West," he answered. In a rather distant voice that didn't sound much like his own, he added, "You must promise me to think on one thing, Qwynlo."

The thick lines in Qwynlo's forehead deepened. "Yes?"

"When I am no longer here, you should take my place and lead the North-West. You are well-liked and you have a sharp mind. You can carry on all of the good work that we have done in the name of progress and improvement-"

Qwynlo cut him off. "I don't have the emotional intelligence that is required to lead, Slyvard. I don't understand people, not like you do. I'm good with statistics and logistics, but you're elected because of your compassion and understanding. What good am I at speaking to people? I merely relate figures and facts of reality to concepts and ideas which you then put into practice to benefit the masses. Without you, I am nothing."

Those sharp words hurt Slyvard. They cut him through to the bone. Qwynlo was Slyvard's closest friend and his greatest ally as well as his trusted advisor. In that moment, Slyvard saw a genuine lack of self-worth within Qwynlo's eyes.

"It isn't your fault that you struggle to relate and speak to people, you know. The brilliance of the North-West is that we have made it a place of understanding and learning. We did that together. I know it and you know it. More importantly, our people know it. How will our people react when the man who has helped them accomplish so much stands as a candidate for leadership? You are worth more than what you are good at, Qwynlo, and there is a great deal more to living than just being good at something. Far more," Slyvard said.

"I suppose you're right. I do always try to understand why people feel the way that they do. I just need more practice at it, perhaps," Qwynlo responded.

Slyvard nodded in support of his friend.

The river narrowed further until the sailboat barely slid through the gap. The village was just up ahead.

Slyvard's shoulders loosened. For so long, the annual visit to Stykricht had bothered him no end. He had to keep so many emotions and ideas locked away whilst he was there, being careful to not slip up even once. Especially around Rancylt, given their intimate history and how well she knew him.

Every part of him wanted to despise her but couldn't. Not entirely. There was something so captivating about her sarcastic wit and her refusal to be anything but as wild as she saw fit. Perhaps that appealed to his ambitious nature and the fact that he wanted what he couldn't handle.

Every year, at Stykricht, he had to resist his true feelings. A part of him still loved her, but she had become so cold and distant over the years. He liked to imagine that their relationship was one of mutual hatred. He told everyone as much, but each year when they met, a tension still hung between them. Every time they came face to face, the room became confined like a little box, a dingy cell.

He didn't love her anymore, not truly, or at least he thought he didn't. Or maybe he just hoped he didn't. She was far too arrogant and too much had happened between them to ever move past what was, on the surface, a disliking for each other, a clash of character.

Then again, he couldn't deny his true feelings, could he? Maybe he still loved her and maybe a part of her still loved him.

Who knows with these things. I can't control such feelings any more than Qwynlo can't stop himself from pushing his spectacles further up his nose.

Slyvard smiled at that thought, and brought his attention back to the present, discarding all the confusion that had been bothering him of late. What was right in front of him required that focus more.

The boat stopped, its white sail rippled more than flapped. Slyvard rose to his feet, as did Qwynlo. They stepped off the sailboat and strolled up the path to the small village. His legs were as stiff as ever, but he made an effort to not show it.

Plumes of smoke billowed out of the chimneys, casting a fog-like net over the entire village. It was a pleasant place full of laughter and joy, the simple things that made life so unique and worth living. There were the usual children running around and throwing leaves at each other. A few of them had wooden swords and sparred as though they were soldiers, very inexperienced soldiers, but it was endearing to witness nonetheless.

Meanwhile, the adults discussed the storm that had been and gone, and the state that it had left the land in, among other things. Politics wasn't mentioned once, though, and Slyvard smiled to hear no mention of that miserable topic.

There was something wonderful about the little details of the village as he followed Qwynlo's lead. The smoke that spiralled up and floated through the air created a calming atmosphere, as did the soft sizzling of food and the laughter of both adults and children.

More often than not, Slyvard found it the case that those with very little or less were the most content within a society.

They settled for wood and stone when many refused to settle for anything but gold and marble. Silk and satin were more frequently argued over than linen and fur, since those that bought the latter would make the most out of the necessities.

Slyvard realised that he had a region full of silk and not of fur, but what use was fur in the powerful heat of the North-West? Thankfully, his people were far from vain, unlike those of the South-East.

In the South-East, where all the power of the South seemed to find its way, Meurd had filled the entire region with pompous fools who overvalued their own self-worth and importance to the world. All the while, the South-West struggled.

Regardless of the poor luck that the innocent souls over here seemed to have, those within this village showed no signs of frustration or upset. That was likely a result of them never experiencing the true potential of genuine investment and care, though. Slyvard aimed to see that remedied before this illness of his dragged him to his death.

On they went, until they crested a hill and were greeted by the distant outline of a North-Western ship. The plate armour of the North-Western soldiers that were gathered around the ship glinted in the sun, beckoning Slyvard forth.

A twig snapped quietly in the distance. He turned his head to the source of the sound, to a wooded area off to his right. The trees, with their orange and yellow leaves, swayed in the gentle breeze, shrouding the undergrowth in dark, shifting shadows.

"Is everything alright?" Qwynlo asked, stopping in his tracks at Slyvard's side.

"Yes, fine," Slyvard answered, frowning at what he could have sworn was the shadow of a cloaked figure among the thick trunks, moss-covered stones and dense vegetation.

He blinked and shook his head, before settling his eyes on the area once more. There was nothing, no sign of anybody. Maybe he was going mad.

"Onwards," Slyvard said, after a moment.

He caught his friend looking at him from the corner of his eye, registering a look of concern on Qwynlo's face. Slyvard ignored the unasked question and marched on, desperate to set sail for Yinfyr.

Reunion

The False Knight had his head in his hands as he leant over the rail of the ship. They'd been at sea for a few days, rocked left and right by the black North-Eastern waves as they lashed against the hull.

Blynkiln's head was full of stupid ideas about how Merek somehow escaped with his life. His heart though, weighed heavily with guilt and sorrow.

If only they'd have fled for the horses when they had that first chance, before Blynkiln himself had ideas of honour and heroism rattling about in his damned thick head.

Maybe they should've let Gylphur, Fyndor and Pyrclo stay back and defend them whilst they turned tail and ran. It would've wound up much the same for those three. Merek would've made it, though, and Henfylt would've been unharmed. *But no, I had to draw my sword like a dolt and encourage everyone to join me, didn't I? Stubborn shithead.*

He let out a deep, ragged sigh. He'd spent the past few nights on the ship tossing and turning in bed as he clamped his eyes shut to try and force himself to fall to darkness for even just a few hours. He'd wake up after brief stretches of fitful sleep to a back coated in sweat and the rest of him all hot and clammy.

That wasn't the worst of it. By day, the ship was as silent as any burial ground and as depressing as one, too. Only the occasional bit of quiet chatter would break things up.

Blynkiln looked up at the overcast sky, taking a deep breath of the sea air as he thought about the situation.

He missed Merek's presence and his stupid jokes. His helpful advice, too.

Gylphur had seemed like a fine man, but he'd died with a hole punched in his gut by that ugly shit who'd caused them all no end of bother.

As for Henfylt, well her leg wasn't as bad as they'd first thought, but it wasn't great either. Jynheln had set to work mending it as best he could, making sure it was bound up and clean, before sending the mercenary into a nice long sleep using some technique he'd learned at The Tarspyk Spire.

The worst, in some ways, was Typhylt. Not only had she been shaken by her own encounter with the man who killed Gylphur, but she also had to deal with Henfylt being bed-ridden and far from her best.

Then there was Aedlyn and Ofryth, the both of them grieving Merek's loss.

It was all a bit much, if he was being honest, and behind it all was his own selfish desire to know if Yunylt had seen Adelyka before he'd left his forge. Blynkiln hadn't found the right moment to ask, since the mood was so flat. It didn't feel right to even think about asking.

The False Knight shook his head and cursed to himself. He was scared, if he was being honest. Terrified.

Footsteps came from across the deck, interrupting his misery. Thalyen, with her feathered hat and leather jacket, approached him. She took off the hat, revealing mid-length, tightly curled, brown hair which matched her amber-flecked, brown eyes and complemented her bronze skin.

An awkward silence hung over them. She must've been trying to talk to him or connect with him to try to make him feel better, but she clearly didn't know where to start.

Without her and Jynheln we'd all be dead, the least I can do is try and speak to her.

"It's a fine vessel you've got," Blynkiln murmured.

"Thank you. It was Slyvard's investment, he made sure it was a fine ship," she replied. "It'll see us to Yinfyr just fine, then we can wait there until Slyvard arrives."

A bit of a break from travelling will do us all some good.

Thalyen seemed quite a clumsy and awkward person. She traipsed more than walked and didn't really know whether to cross her arms or wave them about as she spoke. There was something endearing about her, though.

"I know the circumstances are grim, but thank you for what you did. Without your ship and your involvement, we'd surely all be dead by now," Blynkiln said, breaking the uncomfortable silence.

"I don't think I deserve any thanks. I was told where to be and I was there when I was supposed to be. I'm sorry about, well, everything that's happened," the captain replied. Her eyes struggled to settle on anything much as she transferred her weight from one leg to the other.

"You fought well and it wasn't your responsibility to join in how you did," Blynkiln stated, lowering his gaze to the deck.

"It's kind of you to say. Listen, I didn't know who else to turn to, but I wondered if you might speak to the girl. She hasn't left Henfylt's side at all and she needs help but I don't know her well enough to offer any," Thalyen said.

I should be there for Typhylt. I can't sit and wallow in my own sadness and self-pity while everyone else is suffering, too. I have to try and make a difference. What would Merek think of me, standing here like a dolt rather than doing something useful?

"Thank you for telling me. Me sitting here stuck in my own head isn't helping anybody, is it?" The False Knight replied. He turned and left with an appreciative smile directed at the captain.

The walk to the cabin shouldn't have been such a struggle, but it was. Each step towards the door took a ridiculous amount of effort. All of the negative emotions that had been spinning around in him these past days followed him like a great big storm cloud. He'd suffered enough fucking storms for a lifetime, so he did his best to be rid of the cloud hanging over him.

He had to be there for Typhylt and everyone else and set his own troubles to one side for at least a bit, until the others started to liven up. If they ever did.

His slow, heavy steps became a bit faster and lighter, more rhythmic and less discordant as he realised that his priority couldn't be himself. Everyone else had to come before him. That was how he'd honour Merek's memory.

Blynkiln reached the door to the cabin, knocked gently and opened the door. The room was gloomy, its air thick and oppressive. Whilst Henfylt slept, Typhylt sat at the mercenary's side.

"Typhylt?" he called into the darkness.

He heard a quiet sob and a snuffle.

Blynkiln crept through the cabin, and by the time he reached Typhylt, she broke down into tears in his embrace. He held her firmly as she shuddered and the tears streamed down her face. He stayed there, unmoving, for a while. With each shiver and cry, it was like a knife had been plunged into his heart. Regardless of his own struggle, he remained steady.

These tears weren't just for Henfylt's pain and struggles. They came from Gylphur's sacrifice, Merek's too and Fyndor and Pyrclo as well. Typhylt must've been so afraid in those moments, especially when the grey-haired bastard turned on her and sent her tumbling to the floor after he'd hit her with such force.

"Jynheln has given her a break from the pain for now. As for the others, they helped us, so we have to keep going to honour their sacrifice," Blynkiln said, after a moment, keeping his voice low.

"It's not just that," Typhylt replied.

"What else?" he asked.

"It's my fault Gylphur's dead and Henfylt's leg is how it is. If... if I wasn't so useless... then, maybe-" she broke off and couldn't find the words.

"None of it is your fault, Typhylt. Listen, I can't tell you everything will be fine because it doesn't work like that, but you need to understand that none of this was your fault. It was your first experience of battle, you've seen nothing like it before. You couldn't have done any more. Besides, you saved Henfylt's life by jumping in how you did. Sometimes, in a fight, you can do all the right things and still be beaten. Henfylt's one of the finest warriors I've ever met or seen fight. She did all she could. As for Gylphur, he made the decision because he valued you. That's the effect you have on people, and it's because you're selfless and kind. Don't blame yourself. There's only the enemy to blame, and one day we'll get our revenge. Don't let the guilt consume you," Blynkiln said.

They broke their embrace and Typhylt wiped the tears from her cheeks with the sleeve of her bulky cloak.

"Thank you," she said, after a moment.

Blynkiln nodded his head and offered her a supportive smile.

"She won't be awake for a while. Do you mind if I stay with you, wherever you're going next?" Typhylt asked.

"Of course not. Come with me," Blynkiln answered.

As they left the cabin and were greeted by the salty scent of the sea air, Blynkiln reckoned they weren't far from

Yinfyr now. That's when an idea came to him and he cursed himself for not thinking it sooner.

They were approaching the famed Dwarven forge, where his own sword had been made. A forge where they had access to the rare ores of the North-West. Perhaps, with Yunylt's talents for crafting, and the equipment the forge would no doubt have, some kind of brace could be made for Henfylt's leg. Something made using those rare ores and with Dwarven properties set into it. The kind that could either heal or at least dull the pain? Maybe it was a stupid idea, but he reckoned it was worth asking.

Blynkiln headed up to the helm with Typhylt at his side. The two Dwarves and Jynheln were sitting in silence when they all glanced up at The False Knight as he made his approach.

"Any clue where Aedlyn and Ofryth are?" Blynkiln asked.

"I believe they are somewhere on the lower decks. May I ask why you are wondering?" Jynheln replied, frowning.

"I just want everyone together, to speak to you all," Blynkiln answered.

"I'll go and get them, just wait up here. I'll be back soon," Jynheln said, his red and black robes swaying as he strolled down the steps.

Yuneld and Yunylt were sitting on a couple of barrels. They weren't deep in conversation, their relationship was odd to say the least. The two fought together well, but a tension hung between them, probably thanks to the past disagreements that Yuneld had shared with Blynkiln.

Before long, Jynheln turned up with Aedlyn and Ofryth at his side. Blynkiln signalled for Thalyen, who wasn't far away, to come over as well. The atmosphere was as flat as ever. All eyes were either deeply ringed and red, or fixed off in the distance. Shoulders were slumped and heads were bowed.

"I know things have been downright shit lately. We all feel it, it's only natural. But listen. We haven't come all this way for nothing. We can't give up and fold, not yet. Yunylt, I have to ask, now that everyone's here. When did you last see Adelyka?"

Blynkiln's heart raced in anticipation for the misery or joy that would come with the answer. He hoped it was the second of the two, but the first seemed more likely with how everything had been recently.

"She's fine. Last I saw her was before I set off for Hinsylt. She was planning on setting out on one of her searches for you once I was back. The forge is secure and nobody knows she's there but me and Zinlot. Well, and you lot too," Yunylt answered, speaking in a similar way to his younger brother, but with a deeper voice and a more serious tone.

Zinlot? Blynkiln wondered, before letting out a long-held breath, the strength in his legs fading as the realisation of reunion hit him like a wave of the North-Eastern sea.

He'd see her again, and soon. Unless something had happened whilst Yunylt was away, but how could it have?

He silenced the doubt and slowed his breathing, trying to steady his pounding heart as the excitement, joy and nerves all mixed and mingled within him, making his stomach flutter and churn.

Five long, terrible years had passed since he'd last seen Adelyka. Five years since he'd seen her smile and watched those dark green eyes of hers light up in front of him. Five years since he'd heard her voice and her laugh and shared her company.

Finally, thanks to Henfylt's quest, he was going to see her again. It didn't make up for the loss of Merek, or the sacrifices of Henfylt's fellow mercenaries, but it was their quest and it was Adelyka.

A few brief, genuine smiles appeared on the faces of his friends and companions. Whilst the smiles were tainted by an overwhelming sadness, they meant a great deal to Blynkiln in that moment.

Typhylt placed a hand on his arm and smiled at him. He smiled back, before composing himself once more.

"Thank you, Yunylt, for giving her shelter when she needed it. There was one other thing I wanted to ask. It's about Henfylt." Blynkiln looked at Typhylt who frowned, then he looked back at Yunylt who encouraged him to go on.

"I wondered if you could craft a brace of some kind for her leg. I don't know if it's even possible, and I know nothing about how it could be done if it is. But, if you could craft something that could support her leg or even dull the pain, or both, I'd be even more grateful than I already am. What do you think?"

"Aye, I think I could do something. There're a few designs I can think of off the top of my head. With Zinlot's help we could make something effective, I'm sure. It'd be a quick and easy make, I reckon. It would certainly help her, but she wouldn't be able to move as swiftly as she's used to," Yunylt answered.

The False Knight nodded appreciatively at Yunylt.

Typhylt's eyes glinted with happiness and relief as she thanked both Blynkiln and Yunylt.

"Two good things don't make up for all the bad, I know," Blynkiln said. "But perhaps it'll help. We have to stick together and look out for each other. All that remains is to rest at Yinfyr until the King of Dinshei arrives, if Yunylt will have us. We honour Merek by moving forward. We honour Gylphur, Pyrclo and Fyndor by moving forward. They aren't coming back and it hurts. I know it does. But, what would Merek have us do? Give up and spend our days with no joy in us, no laughter shared? He kept his jokes with him until the end, so I reckon it's only right we try to do the same."

"You can stay at Yinfyr for as long as it takes," Yunylt stated, his tone a bit less severe than it had been earlier.

"Thank you, Blynkiln. It won't be easy and of course we're all sad and feeling a bit rundown, but you're right. Merek wouldn't want us to be this way," Aedlyn said, offering him a genuine smile despite her damp, red-rimmed eyes.

He nodded to her and smiled back.

Loss could never be completely beaten from the mind and soul of anyone, but by turning difficult emotions into weapons with a purpose, Blynkiln was sure that the path ahead would become less challenging.

The False Knight, after a moment, heard a wonderful thing. Conversation. He'd almost forgotten what the stuff sounded like.

The two brothers chuckled quietly together. Jynheln and Aedlyn talked with each other, and Ofryth approached Blynkiln and Typhylt. After a short while, they were talking nearly as they used to, the odd subdued laugh here or there.

Thalyen, however, stood alone, so Blynkiln went over to her. She deserved some company.

"None of this would've happened if you didn't give me that much-needed kick up the arse earlier," Blynkiln said, leaning against the rail.

"I wasn't rude was I? I didn't mean it in a bad way, it's just. Well," she spoke nervously, and scratched the back of her head.

"You weren't rude at all. I needed to hear about Typhylt struggling. It got me out of my own head for a while. So, I owe you my thanks. Again. We all do," Blynkiln replied.

"I don't know about that," Thalyen said, with her head bowed.

"Well, I do," he stated.

She looked from the floor to Blynkiln and nodded her appreciation before looking down at his leg and raising an eyebrow. "Your leg's twitching, you nervous?"

Blynkiln hadn't noticed, but when he looked at his right leg, there it was, twitching away.

"I am. I haven't seen Adelyka in half a decade. Of course, I'm happy, even in these circumstances. But it's been so long."

He remembered the last time he was with her, when everything went from shit to worse. He was in his cell, the iron bars practically frozen. Adelyka came to him in the night, releasing him and telling him he had to go.

He remembered their final embrace, the smell of her hair and the beating of her panicked heart against his own. Blynkiln wanted her to come with him, but she was as stubborn as always. She couldn't join him before she'd brought him more time to escape.

Without that time, it would've been more than a hundred knights he'd have needed to cut through. Instead, it was just those unlucky twelve. He'd trained each of them, sparred with them and commanded them.

He thought back on it with shame, lowering his head to the black waves. He butchered those knights without even trying to disarm them first, slashing each one down until the path ahead had been cleared. All twelve of them like they were nothing, just in his way to freedom, so they had to die. It was a wound that never healed.

"You'll be fine, I'm sure," Thalyen said. "If it's been that long, she'll be desperate to see you too."

"I reckon you're right," Blynkiln replied.

A thin layer of snow blew across the sea in the distance, creating a cold mist that made it hard to make out a distant outcrop of land. *Nearly home.*

Raltyr may have been all he'd known until he had to flee, but it wasn't his true home. His home was wherever Adelyka was, and he hadn't been with her in a long time. The path had been difficult, almost impossible at times, but he'd stuck to it like honey, with that single scrap of faith keeping him going.

"So, Thalyen, what's your story?" Blynkiln asked, stopping his mind from wandering.

166

"Started off a bit rough, I suppose. Years back I had to steal to not go hungry. I'm not proud of it, but I didn't have much choice if I wanted to live, which I did. One day, Slyvard was at the market near where I lived, way out in one of the corners of the North-West, and he saw me stealing. Instead of having me arrested or kicked out, he brought me in and gave me shelter and food. I wasn't the most trusting, but he got through to me eventually, and when he found out that we shared an interest and love of the sea, he had me follow my dream of being a sailor. He said I'd always have a place in his fleet if I wanted it, but he didn't ask me to do anything at all in return. I suppose you could say he bought my loyalty, in a way, but how many people would give a starving orphan a shot at being a sailor?" the captain replied, speaking more openly than earlier.

"There's no shame in stealing for survival, Thalyen. The shame is that you had to steal to survive, and that isn't your shame to bear," Blynkiln said.

Thalyen's features softened as she rested a hand on Blynkiln's arm. "That's kind of you to say. I appreciate it. I get the sense you've been in a similar position yourself."

The False Knight nodded and crossed his arms. "In a way, but I could've lived off the land down in the South, probably. The same can't be said for you in the North-West."

"You've a case of needing to take your own advice and words more seriously, Blynkiln. It can't have been easy, enduring what you did. Listen, I know I don't know you well, but it seems to me like you need to cut yourself a break from all this guilt you're carting around with you. Your shoulders must be sore by now," Thalyen replied, with her eyebrows raised as she patted him on the shoulder.

"Maybe you're right," Blynkiln said, finding that those words of support from the captain did quite a bit to break down his walls.

Whilst she'd started off as a seemingly awkward person, Thalyen appeared to be easy to get along with once he'd started to get to know her a bit better.

"Thank you," he stated as he uncrossed his arms.

"No, thank you," Thalyen replied. "For the advice and for including me."

"Anytime. Speaking of," he said, nodding over to his companions. "Have a chat with a few of them. They're good people and they'll take to you quickly once you introduce yourself properly. Trust me."

The captain looked uncertain as she glanced over at the rest of them. As she looked back at Blynkiln, he nodded in encouragement. She took a deep breath and turned to traipse over to them. Blynkiln smiled to himself.

The False Knight stood alone, staring at the land in the distance that grew larger and larger as the minutes passed by. Casting his eyes up at the bright blue sky, he sighed in relief. Only in the North-East could snow fall despite the sky being clear and blue. Only in the North-East could the air be so fresh and welcoming.

Soon enough, the forge was no longer covered by a distant mist. Thalyen stood at the helm and everyone peered over the rails to catch sight of Yinfyr. Blynkiln stopped at Typhylt's side. The closer they got to the blob of land, the clearer it became. A pink and red leafed tree decorated the courtyard, which was lined neatly with snow-covered hedges and tall, wynluk trees.

Yunylt cackled at the sight of his home. As Yuneld glanced at his brother, he grinned. The snow was heavier here than it had been out at sea, but it didn't tumble down in an aggressive or violent way. It glided down to the earth in the soft wind. To be back among the snow after five years made him realise how much he'd missed the stuff.

Once the ship docked, his mouth dried right up, his throat tightened and his stomach fluttered with nerves. Every time he'd been with Adelyka when they were both younger and just discovering that perhaps there was more to their relationship than simply being an inseparable pair of troublemakers, those same things happened. He relished those sensations, because they told him that nothing had changed, not really.

His head was both everywhere and nowhere as he thought of seeing her once more. Seeing her face, hearing her voice and her laugh. His own cheeks flushed with a youthful heat.

Pull yourself together, he told himself, trying to calm down. Henfylt was still injured and in need of help, and Merek wasn't here to help her heal.

"Should we wake Henfylt?" Blynkiln asked.

"Best leave her to rest until we've got this brace made. It's first on me list, I promise!" Yunylt exclaimed.

"We'll stay with her," Aedlyn said as she placed a hand on Blynkiln's shoulder.

"Go and see Adelyka, Blynkiln," Ofryth said as he stood at his mother's side.

"We'll be alright. You've waited long enough," Typhylt stated as she mockingly pushed him to leave. Blynkiln let out a subdued laugh, thanked the three of them and left the ship.

He wasn't in the mood to stroll. His heart raced with the electrifying feeling of reuniting with her. The closer he got to the end of the path, the more intense the feeling became. The courtyard, the hedges and the trees all disappeared. There was only the path to the door, only the path to Adelyka.

Yuneld stopped The False Knight and roughly brushed his hand through Blynkiln's blond hair. "Ye can't be reintroducing yourself to her with hair like that, all spiky and untidy. Bloody hell, do they teach ye humans nothin' of decency!"

Blynkiln laughed and slapped Yuneld's hand away from him. The Dwarf chuckled heartily.

There was a large wall, but no sign of a door. The False Knight turned to Yunylt who grinned before resting a hand on the smooth structure. The Dwarf closed his eyes and took a deep breath.

With a quiet grumble, the wall disappeared. It grew less and less visible until it vanished entirely. All that remained was a small, hatch-like entrance made of wynluk wood. The latches sparkled. Blynkiln assumed that was because they were made using North-Western ores, but he couldn't be sure.

Yunylt clicked his fingers and the little hatch swung open. He climbed through and Blynkiln followed.

The forge wasn't what The False Knight expected. Adelyka had told him, many years ago, of its brilliance, but Blynkiln had always been a sceptic. It turned out, like with most things, that Adelyka was right.

Yinfyr was a forge, but it was also a Dwarven home. The hall was cosy, with plants decorating the shelves and ornamental lanterns hanging from the ceiling. The sun cast away any shadows as it pierced through the windows. Blynkiln could see the ship and the courtyard in the distance, but he could've sworn that there were no windows from the outside. He assumed it was another Dwarven trick.

The sound of footsteps came from above, interrupting his enjoyment of the architecture. Blynkiln looked up at the landing and the last five years faded into nothing, melting away like ice under a ferocious sun. His heart stopped and he fell to his knees as his body turned to jelly. She hadn't changed a bit.

He finally allowed the years of misery to release as she ran down the stairs and embraced him. The tears streamed down his face. Adelyka's own tears landed in Blynkiln's messy hair. They shared no words, just an emotional silence as they held each other tight. All of his troubles went away the moment he looked up and his tear-filled eyes met Adelyka's.

The warmth of being in her arms once again was like no other. Time stopped. There was no awkwardness, no need for Blynkiln to have felt so anxious about their reunion. Everything was as it had always been, natural and organic. Being apart for such a long period had no impact on their connection, none at all.

The False Knight spent the rest of the afternoon and evening with Adelyka, his focus solely taken up by her. The moon took the sun's place. The stars twinkled and the snow fell.

They were left undisturbed for the whole evening. It was the first night in a long time where he didn't feel alone as he drifted off to sleep with Adelyka in his arms.

He dreamt of nothing much, only a blissful peace with her by his side. It felt as though he slept for an eternity, which came as a pleasant change since he'd been such a light sleeper for the past half-decade, always on edge.

Blynkiln was woken softly by Adelyka. He opened his eyes and was greeted by her broad smile and long, unkempt blonde hair. Her dark green eyes beamed with happiness as he met them.

She leapt out of the bed and outstretched a hand. He grabbed it and followed. She handed him a furry, grey cloak and some fluffy slippers. Her cloak and slippers were as white as the snow outside.

They climbed the stairs that spiralled up a tower until they reached the top and opened the door, heading outside.

The stone was surprisingly warm beneath his feet, heated through by Dwarven fires, no doubt. Adelyka sat down by the edge of the small tower, Blynkiln did the same. He took her into his arms once more as the soothing wind made the tumbling snow dance in front of their eyes.

The sunrise was magnificent, highlighting the snow-covered mountains in the distance with an orange and yellow glow, hints of pink and red too. The sun's blistering colours made the snow-ridden ground sparkle and twinkle as if it was made of stars.

Blynkiln sighed. Finally, he was where he needed and wanted to be.

"I didn't miss a single sunrise, even when I was trying to find you. But, on the mornings when I was here at Yinfyr and we were separated, this is where I'd sit," she said, while looking into his eyes.

"I haven't missed one either. Wherever I was, I always made sure to be awake to watch the sun rise," Blynkiln replied. "Maybe that's what kept me going every cold morning."

"Yesterday was the best day of my entire life, Blynkiln. When I saw you by the stairs, I almost couldn't believe it. I kept the faith over the years, but I wondered if we'd ever be reunited more times than I can count." Adelyka had a sadness in her voice as she spoke.

"It was the same for me. When I asked Yunylt when he last saw you, I panicked. I thought, what if he has no idea? But, here you are. Every day was a struggle," he responded, in a tone that naturally matched hers.

Adelyka held him more tightly and rested her head on his shoulder.

"Every day was a struggle," she repeated. "I'm sorry I couldn't find you."

"You tried, and so did I," Blynkiln replied.

"We did, and now we're together again," she stated.

A comfortable silence followed.

The sun continued to blaze across the snowy horizon. He'd missed the views of the North-East. The sight of snow and the sensation of the soft breeze against his face settled him. Those feelings, as wonderful as they were, paled in comparison to the joy that filled him when he looked to his side and saw Adelyka looking back at him.

"I love you," he said.

"I love you, too," she replied.

Healing

Yesterday morning, Henfylt had been given a small and light brace that Yunylt had crafted for her. He'd said that the brace wasn't just there for support, but that the magical properties set into it would help to heal the leg itself over time.

When he'd clamped it around her leg, Henfylt winced and struggled to keep still. Pain shot up her leg in the same way it had when it was first broken, when she'd been cowering on the cold, rain-soaked ground outside Hinsylt's gate, unable to protect Typhylt or herself. After a moment, a soothing warmth had spread through the limb, a soft numbing sensation joining it. The pain seemed to be steadily soaked up into the brace that gripped her leg tight.

Once she'd stood up and taken a few strides, nearly falling right on her arse straight away, she no longer winced. The joint was stiff and the pain didn't disappear, but it had become far more manageable.

Today, as she headed to the courtyard where the large tree with its pink and red leaves stood tall, the pain had become more of an ache. It was always there, but it never overwhelmed her.

As the snow crunched under her boots, Henfylt breathed in the clear North-Eastern air, looking forward to seeing how well she moved in this sparring session she'd sorted with Blynkiln and Adelyka.

In the distance, the mountain ranges were little more than giant mounds of snow. She wouldn't have guessed that solid rock hid underneath it all.

With the sun at its peak and shining down on Yinfyr, the snow sparkled in different colours. A few thin clouds floated across the light blue sky and a bird with enormous wings soared beneath the sun. It flapped its wings as it carved a path ahead. The flapping stopped and the bird glided for a few seconds before flapping once more. It swirled above the forge in a circular motion before singing a soft and gentle tune.

Henfylt thought of Gylphur, Merek, Fyndor and Pyrclo as she stared up at that bird. The four of them had sacrificed their lives for the rest of the group. Perhaps the bird was acknowledging their efforts. She liked to think so.

Seeing her closest friend die for Typhylt had left her full of grief, of course, but worse still were the frustrating emotions that flooded through her as she thought back on it. There wasn't just sadness, regret and guilt. Joining all of that was anger, maybe even rage. She wasn't just angry at the lanky fucker and herself. She was angry at Gylphur for dying, and how wrong was that? To be angry at her friend for dying? He died saving Typhylt's life. Without such a choice being made, Typhylt would be in Gylphur's place and Henfylt found that a terrifying thought that made her stomach heave. Yet, here she was with her jaw clenched, angry at her closest friend for dying. Thinking that way disgusted her, because she loved Gylphur the way anybody loves a close friend. But, she couldn't stop the way she felt just as the sun couldn't stop rising in the morning and setting in the evening.

If only she was a better fighter. She would've beaten the man who killed Gylphur if that was the case. If she'd done more, Typhylt wouldn't have been hit and thrown to the ground like she was nothing. If Henfylt found her balance, her speed and her strength, rather than whatever the fuck it was that she let happen to her instead, then maybe it would have all been very different. Maybe Merek would've had time to escape with Fyndor and Pyrclo, maybe Gylphur would've gone with them, too. But no. That wasn't how it happened because she wasn't good enough, and that stung more than her bastard leg and maybe even the losses that were stacking up, as bad as that was. Failure was the world's biggest arsehole.

The bird stopped circling over Yinfyr and set off flying on its way once again. The bird moved on. She had to try to do the same, however hard that might be.

The experience of loss and the way grief weighed down her feet made the smallest of things seem like the greatest of challenges. But, she knew that she'd get through it with time and by facing it head-on, rather than slamming it away and letting it burn at the back of her mind for the rest of her days.

Worse than the grief, in many ways, was her fear of not being good enough to defend Typhylt anymore. For so long she'd been as fierce a fighter as any, more than a match for everybody she'd faced. Now, though? She couldn't be sure she was a fine match for anybody. It was something new and terrifying, and right now she didn't need new and terrifying. She needed old and familiar. She needed to be better in order to protect Typhylt.

The only way she could think of improving was by going right back to her roots, where all fighters start. She had to be better. She had to be more. *Typhylt needs somebody better. I'm not able to defend her and protect her. Now, with this brace, I'm next to bloody useless!* Even with such thoughts making her doubt herself, Henfylt had never been one to give up easily. Why break the habit of a lifetime?

175

The snow thinned as she followed the path closer to the tree. The pink leaves with their red veins must've been giving off some kind of natural heat, since no snow was covering them.

Henfylt had heard legends of the Sphynlok trees from Yunylt the previous day, once she was up and about. The trunks were white, just like the trunks of all trees in the North-East. But, the leaves on these trees were unique. Pink, with dark red veins. It was Sphyltyr himself who created them, or so Yunylt had told her.

Henfylt reached the tree, outstretched a hand and placed it on the enormous trunk of the old Sphynlok. She closed her eyes as soft vibrations ran through her fingertips. They were slow and delicate but she could feel the energy of the ageless tree beneath her palm.

She breathed in deeply and took her hand away. A single leaf fell onto her black hair. She picked it up gently and laid it down in her palm. The thick red veins of the dark pink leaf gave off a dull light as it vibrated like a steady pulse, as if it breathed. She looked back at the tree, all of its leaves were also glowing.

"Bloody hell!" came the shout of Yunylt from down the path.

"Why's it doing that?" Henfylt asked. A slight crack ran through her leg as she rushed backwards, away from the Sphynlok. She winced and rested a hand on the brace, but the sharp pain soon returned to its usual dull ache.

"I've no idea!" Yunylt exclaimed.

A rising heat came from the Sphynlok. A few branches grew out and sprouted more pink and red leaves. The base of the tree grew larger, too. The earth cracked and a glowing light shot up from the ground. Henfylt shuffled back a few steps, this time more carefully.

What have I done now? she asked herself as a steaming pool appeared at the base of the Sphynlok. The rumbling steadied, then stopped altogether. Henfylt peered into the pool and saw her own reflection in the rippling water.

"Whatever you've done, Henfylt, it's bloody fantastic!" Yunylt cried out in glee.

A crowd gathered around the tree.

"This is magnificent!" Jynheln said as he swept his hair back from his forehead.

"What is it?" Ofryth asked, crouching by the edge of the pool.

Shocked silence was the only answer he got.

"I've got plenty of books here. Anyone who wants to can help us look for the answer. Anything about Sphynloks will do, Tynuks too. Pools of water, actually, as well," Yunylt rambled.

"Oh, and Henfylt, keep a hold of that leaf," he said, before setting off with most of the others.

The thick leaf continued to glow in her hand as Henfylt stood by the pool with Typhylt at her side. Blynkiln and Adelyka stayed with them. Everyone else left with Yunylt.

The mercenary had been introduced to Adelyka last night. The two had a lot in common and Henfylt instantly understood why she was so important to Blynkiln. She had blonde hair, like Typhylt's, though her eyes were green. Not a bright green like Aedlyn and Ofryth's, but a deep and dark green. She had a roughness to her, a firm look about her, the kind that made her attractive and appealing. Henfylt could tell that Adelyka knew how to handle herself in a scrap.

"Well, we could get to work while we wait for them to get back with some answers," Henfylt said, placing the leaf into her pocket.

"I've brought a spare sword since we couldn't recover yours from the battle," Blynkiln replied, in a consoling tone.

Henfylt took the sword in her hand. It felt strange, as if she held a war hammer rather than a longsword. She swung it around to get used to the weight and balance.

"Henfylt, do you mind if Adelyka works with you and I help Typhylt with her footwork?" Blynkiln asked.

"No, not at all. She's a fast learner, so be careful," Henfylt replied as she smiled at the girl and nodded in encouragement.

The mercenary moved over to Adelyka and sat down next to her on a wall not far from the tree. "So, how is it seeing him again?" Henfylt asked.

"It's hard to describe. It's like we were never apart, not really. But I also remember how each day was difficult because I had no way of knowing where he was at any time, just like he didn't know where I was. I knew he'd survive, it's what he does, but I still worried. I owe you everything, Henfylt. He told me that without you coming to that village, he'd never have been put on the path to come back here. We're lucky the timing worked out and I wasn't out looking for him by the time he got here with you lot, too. So, thank you. I understand what it cost to get here and I'm more than grateful for everyone who played a part in it. If you ever need anything, you let me know and I'll happily help where I can," Adelyka answered. She had a strong voice, a voice that was thick with the unmistakable accent the folk from up here usually had.

"I appreciate that. It'll take time to move on, but we all do eventually. At least we didn't do it all for nothing, that's my way of looking at it," Henfylt replied, while itching her forehead.

The mercenary then stood up, ready to begin.

"Blynkiln told me you're one of the best he's seen. That's high praise from him, so you must be good," Adelyka said, rising to her feet as she unsheathed her sword.

The two of them began slowly. Blocking each swing came easily to Henfylt as she placed more of her focus on technique. The problem came when attacking, as she had to drag the sword more than swing it. Her swings were mistimed, thanks to her not trusting this unfamiliar blade.

Her own longsword may have been old and worn, but it belonged to her and she knew it just as it knew her. This spare that Blynkiln found was awful. Poorly made, ugly too. That, or she'd lost all of her ability over the space of days, which she refused to believe could be the case.

It wasn't long before Adelyka went over to Blynkiln and asked if Henfylt could borrow his sword. He nodded and gave the mercenary the narrow-bladed weapon.

"That's better!" Henfylt said as she swung the perfectly balanced sword around in her hand.

"You should get a sword made here, I'm sure Yunylt wouldn't mind," Adelyka said.

"I might have to," Henfylt replied.

The two of them increased the speed of their attacks. Henfylt tried to face the swings head-on, swatting them away rather than doing her usual of dodging around them. After all, the more she leapt about, the more she risked her delicate leg.

For the most part, it worked. With the other sword, she knew she would've struggled, but with Blynkiln's narrow-bladed weapon, everything became simple.

They broke off after a good half hour or so, turning their attention to Typhylt. The girl's speed and determination were promising, but Typhylt's swings were evidently full of anger.

"She's tough," Adelyka said as she strolled up to Henfylt's side.

"Aye, she is. She's full of rage at the minute, too. Each swing's driven by her anger at not being able to save Gylphur. It wasn't her fault though," the mercenary replied, looking down at the ground.

Adelyka placed a hand on Henfylt's shoulder. "There was nothing you could do, either. Blynkiln mentioned what happened. He told me that the mercenary from The Den was a damned fine fighter. So, I know it's a shit way of saying it, but there's no way it was your fault, either. We all get beaten at some point, and there's no shame in it. We just have to get back to working on ourselves and preparing for a rematch. A rematch you'll get one day, I'm sure of it."

Henfylt's leg tingled as she thought back to the crack it made when it had been stamped on. She placed a protective hand on her shin and twinged at the sensation it brought rushing back to her. With her stomach churning and her heart pounding, she wiped sweat off her forehead and tried to stop her good leg from twitching.

"You're alright, Henfylt. You and Typhylt are safe here," Adelyka said, smiling sympathetically at Henfylt as she patted her shoulder.

She tried to take deeper breaths, slowing the restless spinning of thoughts in her head. It wasn't until Typhylt came over and gave her a long-lasting hug that those sensations and the panic started to die down.

It was, on the surface, a moment of weakness. But the more Henfylt thought about it, the more she realised that once again, Typhylt was a source of strength.

As Typhylt helped settle her down, Henfylt focused on what she could control, instead of letting her head dart about all over the place.

Once in control of her breathing, she asked, "Do you mind if I speak with Typhylt for a minute?"

"Not at all, we'll go inside to Yunylt's library and help the others with finding out what this Sphynlok's all about," Adelyka replied, turning to Blynkiln, who gave Henfylt a supportive nod. The two of them left without another word.

Henfylt looked at Typhylt, seeing that the girl herself wasn't in the best of ways, and decided right then that she needed to get herself in order so that she might then be of some help to Typhylt.

"It wasn't your fault, you know," Henfylt said. "Gylphur made his choice and I miss him. I really do. I won't be able to laugh with him and fight with him ever again, but I'll always remember him. Not just for the laughter we shared and the stories, battles, experiences and all of that, but because he protected you. By choice. He didn't have to, he chose to and that means something. You aren't to blame, Typh, he made the choice. You'll be feeling the same anger that I'm feeling. I know it because it's real. It's ok to feel angry as well as upset by the loss of him and Merek. The others, too. The key is to turn those emotions into something positive. We can't let them control us or our actions, we have to face them head-on. With time, these feelings will weaken until they fade enough that they become manageable. For now, though, exploit them. Turn them into passion and let the passion out through everything you do."

A silence of understanding and closure passed between them. It was a small step forward, something that Henfylt reckoned the pair of them needed.

The anger and sadness didn't simply disappear. It didn't work like that, sadly, but the sharing of both guilt and understanding helped lighten the weight a bit, at least from where Henfylt sat. She hoped Typhylt felt the same.

"I'm sorry they're gone, and I'm sorry you were hurt," Typhylt said.

"I'm sorry they're gone, too, and I'm sorry you were hurt. I'm not in the greatest of ways at the minute, but I'll get there. I promise," Henfylt replied.

"We'll get there," Typhylt said.

They exchanged a smile and sat in a comfortable silence for a short while.

"Reckon we should head in and figure out what's going on with this Sphynlok, then?" Henfylt asked, once she was ready to stand.

"Sounds good to me. If anyone can find out what it's all about, it's probably us two," Typhylt answered, her tone less flat than it had been.

They left the courtyard and headed to the forge, chatting away as they went. All the while, Henfylt felt the warm glow of the leaf that she'd tucked into her pocket. Its presence lent

her an odd strength as she followed the snow-ridden path
back the way she'd come.

A Fine Combination

Blynkiln and Adelyka had traded the cold, sharp air of the North-East for the welcoming warmth found within Yinfyr's thick walls.

He sat cross-legged with his back pressed close to hers, so that they could feel each other's heat, just how they used to sit in the library back at Raltyr when they were children.

The floorboards in that musty room were as cold as ice by night, always managing to creak and groan even when the both of them tried to keep out the way of the most knackered ones.

Those were some of the best nights of his life, when Adelyka should've been asleep in her bedchamber and he should've been resting in his corner of Fuldyn's little room in the barracks. They'd sneak past the guards that were stationed around the fortress, crouching and crawling if it meant they'd get some time in that library. It didn't even make much of a library, really. But, North-Easterner's were better known for doing things themselves rather than reading about things others had done, so libraries weren't really their greatest strength.

They'd been found one morning, their heads bowed as they slept with their backs to each other. Fuldyn laughed about it with Blynkiln and called him a dolt for getting caught sleeping out of his own bed. Nobody really cared, though, which got rid of some of the thrill of sneaking around Raltyr at night. That didn't stop them from enjoying the nights in the library, though, where they'd laugh quietly together and keep their voices low by the light of their flickering candles.

They were children, then, neither of them with any friends their own age. Blynkiln had Fuldyn and some of the other warriors in the barracks that didn't mind having him around, whilst Adelyka had her mother and the kind of love people can have for the daughter of the leader they admire. That was it, until they found each other.

It wasn't until Adelyka turned around to look at him that Blynkiln realised he'd been sitting there doing nothing but getting all nostalgic. Her shoulder rested against his back as he looked around at her.

"Any luck?" she asked.

"None. I was too busy thinking back to when we were younger," he answered.

"The library, by any chance?" she asked, a smile crossing her face.

Blynkiln nodded.

"Shithole, wasn't it," she said.

Blynkiln laughed. "Worse than that. Far worse."

"Good memories, though."

"Good memories," he echoed. "Times are good again now, and I reckon that counts for something."

"I'd drink to that," Adelyka said, settling against him.

He'd missed her more than he thought was possible. He sighed and let his shoulders loosen as he slumped back against her.

How did I manage for those five years? He asked himself, almost amazed at his own strength to have fought through what he had without her at his side. In a way, she had been with him, always in his thoughts, lending him the energy to keep going just another day. To be with her now almost felt like a dream instead of reality. The joy and the gratefulness hadn't worn off yet. He doubted they ever would.

So, there they sat together, scanning over the spines of countless books with the hope of finding some answers to the situation with this Sphynlok tree. Blynkiln himself wondered how Henfylt pressing her hand to the Sphynlok's trunk had awakened it. He was pretty sure she didn't have a trace of Tynuk blood in her veins, so perhaps it was some other factor that made it react to her the way it did. He couldn't be sure of that, though.

"You don't think she's got Tynuk blood in her, do you?" he asked Adelyka, keeping his voice low.

Aedlyn, Ofryth, Jynheln and Yunylt were the only others in the room, and they were busy by other stacks of books and scrolls, which filled the room with the kind of heavy scent expected of an old library. Even so, there was no harm in keeping his voice down a bit as he asked such a blunt question.

"I doubt it. I mean, there's no easy way of knowing, but you'd probably have noticed something by now, right? Faster reflexes, hearing things that I wouldn't be able to hear and so on?" Adelyka replied.

"She's well-trained, quick on her feet, but no more so than you," Blynkiln answered.

Adelyka nodded and smiled. "Are you flattering me, Blynkiln?"

"What do you think?" he asked.

They both grinned.

"On a serious note, though, if you haven't picked up on anything like that then I'm sure she's not got any Tynuk blood in her," Adelyka said, after a moment.

"It wouldn't matter if she did, obviously, but I'm interested in why the Sphynlok reacted that way to her. Maybe, if we knew the reason, we'd know what to do next. Or be a step closer to knowing," Blynkiln replied.

"That's a fine point. Maybe one of these books will have the answer," Adelyka stated, shrugging her shoulders.

"I damned well hope so," Blynkiln replied.

They went back to their scanning of the spines that filled the dark wooden shelves. Some of the colours leapt out at Blynkiln, whilst others were dull and muted, barely making him look at them once, let alone twice.

He didn't even know what he was looking for, really. None of these titles filled him with hope of finding answers since they all seemed to be written about something other than what he was after. *Typical,* he thought, placing a thick black tome back on the shelf he took it from a moment ago.

It was getting quite warm and stuffy. He rolled the sleeves of his thick, dark red shirt up and got to his feet to open the window to let some air in.

Aedlyn was facing one of the many towering bookcases that filled the room, her eyes darting over the books that lined the sturdy shelves.

"How are things?" he asked, aware that he hadn't spent a huge amount of time with her since they'd arrived at Yinfyr.

Aedlyn looked no more deflated than she had done since they left Hinsylt. The dark circles under her eyes were maybe a bit more faded than they had been lately, but her eyes were less bright than they had been when he first met her.

She offered Blynkiln a smile and answered, "They've been better. Been worse, too. The main thing is that most of us made it."

"I know it won't mean much coming from me, but Merek was fighting well when I last saw him. I saw the odds, experienced them like you did... but, he was fighting well and anything's possible with a favourable wind," Blynkiln said.

He wasn't entirely sure he believed his own words, but he wanted to say something to at least try and make Aedlyn feel better.

Her smile widened a bit, but the smile didn't reach her eyes. "Thank you, Blynkiln, for trying. Maybe you're right. Either way, he'd be glad that we made it out in one piece."

"Aye, exactly. I miss him, too, you know. I didn't know him like you did, I know that. But, I miss him. You aren't alone, is what I'm trying to say," he replied.

"Strange thing for me to almost be glad about, but sharing the grief helps lighten its weight, I think," Aedlyn said.

"It's hard to disagree with that," Blynkiln responded.

He reached up for the shutters and opened them, letting in some natural light as well as crisp air to freshen the room.

"That's better, I can actually read without squinting now!" Yunylt's voice boomed from around the corner.

Blynkiln was glad to hear Aedlyn laugh quietly.

He turned to get back to Adelyka, to carry on with this searching for answers that was all beginning to feel a bit pointless.

"Thank you, Blynkiln. For caring," Aedlyn called out behind him.

He nodded in acknowledgment and strolled back the way he came, sitting down on the floor next to Adelyka. She held a thin, clothbound book in her hand. Her eyebrows and the set of her lips told him that she was focusing on the words on the pages about as intently as if she was sparring in a courtyard. That was yet another thing he loved about her, how focused she could be on a task. He stayed quiet, enjoying the peace and the familiarity of her presence.

She looked up from the pages, stared at him, and they shared a smile of understanding. Every time Blynkiln looked at Adelyka he couldn't help but stare, just as he knew she couldn't.

After being apart for so long, their connection hadn't dulled. Perhaps it was thanks to knowing the extent of their efforts at getting back to each other that had actually strengthened their bond. Blynkiln knew that Adelyka had endured what he had, out on the roads looking for him just as he had been for her. Neither of them had given up despite the overwhelming weight of a failing hope crushing them both, and this was their reward to share.

"I've found something… I think," Yunylt called out.

Blynkiln and Adelyka rose to their feet, strolling around the corner to the Dwarf. Aedlyn, Ofryth and Jynheln also came over, all with books in their hands.

The carpeted floor muffled the sound of everybody's footsteps. The chill air was freshening up the hot room.

He was surrounded by people he trusted, by people he'd come to know well over the time they'd spent together. Perhaps what made their connections to each other so rich and special was that they'd shared tense moments where the need for survival outweighed everything else, as well as more cheerful moments.

Throughout the course of his life, Blynkiln had often found that relationships between people developed much more quickly if your backs had been pushed against a wall and you had to face the same threat together in order to survive.

Yunylt stood looking down at the book he held in his hands, mumbling to himself without meeting anybody's gaze. They all waited, exchanging glances of anticipation among the silence.

Blynkiln nearly leapt out of his skin the second Yunylt snapped the book shut.

"Nevermind, false alarm," the Dwarf said, frowning down at the floor.

"I wish I asked Merek about these trees before…" Ofryth stopped himself from finishing the sentence. Aedlyn patted him on the shoulder.

Yunylt shifted awkwardly on his feet before clearing his throat. "He'd know about them for sure. I mean, I reckon he would. You know, he was always a very… capable fighter. Maybe talk to Yuneld sometime about him, he knows Merek better than I ever did. They were always good friends, even when things got in the way."

Ofryth frowned, so did Aedlyn.

"What do you mean?" Blynkiln asked, crossing his arms.

"Oh, err, nothing. Just, you know, if you want any stories about him or anything like that then I'm sure Yuneld would be happy to tell you a few. He's out cutting some wood at the minute. He always liked doing that, finds it peaceful for some reason," Yunylt replied, itching his deeply lined forehead. "But, when he's back, you should ask him about Merek... he's an interesting man."

"You think he's alive?" Ofryth asked.

"Listen, I wouldn't want to get any of your hopes up," Yunylt answered, raising his hands as he looked at Ofryth, then Aedlyn. "And there's no real way of knowing... but don't fully write him off, that's all I'll say. Speak with Yuneld, tonight, after we've cracked this business with the Sphynlok, he might give you a spot more hope. Maybe."

Aedlyn's eyes lit up, just like Ofryth's. Blynkiln raised an eyebrow at Adelyka as she raised both of hers.

Some small scrap of hope grew within Blynkiln. That sensation, joining the warmth that came from Adelyka's presence made for a fine combination.

Whether there was anything in this scrap of hope or not was another matter altogether, but that didn't change the fact that seeing Ofryth and Aedlyn have something to smile about came as a welcome change.

"We can hope," Jynheln said, after a moment.

Aedlyn nodded.

"Well, I'd best get back to it," Jynheln stated, opening the book he held in his hands and strolling out the door.

Blynkiln only hoped that Yunylt's words carried some weight. He suspected they did, but even so, he'd seen the odds Merek had faced alongside Fyndor and Pyrclo. There was no guarantee.

Regardless, the more uplifting mood in the library did him no harm as he and Adelyka got back to their reading.

With Eternal Love and Undying Strength

Henfylt and Typhylt, once back in the warmth of Yinfyr, stopped at the top of the staircase where Jynheln paced around whilst holding an open leatherbound book in his hands. His brow was crumpled as he mumbled to himself, turning pages frantically.

Henfylt cleared her throat and Jynheln looked up, snapping the book shut. "Ah, Henfylt. Typhylt," he said, nodding at the pair of them. "Is something the matter?"

"No, but since you're here, I wanted to properly thank you for what you did for me, getting me through the past few days. Without the rest you helped me find, I dread to think how I would've been. So, thank you," Henfylt replied.

"You needn't thank me, Henfylt. I did what was both right and necessary," Jynheln stated.

"You did more than I would've asked, and I appreciate it," Henfylt replied.

The Tarspyk smiled. "How is the leg, if you don't mind me asking?"

The mercenary glanced down at the brace. That same ache reminded her of what had happened back at Hinsylt. "It's better than it was, and I'm grateful for that much."

"Good. That's good," he replied.

"Any luck with the Sphynlok so far?" she asked, after a moment.

Jynheln frowned down at the book in his hands and shook his head. "Regrettably not. So far it is proving to be somewhat elusive. Though, I have found myself closing in on a few theories and ideas with help from the books. One positive of spending many years surrounded by books in the spire is that I usually have a good idea of how to come to conclusions and come up with theories about this sort of thing. It just takes time, and that is the frustrating part."

"Well, for what it's worth, it sounds like you've got it covered," Typhylt said.

Jynheln smiled at her. "I'm trying, and that's all we can do for the moment. We'll have answers soon, though, I'm sure of it."

Henfylt, hearing mention of The Tarspyk Spire from Jynheln, was reminded of the evening she'd spent in The Sightseer's Shelter, and of Typhylt's potential interest in becoming a Tarspyk.

There's probably no better time to bring it up than now, she thought.

"You've reminded me," Henfylt said, looking at Typhylt then back to Jynheln. "I think Typh here might be keen to learn more about Tarspyks. You wouldn't be up for talking to her about it sometime, would you?"

Jynheln's dark eyes sparkled as he grinned.

"Of course, I'd be honoured to! I'm glad you mentioned it, actually, and I'm glad you're interested, Typhylt," he said, turning his gaze from Henfylt to Typhylt.

Typhylt's face lit up.

"When shall we start?" Jynheln asked, speaking directly to Typhylt.

Typhylt looked at Henfylt.

"It's up to you, Typh," Henfylt said, encouraging the girl to come to the decision that felt right to her.

Typhylt nodded. "How about once you've got a theory about the Sphynlok? One that you're happy with?"

"Of course, if that is your wish," the Tarspyk answered.

"Until then, is there any way we can help?" Typhylt asked.

"Follow me," Jynheln answered, leading them both along the landing.

The sunlight pierced through the windows, highlighting Yinfyr's size and filling the place with natural light. Dark wood and stone surrounded them, all beautifully cut and smooth. Everything was warm and dry to the touch. A thick, rich red carpet covered the floor and deadened the sound of their footsteps as they followed Jynheln's lead.

They turned a corner and walked through the nearest door. Inside, some of her friends were rummaging around among piles of unwound scrolls and opened tomes, trying to find answers to the riddle of the Sphynlok.

Bookcases lined the walls, reaching right up to the ceiling from the softly carpeted floor. Mounds of yellowed paper and tattered volumes were stacked at the sides and in front of the towering bookcases, filling the room with the scent of old books.

Nobody looked up from their scanning and skimming of pages as Jynheln led her and Typhylt in. Henfylt shrugged her shoulders at Typhylt and the pair of them got to reading. They tackled the stacks at the sides of the bookcases rather than the tomes lining the shelves.

The first pile was useless, full of poetry and short tales, but the second showed more promise since it was full of academic texts. There were books on military, political and architectural history.

A thin book with a brown cover caught the mercenary's eye. She picked it off the pile but couldn't read the title since the cover was so badly damaged. Once she'd opened it and traced a finger down the contents page a bit, she spotted the word 'Sphynlok' and turned to the forty-third page.

As she read each word and each paragraph, her attention deepened until her mind blocked all of her surroundings out. She hadn't read something so interesting for years. Scholarly writings of politics and philosophy so often bored her that she'd yawn twice with every word she read. This was different, though. It wasn't packed full of the usual 'intellectual' jargon that plagued most academic works, which came as a relief to Henfylt.

She'd always thought that fancy words were used for the sake of elevating the ego of whoever used them. What happened to just saying what you meant and saying it clearly without the need of making yourself sound like an insufferable tosser?

The book itself, whilst an interesting read, told her nothing very useful. It mentioned that most of the trees had been buried or built over on Ynfleyd's orders many years ago, but there wasn't any information on the pools of water specifically.

Henfylt put the book back on the pile. Before she could try her luck with another book, Jynheln exclaimed, "I think I've got an idea!"

The mercenary and the others in the room gathered around the Tarspyk.

"Yunylt, you merge ores from the North-West with the swords you create, to make them act as the core of the weapon, or at least enhance the blade, is that correct?" he asked.

Yunylt nodded slowly, frowning in thought.

"What if the pool and the leaf work in the same way as the ores? What if they are some kind of enhancing tool? You would make a weapon like you usually do and then set it into the water with the leaf that Henfylt has, and the leaf would act as a core to that weapon. Essentially, the leaf would fuse with the sword," Jynheln explained.

"I think you might be onto something with that, you know," Yunylt said, with a chuckle.

He clapped the Tarspyk on the shoulder in a friendly manner. Jynheln winced.

"I don't want to come across as taking anything for granted, Yunylt, but I could really do with a new sword since... well, I lost my own. Would you consider it?" Henfylt asked.

"Of course, of course. I will make it both elegant and beautiful!" he answered, cheerfully.

"One more thing," Henfylt said, with her arms crossed. "Would you be able to make a sword for Typhylt, too?"

"Certainly! What style are you both after?" Yunylt replied, his eyes brightening as he spoke.

"Something narrow but strong. I'll leave the rest up to you. Thank you for this," Henfylt answered. She glanced over at Blynkiln, who nodded in approval.

"What about you, Typhylt?" Yunylt asked.

"My own sword... I don't know," she answered, smiling, despite her voice being thick with uncertainty.

"I'll get right on with it. Perhaps Zinlot'll help me get some ideas together for your design. First, though, I'll ask him about how the blade will interact with the pool. I should've just asked him to begin with, dammit!" Yunylt replied.

"Who's Zinlot?" Aedlyn asked.

"Oh, I forgot to introduce you to him. He's a Gnome, a good friend of mine. A wise old thing, he helps me in the forge," Yunylt answered, before disappearing in a hurry, leaving everyone else with their jaws on the floor.

"What does he mean about a Gnome?" Blynkiln asked, with wide eyes as he turned his head to Adelyka.

"I didn't say anything because I didn't want to say I told you so, Blynkiln. Remember when I used to tell you about

195

Gnomish legends and you'd shrug them off as fantasy?" she spoke with sarcasm, and in a humorous tone.

Blynkiln, rendered speechless, shook his head and laughed.

Surely he's winding us up. They can't be real.

Henfylt and her friends sat in a contemplative silence for a short while. Soon after, the fires of the forge roared and the clanging of metal rang throughout Yinfyr.

Swords were being made for her and Typhylt, right here in the famed Dwarven forge. It made her head spin, since this was the kind of thing she'd once have dreamed of as a girl, drifting off to sleep as she shivered in the cold of the street with the other orphans. Before Irys, before the Guildhall.

She shook her head, forgetting the past and bringing herself back to the present. Jynheln and Typhylt were sitting down on the floor, starting their talk about Tarspyks. Henfylt thought it best to leave the two of them to it rather than interrupting. Seeing Typhylt interested and cheerful warmed the mercenary to her core. The girl had been through enough recently. They all had.

She left the room and followed the sounds of the clanging and roaring. All throughout Yinfyr, the same dark wood and stone made the structure what it was. The hanging lanterns gave off a warm light, dangling down from the ceiling, attached to fancy silver chains. The rich red carpet muffled and cushioned her footsteps, stopping the ache in her leg from being aggravated further.

The closer she got to the forge, the louder the banging of metal became. Henfylt had an image of it in her mind. She imagined enormous vats of molten lava and racks filled with weaponry and armour, a thick smoke billowing out of a chimney and the scent of hot steel hanging heavily in the air.

As she opened the door, no smoke or powerful scents rushed at her. It wasn't a primitive forge in any sense, the air was crisp and thin. A timekeeper sat on a desk, ticking away quietly in the background as Henfylt took in the sights of the open space.

She'd missed the mark on almost everything. The forge wasn't messy and smoking, just as it wasn't full of weaponry, armour and enormous vats filled to the brim with bubbling lava. In reality, it was far more simplistic and clean.

Yunylt brought his hammer down onto a glowing blade, each blow so strong that Henfylt was amazed it didn't shatter the narrow length of steel into thousands of little metallic embers. He kept an eye on some device that looked to manage temperature as he carried on beating away at the steel.

It was a tidy forge, not like the space Gylphur had at the Guildhall. His forge stank of smoke and sweat, it wasn't very clean either but it did the job just fine. Nostalgia tugged at her gut as she thought about Gylphur and his work. The man had always been there for her, supporting her when she was at her worst and laughing with her when she was at her best.

"Ah, you must be Henfylt!" came a soft voice from behind her, pulling her from her own thoughts.

The mercenary turned to see a small figure standing at her feet. He had a face beaming with joy as he extended a hand up to Henfylt. She shook it graciously and smiled at him, struggling to take her gaze away from his eyes that were the colour of a blistering sunset.

"I'm Zinlot, by the way," he said, gently.

Zinlot had a thick white beard, rosy cheeks and a little round nose. Wisps of white hair curled out from under the brim of his orange flat cap. He was smaller than Yunylt and Yuneld, and Henfylt got the sense that he was far older than them, too. He didn't look all shrivelled up and ancient, or walk around with a gnarled old walking stick, though. Instead, he stood straight and lively, wearing a buttoned shirt with straps of leather looped neatly over his shoulders from the waistband of his trousers.

The mercenary had heard tales of the ancient race and how they had supposedly lived in Undysvold before even the Tynuks. Even after Yunylt had mentioned the Gnome, she still thought he couldn't be real. Yet, standing before her own cynical eyes, was this wonderful Gnome with a radiant smile across his face.

"Here are the designs for your sword and Typhylt's," Zinlot said, handing a small and tattered book to Henfylt.

"These are... beautiful," the mercenary replied, staring at the hand-drawn diagrams that were set within the thick pages of the Gnome's leatherbound book.

Her sword was drawn on the left, Typhylt's on the right. There were notes about the dimensions of the swords at the side of each sketch.

Henfylt's blade was drawn long and narrow, its pommel was diamond-shaped and the guard was straight with no unnecessary flourishes. Typhylt's was bolder, the blade slightly shorter and narrowing more gradually, whilst being wider at the base.

Zinlot's sketches were perfect. Henfylt had never seen such detailed drawings before. The swords looked real even on the page.

"So, it will suffice?" the Gnome asked as he swept some white hairs back under his cap.

"Beyond that, Zinlot. It's simple, which is exactly what I wanted. And Typhylt's... well, it'll suit her perfectly," Henfylt replied, with gratitude in her voice.

"Oh, it is not simple Henfylt. No, no. It is elegant and fierce, a symbol of protection and aggression. It is stronger than steel and as brave as can be. It is, and will always be, reflective of the one who wields it. That is the secret to any good weapon, a weapon forged to the specifications of the one it will serve," Zinlot said, with passion and confidence.

In such a brief moment, the Gnome had understood and summarised her perfectly. Henfylt had never thought of herself as any of the things that he described her so carefully and deliberately as, and yet, when he spoke the words, they resonated with her as if they defined her entire character. Her entire being.

"Well, thank you. I don't know what else to say. Truly, thank you," Henfylt replied, totally dumbstruck.

"Listen, Henfylt. Typhylt will face many challenges in her life. You must be there for her as she grows and changes. This sword of hers will see her through much, but her mind is brighter than the stars in the night sky and the sun at the peak of daylight. She is destined for a life filled with adventure, discovery and great achievement. There will also be heartbreak and despair, as with any life, but she will be wonderful. Especially with your help. The Gnomish say that life comes from three places: the mother, the father and the earth itself. She must follow the earth beneath her feet, because if she does not, I see only arrogance and ambition ahead of her. They are two very dangerous things when merged into one and left untempered." The Gnome's orange eyes were damp but bright as he stared into Henfylt's soul, almost blinding her.

All she could manage was a nod as she handed Zinlot's book back to him. He smiled at her in an understanding way and strolled over to Yunylt who still banged away at the glowing steel with his hammer.

Henfylt left the forge without another word, struggling to understand what the Gnome meant and how, without even seeing Typhylt before, had seen such a future for her. *Perhaps he does know her somehow, but how could he? He must know of her, otherwise, how could he say something that feels so true? What am I thinking?*

Her head spun in a wheel of a thousand questions and no answers offered themselves up to her. She wished she could ask Merek for an answer. He may have had something wise to say in response, or at least something funny. But, of course, he wasn't there. He'd never be there again.

As she strolled the way she'd come, a heaviness filling her head, Henfylt bumped right into someone. She took a step towards whoever it was she'd nearly knocked to the floor and rested a hand on their arm.

"Shit, sorry," she said, cursing herself for not looking where she was going.

It was Thalyen who looked back at her. The captain stumbled awkwardly on her feet and apologised.

"I took the corner blindly. Sorry, Thalyen," Henfylt said whilst she stood uncomfortably close to the captain, her hand still resting on Thalyen's arm.

The mercenary knew she should step back to give her some space, but she couldn't. Her body told her to stay put, not letting her move an inch. The captain didn't move either. Henfylt's cheeks became warmer than the hearth in her Guildhall.

Thalyen's amber-flecked eyes were so inviting and captivating, she couldn't bring herself to look away from them. Her throat tightened and her mouth dried right up as her heart started hammering away in her chest.

The captain cleared her throat. "I'll get out of your way now," she said as she stepped around the mercenary.

"Thank you! For bringing us here, I mean," Henfylt blurted out, her stomach fluttering. She cursed herself, but she'd chosen her path, so now she had to stick to the fucking thing. "I didn't have the chance to say earlier since I couldn't find you, but none of us would've made it if it wasn't for you. So, thank you."

Thalyen turned around and smiled, acknowledging the mercenary's words with a slight nod before continuing on her way.

Henfylt leant against the warm wall and slumped down in a sort of frustration that she hadn't felt in a long time, if ever. *You could have been less awkward or tried to make conversation, but no, you just had to freeze like a total idiot didn't you? Well, fuck. Pull yourself together.*

She rose to her feet once more and her leg let out a quiet crack, spreading a sharp pain through her knee, thigh and calf, as if warning her to not forget about it still being damaged.

Once she'd taken some weight off the bloody thing for a few minutes and stretched it to get rid of the stiffness, she strolled in a deflated way back to the others. The pain dulled until it returned to its usual, manageable ache.

"Ah, Henfylt! Have you got a moment?" Jynheln asked, waving her over. He was still sitting on the floor with Typhylt.

"Of course, what is it?" she asked, walking over to them both.

"Typhylt and I have been having a good, honest chat about Tarspyks. Well, she's certainly capable of finding her path to success at the spire. I thought I would let you know. It's just a case of you two discussing the matter of when she begins, if that is what she truly wants, of course," Jynheln answered, his voice full of pride as he spoke. "I shall leave you two alone. Typhylt, you should know that there is no pressure or rush to make this decision right away. It has come about rather suddenly. Whether you choose the spire, something else or nothing at all, always have confidence in your emotional intelligence and wisdom."

The Tarspyk bowed his head and left the room, his red and black robes swishing behind him as he strolled for the door.

Henfylt lowered herself down at Typhylt's side, taking care as she stretched her bad leg out in front of her. "So, what are you thinking? If you have any ideas at the minute, that is," Henfylt asked.

"I know I want to try, but I also know that I don't want to leave you. We should, at the least, see this job out. Is that alright with you?" Typhylt replied, turning to face Henfylt.

"Of course. Stay with me as long as you need and like. I can keep training you as well, if that's what you want," the mercenary said.

"I'd be grateful for it. Thank you, Henfylt. I really mean it," Typhylt responded, leaning over and resting her head on the mercenary's shoulder.

Henfylt wrapped an arm around Typhylt and the two of them sat like that for some time, with the odd bit of mindless chatter every now and then, a few quiet laughs here or there.

She noticed the dull, silver necklace that had always hung around Typhylt's neck. As the upside-down triangle caught the light, its dent-filled and battered surface was highlighted.

"Typh," she began.

Typhylt looked at her. "Yes?"

"Do you mind if I ask you about that necklace you wear?" Henfylt asked.

Typhylt sat upright and shook her head. "No, not at all."

She took it off and held it in her palm, the neat silver chain matching the triangle in the dullness of the metal. It looked as if it had been hand-made by someone with little experience in the way of metalwork, but something about it made Henfylt smile.

Typhylt ran her thumb along the triangle and handed it to Henfylt with a smile on her face. "Here, have a look."

It had hardly any weight to it as Henfylt held it in her palm. "It's a sturdy thing," the mercenary said, surprised as she felt the beaten metal and the bumpiness of it.

"I've had it my whole life, and I still don't know where it came from. My parents, I suppose, or one of them... at least," Typhylt said, picking at the skin around her nails as she bowed her head.

"Well, it's beautiful," Henfylt replied, passing it back to Typhylt.

"You think?" Typhylt asked, raising her head again. "I know it's not shiny or expensive. I mean, the sides aren't even the same length. But, I like it."

"I get that. Expensive things are often overrated. This was made with love and care, I can tell. Hand-made, too," Henfylt replied.

Typhylt flipped it over in her hand and ran her thumb along a tiny inscription.

"What does it say, if you don't mind me asking?" Henfylt asked, curious, but not wanting to be too nosy.

"It says: *With eternal love and undying strength*," Typhylt answered.

"With eternal love and undying strength," Henfylt repeated.

"I don't know why it ended up with me... but, I've always found it comforting, in a way," Typhylt said.

"It's a nice inscription, and it came from something special, no doubt," Henfylt replied.

"It's good to have something... of them," Typhylt stated, slipping it back over her head.

"They'd be proud of you, I reckon," Henfylt said.

Typhylt smiled. "I hope so."

After a brief silence, they moved on from that topic. The mercenary spoke about meeting Zinlot, leaving out the details about Typhylt's supposed future. They laughed together when Henfylt mentioned her own awkwardness around Thalyen and how, actually, it was more amusing than embarrassing.

Time passed slowly as Henfylt listened carefully to every single word that Typhylt said. It was a moment of peace. Even when things had been relaxed in the past, there was always something waiting around the corner for them. But, in those moments, there was nothing but the two of them and their shared laughter.

Henfylt waited and waited for her sword to be finished. The conversation with Typhylt helped to distract her from the frustration of waiting. She hated waiting, but she had to be patient. It was so much harder than just relaxing and watching time tick by. She had something to look forward to, something that was never far from her mind.

Plenty of time had passed since Yunylt started crafting the swords, when Yuneld finally came to fetch Henfylt and Typhylt. He'd been sent by his brother. Henfylt rose to her feet, as did Typhylt. The two of them got a move on, not wasting any time.

Typhylt had a bounce in her step, struggling to keep her excitement contained, as they followed Yuneld down the corridor and reached the dark wooden door that led into the forge.

Yunylt stood by the desk that had the timekeeper on it. Ticking quietly, the cogs inside the machine rotated, moving the fastest pointer along regularly. Typhylt stared behind the desk, where Zinlot was standing with a smile on his face.

"Well, what do you think?" Yunylt asked as he laid a bundle of fine cloth onto the table and opened it to reveal the two swords.

Henfylt's sword was identical to Zinlot's drawing. As her eyes rested on the fine work of art, she realised it was actually real this time, rather than being set in a page of a book. Seeing it in the form of steel made Zinlot's drawing all the more impressive and beautiful for how accurate it had been.

"This is... bold," Typhylt said, splitting through the silence.

"Do you like it?" Zinlot asked.

"It's brilliant," Typhylt answered, grinning.

"And you, Henfylt?" Yunylt asked.

"It's beautiful. Thank you both," the mercenary replied, smiling as she spoke.

"Excellent!" the Dwarf and the Gnome announced in unison, whilst crossing their arms.

"All that's left, when you're ready, is to put them in the pool with that leaf you've got. Then our work is done," Yunylt stated.

Henfylt had almost forgotten about the leaf, despite feeling its warmth from her pocket even as she stood here without looking at it or holding it in her palm.

"Let's go," Henfylt said, nodding at Zinlot and Yunylt.

They left the forge and headed for the Sphynlok, calling out to everyone to let them know where they were going and what was happening.

I wonder what'll happen. Will it even work? Henfylt asked herself as they left the building and followed the path to the pink and red leafed tree.

They reached the pool at the base of the Sphynlok. More and more of the mercenary's friends arrived. One by one, they came up the path until everyone was there. Most of them tried to not stare at the Gnome, but curiosity got the better of them.

"We've forged the swords, now all we have to do is lower them into the water and put the leaf in with them," Yunylt said, formally, as he held the piece of cloth that covered the two swords in his arms.

He nodded at Henfylt and she reached into her pocket to take the leaf out. It was glowing just as it had been earlier, its red veins pulsing. All eyes were on the mercenary for a moment, but the only gaze she felt was Thalyen's. The rest she was comfortable with, but Thalyen made her stomach flutter and her heart skip the odd beat.

Zinlot took the blades from Yunylt's grasp and lowered them into the pool. He turned his head, and the sunset gaze of the Gnome fell on Henfylt. He signalled with a nod.

She cast the leaf into the water. Everything was still. Then a slight rippling came, a few bubbles sprang up and popped softly. A rising steam whirled in the cold air. The two swords didn't sink, they floated on the surface, bobbing up and down.

A sudden warmth and a brighter glow leapt up from the pool, a quiet hissing, too. The water lit up pink and red, rising up and settling back down. A spark of orange and yellow came next as the leaf split in two and fused with the swords, sending up thin tendrils of smoke. The bubbling and steaming grew stronger and more violent with each passing second. The water rippled and splashed over the sides of the pool, dissolving any snow at its edges.

Everyone took a step back as the pink and red came back. This time, the two colours spiralled on the surface of the water, winding around the swords. Thousands of thin little lines twisted together and made fizzing sounds as they tightened their grip of the steel. The dark pink and the red veins merged until they were melded together by bright sparks of orange and yellow. The dancing colours stuck to the blades like a shirt to a back soaked with sweat, never letting go until a shattering sound echoed around the Sphynlok and the light went out. The pool rippled, but the sizzling, bubbling and hissing stopped. After a few seconds, the water was completely still once more, just as it had been before.

Two swords sailed across the surface in silence. They were not ordinary swords anymore. Where there had been the shiny silver-grey of well-worked steel, there were now dark pink and red blades. Henfylt reached into the pool and grabbed her sword, whilst Typhylt grabbed hers.

The mercenary formed a connection with the perfectly balanced sword straight away, feeling it in her heart somehow. It didn't feel like a new weapon, it felt as though it understood her and she understood it. It was beautiful and elegant, even more so than before, thanks to the red veins that shot through the dark pink steel.

Henfylt turned and looked at Zinlot. The Gnome's orange eyes told her all she needed to know. This wasn't a coincidence. She couldn't put all of this on chance and say it was just some random series of events anymore. How could she? Her connection to Typhylt no longer stemmed solely from their chance encounter. Perhaps that encounter wasn't even one of chance to begin with. Their connection had been enhanced by the swords they now held in their hands. Both weapons were made what they were by a single leaf, a shared core.

Henfylt understood that this had happened for a reason. All of it. Zinlot gave as much away. She just didn't know what the reason for it all was. *I probably never will,* she thought, as she saw her own reflection in the tinted blade of her new weapon. She sensed that these swords would have a significant part to play in what was to come.

Love is Easy, it's Letting Go That Isn't

W hat a strange day it'd been. Blynkiln had watched on in nothing short of awe as the leaf fused with the blades Zinlot put into the pool beneath the Sphynlok.

The way the two things reacted to each other was unlike anything he'd seen before. He'd undone the clasp of his cloak to let a bit of cool air in since the heat that came from the pool did its share of keeping his teeth from chattering.

Once the sun had fallen and the moon and stars had taken its place, Yunylt had gathered them all inside his cosy hall for a warm meal. Blynkiln was taking a long sip of his beer at present, enjoying the rich taste as he reflected on the day's events.

The sparring session he and Adelyka had with Henfylt and Typhylt was the best to date, not that there'd been many. It seemed to him that the new swords were doing the trick just fine, evidently nice and easy to swing, quick to raise for defence and quicker still to strike in offence.

Anyway, enough of that. Enjoy the present. Enjoy the beer, he told himself, seeing Adelyka's smile as he glanced at her.

The chatter around the great big table filled the cosy Dwarven hall with a cheerful atmosphere. The colourful squares of cloth that were strung up by the dangling lights contrasted the room's dark wooden furniture, making it a homely space.

There was a fine art to getting the balance between cleanliness and homeliness struck just right, Blynkiln reckoned. Some places were too clean, so they seemed clinical and cold. Heartless, even. Others were so full of clutter and dust that any sense of homeliness about the place was lost by the lack of it being scrubbed and tidy. But here at Yinfyr, Yunylt's home was in order. Enough order so that everything was spotless, but not too much so that it seemed more of a blank space with no personality rather than a home.

Aedlyn was laughing with Henfylt and Yunylt just opposite Blynkiln, whilst Ofryth was chatting away with Typhylt, Yuneld and Adelyka. Seeing everyone enjoying their evening made it impossible for Blynkiln not to smile, especially for Aedlyn and Ofryth. After all, the loss of Merek, if it was indeed a loss, had hit them hardest of all.

"So, Blynkiln," Thalyen said, leaving Jynheln and Zinlot to carry on their conversation without her.

Blynkiln leaned over a bit, so he could hear her better.

"I haven't had the chance to speak with you properly since we got here, but I was wondering if those nerves you were feeling have gone by now?" she asked.

Blynkiln smiled. "They went about as soon as I saw her. You were right when you said I'd be fine."

Thalyen clapped him warmly on the shoulder after taking a slurp of her own beer. "I'm happy for you."

Blynkiln nodded his appreciation before asking, "And you? Are you happy?"

The captain frowned down at her tankard. "I've got beer and good company."

Blynkiln chuckled quietly, shaking his head. "That's not what I meant, but if you're sure."

Thalyen's frown slipped as she cast her amber-flecked eyes about the table, her gaze lingering on a laughing Henfylt.

Blynkiln raised one eyebrow as he looked from the mercenary to the captain. Thalyen blinked a few times before leaning back in her chair and acting as if she hadn't been staring at anybody in particular.

Blynkiln shuffled his chair along, moving a bit closer. The captain watched him with her eyebrows drawn close together.

"Speak to her," he said.

"You what?" Thalyen stuttered.

"Speak to her," he repeated.

She shook her head and Blynkiln smiled, taking matters into his own hands. Thalyen protested, but before she could stop him, he'd caught Henfylt's attention.

"Something wrong?" the mercenary asked, staring dumbly at Blynkiln and then Thalyen.

"Nothing's wrong, just wondered if you two have had the chance to properly speak to each other yet?" he framed it as a question, but he knew the answer.

Henfylt glanced at Thalyen and took a breath before shaking her head. "We haven't, actually," she answered, smiling awkwardly at the captain who smiled back.

"Bear with me," Henfylt said, rising to her feet as she dragged her chair over to Thalyen and Blynkiln.

As Henfylt had her back turned to them, Blynkiln nodded to Thalyen. "Nothing to lose," he said.

Thalyen's posture became less rigid as she smiled and replied, "Thank you."

Blynkiln shuffled his chair back to where it'd been. He'd done his bit for two friends, hopefully inspiring some confidence. Who knew what would come of it, maybe nothing, but maybe something. *A bit of courage goes a long way,* he thought, feeling quite happy with himself.

The night went on in a similar way, with Blynkiln dipping into conversations with different people, sharing some laughter and the rest, all until the more tired among them headed off to bed.

Blynkiln, Adelyka and some of the others followed Yuneld's lead into a lounge with padded sofas surrounding a circular table. A fire flickered away in the background, giving off a steady heat and a gentle ambience.

The Dwarf tossed some fresh logs onto the pile of charred wood. They smoked and hissed until they caught fire and turned the low, soft glowing of embers into raging yellow and orange flames.

Blynkiln and Adelyka sat next to Yuneld, whilst Henfylt and Aedlyn took up one sofa, leaving Typhylt and Ofryth the last. Everyone else had called it a night.

Blynkiln sank into the sofa and sighed. He'd eaten more than he should've, the same could probably be said for how much he'd drank, too, but his mind was slightly foggy and his mood was too high for him to give many shits about that.

Trading a seat at a table for the comfort of a padded sofa seemed a damned fine thing to him then, as the warmth of the growing fire soothed his back, and the tightness in his legs and arms faded away.

"Yuneld," Aedlyn said, breaking the restful silence.

"Aye?" the Dwarf asked.

"I've been meaning to ask, since Yunylt mentioned it earlier, how well do you... did you know Merek?" She replied.

Yuneld swallowed audibly, frowning down at the carpet before meeting Aedlyn's gaze. "I've known him for... quite a while."

"How long is quite a while?" Henfylt asked.

Yuneld offered her an awkward smile. "A good few years. Many years."

"And do think..." Aedlyn couldn't finish her sentence.

"Do you think he's... dead?" Ofryth asked, for her.

The atmosphere became more tense than restful as they all stared at Yuneld, waiting for his answer.

He leaned in and clasped his hands together. "I couldn't possibly say for sure. But, I'd be surprised if he was dead."

Blynkiln found his breath again. Sighs of relief filled the cosy room.

Yuneld raised a hand. "I don't know for sure. Truth is, I wouldn't have said anything to ye all if ye hadn't asked. Uncertainty's a tricky bugger, far worse than believing something with all your heart whether that thing's the truth or a lie."

He makes a good point, Blynkiln thought, but he couldn't lie to himself about not being glad Aedlyn and Ofryth had asked anyway.

"How can you be so close to... certain?" Typhylt asked.

Yuneld let out a deep chuckle. "That would be a story for Merek to tell ye, assuming he is in fact alive. All I'll say is that he's a tricky man to kill, more tricky than you'd think, the sly old bugger."

Aedlyn thanked Yuneld for his honesty, her mood evidently on the rise. Before long, the Dwarf said goodnight to them all and left to find his bed.

The six of them spoke for a short while about their journey here, and a few of them asked Adelyka about herself. It was nice to see them take to her so quickly. Blynkiln reckoned it must've been nice for Adelyka, too.

She must've felt as alone as I did, her only friends being Yunylt and Zinlot for such a long time. She'd only have seen them when she came back here to resupply, anyway. That didn't stop her from giving up, though, Blynkiln reflected.

There were no new heights for his opinion and love of her to reach, they already breached far past any clouds in the sky and beyond, but the sacrifices she'd made leading up to their reunion meant a great deal to him just the same. He'd never forget.

Blynkiln refocused on the conversation, meaning to live solely in the present, despite his ever-wandering mind.

"... So, you both learned to fight together?" Ofryth was asking.

Adelyka nodded. "I don't know if Blynkiln mentioned a woman named Fuldyn to you, but she trained us both. She trained nearly everybody living in Raltyr at that time."

"Was she a good teacher?" Typhylt asked.

"Aye, a fine teacher. She was headstrong, didn't let much slide when she was in the sparring yard. Outside of it, she was one of the kindest people you could ever meet," Adelyka answered.

"And she brought you up, Blynkiln?" Ofryth asked.

"She did. Kept me fed and made sure I slept, or at least tried to," Blynkiln answered. "Adelyka's only a year older than me, so Fuldyn had us spar as a pair. I had more time to be taught, since I didn't do anything else, really, which was probably just as well."

Typhylt frowned.

"Slow learner," Blynkiln said, tapping his temple as he smiled.

Adelyka patted him on the back. "Once you learn a thing you're damned good at it."

"Are you flattering me, Adelyka?" Blynkiln asked.

"What do you think?" she asked back.

They shared a knowing smile.

"So, how long do you think it'll be before Slyvard gets here?" Aedlyn asked Henfylt.

Henfylt crossed her arms. "No clue. He'll have been at that meeting at Stykricht, and I reckon he'll have been coming directly from there to here, but I don't know for sure. Thalyen or Jynheln might have a better idea."

"I just hope that Merek knows where to find us. If he's alive," Aedlyn said.

Henfylt rested a hand on Aedlyn's shoulder. "He'll know. We can always wait here for a bit, I'm sure Slyvard would understand."

Aedlyn smiled at the mercenary. "You're probably right. Thank you."

"You don't mind if I ask how you met Merek, do you?" Henfylt asked, after a moment.

Aedlyn shook her head. "No, not at all. It's not the… happiest story."

Ofryth offered a supportive smile to his mother.

"If you don't want to talk about it, that's fine, I get it," Henfylt said.

"I appreciate it, but I'd like to share," Aedlyn replied. "It might give you some insight into the kind of person my mother is and the kind of person Merek wa- is."

Henfylt nodded.

Blynkiln shuffled forwards a bit, Adelyka did too. Typhylt had a look of concern on her face, Ofryth looked hurt for his mother's sake, and Henfylt was there at Aedlyn's side, all of them ready to listen.

"Merek is the reason we're both here," Aedlyn said, looking at Ofryth and then at the rest of them filling the sofas. "I was carrying Ofryth when I met Merek at Lyen-Saithe. If he didn't help get me back to strength and then help me deliver my son… you see what I'm trying to say."

Blynkiln nodded, the others did too.

"He could've turned me away. It was only by chance that I found the village, but when I did, he was out cutting wood and he just stared at me for a minute. I'd been on the road for a while, and I knew I was a mess, not just physically. I was about to try and run off when he smiled at me, put his axe down and said, '*I've seen wild dogs fresh out a bog look less buggered than you. Come on, now, let's get you a warm drink.*' He slowly reached a hand out and I took it, almost laughing at how he compared me to a wild dog. I trusted him right away, and I still don't fully know why, but I'm glad I did," Aedlyn stopped for a minute.

"That sounds like Merek," Blynkiln said, softly.

Aedlyn smiled. "Before Ofryth was born, Merek was there for me, keeping me company and helping me back to full strength. Once Ofryth was born, the three of us were often together. And here we are. So, that's how I met him. How I got there, that's the unpleasant part of the story."

As Aedlyn's eyes grew watery, Henfylt took her hand.

"Stop if you like," the mercenary said.

Aedlyn acknowledged Henfylt's words but took a breath and carried on telling her story. "The short of it is that I was close with Ofryth's father. We were young and we weren't 'together' in Ghoslyn's eyes, as my mother put it. I got pregnant and Meurd inevitably found out about it. She locked me in a cell and had Ofryth's father killed. Some of the guards around Tymur cared about me because I was always kind to them, so a few of them helped to get me out. I still don't know where they are now, if they also fled, or if Meurd had them killed. I can only hope they went undiscovered or left the palace themselves." Aedlyn spoke with a bluntness that told Blynkiln she didn't want to dwell on this for too long.

Old wounds are often the deepest, he recalled Fuldyn once telling him.

Blynkiln's heart sank and the room grew quieter than any burial ground. Henfylt embraced Aedlyn.

"We all have a past and mine's behind me, so I don't want any of you looking at me differently, with pity in your eyes every time you speak to me," Aedlyn said, with a few tears running down her cheeks.

"I'd be more likely to look at you with admiration, being honest," Adelyka said, going over to Aedlyn and giving her a big hug. "Going through all that and being as good as you are, that takes something more fierce than courage."

Aedlyn thanked Adelyka for her words.

There were more words of support, more shows of it, too. By the time the fire had well and truly gone out, everybody had given Aedlyn a hug, even Blynkiln, and he wasn't the sort to hug many people.

"For what it's worth, I'm sorry you lost him," Blynkiln said.

Aedlyn nodded in acknowledgment. "Even after this long, I still miss him. Love is easy, it's letting go that isn't."

Blynkiln reckoned she had a point with that.

Despite the mood becoming sombre, Blynkiln felt the strengthening of his relationships with everyone in the room.

He'd always thought that friendships were tightened the most by either a great load of laughter or a great load of sadness, always the more extreme emotions on either end of the scale. He reckoned that tonight was proof of that much.

Soon enough, everybody was yawning, and they were all rising to their feet to say goodnight to each other. Blynkiln put the heavy fire guard up, not that anything was burning, but it was best to be safe.

He said goodnight to Ofryth, Typhylt and Aedlyn one by one. When he got to Henfylt, she surprised him by embracing him.

Blynkiln frowned over her shoulder. "What's this for?"

The mercenary held him out at arm's length. "For how you helped Typhylt on the ship here. She told me that she was lost until you spoke to her. Thank you, for being there for her when I wasn't. Also, it's for the idea of the brace. Yunylt told me you came up with it. Thank you, I mean it."

"I didn't do much, just an idea that Yunylt would've come to himself and some words to Typhylt, but you're welcome. It was Thalyen who gave me a shove in the right direction with Typhylt, I just went from there," Blynkiln replied.

Henfylt's features softened. "She did?"

"Aye, she did."

"Well, I'll thank her too. You still helped Typh, though, and I won't forget that. I won't forget the pain this brace is keeping at bay, either," Henfylt said.

Blynkiln smiled. "I owe you for getting me here, to Adelyka, so we'll call it even."

The mercenary laughed quietly. "Fine, even it is."

He clapped her on the shoulder, and Henfylt said goodnight to Adelyka before leaving the room.

There was no rush to get to their room, so Blynkiln and Adelyka enjoyed the sights of the forge as they strolled about the corridors and up the stairs, talking quietly to each other as they went, not wanting to wake anybody up, or stop them from finding their sleep.

It had been a fine evening, one of the best, even with the heaviness of Aedlyn's story. In some ways, that was what made it so unique. A night of understanding and friendship, the kind Blynkiln valued a great deal.

He wondered what tomorrow would bring. More sparring and plenty of conversations, he hoped. Either way, by the time he and Adelyka had got upstairs to their room and into bed, Blynkiln was knackered. He drifted off to sleep with the familiar warmth of Adelyka at his side, knowing that he'd sleep more deeply than ever.

Reflections and a Stranger

The sounds of the frothing waves crashing against the hull of the ship made Slyvard smile as he leaned on the railing, breathing in the salty sea air.

They were well on their way to Yinfyr, the Dwarven forge, so he was enshrouded in a thick fur cloak to protect him from the cold that grew more intense the closer they came to reaching their destination.

The last time he had been to the North-East was some time ago, and he certainly hadn't missed the misery that was the biting cold. Rancylt had always gone on about loving the freshness of the air and the joy at not suffering under a sweltering sun. All Slyvard knew of the North-East was that if one were to go there, they had better be carrying enough layers of heavy clothing to weigh a mule down.

He drew his cloak tighter around him before clearing his throat and letting out a cough or two. His limbs were stiffer than ever, yearning for some heat to loosen them up even just a small amount. But, no, they would find no heat here in this wretched region of Undysvold. He would have to suffer in silence. It wasn't unbearable, it was just a frustration. Problematically, that was how all terrible things began, as mere frustrations.

Slyvard shook his head and chuckled quietly to himself. He had to stop feeling sorry for himself sometime soon. Self-pity was a slippery slope, leading only one way: down into the depths of bitterness itself. He didn't want to be the kind of person who enjoyed writhing about in his own misery, constantly complaining about how unjust this or that was. He wanted to be better than that, to rise above such pettiness. After all, how difficult was it to rebuke himself if it meant he would get back on track almost right away?

Most problems have simple solutions, people just want the solution to be complicated so that they have a 'right' to not be in control of themselves for just a little bit longer. All it takes is those few stern words and a simple adjustment of the mind to get back on track. I've no time for complicated, lengthy solutions when a quick and easy one will do much the same. I don't have the luxury of time, Slyvard thought.

He drew back from the railing and sighed, watching his breath drift through the sharp air. He had enjoyed the view of the black, open sea and the sensation of the rocking deck beneath his feet for long enough. He needed the comfort of warmth, so he headed across the dark wooden deck and opened the door to the cabin.

Qwynlo was sitting in a chair at the side of the heavy, bolted-down desk. He looked up from his letters, the scratching of his quill fading until it stopped altogether.

"We're making good time," Slyvard said, as he lowered himself into his own chair.

"We are," Qwynlo replied, rolling the lightly ink-stained sleeves of his thick white shirt down. "We should be there late this afternoon."

"Indeed," Slyvard said.

"Is something the matter?" Qwynlo inquired.

Slyvard leaned back, letting his clasped hands rest on his stomach. "I must admit, I'm almost concerned with how... easy this has been. I didn't think it would be impossible, but I thought we would face at least some resistance along the way. Yet, here we are. Perhaps that business at Hinsylt was the only bit of bother that there will be."

Qwynlo pushed his spectacles further up the bridge of his narrow nose before crossing his thin arms and regarding Slyvard from under his thin, brown eyebrows. "Is there something you are worried about specifically?"

Slyvard shook his head. "Not specifically, no. I just think it's been all too easy. Granted, there were a few more people in the party than I thought, and they lost some good friends which is tragic enough without the need of anything else going wrong…"

"But, even so, you feel as if there may be some danger lurking around the corner?" Qwynlo asked.

"I really don't know, Qwynlo. Perhaps I'm becoming something of a cynic?"

His closest friend raised his eyebrows, the trace of a smile establishing itself on his face. "I severely doubt that. Having some… reservations is perhaps no bad thing, though."

"Perhaps," he replied, pensively.

Slyvard would never tell his friend and advisor to be quiet, of course, but Qwynlo had always been good at sensing when Slyvard needed his peace. So, Qwynlo kept silent whilst Slyvard allowed his mind to drift freely. It was a strange sort of sensation, almost like hearing things but not listening to them.

A leader needs his silence just as any man or woman does. Silence allows contemplation and contemplation allows growth. Without silence, a man or woman cannot grow, much like a plant without water.

The truth of what troubled him wasn't so much that things had gone all too smoothly, it was more that with these first steps out of the way to bring about change in Undysvold, Slyvard now had to answer a question he had put off answering for quite a long time. How would he deal with Rancylt?

Meurd was easy. He had no fondness for her in his heart, so he could have her imprisoned for the rest of her days and not feel too upset about it. But Rancylt? Someone that he had loved and who had loved him? Someone he had nearly created such a fine life with, if only...

He closed this branch of thought with a twinge in his gut and the ache of loss weighing heavily in his heart. *Is it pathetic to feel this way? To fail to address such a vital question? I cannot kill her, not after what we had, what we could have shared for eternity. But she will not see it as a kindness to replace her with another, either.*

Of course, the trouble with solutions was that they rarely leapt out of hiding when one most needed them to. Slyvard knew he would have to tease them out if he were to get anywhere with this problem.

"You know, Qwynlo, for all of the good years and the bad, for all of the experience I have gained over my life so far, it always seems to be the simplest of things that keep me awake at night, never the complex," Slyvard said as he shuffled upright in his chair.

Qwynlo tapped absently at the tabletop. "The simplest problems require the simplest solutions, as they say."

Slyvard snorted. "Quite the contrary, my dear friend. We live in a world of opposites. That is why complex problems are the simplest to solve, and the simplest problems are the most complex to solve."

"That is certainly a... an interesting theory, Slyvard," Qwynlo replied.

Slyvard slapped his knee before rising to his feet. He had come in here for some warmth to soothe his joints, only he had been greeted by the air of a stuffy cabin instead.

"I shall leave you to your letters," he stated.

"Very well," Qwynlo replied as he rolled up his ink-stained sleeves once more. "We will make it to Yinfyr before dark. I'm sure there is nothing to fear for our allies that are already there."

Slyvard looked from the cabin's hefty door to the large desk instead. Qwynlo was back to writing another letter.

"I'm sure you are right. Let us hope so, anyway," Slyvard said, before strolling out into the fresh air and closing the door behind him.

This vessel was like any other North-Western ship, made with reliable wood and to the highest of standards by the finest shipbuilders in Blantyrn. The large, billowing sails would intimidate any other ships sailing these seas, whilst the equipment and the crew manning the vessel would comfortably see anybody off if such an event ever did arise.

Slyvard almost felt safer out at sea than he did at Dinshei, but that had always been the case. He sometimes wondered what he would be doing if he wasn't leading the North-West. Would he be discovering unchartered waters with a crew like he had done many years ago for that brief spell when he was a young man?

He shook his head and countered the latest powerful wave that nearly sent him tumbling to the cold deck. This wasn't the time for reminiscing on days gone by, or for thinking about things that could have been or perhaps should have been. Such a line of thought was as slippery a slope down to insanity as self-pity was to bitterness, and he had no true desire to pursue it any further.

As Slyvard was admiring the way the thin clouds drifted through the blue sky, he was disturbed by the sound of armoured footsteps pounding against the ship's deck behind him. He turned, greeted by the plate armour of a North-Western soldier glinting as the sun glared off the bright, polished metal.

The soldier, who he deemed to be Rynto when she got close enough to him, was slightly red-faced from the chill air as she halted in front of him. She had thick brown hair that was cut short, and dark brown eyes. Her tanned skin and freckled face told Slyvard that she had spent plenty of time out under the North-Western sun. Her muscular frame reinforced that idea. No doubt she trained tirelessly outside.

"Is everything alright?" Slyvard asked.

"Yes and no," Rynto answered right away, drawing herself upright. "We have eyes on whoever he is so there's no immediate danger, but there's a man down in the lower deck, tucked away by some barrels. I came to let you know and to ask what you want us to do about him."

Slyvard frowned. "I see. And, do you know this man? Could you describe him to me?"

"We haven't approached him yet, just keeping an eye on him for now. He's got his hood up so it's hard to tell. I'd say he's average height, broad about the shoulders. He carries a sword, too. That's about all I know."

"Interesting. A stowaway," Slyvard replied, thinking back to the hooded figure he could have sworn he had seen hiding among the trees before he and Qwynlo had reached the ship. "Well, thank you for telling me, Rynto. If you would be so kind as to lead me to him, perhaps I will introduce myself."

Rynto's eyebrows drew closer together, emphasising the heavy lines in her forehead. "Don't get too close. He could be dangerous, that's all I mean. My King."

Slyvard smiled. "There is no need to call me 'King', Rynto. Please, we are all equals."

Rynto nodded awkwardly, smiling back. She turned and led him from the top deck down to the second. They passed barrels and coils of unused rope, a crate of fruit and a cabinet lined with spears, swords, shields and bows. The air wasn't stale, nor was it particularly fresh as they greeted those they passed until they reached the stairs leading to the lowest deck.

Slyvard muffled a cough and steadied himself on the rope at the side of the stairs as he followed Rynto down. He brushed the usual strands of his thick hair back with the rest.

They were forever falling back over his forehead, always doing what he didn't want them to do.

The lowest deck was the hottest and stuffiest of all, one half used as sleeping quarters for the crew and soldiers, the other for cargo. A group of soldiers were standing guard by the entrance to what was practically a maze of barrels. They acknowledged Slyvard and Rynto as they both arrived.

"He's just through here," a soldier called Yaryk stated, pointing a thumb over his shoulder.

"And we really know nothing at all about who it is?" Slyvard asked.

They all shook their heads.

"Afraid not. We assume he snuck on before we set sail," Yaryk answered.

"Well, obviously. He didn't swim for five hours before climbing aboard, did he?" Rynto replied, sarcastically.

Yaryk shook his head, sharing a smile with her. "I was just clarifying, making it known."

"Well, thank you Yaryk," Slyvard said, smiling to himself. "Thank you all, for keeping an eye on him, and for fetching me, Rynto."

"Of course," she replied.

"Well, I had better have a talk with our stowaway," Slyvard said.

"Allow at least one of us to accompany you, just to be safe," Yaryk replied.

Slyvard waved him down politely. "There is no need for that. Follow if you like, but if this man wanted to kill me, he would have made a start by now. Perhaps he wants to be found now that he has safely made it onto our ship. Who knows? Maybe he thinks we won't throw him straight into the sea."

Rynto and the others wore shocked expressions on their faces. Slyvard laughed to himself. "I'm only joking," he said, smiling as they now registered his sarcastic comment.

Qwynlo would have been reprimanding him for this. Not for making an unoriginal joke, but for how stupid it was to go towards a man with a sword at his hip without a guard at his side. However, Slyvard had seen his share of battles and could defend himself perfectly well, even with his slightly stiff limbs hindering him. Besides, he knew that his faithful soldiers wouldn't be far behind him, and even so, he meant what he had said. This man was no threat, otherwise he would have acted sooner. Slyvard was sure of it.

He strolled through the maze of crates, barrels and the like, the steady but weighty clanking of armoured footsteps thudding behind him.

A hooded figure was slouching against the very back wall of the ship, trying to make himself small despite his broad shoulders betraying him. Curiosity gripped Slyvard the closer he got to reaching the feet of this stranger.

The man's eyes were fixed on Slyvard as he came into the figure's line of sight. He made no move as he remained slumped against the wall, with one leg stretched out, the other with his foot planted on the wooden boards, arching his leg up.

Slyvard stopped and clasped his hands together in front of him, determining nothing about the man that sat before him since his face was covered in shadows both thick and dark.

The man rose steadily to his feet, keeping his hands away from the hilt of his sword. A pink and red leafed tree adorned his leather sheath. He had big, pale hands and stood at a similar height to Slyvard himself. Despite that, Slyvard felt much like a child standing in the towering shadow of a god, and he didn't particularly know why. But that was the sensation that ran down his spine as the broad-shouldered man removed his hood...

An Unexpected Visitor

The state of being alone wasn't half so bad as the feeling of loneliness. After years of that being all he knew and experienced, Blynkiln had come to hate his own company. There was only so much a man could take of his own thoughts rattling about in his head if he had nobody to share them with, after all.

Thankfully, he no longer had to worry about that being a problem. He looked to his left and his eyes met Adelyka's. He was standing in his thick, grey cloak that kept the chill off his back well enough, and she was standing in her white and silver cloak that was hopefully doing the same.

Was it luck or fate to be reunited with her? He asked his gods.

The only answer he received was a cold snowball to the back of his head. Adelyka laughed as Blynkiln wiped the snow from his hair. Yuneld, in the distance, grinned like an idiot with another snowball ready in his hand.

The False Knight gathered up some snow for himself, his fingers and hands going numb as he packed it all firmly together. Once he'd flung it at Yuneld's face, the snowball burst into thousands of little flakes. All three of them chuckled, red-faced from the cold.

"Right, get here!" Yuneld exclaimed, playfully, as he gathered up more snow.

Before Blynkiln could organise his own defence from Yuneld, shivers ran all over his body as a huge pile of snow had been dropped on his head. Adelyka's familiar laugh came from behind him as the snow melted in his hair and streamed down his spine, chest and shoulders.

Yuneld started pelting him with more and more snowballs, too, cackling as each one crumbled against Blynkiln's head and body. He could do nothing to shield himself, so he accepted his fate with a smile on his face.

As Yuneld and Adelyka turned on each other, their alliance no longer holding up so well, Blynkiln managed to get back into the battle. Whilst Adelyka was distracted, Blynkiln rolled snow into snow until a great big dome of the stuff sat in front of him. With all his might, and once he'd packed it all together, he lifted it up and up until he couldn't reach any higher.

Adelyka stepped back to gather more snow, defending herself from Yuneld's constant pressing. The Dwarf gave nothing away, he just had a wide grin on his face.

As Adelyka got closer and closer to Blynkiln, unaware that he was even there, he dropped the huge mound of snow right over her head. It covered most of her since she'd been crouching. All he could hear was muffled laughter. She popped her head through the pile and had that same enchanting smile across her face that had helped him fall for her all those years ago.

She leapt at him through the snow, knocking him clean off his feet with her strength. Their eyes met as they were both grinning and breathing heavily. Her green eyes were so full of love, that he forgot about everything else around him. The coldness of the snow underneath him and the dampness of his clothes no longer bothered him. Even his hands didn't feel numb as he placed them on her hips. There was only the warmth of love and desire as strands of her thick hair hung down in front of his face, her lips parting slightly, her eyes never leaving his.

He hoped that Yuneld had found something else to do and somewhere else to go. The childish part of Blynkiln felt bad for abandoning the war in the snow, but there was always another time to end that war. As any experienced soldier knows, a war is made up of many battles and each one could have a different winner.

Some time had passed and the sun reached its peak. Blynkiln and Adelyka had gone inside, needing to warm up properly after their time in the snow. Their cloaks needed to dry by the heat of a large fire, too.

"So, are we really just waiting here till King Slyvard makes it?" Adelyka asked, leaning back in the chair by the fire. The wood cracked and hissed as the flames burned through it.

"As far as I know. Thalyen told me as much, and Jynheln confirmed it the other night," Blynkiln answered.

"Is it what you want, to rule the North-East again?" he asked, after a moment. He was almost afraid of what the answer might be, but her needs and wants were his priority.

"I don't know. Sometimes I think it is, because they're our people and they need our help. Part of me, as bad as it sounds, wants nothing to do with it because of the responsibility it comes with. I just want to live by your side. On the road for a time, maybe. Waking up when we want, where we want. Breathing in the air, swimming in lakes and travelling to all those places we both want to visit. All that, with little responsibility. That's the dream. Even so, I'd maybe feel guilty for leaving my post," she answered.

"Elensfyr would be nice to visit. We could read as much as we wanted and stay as long as we wanted. It's a tough decision, one that I can't really help you with. All I'll say is, whatever you choose, I'll support you however I can," Blynkiln said.

Adelyka smiled at him and rested her head on his shoulder. "You always have, but it isn't just about what I want."

His thoughts turned to Merek, since they'd spoken about Elensfyr back in Lyen-Saithe. He remembered Merek's joke, the image of him being rolled in a barrel. All of that, just to get to this library. He hoped he'd see Merek again, he really did.

"I haven't forgotten how difficult it must've been for you to choose between me and the entire region back then, you know," Blynkiln said.

"It wasn't a decision, Blynkiln. I'd do anything to keep you safe and to be with you no matter the consequences. You know that. If I have to abandon you in order to be Queen of the North-East, then the title can sod off," she replied.

He held her tightly as he said, "Nothing will break us apart again."

"Nothing will break us apart again," she repeated.

A comfortable silence followed as they sat together and shared their peace, with nothing but the soft cracking of wood in the background. The rich scent of the burning wood hung in the air.

As for the day ahead, he and Adelyka had their daily sparring session with Henfylt and Typhylt which he looked forward to. Yesterday, things had gone well with big improvements made. Henfylt was moving better as she'd sparred with Blynkiln, and Typhylt was picking up the drills nice and fast under Adelyka's guidance, no doubt helped by her new pink and red bladed sword.

The weapons that had been placed into the pool at the base of the Sphynlok were like nothing Blynkiln had ever seen before. The steel became a dark shade of pink, more of a tint than anything, and the dark, subtle red streaks that looked like veins stretched up the entire length of the blade.

Henfylt had an elegant, simple sword that was similar to Blynkiln's in shape. Typhylt's had a wider base, more like a normal longsword, but the blade narrowed down almost imperceptibly to its point.

When Blynkiln had been handed the sword, he could've mistaken it for a feather with how little it weighed. Despite that, the enhanced steel was sturdier and sharper than even his blade. He had to admit, a shred of envy ran through him at that fact, but he was happy for Henfylt and Typhylt. Besides, his own sword had made him feel close to Adelyka when they were apart. It had also got him through his share of scraps over the years.

Adelyka had told him how impressed she was with Typhylt after their session the previous day, saying how the girl could get her guard up quickly and was nice and light on her feet. As for Henfylt, Blynkiln already knew how good a fighter she was. But this new sword only increased the speed of her swings and the intensity of her blows.

With that in mind, he turned to Adelyka and said, "We'd best go and see what Henfylt and Typhylt are up to."

"Let's go," she responded, stretching and yawning as she stood up and fetched their cloaks which were now dry thanks to the heat of the fire.

They only had a short way to go. Through the corridor, down the stairs and out the hatch until they reached the courtyard. It was colder than it had been earlier, and the wind had picked up in strength, too. Even his fur cloak struggled to stop him from shivering.

Henfylt and Typhylt were waiting in the distance. The mercenary wore a black cloak, more fitted than Blynkiln's, and the girl was swallowed whole by this enormous white thing that looked more of an oversized blanket than a cloak.

As they came within a stride of their sparring partners, a cry of warning echoed out from behind them. "Inside! Inside now!" Yunylt shouted.

His heavy brown cloak flapped as he sprinted up the path and past the Sphynlok. Once he reached them, he bowed his head and rested his hands on his knees as he tried to catch his breath.

"What's the matter?" Adelyka asked.

"Ship," followed by a harsh intake of breath. "There's a ship. On the horizon. Best get inside!" Yunylt exclaimed.

"Could it not be King Slyvard?" Blynkiln asked.

Yunylt shook his head. "This ship's not North-Western. It's white. Wynluk wood."

Blynkiln and Adelyka frowned at each other, then at Henfylt and Typhylt, but they all listened to Yunylt and made way for the cover of Yinfyr, just to be sure. It was the right thing to do, especially since Blynkiln hadn't seen Yunylt so shaken and cautious before.

It didn't take them long to get inside, warm up, and be joined by everyone else who rushed down to see what the commotion was all about.

"As you know, you can see out the window but nobody can see in it. I'll go out and see who it is. Stay in here where it's safe. Do not go outside, no matter what," Yunylt said, once he'd caught his breath.

"I'll come out with ye!" Yuneld exclaimed.

The two Dwarves nodded at each other and left without another word. The False Knight stayed with the others. His heart pounded as he stared out of the window.

Whoever the ship belonged to had come when the sun had risen to its peak, showing no caution. A single ship was all that was necessary for whatever the purpose of this visit was.

The vessel broke through the icy mist, its long bowsprit casting a shadow as it led the way. Blynkiln could do little more than pray it was a traveller or a merchant. At least they could be easily sent away.

As the vessel became larger, the fear deepened within him. The ship, well-made, had an all-white hull just as Yunylt had said. A North-Eastern ship that size with such large sails could only belong to someone with coin, resources and power. *Why would Rancylt come here?*

The ship docked and a company of North-Eastern warriors marched out, each covered head to toe in thick chainmail with fur laid over their shoulders and pouring out the tops of their boots. None of them wore helmets.

In five years, the uniform of the warriors of the North-East hadn't changed a bit. It was exactly as Blynkiln remembered.

Whilst there weren't hundreds of warriors, there were a good chunk more than a handful, which confirmed The False Knight's cynical expectations. It was indeed the Queen of the North-East.

After the warriors lined up with their swords at their sides, they stepped back to leave a narrow walkway behind them, fit for one person to walk down.

To contrast all of the black and silver, Rancylt wore a pale pink cloak with delicate sky-blue flowers embroidered into it. The cloak, satin or silk, seemed so out of place as it rippled gently with each of her elegant but commanding steps.

The closer she got to Yuneld and Yunylt, the more rapidly Blynkiln's leg bounced up and down. Adelyka took his hand in hers, and he turned to stare into her beautiful eyes. His heart raced and he thought she might settle him and calm him down. He was wrong. It only made it worse as he realised that after enduring half a decade of fighting for his own survival, he'd forgotten how to fight for someone else's.

An anger rose in him, then. He'd not long reunited with her and now they were being threatened again. *Why is this happening? Haven't we suffered enough?* He was angry with himself, with the world and with his gods. They were sat in the heavens, living a pleasant life of peace and prosperity, but they couldn't allow him that, could they? Not yet, clearly, the bastards. He had to endure more pain, more loss and more tragedy. He reminded himself that it wasn't their fault or responsibility, but that didn't help. In fact, it made him feel even more helpless as no divine power could intervene when he most needed them to. Or could they?

He'd experienced these emotions many times before. They visited him now as old friends would, checking in on him, making sure that he hadn't forgotten about them. The worst feelings always made their return after an experience that was too good to be true.

He refocused himself, gathering the years of resilience and perseverance up until there wasn't anything else, only a fierce determination to protect Adelyka, his friends, and himself. The feeling rose within him, offering some small comfort and warmth to hold onto. A strength he hadn't experienced before awakened within him.

He focused back on the meeting between Yuneld, Yunylt, and Rancylt. She now stood an arm's length away from the Dwarves. Her warriors were emotionless statues staring off into the distance.

"Your illustrious majesty," Yunylt said, with a humbling bow.

"You flatter me, Yunylt," Rancylt replied, in a soft and delicate voice.

She hadn't changed much over the years. Her sharp cheekbones were hard to miss and her hair was as long as it always had been. It would've been hard to think of her as anybody but Ynfleyd's daughter. She had the same blonde hair and the same blue eyes, even the same sense of presence as her mother had done, and Blynkiln had only seen Ynfleyd a few times when he was a boy. It didn't surprise him how much they looked alike. Every child's hair and eyes naturally matched their mother's rather than their father's, after all.

He brought his attention back to the meeting between the Queen of the North-East and the Dwarves.

"How can we be of service?" Yuneld asked, crossing his arms.

Rancylt called to her warriors, "Bring over three chairs and a table."

Four of them left in a hurry and an uncomfortable silence followed. Rancylt, in her colourful dress and with an unsettling smile on her face, stood as still as a stone.

Soon enough, the warriors came back and set the table down with the chairs around it. Rancylt signalled to the Dwarves, offering them both a seat. They exchanged a glance, then cautiously took their seats.

"Now that we are all sat down, we can begin," Rancylt stated, as she leaned back in her chair and folded one leg over the other, smoothing any creases in her fancy cloak.

"There's a beauty to History, don't you think?" she asked, after the brief pause.

"I'd say so. A lot's happened and even more's changed over the years," Yunylt responded.

Blynkiln struggled to hear, but he could just about make out what was being said after focusing on the distant voices. He doubted anybody else in the forge could hear them. He thanked the gods for his Tynukei blood, then, for making his hearing so sharp.

"You've both seen double my years or more, I suspect. How old are you both? Over a century or so?" she asked.

"A few years shy of ninety, myself," Yuneld answered. "Yunylt's five years older than me."

"Incredible, how we all age. I'm only a few years off fifty, yet I look older than both of you," she replied, her eyes gliding off into the distance.

"If it's any consolation, you have smoother skin than most humans who are half your age!" Yunylt exclaimed.

Rancylt laughed. "You flatter me once more, dearest Yunylt. I'm afraid to say that I'm not here just to talk about age and history, though." Her voice didn't grow colder, it was just as soft and warm as it had been to begin with.

"History has always fascinated me, you know. It was many years ago when my mother ordered the death of all Tynuks. I still think she was wrong to do it. They were interesting and capable of such wonderful things, yet she chose to stamp them out as though they were nothing more than old relics. Aside from that, you can't just wander around wiping out an entire race of people because… you felt like it, can you? Anyway, my mother also tried to cut the Sphynloks down, and when they grew back she had them built over and covered in all kinds of different ways, as I'm sure you both know. All but one. That one over there," the Queen of Raltyr pointed to the pink and red leafed tree that stood not so far away from them all.

"She allowed it to stand as a symbol, I believe," Yuneld interjected.

"Exactly right. So, all of the trees of Tynuk origin are covered up, dormant, apart from this one. I'm here because I was hoping that you could tell me if you've done anything to that tree lately. You see, I was rudely awakened a few days ago as I found an enormous tree with pink and red leaves growing rapidly through my bedchamber. It had ripped through the floor and startled me greatly, as you can imagine. So, have you done anything to that Sphynlok recently?" Rancylt asked, her tone growing colder.

"Well, I did touch it, but didn't think anything of it at the time," Yunylt said, his left leg starting to bounce ever so slightly.

"You touched it, you specifically?" she asked.

"Well, yes. Yes I did," he lied.

Blynkiln's stomach churned.

Rancylt's cold gaze fixed onto Yunylt as she clasped her hands together and leaned forwards. "I have a theory. I don't think you touched that tree. At first I didn't know what to think, I was on my way here simply to ask you the question. But, as I approached, I noticed a ship harboured just over there," she pointed at Thalyen's ship.

"It's new," Yuneld commented.

"Don't take me for a fool and don't interrupt me. You're lucky my mother showed you mercy after the war, all those years ago," Rancylt snapped.

Yuneld bowed his head in apology.

"It's a ship from the North-West. I can tell as much because it's perfect, and only Slyvard's shipbuilders could create such a beautiful vessel. My own shipbuilders are useless in comparison," she said, sounding more frustrated than angry. "I could get past that, though. Perhaps it was new and you just thought to buy it. Then, as I arrived, you didn't invite me inside. Now, if any of my other subjects refused to invite me inside, I wouldn't even question it because people are so rude and inhospitable these days. Dwarves, however, are the complete opposite. It is in your very nature to be hospitable, it is part of the reason why I have such a love of your endearing race. So, I will ask you once and only once. Who have you got inside?"

Blynkiln's heart pounded as his head spun with all kinds of potential solutions to this problem. He needed to act but what could he do? There was only one way out of the forge, and he'd only just got back to Adelyka. How could he risk it all by storming out there like a dolt? He could answer the question for Rancylt that way, though, leaving Adelyka and the others safe in the forge. Or, could they all go out and take the fight to the North-Eastern warriors? They might've been outnumbered, but perhaps it could be done with a bit of luck on their side. He turned to his friends as if they could answer his questions, but of course they were all clueless to the situation.

"If I were to guess," Rancylt began, breaking the silence, "I would guess that a Tynuk of some description is in there. One who has been lost for quite some time. One who can hear my words when nobody else but you two should. I don't understand the nature of Sphynlok trees, so I could be well wide of the mark here, but if they were to awaken, which they have, then it would most likely be at the hand of a Tynuk or Tynukei, wouldn't it? Someone with a shared background to the trees themselves. As far as I am aware, there is only one left in the entirety of Undysvold-"

Before she could finish, Blynkiln leapt up and darted out of the hatch. He'd looked at Adelyka one last time before he left. He couldn't risk anyone else, not when he'd already been found out.

"Bravo! Look who it is!" the Queen of Raltyr cried out, clapping her hands together as if she was watching some entertainers perform for her.

He strolled over to the two Dwarves and Rancylt. The snow drifted down from the sky and landed softly on his head, damping his hair and covering his shoulders. He had his narrow-bladed sword sheathed at his side. He was ready.

His cloak no longer protected him from the cold, he'd thrown it to the ground. Strangely, with each stride he took, the energy and fearlessness grew within him. Maybe putting some distance between himself and Adelyka calmed him because there was a kind of barrier between Rancylt and her. He was ready to fight, but he was far from ready to die. That made for a dangerous combination, he reckoned.

"The False Knight! Here at last. How long has it been? Five years or more?" Rancylt asked, once Blynkiln had stopped just behind Yuneld and Yunylt who were still sitting down.

"Something like that," he answered, knowing how to play her game, or hoping he did.

"The years haven't been kind to you, I see," she said.

"I'd say the same for you. I think Yunylt was being polite earlier," Blynkiln replied, knowing he was talking a load of shit, but hoping it would rattle her all the same.

Rancylt's eyes narrowed. She took his insult to heart as he'd hoped. "You remind me of Slyvard, though you're far less intelligent and charismatic. The way you bite back so viciously when provoked. On him, it's always been far more attractive and charming."

The False Knight kept his silence.

"You think you're being clever, by acting so confident yet allowing me to control the conversation. I know what you think you're achieving, but you've helped me deduce that you were not alone in there," she said, attempting to provoke a response.

The fear formed in the pit of his stomach, but he blocked it out.

"You seem upbeat and happy, focused and ready. I'm willing to bet that if I were to order my faithful warriors to march into that forge, your expression would suddenly change. You would either beg or you would lash out and attempt to kill me. Is it Adelyka in there?" she turned her cold glare to the Dwarves who remained silent.

"If that's how it is, then we must abandon polite conversation in favour of violence and desolation," she said, so calmly. "Take the three of them prisoner."

She stepped back and took off her cloak, revealing a dress of chainmail and fur underneath. There were two daggers at her sides. She unsheathed them both and stood at the side of the approaching warriors of the North-East.

The two Dwarves leapt up, grabbing their hammers. Blynkiln, Yuneld and Yunylt formed a tight arrowhead. He stood at its point with his sword in hand.

The three of them backed up to put some distance between themselves and the approaching enemy. The tables and chairs were kicked out of the way and shoved to the side.

Blynkiln's heart pounded, but in anticipation rather than fear. Waves of strength flowed from his heart throughout his body as he made his mind a blood-filled space.

When he was least expecting it, a ball of flame and smoke flew overhead, landing between him and Rancylt.

"Run back while the flames burn, we'll make for Thalyen's ship!" came the cry of Jynheln from behind.

Blynkiln turned and ran. Yuneld and Yunylt were just ahead of him. A volley of arrows whistled and stabbed as they flew through the air and plunged into the cold ground behind and around The False Knight.

Jynheln launched another ball of flame. The screens were loud and the stench was horrendous as the flames found their feast among the archers.

Blynkiln heard no footsteps behind him.

"They're cutting off the route to the ship!" he shouted, hearing the enemy form up to his right.

"Ah, bollocks!" Yuneld shouted, over the desperate screams of the burning.

Adelyka and the rest were soon with Blynkiln, Yuneld, Yunylt and Jynheln.

"We'll have to form up and face them!" Henfylt exclaimed, unsheathing her pink and red bladed sword.

"Keep Ofryth and Typhylt in the middle, the rest of us push up!" Aedlyn shouted through the screams that still raged on in the background. She had an axe in her hands, smaller than Gylphur's had been, but big enough and sharp enough to cause their enemies some damage.

Blynkiln led the line, Adelyka to his right and Henfylt to his left. He had no time to check where everyone else was, but he knew that the boy and the girl were in the middle, safest of all.

They all marched forwards. The cold air tried to freeze Blynkiln in place, but the fire within him kept his joints from seizing up. There was no turning back now that they'd reached the enemy.

Jynheln struck the first blow, launching a great stream of fire at the line of North-Easterners. Most of them leapt out of the way, having sensed it coming, but a few were caught out. The skin of the unlucky ones blistered and burned brightly among the white of the snow. The Tarspyk settled for launching smaller balls of fire after that, targeted where more of the North-Easterners were huddled together in small groups.

Soon enough, blood flowed as did Blynkiln's burning rage. He swung and swung, too quick to counter or dodge, cleaving through the North-Eastern warriors that stood in his path to freedom. He glanced at those around him every now and then, making sure that nobody was getting overwhelmed.

Blynkiln targeted the weaker places of the enemy's armour which he knew so well. The slashes caused guttural screams and yells of pain to ring in his ears, whilst the beheadings brought only silence, blissful and calming. He was made for violence.

As he expected, another group pushed up, trying to box them in. He commanded the Dwarves and the Tarspyk to focus their efforts on the flanks, keeping Typhylt and Ofryth as safe as possible in the heat of battle, which was no easy thing. But, with each blow Blynkiln became more powerful, more unstoppable. Every swing was strong, fast and calculated. Every swing found its target.

They were managing the threat well, for a time. Blynkiln even thought perhaps they'd manage to win the day. Of course, fatigue soon set in, shattering that brittle hope in front of his eyes and stealing much of the air from his lungs and some of the venom from his swings. Time had a funny way of cursing everything and everyone, it really did.

A deep grunt and a low cry came from somewhere on his right as someone collapsed. With the battle at such a chaotic point, it was hard to tell whether the body was a friend or a foe.

Meanwhile, Adelyka and Henfylt were holding their own well enough, but they soon began to tire. Adelyka was trying to control her breathing and Henfylt's bad leg was shaking, any strength in it seemed to be leaving her. Despite the blood in The False Knight's veins that heightened his reflexes, enhanced his senses and offered him some more stamina, Blynkiln's swings slowed and weakened until Rancylt called her warriors back.

The Tarspyk had thrown his last fireball. It was more of a spark of flame than anything, and after it had landed he collapsed in exhaustion, sweating as if he had a terrible fever. Typhylt and Ofryth were safe in the centre. Yuneld was still standing but his broad chest rose and fell at a worrying rate as he wiped a thick sheen of sweat from his red face. Adelyka and Henfylt, who were standing at his sides, were also in the same state. Aedlyn and Thalyen, who guarded the blonde-haired girl and the brown-haired boy, were on their last legs, struggling to draw in enough breath to go on just a little longer. There was no sign of Yunylt.

Rancylt's warriors looked no better, but the ones that were left stepped back and a new group stepped forward, fresh and ready for battle. Blynkiln and his friends had killed their share of North-Eastern warriors today, and whilst the numbers against them weren't as bad as they had been to begin with, he struggled to see a way out of this. Panic gripped him as he glanced at Adelyka and she looked back, holding his gaze.

"You all fought valiantly and took a frustrating number of my faithful warriors to their deaths, and I commend you for that. I truly do. It was a worthy effort! But look at you all, you're exhausted. Meanwhile, I have more warriors keen to jump in and kill each one of you," the Queen of Raltyr stated. Nobody would argue even if they had the energy to. She was right.

Rancylt made a signal with her right hand and two North-Easterners brought a limp body forwards.

"This is what happens," she said as the warriors dropped the body to the floor. It was Yunylt, a shell of his former self.

Yuneld leapt forward, Blynkiln held him back.

"Ye get your filthy hands off him!" the Dwarf roared in pain, struggling in Blynkiln's arms. He kicked, wriggled and screamed, but Blynkiln couldn't let him go.

"He's dead, Yuneld. It's what happens in battle," Rancylt said, in a tone as cold as the snow that fell around them. "Not everyone gets a glorious send off. You should know that I liked Yunylt very much, on the whole. I truly did."

Yuneld couldn't speak. After he gave up trying to escape the iron grip of The False Knight, he wailed. The cries were haunting, so full of pain and suffering, caused by the severing of a bond only brothers knew.

Blynkiln kept his own tears at bay, but seeing his friend in such pain did him no favours. All spirit that was once so strong among the group had been beaten out of them. There was nothing righteous or holy about what had happened here. Blynkiln saw only blood, charred corpses and death. But this was his world, as a warrior himself. Violence, fighting and death made him who he was, what he was.

A tear rolled down his cheek, growing cold almost instantly. Yuneld's head was bowed as he grabbed and squeezed the sleeve of The False Knight's shirt. He wept and shuddered, but Blynkiln could do nothing to ease such an intense sorrow. He couldn't make it right. He had to hold Yuneld and feel the burning pain with him.

He looked at the faces of despair that surrounded him, knowing that nothing could be done. The fight had ended and they were all at the Queen of Raltyr's mercy.

"Drop your weapons," Rancylt commanded.

Silence. He was about to drop his sword when a voice came from behind him. "No. You don't get to order us around, we won't listen. You'll have to take us yourself," the voice was Typhylt's.

"Who's this little cherub? So sweet and angry!" Rancylt replied, grinning wide.

Before she could get a response, she'd been knocked off her feet. Blynkiln hadn't been able to stop Typhylt as she sprang out of his reach like a bolt of lightning.

Typhylt hit Rancylt in the face three times before Henfylt got involved. Blood shot up everywhere. Blynkiln, instead of releasing his sword, tightened his grip and got ready to attack the North-Eastern warriors once more as they stepped in to defend their leader. Adelyka and the others, as tired as they were, joined him. Even Yuneld, now with his tears behind him and his knuckles white around the handles of his hammers, followed Blynkiln into the heart of battle.

Each swing came to him more powerfully than the last. This energy within him was fuelled by an intense anger. It spurred him on as he let it take complete hold of him. He swung with little thought, allowing his senses to take over. All around him, his friends fought without hope but with a blind rage and fury that was all the more useful.

He pushed on, slashing and slicing with nothing else on his mind apart from the death of his enemies and the death of Rancylt. He could see her, blood running from her nose down her chest and even in her hair. Blynkiln wanted to end her for good, so he pushed on through the warriors between them until there were so few left in his way.

He blocked out the fatigue, forcing himself on, until somebody flew into him, knocking the wind out of him and sweeping him right off his feet.

His head met the cold ground and the world started to spin as a vicious pounding set off in his head. He placed a soft hand on the back of his head, his fingers becoming unpleasantly warm and sticky. He raised his hand to his eyes, seeing his blurry fingers slick with dark red liquid. Blood.

He tried to get himself upright as darkness closed in from the fringes of his blurring vision. He got to his knees before he flopped back down again, his dizziness sending the world spinning ever-faster around him.

The clanging of steel on steel grew louder and louder, banging in his head as the sound rang endlessly in his ears. Any remaining strength in his limbs left him as he saw only darkness and felt only numbness, falling into oblivion.

Choices

Henfylt's heart pounded in time with the flares of pain
that lashed up and down her bad leg. She'd been
shoved to her knees and had her hands tied together
by some harsh rope that rubbed against her wrists. Her sword
had been thrown onto a pile of steel not so far away.
Everyone else was in the same position.

Typhylt had been put between Adelyka and Yuneld, a
short distance away from Henfylt herself. The Dwarf wasn't
crying as he had been earlier. He seemed to be more of a pale
ghost, emotionless and unmoving, instead of a living thing.
Adelyka, meanwhile, stared at Blynkiln, who still hadn't
woken up.

Yunylt's cold corpse was left by itself, all dried blood and
tattered clothing. Like some pile of unwanted, useless waste.

Henfylt turned to face Jynheln who sat at her side. The
Tarspyk couldn't even keep himself close to upright. His hair
flopped over his sweat-slicked forehead, dangling in front of
his eyes as he shivered in the cold.

Henfylt shivered, then. Her weak breaths wavered out in
front of her like they came from a wounded animal. All of
her friends shared the same problem, the unrelenting cold of
the North-East.

They'd all chucked their heavy fur cloaks to the ground before they'd rushed headfirst into battle. They were probably all regretting that now. Henfylt certainly was.

The soft wind blew through her messy, blood-streaked hair as she cast her eyes up to the blue sky that was as bright as ever. A few clouds hung up there, but not many. The sun didn't do much to make her feel any better, either. It floated so high up, so far away, offering no heat or help. What use was that?

Henfylt had been beaten again, and her heart raced and raced at the building dread. She worried about Typhylt, the girl she'd grown so fond of, especially after her attack on the Queen of Raltyr.

At least Zinlot was safe in the forge, for now. Henfylt thought back to when she'd ordered him to stay inside since he was of no use to anyone in a battle. The Gnome had looked at her in a strange, philosophical way, as though he knew everything there was to ever know.

"Go with true faith in your heart and a raging fire in your stomach, Henfylt. When the sun is eclipsed by the clouds and vengeance itself comes calling, you shall know that you are saved. Praise the greyness, the wind, the rain, the thick fog and the fierce storm, for its coming oh so quickly," Zinlot had said to her before she left in a panic with the others.

Henfylt was as confused then as she was now, waiting for Rancylt's return. The Queen had disappeared once they'd all been tied at the legs and arms like helpless fish being dragged out the river and thrown in a bucket.

Soon enough, Queen Rancylt returned with her hands clasped together in front of her. She wore an icy blue cloak this time, clean and uncreased. The delicate, well-fitted cloak revealed Rancylt's athletic figure. She'd cleared the blood from her nose that previously dripped down her chin and speckled her shiny hair.

Whilst it was a dangerous thing to do, Henfylt was proud of Typhylt for attacking Rancylt how she did. It had been a blur of blonde and blonde, hardly a battle, more of a one-sided beating.

Henfylt's thoughts were interrupted.

"Well, that's better. I'm all clean and beautiful again!" Rancylt exclaimed.

The mercenary couldn't argue with that. The Queen's blue eyes sparkled with charm and arrogance. Her thin lips curved into an oddly warm but somehow unsettling smile. Her cheekbones were as sharp as her skin was smooth. Yet, even with those striking features, Rancylt was evil, and Henfylt wished for nothing more than to crush her pretty face beneath the sole of her boot.

The Queen of Raltyr strolled over to Typhylt. Henfylt struggled, wincing as she tried to wriggle out of the rope that grated against her wrists with every slight movement.

"What's your name, vicious cherub?" Rancylt asked, crouching down by Typhylt.

Answer the question, don't try to be clever. Please.

"Why do you care!" Typhylt snarled. She sounded more like a battle-hardened warrior rather than the young woman that, in reality, she was.

Henfylt bowed her head and held her breath, her heart thumping away more quickly than ever.

"So feisty and brave. I admire you. I admire you greatly," Rancylt replied.

This time, Typhylt was about as silent as the corpses dashed around Yinfyr's grounds. The Queen kissed her softly on the forehead before jumping to her feet.

Henfylt reminded herself to breathe.

"What's up with him?" she turned to her warriors, pointing at Blynkiln. The False Knight was lying in a heap among the snow.

"He's unconscious, isn't it obvious?" Adelyka replied, before any of the North-Eastern warriors could.

Rancylt chuckled, turning to Adelyka. "He'll be fine. With that blood in his veins, he'll be up soon. Sooner than you or I would be, by any measure."

She cast her cold eyes over all of them, letting them know that she had won and that they were all sitting here at her mercy, waiting for her judgement.

"My dear, dear mother, Ynfleyd, was awfully misguided you know," Rancylt began, after a moment, pacing left and right as she spoke. "I loved her as any child loves their mother, despite her cruelty. But, she was foolish to have all of the Tynuks hunted. They had so much power in them, power that would've been better to keep for all, rather than to just stamp it out like she did. She should've found a way to work alongside them after the war, she really should've. But no, she was a fool."

She paused for a moment, shaking her head. "It's said that Inshelt, my mother's nemesis, used to pluck children off the streets in the dead of night. He would experiment on them, you see, and take their organs to create strange potions. He was driven so much by his desire to join his closest friend, Sphyltyr, in extending his life, that he experimented on children. How low could he go? It really is quite disgusting. He thought that us humans, when young, had some strange properties that could perhaps, with some encouragement, awaken his ancestors' blood within him. He was misguided, of course, like some zealot of Ghoslyn, up until even Sphyltyr had had enough of him and plunged his sword into Inshelt's black heart after their lengthy duel. Anyway, here's Blynkiln! The last of the Tynuks, and he's... sleeping. I need him to wake up and make a decision about the future of Undysvold. It is only fair that we grant him one last wish, as one of the last of his kind."

Henfylt looked up at the sky again. It was still blue. There was no greyness, no rain or storm in sight. She wasn't the sort to believe in the supernatural, or in prophesies. But, something about the way Zinlot spoke about things made it almost impossible to doubt him. Even so, that thought didn't stop the roiling in her stomach or the pounding that started at her temples.

The Queen of the North-East strolled over to Blynkiln and kicked him in the ribs. Henfylt winced, feeling the impact herself, or near enough. Adelyka stared daggers at Rancylt but thought better than to say anything.

The False Knight's head flopped over as he opened his eyes slowly.

"Blynkiln, up here!" Rancylt exclaimed as she clicked her fingers in front of her face.

Turn grey, start raining... please. A storm. We need a storm, Henfylt thought. An acidic taste started to rise at the back of her throat. She screamed within herself up at the sky, as if some deity was listening to her. *How stupid. No rain or clouds will come. Nobody can save us. They were just some useless words of prophecy.*

Blynkiln blinked a few times, then stared up at Rancylt. His eyes were so dark and full of hatred.

"Good. Now we can begin," she said, with a devilish smirk across her face.

"What do you want from him?" Aedlyn asked, through gritted teeth.

The Queen looked at Aedlyn. "It's nothing personal, but you and Adelyka are... problematic to say the least. You see, I'm aware of just how popular you both are. Adelyka among my people and you, among yours. If you were to stand against your pious bitch of a mother, you would win with the love of your people. I don't doubt it, and you now hate me more than she ever could. Sadly, I must recognise my own shortcomings as well. So, if Adelyka stood against me, I would be deposed and probably killed. At present, though, there is no fear of my rule being shortened."

Rancylt crossed her arms and went back to pacing left and right for a few moments. The pause was clearly theatrical. She was playing with them, taunting them. Letting their lack of power sink in further, deeper.

"I don't want to kill both of you, especially not in front of your son, Aedlyn, and in front of your precious Blynkiln, Adelyka. But, what should I do? How can I handle this situation? This business of going behind my back and plotting… something, cannot go unpunished, I'm afraid. I don't kill or hurt children, so they are safe. I might keep the cherub. With some instruction and time, she might become a loyal warrior," Rancylt said.

"Don't you fucking dare," Henfylt interrupted, allowing her fury to boil over.

"Oh, so very protective. She isn't your daughter. Please, be silent," Rancylt replied.

Henfylt listened. She had no choice, not really.

"Naturally, I will ask one of my subjects for their advice, as any good queen would," the Queen of Raltyr stated, as she strolled back over to Blynkiln who glared up at her. "Say one name and I will spare whoever you choose. No tricks. Your lover, or the boy's mother. Oh, it even rhymes! How wonderful."

"Don't do this, Rancylt," Adelyka said.

"I must," she replied, in a voice without emotion.

"I'll leave, go back to some village and not get involved in politics. I promise! My only care is Ofryth, not some title. Please, just let us go!" Aedlyn pleaded.

"You might. You might not. Why would you not ensure his safety by being the most powerful person in the South, maybe even in all of Undysvold?" Rancylt asked.

Aedlyn's eyes dropped to the floor. The acidic taste in Henfylt's throat grew more intense. Ofryth had tears in his eyes as he looked at Blynkiln, then his mother. Nobody moved, nobody spoke. Henfylt could've sworn that nobody so much as breathed.

"Choose!" Rancylt shouted, making Blynkiln and everyone else jump.

"Adelyka," was the response that came, so fast and sudden. Blynkiln's voice was half-adamant and half-cold. There seemed little hint of doubt in the words he spoke, despite the tears in his eyes and the look of horror across his face.

"Very well. Speak your last words, Aedlyn," Rancylt declared as she reached to her side and unsheathed one of her daggers, waiting. She frowned down at the blade in her hand for a brief moment, before fixing her cold eyes on the brown-haired woman she was going to kill.

Aedlyn looked at her son, her bottom lip trembling. "I love you, Ofryth. More than anyone could love anything. Be brave and strong, but above all else, be kind and have nobleness in your heart with everything you do and every action you take. I'm so proud of you and I always will be. Now, look away, my son. I love you," she said, forcing a smile even with the tears forming in her eyes and streaming down her cheeks. Her voice was weak and cracked.

"I love you," Ofryth managed, in a broken whisper, before Aedlyn nodded and he did as she'd told him.

He closed his eyes and looked away, facing Henfylt and the others that sat to his right. He broke down into tears, his whole body shivering and shuddering as he tried to take deep breaths with his head bowed.

Henfylt met Aedlyn's defeated, fearful gaze before looking away. The sound of a blade being ripped across someone's throat couldn't be mistaken for anything else.

There was a gurgling sound as the blade bit deep, followed by a thud, as fresh flecks of warm blood spattered across the mercenary's face. The blood of her friend.

Henfylt's whole body shook as she shivered so intensely, her eyes locked onto the snow-ridden ground. The warm blood of Aedlyn countered the cold of her own freezing tears as they ran down her cheeks. Her throat was so dry. All she could taste and smell was blood and bile. In the background, Ofryth whimpered and wept. Someone, somewhere, retched.

Rancylt didn't speak as she scrubbed her blade clean, bloodying her cloth as her eyes focused on anything but the corpse she'd just made.

Henfylt focused her mind on her breathing as she trembled in the cold. A terrible quiet hung in the air for well over five long minutes as nothing could be heard but the sounds only the grieving can make. Awful sounds of loss, failure and defeat. The kind of sounds that stick with you for a long, miserable while. Knowing she'd never have a quiet chat with Aedlyn again, see her smile or hear her laugh, Henfylt looked to the sky through her blurred vision.

Clouds formed up. White at first and thin, they merged and merged until the sun was almost entirely blocked, its rays breaking through a little until the clouds darkened, turning from white to grey then grey to a black as dark as the inky depths of the North-Eastern sea.

The snowfall slowed, becoming lighter then stopping altogether. A rumbling, so loud, heavy and angry, followed. Then the rain came, washing Henfylt of the dried blood that lay thick in her black hair and over her clothes. Each drop hit the ground with more power than was natural, soaking through the thick layer of snow and frost until they dissolved.

The wind came next. Quiet whispers of faith and hope soon turned into angered yells as the speed of the wind increased, howling and whistling loudly around her. The storm came from nothing and nowhere, but it came too late. The cracking and rumbling boomed again, the downpour increased, but it all came too late.

Darkness enveloped Yinfyr, and finally, the fog arrived. It started out as a soft, frozen mist, but soon turned into something far more frightening. Something thick, blinding and suffocating. The rumbling and cracking raged on as everything became colder with each passing second. It had all come too late. All of it, far too late. The sheets of lightning lit up the world as the sharp, jagged forks tore through the dark fabric of the sky. There was fury in the storm as it became darker and darker.

Everyone remained silent, even Rancylt had a look of fear dancing across her face. She grew pale and ghost-like as her wide eyes locked onto something that shifted in the distance. She held her knife in her right hand, pointing it at the all-devouring fog. Henfylt followed the knife's sharp, glinting point until she spotted a man of average height with the broadest shoulders she'd ever seen. He strolled through the cold mist, each step more angry than the last. Every time his foot met the cold earth, a dull thudding echoed around the area, louder and louder, impossibly so. The closer the figure got, the more familiar he became.

The white hair and the scruffy white beard, the blue eyes that were darker than a starless night sky set against pale skin. *Merek?* Or were her own eyes playing tricks on her, was he really here? The fog was thick, but he stood close to her now and it must've been Merek. Yuneld was right, he was alive. The set of those broad shoulders and the angular nose couldn't be anybody else.

Merek, who usually had such a kind face, was the very picture of a vengeance so dark and bloody as he stood perfectly still in the harsh rain that battered down on his head and the ferocious wind that whipped at his long, thin cloak. His brow was crumpled and his eyes were narrowed, lending him the look of a man so furious it set Henfylt's teeth to chattering and her whole body to shivering.

"Slay this man!" Rancylt commanded, retreating into the fog.

Merek drew his longsword from a leather sheath that had a small symbol of a Sphynlok tree decorating it, standing firm and ready.

A few soldiers ran at him, each one swung and each one screamed as they fell to the ground. He blocked each attempted slash with ease, whirling around when necessary to position himself for his next kill. There were many, but they came one at a time at first, then they changed their strategy, and bigger groups tried to attack him from multiple sides. He slapped every blow aside and cut through legs, arms and heads with such ease. Henfylt had never seen anything like this before. Merek was a demon, vengeance incarnate.

Henfylt tried to break through the rope that bound her but couldn't. Merek didn't need help though. It was as if Sphyltyr himself was fighting his way through an entire army, like some kind of tale that would be told in a tavern on a cold and rainy night. He was noiseless with each aggressive, powerful slash. The wind didn't hinder him, neither did the rain. He was a veteran of war, a bearer of chaos, and a bringer of death.

His swings were inhumanly fast, he wasn't tiring, he wasn't breaking a sweat. *He must actually be...* she stopped herself from thinking it.

Merek had slain more than a score of Rancylt's warriors, a good deal more, and whilst he looked keen to keep at it, more North-Easterners poured out of the wynluk ship. They stormed through the fog whilst Merek stood perfectly still, holding his blade out in front of him, thick ropes of blood dripping along its length and sliding down its point.

The enemy came closer and closer, the many boots stamping the ground down like one huge herd of cattle. Merek didn't shift. He was a statue of calm after what had just been a display of untamed hatred and rage.

A retinue of soldiers dressed head to toe in polished plate armour stormed past Merek. Some had spears, others had swords and shields.

The Noth-Western soldiers stormed across the field with their leader at the front, leading the charge. The King of the North-West flashed by, shouting encouragement to those at his side, his brown hair flapping in the harsh wind as he led his people into the thick of the battle.

A soldier came over to Henfylt, untying her with haste whilst the battle raged on in front of them all. A woman helped her to her feet and patted her on the shoulder.

Henfylt ran over to Typhylt and embraced the girl, ignoring the pain shooting up her bad leg. Then she helped the soldiers get Thalyen free, sitting with her for a moment to make sure she was as alright as someone could be after all of this.

Out of the corner of her eye, Henfylt saw Merek cradling Aedlyn in his arms as tears streamed down his face. He held her corpse tight, and Ofryth joined him. He hugged the boy who shuddered and shook with uncontrollable sadness.

Blynkiln and Adelyka sat together, holding each other. There were no words. The False Knight wept in her arms like a child.

Jynheln was being helped to his feet by a man wearing spectacles, the same man she'd seen in the academy back in Hinsylt.

Typhylt was now with Ofryth and Merek. The fierce, white-bearded man had let go of the boy so that Typhylt could comfort him.

Never puts herself first, Henfylt thought, as she watched on in pride, a few tears sliding down her cheek.

Typhylt, after a few moments, returned to Henfylt and they both went over to Yuneld. The Dwarf, free of the rope, sat still and shivered with only Zinlot for company. Yuneld's eyes were empty of emotion. Typhylt shed a tear and held him as he began to weep once more. Henfylt stood over them, resting a hand of sympathy on the shoulder of the Dwarf, feeling his anguish as he shuddered in pain and grief. Zinlot rested one of his hands on Yuneld's other shoulder.

The clouds cleared, the fog dispersed, the rain and the wind stopped and snow began to fall once more. The blue sky brightened, and whilst Henfylt and her friends were free, she saw only suffering and misery all around her. Tears of both fear and loss.

Nobody cared about their freedom in those moments and why would they? There was too much loss and too much pain surrounding them. To her, there was no battle. She wasn't willing to fight. She was exhausted, both physically and emotionally. Her friends needed her and she needed them, so that they could all grieve together.

The battle continued in the background, but she didn't care to look. The hatred within her had turned to fear and sorrow, melted away like snow under a warm sun.

Typhylt released Yuneld from her embrace, allowing Henfylt to take her place and help him through the pain. The girl remained close, looking at Henfylt with tears in her eyes.

Zinlot patted Typhylt on the shoulder as Henfylt wrapped her other arm around her, nodding her thanks to Zinlot as she did.

There were a number of soldiers keeping watch over Henfylt and her friends. They'd fetched all of Henfylt and her companions' weapons and now stood as still as statues, scanning the battlefield ahead.

Before long, more North-Westerners were forced back by the North-Eastern forces. There was no battle to be won here. Only more deaths to tally up, and Henfylt reckoned the tally was already steep enough.

The soldiers had Henfylt and her friends gathered into a circle of sorts as the King of Dinshei hurriedly spoke to them all.

"This is not a good time, I know, but we must leave for Blantyrn immediately. We do not have the strength they do, not quite. I know you need to grieve, but we can secure the bodies of your dead and hold a ceremony for them once we are safe. Thalyen, your ship is still anchored and in good shape. Take it and anyone else, but leave straight for Blantyrn with a few of our soldiers to keep you all safe. We'll leave by the ship we used to get here once we've seen you to safety."

Thalyen nodded at the command, and a flock of North-Westerners followed her as she went. Meanwhile, Slyvard sprinted back to the soldiers that were fighting to instruct them on their own escape.

Merek approached Blynkiln and whispered something in his ear, resting a supportive hand on his arm as he did. Ofryth looked on, his eyes darkening. The False Knight nodded, and with Adelyka, followed Thalyen to her ship.

Merek cast a pained glance over at Henfylt, but he managed to smile at her and Typhylt. The mercenary, even with such little energy, summoned the strength to jog over to the formidable warrior who'd helped save them. She threw her arms around him in a show of gratitude.

"I don't know what to say," she said as he held her firmly, calming her down.

"Then say nothing, Henfylt. We will arrive at Blantym and speak again. Keep your words until then, hold them close," he replied, releasing her from his embrace.

She turned and strolled back to Typhylt. The two of them followed Thalyen, Blynkiln and Adelyka.

As the North-Western soldiers eased off and started to retreat for the ship that had brought Slyvard, Merek took Ofryth, Jynheln, Yuneld and Zinlot towards it. Perhaps it was wise to keep The False Knight and Ofryth separate after the choice he'd been forced to make.

The soldiers carried the bodies of Aedlyn and Yunylt onto Slyvard's ship, also carting the few injured and dead soldiers of the North-West that they could back to the ship as the defensive line eased off more and more, until they held barely a scrap of land against the North-Easterners.

Henfylt took one last look at Yinfyr. It had been their paradise for a time, but death had chased them away. She thought of Yunylt, his joyous smile and uplifting laugh. They hadn't known each other long, but he'd had a positive impact on her. She rested a hand on her sword's diamond-shaped pommel, thinking that a part of Yunylt would live on in that blade, since he'd beaten it into shape and forged it into existence.

She was the last to get to Thalyen's ship. The captain helped her up, reaching a hand out which Henfylt gladly took. Thalyen's hand was soft and smooth, but very cold. As Henfylt hopped up, she stood close to the captain, the pain in her leg making it hard not to wince. Their eyes locked, sharing a message of weariness but also of support. An understanding passed between them in that moment, a sort of connection.

The circumstances stopped them from acting on primal urges. It was wrong to even think about such things, but battle sometimes did strange things to people.

Regardless, the mercenary tore her gaze from the captain and the two of them found their way to Typhylt, Blynkiln and Adelyka.

Most of the North-Western soldiers stayed on one of the lower decks, but their presence comforted Henfylt.

The others had made it to Slyvard's ship not so far away, and the last of the North-Westerners were sprinting on board, ready to flee.

Henfylt knew that the forge would be burned. At least the Sphynlok would survive. Even so, the thought of the last real memory of Yunylt being wiped from Undysvold hurt her.

I have the sword to remember him by. The brace, too, she thought, as she stood at Typhylt's side and watched the powerful waves slap at the hull of the ship, rocking it side to side.

Once they were a safe distance from Yinfyr, and Henfylt had caught sight of Slyvard's ship following Thalyen's, she let herself slow down and breathe properly. She thought of Aedlyn, Yunylt and Gylphur, feeling the weight of their deaths more deeply than ever.

She still had Typhylt. Merek had come back to them all, too. It didn't put things right, but it helped her to think of what she fought for and of what hadn't been lost. Within the mercenary, there was a greater drive than ever to see Slyvard's vision come to be.

The Weight of Grief, the Strength of Friendship

Night and day merged into one down on the lowest deck of the ship. He couldn't say how long he'd sat, unmoving, with his own mind threatening to swallow him whole. If not for Adelyka, Blynkiln would've long since drowned in his own torment.

He was cold despite the weight of his heavy cloak around him. He was cold in his heart, like something was wrong with him and he could never feel warmth again. Maybe he had no right to comforts of any kind after what he'd condemned Aedlyn to, what he'd taken from Ofryth and Merek.

He was plagued by nightmares, in the rare instances when sleep found him. Nightmares where he was the one standing over her corpse with the bloodied dagger in his hand after drawing it across her throat. He took the life of a woman who'd supported him, helped him and become his friend. More importantly, he took the life of someone who was kind.

Adelyka squeezed his hand. She was the only bit of warmth, love and comfort he'd felt these past however many days they'd been at sea.

She'd tended to his head wound, bandaging him up, just how Merek had bandaged him up when he first met Aedlyn and Ofryth, two people whose lives had been either ended or ruined by him and his actions. And yet, worse than all of the grief and the pain at what he'd taken, was the fact that Blynkiln couldn't regret his decision. He couldn't bring himself to wish he'd acted differently, and what did that make him if not the worst kind of man? A monster.

The ship shifted left and right, up and down as the waves rocked it. Every now and then, over the past days, Henfylt, Typhylt and Thalyen had checked on him and Adelyka, bringing them something to eat or drink. Blynkiln struggled to force down anything they handed to him. He struggled to listen to them as they told him there was nothing he could've done, not really.

I could've delayed her a bit, he thought, then he realised that even if he'd somehow managed to delay Rancylt for a few minutes, she probably would've killed Adelyka as well as Aedlyn. That thought made him feel even worse. Far worse.

"I'm sorry," he croaked, with a dry throat as he looked at Adelyka. "For being useless these past days."

"There's nothing to apologise for. You need time to wrap your head around things, you need to eat something and you need rest."

"You do too," he reminded her. He wasn't too stuck in his own head to work out how shit she must've felt.

Adelyka bowed her head, her stomach grumbling. "I don't feel much like eating, to be honest. I know you don't either."

"I'm grateful that you're still here, with me. Really," Blynkiln said.

"I am too. Despite everything. It feels wrong, though," Adelyka replied, taking a deep breath to compose herself.

"I know," he stated.

The footsteps of the North-Westerners scraped and thudded along the floorboards above as a silence of shared grief stretched over Blynkiln and Adelyka. If this was how he felt, Blynkiln couldn't imagine how heavily the pain and loss must've been weighing on Ofryth and Merek on the ship that was trailing behind them.

He was lucky that Merek hadn't cut him down where he stood. Instead, the man who summoned a storm just put an arm around Blynkiln, patted him on the back and told him that he understood. Even after Ofryth must've told him about how Aedlyn was killed and why, whilst the both of them grieved, Merek had practically told him that there was nothing to forgive. That didn't stop Blynkiln from blaming himself. Nothing would stop him from blaming himself. He'd as good as killed Aedlyn himself and damned Adelyka to the unforgiving weight of guilt in the process.

Henfylt, Typhylt and Thalyen came down the stairs and ambled over to Blynkiln and Adelyka. Adelyka rose to her feet and spoke quietly with the three of them. Blynkiln didn't have the heart to listen in, but his damned hearing made it impossible not to.

"How is he today?" Thalyen asked.

"Similar to usual, maybe slightly better," Adelyka answered.

"And you?" Typhylt asked.

Adelyka patted the girl on the shoulder. "I'm in a better way than some of us no doubt are, thank you. Are you all alright?"

Typhylt and Thalyen nodded.

Henfylt said, "Aye, hanging on."

Blynkiln, with his stomach grumbling, his body sore and his head still swimming with pain from the blow he'd taken, struggled to his feet and stumbled over to them.

They all looked at him with raised eyebrows and wide eyes. It was the first time he'd risen to his feet outside the times he needed to piss or shit, after all, so he didn't blame them one bit for their reaction.

He cleared his throat and took a deep breath. "It's about time I thanked you all properly. For giving a shit. I'm sorry I've been so..." he couldn't find the right words, but they all seemed to understand what he was trying to say.

Typhylt nearly knocked him off his feet as she embraced him, telling him that he really couldn't have done anything and that she was so sorry for the position he'd been put in by Rancylt. All the while, Adelyka locked eyes with him, giving him the strength to pat the girl on the back and thank her for her kindness.

Thalyen and Henfylt clapped him warmly on the shoulder, and they all gave their support to Adelyka as well. Support didn't bring Aedlyn back, neither did it make Blynkiln feel any less guilty, but it did make a difference.

There was a chance in this moment to get pulled back into the world of the living, rather than being stuck in this purgatory he'd made his home for however many pissing days had passed since Aedlyn's murder.

"Some fresh air might do us some good," Adelyka suggested.

Blynkiln nodded. "You're right."

Thalyen led the way up the stairs where the air was fresher.

Blynkiln took a tight grip of the rope that led up to the top deck, the brightness of the sky at sea beckoning him out the shadows.

The steps were solid under his weight, his weak legs somehow managed to carry him well enough as he emerged from the dimness. The brightness of the world made him cringe as pain flashed in his head, behind his eyes. He'd been so used to the dark that it took a few minutes for his sight to adjust to the blinding light of the blue sky and the openness of the vast sea.

Adelyka shielded her own eyes from the sun and took a deep breath of the salty air as she looked back at him. Blynkiln took a leaf out of her book and felt better for it. There was freedom in being at sea, an indescribable kind of freedom.

His guilt, his grief and his fear weren't all cured by the sea air, but seeing the waves collide with the hull of the ship and nearly rock him right off his feet lent him a bit of perspective. He had to carry the cost of his choice with him, and he'd do his best to bear it with honour, but Adelyka's life hadn't ended and neither had his. What would be the point in living if he was going to spend his days sulking, cursing himself and making the woman he loved more than anything in the world more miserable than he currently was?

He'd played a part in Aedlyn's death, and he missed her even if he didn't maybe have the right to. He'd remember her and honour her memory as best he could.

Perhaps Adelyka and the others were right. Perhaps he couldn't really have changed anything about the choice he made. The shame he felt in himself came from his lack of bothering to try. He could've tried to delay things. He could've at least tried to plead with Rancylt. He refused to believe she had no heart at all, just a very cold one. But, he didn't bother to try, did he? The fear of losing Adelyka was too much for him to bear for even a minute, and that was why he couldn't bring himself to regret his decision. If he hadn't made it, she wouldn't be standing there looking at him now, taking his hand in hers and holding it in that way that made everything just a bit easier.

He closed his eyes, took a deep breath and held it for a long moment, thinking about Aedlyn, Ofryth and Merek as he did. He knew the part he'd played, he recognised it and let the guilt settle in his gut as he pushed the breath out and opened his eyes, composing himself.

"Thank you all, again," Blynkiln said, after a moment. "I owe you."

Henfylt let a half smile across her face as she replied, "Repay us first by freshening up and changing your clothes. Please."

The simple joke made them all exchange smiles and chuckle quietly.

"You have a point. I'll get right on that," he stated, feeling far from clean all of a sudden.

"Before you do," Thalyen replied, handing him a brass baton-like thing. "Look over there."

He stood frowning down at this thing she'd pressed into his palm. It was quite heavy and well-made.

"It's a telescope," the captain said, drily. "You look at things a distance away through it to see them more clearly. It sort of... makes things look nearer than they actually are."

Blynkiln nodded and raised it to his eye. Thalyen extended it a bit and told him to close his other eye, then she angled it right until he saw a distant chunk of land.

"That's our destination. Blantyrn," Thalyen said. "A fair few hours away, but it's somewhere safe, somewhere to rest for a time."

From so far away, even with the aid of this... telescope, it looked little more than a blob. Blynkiln reckoned she showed him this distant blob not to amaze him or excite him with how magnificent a blob it was, but to give him some hope about a place where he and the others, Thalyen included, could rest and recover.

"Can I see?" Typhylt asked.

"Of course," Thalyen answered.

Blynkiln passed the telescope to the girl. Thalyen angled it just as she had done for Blynkiln, telling Typhylt about the famous port city and how wonderful it was up close.

"I could use a rest. We all could," Henfylt said.

"You've got that right. Been a shit run lately," Adelyka replied, solemnly. "Worse for you lot, by the sounds of what went on outside Hinsylt."

"Not been the best, but we'll get there I'm sure," Henfylt stated.

After Typhylt finished, Adelyka had a look, seeming quietly excited to see a new part of Undysvold. Neither of them had been to Blantyrn before, and whilst Blynkiln knew he and Adelyka would both despise the sticky heat, he couldn't deny that it would be at least interesting to spend some time in a place he'd never seen before.

"Henfylt?" Thalyen asked, offering the telescope out to the mercenary.

Henfylt stepped up, awkwardly leaning back as the captain tried to guide her arm to point the telescope right. With Henfylt's lack of ability to listen to instructions, both the mercenary and the captain were laughing in a subdued way before long. Laughing in the kind of way only grieving people could laugh, almost guiltily, as if they thought they shouldn't find anything funny ever again. It was still comforting to feel a little more relaxed and not so depressed.

"I'm trying to help you, woman! What are you working against me for?" Thalyen asked, in that awkward way of hers, struggling to keep the humour from her voice.

"There's no helping me, I'm too far gone," Henfylt answered.

"I can see that," Thalyen said, sarcastically.

"You cheeky woman," Henfylt replied, as she took the telescope from her eye and looked at the captain for a moment.

Thalyen took the telescope from Henfylt, shaking her head as she smiled.

Blynkiln, Adelyka and Typhylt exchanged a knowing glance.

"Should we leave you two alone?" Typhylt asked.

Blynkiln struggled to stop the smirk from spreading across his face. Adelyka had the same struggle, it seemed.

Henfylt and Thalyen's cheeks must've been hot enough to burn through wood, then, as they stood awkwardly next to each other, exchanging one last glance.

The afternoon went on in a similar way. Sometimes Blynkiln would fall to a grim silence, or someone else would and they'd be lifted out of it by another in their company.

Time passed and they grew closer than ever as a group. By the time the moon had taken the sun's place, they headed back out to the deck, with no need for their heavy cloaks as they approached Blantyrn's sprawling dock.

"Stars are clearer than I've ever damned well seen the things," Adelyka said, slack-jawed.

Blynkiln nodded, finding no words.

"What do you think, Typh?" Henfylt asked.

Typhylt shook her head. "Same as Adelyka. Never seen anything like it before."

"It's a fine sight, a fine place," Thalyen stated.

"Hard to disagree," Blynkiln replied.

As the ship moved in closer to the dock, he found it impossible to not be filled with relief. His body ached, he was tired, hungry and in need of a great deal of rest and recovery in a safe place, where he knew no harm could come to Adelyka, his friends or himself.

They were all struggling to not smile at each other as the ship's anchor rattled down and the vessel came to a stop. Blynkiln reckoned they'd earned a break. Ofryth and Merek needed this as much as anybody, too, and they weren't far behind.

Despite the past days being so rough and despite the tragic losses of Aedlyn and Yunylt, Blynkiln looked at Adelyka and his friends, determined to make up for his wrongs, determined to help them see this quest of theirs through as best he could. As Adelyka looked back at him, he could see that same determination in her dark green eyes, and that was enough for him. They'd be doing this together.

Warfare

What separated the true leaders from the false ones was how they acted in times of warfare. Slyvard had wanted to avoid war at all costs, but he no longer had a say in the matter did he? It had been taken out of his hands the moment Rancylt decided to slit Aedlyn's throat. Perhaps even before such a tragedy had come to pass.

He had thought nothing of trouble as he and Qwynlo sailed across the North-Eastern sea. All he had been aware of was the hooded figure that had stowed himself on board, the figure who turned out to be a friend to Henfylt and something of a father figure to Aedlyn.

He shook his head as he stood over the unfurled map of Undysvold. If only they had been quicker. If only they had the gift of perceiving events that were yet to happen. *Foolish thoughts from a foolish man's unfocused mind,* Slyvard thought.

He hunched over the map, analysing where best to attack and where he would most likely need to defend. He would have to set up the necessary squares on land and blockades at sea, as well as supply lines to keep all of his soldiers fed and healthy, all the while rising above Rancylt and Meurd's petty games that would no doubt cause him a number of headaches over the period this war would likely stretch.

How long? How many will die? We minimise losses by acting quickly but with wisdom. We minimise losses by strategising with caution.

Slyvard slowed his racing mind down with a few stern words to himself. He had to be as calm as possible, otherwise he would make a mistake. Most people could afford to make mistakes, he could not. One mistake and people would die. That was the reality of leading in times of warfare. That was the reality of trying to change the order of the world.

Rancylt will struggle, her people detest her and yearn for the days of Adelyka's rule to make a glorious return. Meurd is the greater threat. Such a large force, well-organised on land, particularly in the East. Weak at sea, though. We will exploit their weaknesses, we must. Who will take her place now that Aedlyn is no longer an option? The boy, Ofryth? Would he want that? Would he be capable of leading?

The questions kept coming, but no answers came to his aid.

Slyvard detested war. It was a last resort, but he had known it was a possibility all along. Perhaps he should have opened Meurd and Rancylt's throats back at Stykricht. *No, the risk was too great.*

A knock at the door interrupted his train of thought. He looked up from the map and its vivid colours. Jynheln was standing before him.

"You wished to see me," he stated.

"Yes. I hate to call on you once more, old friend, but I desperately need you," Slyvard replied

"I will help where I can," Jynheln said.

"For what's coming, we cannot allow the enemy to get their hands on valuable allies. I would ask you to go to The Tarspyk Spire and seek the assistance of your fellow Tarspyks. It is far away, I know, but we can't allow them to side with Rancylt or Meurd. You are the only one they might listen to. So, what do you say?" Slyvard asked.

"Of course, I will go. It has been some time since I was last there. Perhaps, if she wishes, I could take Typhylt so she might begin studying with the aim of becoming a Tarspyk one day. We have spoken about it before, and with the situation as it is, perhaps she now feels it to be the right course of action. May I ask her?" Jynheln inquired.

"If she wants to, I see no reason to deny her such a chance. Consult Typhylt, of course, and the mercenary, Henfylt, on the matter. Good luck, and be safe, my friend," Slyvard answered, clasping his hands together in front of him.

Jynheln nodded as he turned to leave, closing the door behind him.

Slyvard's throat tickled in that irritating way that he had become accustomed to over the past weeks and months. He coughed a few times onto the back of his hand, his legs trembling as a sharp pain shot through his chest. He flopped down into the chair in front of the map, leaning back as far as he could, catching his breath once the brief coughing fit had passed.

He got his breathing back under control and looked at the walls around him, which were usually blank, but had diagrams of Dinshei, Tymur and Raltyr pinned to them at present. They were incredibly accurate diagrams, featuring dimensions, strengths and weaknesses, known points of entry and so on. He stared at each one for a while, frustrated at the fact that none of them were Stykricht. After all, he had successfully infiltrated Stykricht before, on the stormy night when he watched the life drain from Ynfleyd's blue eyes as he dragged the blade of his knife across her throat to put an end to her tyrannical rule.

After that night, when the blood had spurted out of Ynfleyd's throat like a fountain, Slyvard had risen and risen. Part of him wondered if he would still have the adoration of his people if they knew the truth. Perhaps he was a coward for doing what he had done. Or, perhaps, he was simply opportunistic.

She was no better than Inshelt, a betrayer of promises and responsible for near genocide, he thought, before returning to matters of strategy.

There could be no details left unexplored. He had to draw up points of interest, positioning, battle formations, tactics and the rest. All of it made his head sore because it would all likely change in the heat of battle anyway. Nevertheless, preparation was vital.

He sighed, lowering his head onto his folded arms. This had all happened before, when he caused the Civil War by killing Ynfleyd and encouraging the people to rise up and fight for their independence. The thought of the lives that would be lost bothered him as much this time as it had before, taking more and more of his humanity away from him. Yet, here he sat, aware of the part he had played in not just one war, now two.

It's just men and women, sons and daughters, mothers and fathers left in pain at their losses. Every time there is a war, the people suffer. It won't be any different this time. It will be even worse. There is no unity to be found, no shared joy at being rid of Ynfleyd this time. Nothing to hide behind until someone wins it all. What does it matter to Rancylt and Meurd? They will be laughing at the prospect of gaining land, Rancylt for herself and Meurd so she can turn everyone into Ghoslyn's foot soldiers. It's all about control. How do we gain control so that we might limit casualties? By acting quickly, but what do we take first to tell the world that we mean to win?

The answer came to him just as he was about to start tearing his hair out. Minimising casualties had to be his job. It wasn't as if Meurd or Rancylt cared.

He leapt from his chair, leaving the stuffiness of the little room in favour of the warm North-Western air. The heat rushed at him as he marched through the canopied corridors and strode down the smooth sandstone stairs that had bannisters made of wynluk stuck at their sides.

The sun's fiery rays shot down on Slyvard, no wind bothered him as he went on his way, storming through Dinshei until he found the mercenary. She was speaking to Typhylt, and the conversation looked to be one of a serious nature.

After a few moments, she turned to face Slyvard.

"Apologies for the interruption," Slyvard began, wiping the hair from his forehead. "I would be greatly appreciative of your help if you will offer it once more, Henfylt. Of course, you can decline, I'm no tyrant."

The mercenary strolled closer, her dark brown eyes locking onto him as she crossed her arms. "Go on."

"I would ask that you go, with a group of fighters, and take Dansphylt. If we gain and hold the border, we gain some control over the South-West. We have to act quickly, so you would need to leave soon. What do you say?" Slyvard asked.

Henfylt turned to Typhylt, and the girl nodded.

"I'll go," the mercenary answered, with a glint of determination in her eyes.

Slyvard couldn't help but smile. He had made the first move and it was a wise one.

"I'll join you," came the voice of Merek from nowhere, without warning.

"Very well, is there anyone else from your group that you wish to take with you?" Slyvard asked. "Aside from Blynkiln and Adelyka, I'm afraid to say that I need them with me."

"I'll have Yuneld, if he's willing. What about Thalyen?" Henfylt replied.

"Excellent. I'm afraid she is captaining her ship, though she might be willing to defend Dansphylt from the sea and join you later," Slyvard answered.

The mercenary nodded and turned to Typhylt once more. Slyvard didn't listen in, but it seemed as though they had two very different destinations in mind. There were utterances of both confirmation and reassurance as the two of them spoke.

Slyvard was left standing at Merek's side. The powerful storm-summoner had such a presence about him. Not the presence of a commander or a captain, nor even a king. His presence was something altogether more intimidating and humbling. After witnessing the storm that Merek had created from nothing but his own fury, Slyvard felt as though he stood in the presence of a wise and experienced god-like soul. A man who cut through more than a score of North-Eastern warriors without help, without his swings weakening even a bit.

Henfylt turned to face Slyvard once more. "I'll leave here with Merek and hopefully Yuneld, by ship."

"I'm going to The Tarspyk Spire with Jynheln and Zinlot. I'll try and convince Ofryth to come too," Typhylt stated, rather formally.

"Excellent," Slyvard replied, clasping his hands together behind his back. "Thalyen will take you, Merek and Yuneld to Dansphylt and I shall work alongside Blynkiln and Adelyka."

Then, turning to Typhylt, he placed a hand on her shoulder. "You have a vital job, Typhylt, but you will be safe. Jynheln will try his best to get the rest of his people on side, but I would ask you to try, too. There is something about you... I think they may listen to what you have to say. Of course, your priority is to learn what it means to be a Tarspyk. I'm sure you will be wonderful." Slyvard spoke from the heart. He had a feeling that this girl would go far. She had something to her, a personality and a strength of sorts too. A strength he recognised.

Typhylt nodded. "I'll do my best."

"That's all any of us can do," Slyvard replied, with a smile on his face.

He spoke to Henfylt and Merek, turning away from the blue-eyed girl. "Take control of Dansphylt with the help of the soldiers I will send with you. Then get word to me so I know what is happening. Once that is done, and if you still wish to help, advance into the South-West and push through to Hinsylt. Take some of those soldiers with you as you go. That way, the pressure will all be on the South-East which will certainly be a positive once they are boxed in. As for the North-East, with Blynkiln and Adelyka's help, I will push into Rancylt's region and end her reign for good. Then, naturally, all of our swords point to the greater threat of the South, its Eastern side specifically."

He received nods of understanding and agreement.

"I take it you'll dispatch ships to patrol the seas?" Henfylt asked.

"Of course. You focus on the land and I will make sure that you are protected from the sea. War on the waves is easy, it's simple for my people. The problem will be watching the land," he answered.

"It's wise to move fast. If we make the first move, we have the upper hand," Merek said.

"Precisely. Good luck to you all," Slyvard responded.

"We'll meet again," Merek stated, speaking the words in a way that left little room for doubt.

Slyvard bowed his head in response.

Henfylt, Typhylt and Merek left. The mercenary had an arm around the girl, and Slyvard found himself alone once again as he looked at the fountain and watched the water pouring out and flowing into the little bowl, then filtering down until it landed in the base from three different directions.

A faint smile crossed his face as he basked in the warmth of the sun, the trickling and splashing of the fountain continuing in the background.

With no wind in the air, everything remained perfectly still and hot, so very hot, as he allowed himself a few moments of total peace. He had no idea when or if he would ever return home once he had left for the North-East, so he had to enjoy what time he had here.

Dinshei's courtyard made use of simplistic, but striking, architecture. The many pillars were wide at the bottom and narrow at the top, all equal in shape and size. They held up the canopied corridors that cast heavy black shadows underneath them. There were benches placed in the shade and some by the bright green hedges.

He adored the courtyard, a place that welcomed all, but one that had been presently abandoned with only himself wandering its grounds.

Sometimes, the price of being the King of Dinshei was something as simple as loneliness. He would pay such a price with a smile on his face if it would guarantee that his people would always live as they do now, though.

Footsteps sounded through the courtyard as Qwynlo approached.

"Are the ships ready?" Slyvard asked.

"Yes, all ready for departure," his closest friend answered, pushing his spectacles up his narrow nose.

"Excellent. Thalyen will take Henfylt and a few others to Dansphylt. That way we can control the border and keep the South at arm's length. I intend, with Blynkiln and Adelyka's help, to venture into the North-East and establish a stronghold along the coast. With the ships forming a blockade, we will be able to receive all the resources we need. Food, clean water, any medicine we may need and warm clothes, in particular. We're in a strong position, Qwynlo. A very strong position indeed. Yet, I fear for the soldiers that will fall, I fear for their families and their friends. I fear for all of Undysvold," Slyvard stated.

"Is it wise that you go to the frontlines?" Qwynlo asked.

"You have to ask yourself who you want to be, my friend. Do you want to be a ruler, sending all of your little wooden soldiers into battle whilst you warm your feet by an open hearth, stuffing your face like a pig? No, you do not want to be that, because it is very easy to be a ruler. You want to be a leader, the one that your people look to for inspiration, the one that your people love and trust. You want to lead and you want to be an equal to those that fight at your side, and in your name. You let them make their own choices, whether they fight for you or not. That's the crucial difference, Qwynlo. Our people are proud and caring, but they have their own minds and I acknowledge it, you acknowledge it. We do not order them to fight for this place, they choose to," Slyvard answered.

"Very well. You stay true to yourself even with a great threat looming over your head. It's admirable and brave, but I think it is perhaps foolish, too," Qwynlo responded, rather sharply.

"Why is it foolish?" Slyvard inquired, his brow creasing.

"If we lose you, we lose the war, Slyvard. Without you, this region grows unsteady and panicked. Is it worth risking it all so that you can call yourself a leader and not a ruler?" his advisor asked back.

The words stayed with Slyvard as he watched his friend stroll off without another breath passing between them.

He knew that this would be the last day of order and reason for a long time. What came next could only be chaos and destruction. He only hoped that he would live to see the new Undysvold, one that had been forged from chaos, but had become free. Truly free. A place of happiness and safety, where none suffered.

As unrealistic as this vision of his was, Slyvard asked himself who cared for reality. He had always found the power of living to be in the vision of idealists, in the joy of dreams.

Whilst his hopes were perhaps foolish and misguided, he thought it was better to try to do good and fail, than to not even attempt to make such an effort to begin with. Watching from afar was easy and pointless, but jumping in and fighting with passion and for what was right took courage and strength.

Throughout his whole life, Slyvard had fought for what he thought was right. He had made his dreams a reality for his people, despite coming from nothing himself. He intended to continue doing that for whatever time he had left in this world.

He rose to his feet, concerned about the frightening nature of the future as he left the peace and calm of the courtyard, with the sun at his back, in favour of the port in Blantyrn. It was time to listen to the screams of warfare and to abandon all sense of calm, for momentum and passion were everything in times of war...

Acknowledgements

I'll start this by saying thank you to you, the reader. Whether I know you personally or not, thank you for picking up this book. There are many people who contributed to making the book you hold in your hands exactly what it is, and I'll be thanking them all in turn. I hope that I've repaid the trust you put in me when you chose to read this book by giving you an enjoyable story to dive head-first into. If I didn't, then you either have really poor taste or I'm just a shit writer. Thank you, though, seriously.

I wouldn't be here without my mum and dad, so I reckon that gives them the right to a mention. You two gave me the chance to pursue this dream of mine by working hard and always encouraging me to follow my own path. That's probably one of the greatest things a parent can do, so thank you both for that.

As for my older brother, Sam, well he's alright isn't he? Realistically, he's my closest friend and a fine one to have at that. Thank you for being you, Sam. We have our share of laughs, don't we?

I've also got to thank my four cats. Sadly, they can't read but they deserve a mention. They spend their share of time around me and they're a great comfort, even when they don't stop whinging for their tea.

As for anybody who's unfortunate enough to call me a friend, thank you. Whether ours is a friendship that stretches back a fair few years or if it's one that's more recent, thank you. If it's one where we spend our time laughing senselessly at 2am in the morning at the most unfunny things known to humankind, you have my thanks and my appreciation.

A few more specific thanks go to the following, all for different reasons:

Mum, again – the first person to read this book in its earliest stage and its later drafts too. Thank you for all the reading and rereading, for suggesting trimming the bits where I waffled on, and for always being happy to listen to me yap about the ideas bouncing around in my head.

Sheila Dowton – the second person to read this book at an early stage. Thank you for letting me know what worked and what didn't, and for highlighting plot inconsistencies along the way. Your feedback was vital for making this book what it is.

Dad, again – for encouraging me to use the map I designed, for your hard work at making it look far better than I could have hoped, and for putting me in touch with the fantastic designer of this book's cover. Without that I worry what the cover would look like today…

Tim Ellis – the designer of this book's cover. You might think you're no Frank Frazetta, but you'll more than do for me. Thank you for making the cover what it is, I really couldn't be happier with it.

Katharine Tucker – developmental editor. Thank you for highlighting the weaknesses as well as the strengths of the version of the book you saw. Your feedback was critical and it made me go through a final round of editing that led to big changes being made in order to make this book as good as it could be.

Rob Ivinson – he's like a young Roger Federer, he really is. Your coaching on the tennis court got me off my arse and saved my neck from being craned at horrendous angles all day every day. Perhaps more importantly, your work at strengthening my mentality has helped me stick to this path and never stay in a rut for too long. Thank you.

Shona Dawson – thank you for always being interested in, and supportive of, my writing. Thank you for the many conversations over the years, I always enjoy them. There is no one more skilled with a pair of scissors than you.

K Simkins – thank you for always supporting me, encouraging me to never give up and to always follow my dreams. Without your kindness and your desire to get the best out of me for so many years, I know for a fact I wouldn't have written this book. You're a remarkable teacher of English and somebody I count myself extremely lucky to have been taught by and to have known.

J Harris – this book wouldn't exist without you, simply put. Thank you for putting so much time and effort into your creative writing club, without that I never would've started writing. Thank you for putting up with me babbling away at you long after a school day had ended, too. You're an incredible teacher who always managed to get the best work out of me.

M Shearer – thank you for having such a great sense of humour that made harder days worth smiling through. As well as that, I owe you thanks for being such an out-the-box creative thinker. Your unique approach sticks with me to this day.

Finally, at long last, back to you. If you made it this far through my ramblings as well as the actual story part of this book, then I owe you a debt that probably can't be repaid. Thank you for being willing to take a chance on this book, I only hope that you enjoyed the journey as much as I enjoyed writing it.

I wish you all the best for the future and if you're not there yet, I hope you find your voice soon.

Read on for the first two chapters from
book two

In the Midst of Chaos

Nobility and Convention

The windswept landscape of the South-West was a vast expanse of beaten and battered terrain. Henfylt shivered. The South-West's gigantic scale was laid bare from the heights of Dansphylt. The light drizzle and harsh wind brought childhood memories back to her, nostalgia stabbing in her gut.

Few things compare to this sight. I'll bring Typh here one day, show her the beauty of the view. She'd love it. S'pose my own enjoyment of the weather here is affecting my judgement, but I reckon she'd like it, Henfylt thought, crossing her arms and sighing.

"Everything alright?" Merek asked as he sharpened his sword, each stroke timed to perfection by the hands of the seasoned veteran of war.

It was a fine sword. A simple thing with a coin-shaped pommel and a leather-wrapped grip. The blade itself was average in both length and width, but practically black in colour.

Seeing such a plain, unremarkable weapon in Merek's hands was a bit odd to say the least.

"I'm alright, just admiring the view," Henfylt replied.

Merek rose from his perch and approached her, sharing a few minutes of silence with the mercenary.

"It is beautiful."

Henfylt lowered her gaze, her thoughts falling back to those she'd lost. Beauty wasn't something she'd thought about much lately. They still haunted her, the faces of the dead and honoured. She cared for each of them, but they didn't allow her peace. Perhaps guilt kept them tied to her, but guilt from what? Henfylt hadn't caused their deaths, but she couldn't escape them.

"Are you thinking of Typhylt? Worried about her, or simply missing her?" Merek asked.

"In part. Seems foolish to feel this way, especially after what we've lost. Maybe that's what's bothering me so much," Henfylt answered.

"There's no shame in it, she's important to you and you've grown used to having her around. Praps all you need is more time to adjust. Then again, you'd probably miss her even if years were to pass. That's how it is with these things," Merek stated, sitting on his perch again as he clasped his hands together, around his knee.

His blue eyes were haunted by the same sadness that had made them closer to black since Yinfyr, when he'd cradled Aedlyn's lifeless body, peering down into her colourless eyes, his own tears dripping onto her pale face.

"You're probably right. She'll be fine anyway," Henfylt said, tearing her gaze from Merek to focus on the landscape instead. Forgetting wasn't her intention, but moving on had to be.

She's better off with them rather than me. At least they can protect her properly. She'll be learning a lot more too, at the spire.

Soft droplets of rain fell onto her hair and shoulders, trickling down the sleeves of her shirt.

"Right, I'm back with good news."

Henfylt raised her head as Yuneld appeared, brown cloak clutched tight around him, in an attempt to fend off the ruthless weather.

"We're good to go, Slyvard says we should set off for Hinsylt as soon as possible."

The Dwarf had a half-smile on his face, but the same misery that had possessed him on the day his brother was killed still darkened his green eyes.

Finally. Been stuck here with nothing to do for too long. Maybe that's been good though, it's allowed us to manage everything better, given us time to prepare for the real battle.

Henfylt looked expectantly at Merek, the Dwarf did too.

"What you both looking at me for?" he asked, his tone slightly humorous.

"I don't actually know. Ye just seem to be the de facto leader of our little trio," Yuneld answered, as he crossed his muscular arms and tilted his head to one side.

"In that case, I better give the order then. Get yourselves together, we march for Alkyn!" Merek jested.

It was the first time he'd spoken in his usual light-hearted voice since Hinsylt.

The border's interior, lined with dust, was bland and unpleasant. Where Yuneld's home had been so full of character and cosiness, Dansphylt seemed to focus entirely on function and little else. The border had no personality or beauty and it showed no desire to even try to dress itself up.

I wonder if they'll ever renovate this place. Maybe there's no need to, but they could at least get rid of the dust and give it a good clean once in a while. That wouldn't hurt, surely, Henfylt thought as she descended.

The creaking stairs wound around and around in a spiral of sorts, a cramped little spiral where the air grew stale and the scent of sweat was all that could be smelled.

"They need to ventilate this place better, bloody hell," Yuneld said, gripping his thick cloak up to his nose.

"I'm relieved this is the last time we'll have to walk down these bloody stairs," Merek stated, looking over his shoulder at Yuneld and Henfylt.

3

Dansphylt had been a disappointment. Passing through the border had almost been nostalgic, reminding her of the Guildhall. The interior of the thing, though, made her feel flat and uninspired.

Before long, the trio found their way to the first of the three gates. Each gate, thick and heavy, sat like a dormant beast. The chains at the side were so sturdy and hefty, straining and growing taut as they clinked and rolled into a tight ball around a metal cog that sat high up the walls. The weighty wood creaked and the dark metal groaned as the gate lifted from the ground.

Clouds of dust flew up since it hadn't been raised in such a while. Henfylt flapped her hand in front of her face as the dust whirled in the air. Merek sneezed and Yuneld coughed.

"Fucking dust," the Dwarf grumbled as he coughed once more and let out a houndish sneeze that rocked Dansphylt's walls.

Rynto strolled up to the mercenary's side.

"You've been allocated a reasonably sized force. The bulk of us are staying here to ensure total control of the border for the rest of the war. Slyvard hasn't given specific instructions on how you should take Hinsylt, but I believe he has enough faith in the three of you to come up with something, 'creative and unconventional', he said."

"He might live to regret that decision, but I'm not complaining," Henfylt japed, eliciting smiles from those around her.

"It's been a pleasure, Rynto, you keep this lot in check. We'll see you soon," Merek stated.

"Thank you for saying so, without you three, this would've been so much harder. We'll all miss you, but it's been an honour to work for you," the soldier replied, outstretching a hand.

"In truth, Rynto, ye haven't worked for us, we've worked together, as one," Yuneld said.

4

The Dwarf gripped her hand and shook it firmly. Merek did the same, as did Henfylt.

Rynto had fairly short, light brown hair. She was tanned, but that was hardly a surprise since she'd grown up in the North-West and had barely left the region in her thirty years of living. Most of the soldiers were tall and muscular, and whilst Rynto had a muscular frame, she stood a bit shorter than the average soldier but seemed a match for anyone in a scrap.

"Good luck," Rynto said, as she turned to leave.

Henfylt and her two friends moved through to the next gate, raising and lowering the enormous things wasn't a simple task, and it took its share of time. Each one was operated by two wheels that had to be turned in order to activate the pulley system which then lifted the heavy gates.

A century had passed before the last two gates had been raised. Finally, after the long wait, they were free to leave the safety of Dansphylt and enter the hostile territory of the South-West.

Merek turned around, so Henfylt did the same, Yuneld too. A few hundred soldiers, all covered head to toe in the finest plate armour of the North-West, stood waiting. They were like miniature statues when compared to the border's walls.

The sun, now unblocked, set line upon line of shining silver to glistening. Helmets glimmered and the blades of swords and spears sparkled as the narrow shafts of light bounced off them. A soft dinting sound rang in Henfylt's ears as droplets of rain pattered down on the expansive sea of steel.

"We march for Alkyn, remain vigilant. I'd expect there to be some kind of resistance on the way there, and at Alkyn itself, of course. But, we're more than a match for any force," Merek said, speaking in a commanding tone.

"The tactics they will employ are most likely to surround us on the road, so watch the forests and the dips because at any moment, the enemy may strike!" he shouted, with a voice so loud and clear it boomed across the land, reaching all ears and no doubt sending birds flapping out their nests in the trees.

"Anyway, enough of the silence! Talk to your friends and fellow warriors, enjoy the journey!"

With that, Merek turned once more and led the march to Alkyn.

For too long, Henfylt had watched over the lands of the South-West from the top of Dansphylt where it seemed like nothing could possibly go wrong. Yet, down on the ground, unprotected, she was at risk. They all were.

She peered out of the corner of her left eye then her right. Typhylt was nowhere to be seen. Her shoulders dropped and her limbs loosened. As she realised that she couldn't see the girl's smile or hear her laugh, a sadness hung over her.

Is it worth losing that just so I can feel less on edge? Maybe. We're at war after all. I have to be at my best and my own care for her would just get in the way. There's no room for it, not now. I need this to be done and then I can settle down. Maybe I'm just being unreasonable.

The trees creaked in the wind, but the rain eased off after a while. It had been an uneventful march until Henfylt caught a glimpse of steel, shining amidst the forest's dark shadows.

She nudged Merek and whispered, "On the right, in the forest."

He nodded and turned to Yuneld.

Henfylt couldn't make out what was being said, she only heard the Dwarf's response, "Aye, we've got a few on the left an' all."

Henfylt kept her eyes front as they marched, glancing right every now and then. More and more lined the trees. What had been a few glimmers, soon became many.

"I say we fall in the crowd and slip into the forests," Yuneld muttered.

"Agreed."

"Agreed."

Henfylt slowed, dropping back and allowing herself to be swallowed by the ranks of North-Western marchers. As they encircled her and carried on moving forwards, she alerted them to the threat, hoping the message would spread quickly.

She spied Merek to her left, and Yuneld further down. The Dwarf nodded at them both, and Henfylt went over to him.

Merek took the right bank, disappearing into the thick foliage and moss-covered ground. The mercenary shrank into the tall trees with Yuneld close by. The marching of their comrades continued, the soft clanks grew quieter and quieter as did the dying chatter.

"Right, let's go," she said to Yuneld.

They moved as shadows, silent and unnoticed. A few twigs snapped under the feet of their enemies, not far ahead of them.

A soldier was crouched in front of Henfylt, surveying in silence. She unsheathed her knife, no sound, and plunged it into the soldier's bare neck, blood running down his right side, joining the rain in its pattering onto the ground.

Yuneld leapt up at another soldier's neck, dragging them to the cold floor and twisting at the neck until the body became limp and the twitches stopped altogether.

Up ahead, a troop of twenty or so were well spread out, following the North-Westerners from the supposed safety of the trees and foliage.

A woman of medium build stood in front of Henfylt, keeping cover behind a tree. The mercenary placed a hand over the soldier's mouth, muffling any screams as she lodged the blade into her enemy's side, ripped it out and stabbed again and again until there was nothing but a corpse slumped in her arms and blood slicking the knife's grip in her hand.

Yuneld slunk off down a hill whilst Henfylt focused on her own task, stalking the Southerners through the trees and undergrowth. She wiped her hand clean of the blood, ready for whatever came next.

Two soldiers were moving their hands in strange signals. One was a dark-haired man, the other a fair-haired woman. The mercenary approached, unsheathing her longsword quietly. With her arm outstretched, she angled the blade at their bare necks, the pink and red blade thirsty for blood.

She let free one rapid slash followed by another for good measure, and the two corpses spurted blood as they toppled over like thin trees in a vengeful storm.

She moved on, sheathing her sword again. Her footsteps were unnoticeable, shielded by the intensifying rain and howling wind that ripped through the forest in a blind rage.

Yuneld reappeared up ahead, his black hair speckled with blood.

Henfylt spied eleven enemy soldiers. Whether they were scouts or a small party planning on assaulting the North-Westerners when night came mattered little. They couldn't be allowed to walk away with their lives, not today.

She continued, crouching, through the moss-covered ground. The earthy scents rushed into her nose, but there was something else in the air, too. The rich scents of metal and blood. The stench of war and chaos.

Her senses narrowed the more she focused on her next target. Yuneld vanished from her vision as did the humanity from her soul.

She forced the next soldier to the ground, smothering him and slitting his throat among the taller blades of grass. Little bursts of crimson leapt up at her face as she stared into the dimming eyes of her enemy. She let go once the light left his eyes and he stopped struggling.

As she peered down at the soldier, she realised he was just a boy. A boy so young, a life so short. Her hands were wet with the blood of this boy. The world grew dark around her. Those eyes, green eyes, stared at her, empty of a soul. Void of life.

The rustling startled her, tearing her attention from the corpse of the boy that lay in front of her to the imminent threat that approached.

Henfylt leapt up, sheathing her knife and unsheathing her sword, slashing at the enemy blindly. They parried the strike, knocking her off balance. She stumbled backwards, crouching under her attacker's next swing. Henfylt spun around, rose to her feet and met the blade of the soldier just in time, steel ringing. She pushed against her enemy with great force and strength, shoving them to the cold ground and knocking the sword from their gloved hands.

The soldier faced the point of the mercenary's weapon. Joining the fear on his face was a look of regret, the face of someone with a troubled past. His mouth twitched, opening in an attempt at calling out. All that escaped his lips was a harsh gasp for air and a cough of blood as Henfylt plunged her sword's point into the soldier's straining neck. The essence of life drained from her attacker's eyes until nothing remained.

The mercenary panted for breath, shifting her head from left to right hoping that nobody had been alerted to her presence. Of course, she wasn't so lucky. A fair few soldiers closed in around her like a pack of hungry wolves.

Yuneld cracked one of them over the head with his hammer, having leapt up in the air and screamed as he brought it down in a savage swing. The body twitched, but that was about all it could do.

Still panting for breath, Henfylt angled her sword and twisted on the spot, grabbing her knife once more. Eight soldiers remained. Four ran at her whilst the others sprinted at Yuneld.

She deflected the first blow, tearing her knife through the air and dragging it across someone's arm. She ducked and regained her balance, spinning around and delivering a fatal blow.

Three remained.

They circled her, intent on avenging their friends. All the while, she waited, baiting a foolish attack. It came and she parried it with a clang, barging into her enemy and headbutting them, sending them to the floor with a dull thud.

She used the delay to launch an assault of her own on the last two. She swung with her longsword and plunged her knife into the stomach of one of the Southerners. There was a scream. She kicked the enemy away and turned to her last opponent. An easy parry, sparks flew. With a half-turn and a jab, she knocked the wind from her foe. Henfylt hit the soldier with the hilt of her knife repeatedly until they tumbled to the floor. To finish the job, she thrust her sword into the heart of the fallen attacker, ripped it out from their chest and positioned herself, ready to meet the disoriented blow of the woman she'd sent to the floor a few moments ago. With a parry and a diagonal slash, the job was done.

Henfylt's good leg was heavy, and her bad leg felt like it was on fire. She could've done with flopping to the ground to catch her breath, but Yuneld was in danger. He'd dispatched one of his foes, but three remained and they were overwhelming him.

Henfylt lifted her sword and dashed over to the Dwarf. Once there, she cleaved through the legs of one of his opponents who screamed from the pain and impact of the blow. She then jabbed her knife into the shoulder of another soldier, who released a guttural shriek.

With that, she was finished. Yuneld brought his hammer down on his final enemy, cracking a few ribs by the sound of it and not stopping until no more breath could be drawn. The one with the knife in his shoulder tried to fight back, but the Dwarf swung for his head and the crunching resounded throughout the entire forest.

Yuneld collapsed at Henfylt's side, panting frantically. She allowed herself to rest, since no immediate threats remained.

"Bloody hell. I. I tell ye. I'd have been dead if it weren't. For you, and that speed of yours," Yuneld managed, through deep breaths, his chest rising then falling as he spoke.

"It's what friends are for," Henfylt replied in a rapid outpour of words.

She breathed deeply in and out for some time, lying amidst the blood and the grass. Strange business, really, resting in a place of chaos and death.

The wind and rain continued to assault the lands of the South-West. Trees creaked and groaned, whispered and whistled all while Henfylt lay in silence at the side of Yuneld.

Beads of sweat lined her forehead, she wiped them away in an unrushed movement. Guilt danced in her stomach, not for the other soldier's she'd slain, but for the boy. Was it guilt or shame? She remained unsure, perhaps both found a home within her.

It's war. The boy knew what could happen to him. How many people had he killed before I ended him? I'll never know, so it isn't worth losing any sleep over, right? Henfylt argued with herself.

"Looks like you two had quite the scrap," Merek interrupted her thoughts, looming above them both.

Henfylt looked up at him, hardly a speck of blood or a single show of effort clung to the wise man's body or face.

"On the other hand, ye look quite like you've done a grand total of fuck all!" Yuneld exclaimed, crawling to his feet in an inelegant motion. The Dwarf spoke in a tone thick with sarcasm.

Merek clapped Yuneld's back with a firm hand and smiled at him.

"Quite the trio we three make. Praps we ought to do this more often," he said, chuckling, before growing solemn once more.

Henfylt pushed against the ground, supporting her aching leg in getting her upright once more. She had a shallow cut just below the knee on her good side, but other than that only the stabbing pains in her bad leg bothered her.

"How many did we lose?" Henfylt asked, fiddling with the brace through her fleece-lined trousers.

"None," Merek responded, a ghostly smirk crossing his face.

"Seriously? Not a single one?" Yuneld asked.

"Not one. They were scouts, but I reckon they'd have attacked us at night with a greater force at their side," Merek answered.

"Least the plan worked, means we're doing something right," Henfylt said.

She heard the distant clanking of the North-Westerners on their march.

"Well, we'd best follow. Onto Alkyn," Yuneld stated.

"The only thing left to discuss is how we infiltrate Hinsylt and ensure we maintain it as an outpost," Merek said, looking to his left and then to his right, inviting the Dwarf and the mercenary into a discussion.

"Oh. Well, about that, I have an idea," Henfylt replied, smiling.

"Do tell," Merek replied, motioning for her to continue.

"Well, it isn't particularly noble and conventional..." she said, casting a glance at Yuneld and Merek, with her eyebrows raised.

"Fuck nobility and convention!" the Dwarf replied, to which Merek nodded and grinned.

The mercenary laughed, a wave of relief washed over her as her two friends chuckled as well.

She explained the idea that had come to her some time ago, when she overlooked the South-West of Undysvold from the very top of Dansphylt. From so far up, she'd felt capable of just about anything.

The Tarspyk Spire

The prow of the ship ripped through the dense fog. Waves lapped against the hull as the vessel tore through the open sea.

The Tarspyk Spire loomed in the distance. It reached so high into the sky, poking through the clouds that encircled it. It shone like a lighthouse as the sun's rays bounced off its tip, casting colourful lines in all directions. All Typhylt could do was look at it in both disbelief and wonder.

Even from so far away, she could admire the spire's architectural brilliance. The base of the structure forced itself into the rock it stood on, looking almost natural as it did. A few little towers shot off in different directions from the spire's main body, each capped by a red, cone-shaped roof. Being an academy of sorts, it had to instil a sense of wonder in its pupils, and it had certainly achieved that much.

For a school of magic, the building ought to have been made using some unique resources that nobody had ever heard of, Typhylt thought, but she found the simplistic nature of the material used to be a show of modesty. A much needed one in a world led by people like Queen Rancylt.

The thought of the North-Eastern Queen caused her fingers to itch and her throat to tighten. She shut those thoughts out and focused on the spire once more.

The structure, which was so tall and narrow, perplexed Typhylt. She'd grown up surrounded by short and fat houses, after all. Even Hinsylt boasted an array of crude buildings, most of which seemed wide and vastly inelegant. She'd only been there once and it hadn't inspired her at all. Though, perhaps she allowed the memories of her time there to influence her perspective of the place.

The spire, however, was exciting, as it invited her to pursue the dream she felt within herself. A dream without limitations, where anything and everything was possible.

As she stared through the thin veil of icy mist in the distance, Typhylt felt the same desire for betterment, the same desire for more, that she'd carried with her for most of her life. She recalled a passage from a book she'd read some time ago, thinking it was wise to keep its teachings close to her.

Ambition is a precious thing, a delicate thing. If you don't have it, then what is the point? To not aspire to anything other than what the norm permits? However, you must cast your ambition to one side when those around you are burned by your own selfishness. For what is ambition worth when one walks this world alone?

She took one last look at the very peak of the spire as it pierced the clouds, before abandoning the upper deck in favour of the lower decks, where she could seek out Ofryth, the boy who had lost so much.

Typhylt often worried about Ofryth. He hadn't spoken much of late, understandably so. He seemed distant and stranded, as though he was lost to grief's commanding current. She just wanted to help him, to keep him from drowning.

The wind whistled through the lower decks. Since she was wearing her black cloak, the chill didn't bother her. The thick layers of fur may have kept her from shivering, but she knew her nose, cheeks, and the tips of her ears were probably bright red.

The ship groaned and creaked. Two nights ago, there had been a storm, a terrible, violent storm with a whipping wind, flashes of lightning and deep rumbling thunder. It had rocked and battered the ship, slowing it down on its path to The Tarspyk Spire.

Typhylt adored storms, she had always loved them. Growing up in the South-West was practically impossible for someone who detested storms. They'd live in constant fear and spend many days of the week hiding under their thick blankets in the foolish hope that the loud cracks and fierce whistling would cease.

Typhylt believed that storms arrived when nature grew angry. Part of her admired the chaotic and unruly nature of them. She understood their anger, that feeling of rage as it bubbled under the surface waiting to explode. She envied nature, for it could release whatever anger it felt whenever it wanted to and nobody could do anything to change that or stop it.

It's a good thing that our actions have consequences. Without those consequences keeping us in check, we'd be no better than monsters, Typhylt thought, as she continued through the lower deck.

Before long, she came across Ofryth and Zinlot.

The Gnome had his orange flat cap on, as always. Thin wisps of his white hair peeped out from under its brim. He wore little boots which were an autumnal brown sort of colour, soft and warm in shade. Even at sea, where the roughness of the waves bothered many people, the Gnome remained perfectly still and calm.

As she approached, Ofryth's emotionless gaze drifted over her. He was a mess, brown hair all tangled and unkempt, with heavy circles under his once-bright eyes.

The Gnome welcomed her kindly, as always.

"How are you today, Typhylt?" he asked, peering over some little spectacles he had perched on the end of his round nose.

"I'm…" she looked at Ofryth, seeing the state he was in. "I'm alright, thank you," she answered.

"And you?" she asked.

"Much the same," Zinlot answered.

She moved over to Ofryth, slowly lowering herself to sit by his side.

How could she know what to say? Everything had become so complex and miserable after the events in Hinsylt and then with the arrival of Rancylt at the forge. Nothing felt right anymore. Could she ask him how he felt? No, the obvious answer was "not great".

So, she just sat there at his side in silence, reaching for the chain of her necklace, the necklace that comforted her. That was all she could do. Maybe it was enough, to just sit at her friend's side, to let him know that she cared.

Time is what he needs. Time and kindness. He knows that we care and he'll learn to manage his grief with time, though I doubt he'll ever be his old self again, but that's ok.

The weight of sorrow made her think back to Gylphur. Part of her still blamed her own stupidity and lack of action for his death even after what Henfylt and a few others had said to her regarding the matter.

Soon enough, the ship rocked to a halt. She leaned forward from the jolt, rose to her feet and offered a hand to Ofryth. He stared at the outstretched hand for a moment, something resembling mistrust darkening his eyes. Without thought, she smiled at him encouragingly. He raised a hand in a timid fashion, then gently gripped hers. Typhylt pulled him up in a soft movement, and the distrust in his eyes diminished somewhat.

It will take time. This is the first step, I think. I hope.

She instinctively released his hand once he'd gained his balance.

Shadows enveloped the lower deck, floorboards creaked under her weight. It was a sturdy vessel, but the weakest in Slyvard's fleet, the oldest too. The King had placed Typhylt and the others on it for the purpose of getting to The Tarspyk Spire safely. The chances of conflict on the open seas at such an early stage in the war seemed minimal, but he insisted on a number of his soldiers joining them on this ship that hadn't seen active battle in years. It resembled a merchant's ship, posing no threat to any Schooners that scouted the North-Eastern and Southern waters.

Typhylt found it amusing that this ship would be deemed powerless by most even though it carried a large crew of North-Western warriors on board. Boasting cannons wasn't necessary, that would only expose the vessel as one bred for battle and warfare. A quieter approach seemed logical to Typhylt, especially when gathering potential allies who could so easily join the other side.

As she strolled towards the set of stairs, scents of orange and lime rushed at her as did the smell of damp wood. Over the past week, she had grown accustomed to such smells. They were far more pleasant than the odour of sweat which hung heavily in the air around the sleeping quarters, that much was certain.

A rope stretched along the side of the tall, narrow steps. She had to lift her left leg up as high as it would go before she reached the next step, then she moved her right to join it. The power of the waves slapped at the hull, rocking the ship even though it had docked. She made sure to hold onto the rope.

Soon enough, the sea air greeted her and she breathed in for a long spell, allowing the blunt saltiness to invade her nostrils.

Before admiring the spire, she turned to help Zinlot up. The steps were too tall for the poor Gnome to climb with ease. He smiled at her in thanks as she extended a hand. His skin was smooth and soft as his hand delicately gripped hers. Once he had straightened his braces and smoothed his shirt, he looked at the spire and then at Typhylt.

"It's beautiful, isn't it?" he asked, placing his hands on his hips.

She took a moment before responding, offering a hand to Ofryth as he took one step at a time. He declined, though not unkindly.

A strange sensation formed in her stomach and her chest as she turned and stared up at the spire once more. The structure was still standing a way away from the dock's end, but she stood closer to it now and it amazed her even more.

The 'simple' light grey stones that gave The Tarspyk Spire its form were all etched with delicate details. Even from this far back, she could see the spirals and swirls, the strange shapes and symbols that adorned every inch of the building. The cone-shaped red roofs also featured multiple dangling crystals that spun and flared in the whistling wind. They danced and sparkled as the sun's rays caught them, sending colourful beams in all directions.

"It is beautiful," she answered, glancing at the smiling Gnome.

"So, this is The Tarspyk Spire. What do you think?" Jynheln inquired, once he strolled over to Typhylt, Zinlot and Ofryth.

"It's amazing," Typhylt answered.

They left the ship, first climbing down onto the wooden dock and then following it until a cobbled path took its place. The spire grew larger and larger with each step she took.

"You see, this stone was found in the ice caves by the original Tarspyks. They were a nomadic tribe all those decades ago, mainly living in the caves and moving through tunnels like the miners in the North-West. They finally realised that there were better, more civilised ways of living once this area of Undysvold became more populated."

The Tarspyk spoke with passion and interest, pointing at the large grey stones and making gestures associated with tunnelling as he did.

"Anyway, here we are. Back home," Jynheln said, a hint of sorrow tainting his words.

He grew silent as the wooden door swung open.

"Jyn! How long has it been?"

An elderly woman came storming out of the door with a stick in her left hand, tapping against the snow-ridden, cobbled floor. She had silver hair and wore robes that were striped pale blue and silver.

"Maghun, you haven't aged a day!" Jynheln exclaimed, as he outstretched his arms and embraced the elderly lady.

She laughed and then released him.

Maghun's ghostly grey eyes landed on Typhylt.

"And who is this girl?" the lady asked, turning her head from Typhylt to Jynheln in a smooth and slow motion.

"Ah, this is Typhylt. She is something of a prodigy. A keener mind for her age, you will not find," the red and black haired Tarspyk answered.

Maghun approached Typhylt, moving her stick forward in an abrupt manner. The stick released muffled sounds as it met the lightly snow-covered cobbled path.

The closer she got, the more unsettled Typhylt became. Feeling so tense was unnatural for her, yet tension gripped her for a reason she could not place.

Maghun stopped and leaned forwards. She had some wrinkles, mainly on her forehead and around the corners of her eyes. A loose strand of her silver hair flapped in the wind as her eyes narrowed.

"Intriguing. The name of a South-Westerner but the hair of a North-Easterner. Where do you come from, Typhylt?" Maghun inquired, straightening herself.

I don't know. I can't say that though. I arrive at this brilliant place of such high standards and I don't know where I come from. I never felt truly at home in Tynylt, but close enough, perhaps. I didn't feel at home in the North-East, either, not that I was there long. Where do I come from? Home was with Henfylt.

Her cheeks became unpleasantly hot as the silence stretched. She picked at the skin around her nails as her throat tightened. She itched at the back of her head, not knowing what to say. She shifted her eyes left and right, searching the air for an answer. It gave nothing of the sort.

Maghun tilted her head to one side and answered the question for Typhylt, "An orphan?"

Typhylt nodded, then lowered her head. *An orphan or unwanted, makes little difference. Maybe they are both dead.*

The elderly lady approached Typhylt, placed a gentle hand on her shoulder and smiled at her, revealing a set of slightly crooked teeth.

"My dear, there is no shame in being an orphan. Not knowing where you come from can make you the most fascinating person in any given room. Jyn will tell you the same, he didn't know his parents either. Be proud that without the luxuries of other children you still have more to show for yourself than most do."

At that moment, Typhylt realised that she had misread Maghun. She had mistaken her for a figure of authority, a commanding matriarch. Yet the opposite seemed true, for Maghun's ghost-like grey eyes were not transparent and empty, they were actually full of kindness.

"Follow me and we'll get you all settled in," she said, turning for the door.

Typhylt moved her head right and then left, taking in the sight of the tumbling flakes of snow. She breathed in, the air so fresh and pure as she looked up high at a window, seeing a purple-robed figure glaring down at her. She shivered, but not in reaction to the cold. Jynheln hung back for a moment, leaving Zinlot and Ofryth with Maghun. Typhylt ripped her eyes from the window and the cold face.

"You lost your parents?" Typhylt asked, once the others had left.

"Yes I did, but as Maghun said, there is no shame in it. Do you know why there are so many orphans throughout

Undysvold?" Jynheln asked, as he brushed his hair away from his forehead.

"So many died in the wars over the years, leaving not much behind," Typhylt answered.

Jynheln nodded. "Precisely. You are not alone," he said, smiling at her kindly.

"When did you start to... feel like you fit in properly?" she asked, her face glowing red once more as she looked back up at the same window. The purple-robed figure had vanished.

The Tarspyk placed a reassuring hand on her shoulder and looked into her eyes.

"I didn't. If I'm being honest, I still feel like an outcast. The thing to remember, Typhylt, is that none of it actually matters. Whether you fit in or not is irrelevant. What matters is this," he pointed to her head, "and this," he pointed to her heart.

"It may be a cliche, but it's true. If there is a king who fits in, feels righteous and deserving of his status, whyever that may be, but he has no head for strategy or heart for caring, then what is his purpose? What is his worth? Say the opposite is true for a queen, in this example of mine, say she has a head and a heart but seems to not fit into a position of authority, what is her worth? Far greater than that of the king, in my eyes. Status, title and all such things can define a person, but it is those people that make for the worst company and even worse leaders."

Jynheln's words settled Typhylt. The heat in her cheeks died down, disappearing altogether after a few seconds.

"Thank you, Jynheln," she said, smiling at him.

"Anytime," he replied, before leading the way to the entrance.

Before Jynheln strolled through the door, he turned to Typhylt and spoke in a quiet but clear voice. "Try to steer clear of anybody in Trynphor's Company. They usually sit huddled in a group away from the rest of us. You'll be able to tell who they are very easily. Best not roam around alone either. There aren't many of us Tarspyks, but unfortunately most of us, as you'll soon learn, make for poor conversation and even poorer friends."

"Trynphor's Company, are they a sect within the Tarspyks?" Typhylt asked.

"No, we give them a place to stay. We shouldn't, if you ask me. They're criminals, pirates. Either way, best stay out of their way. We have a… challenging relationship with them, to say the least. The council keeps them here because we occasionally rely on their skills to get information on the goings on around this world. Anyway, enough of my lecturing, let's go," Jynheln answered, with a nod.

Pirates? I didn't know there were any in Undysvold. I suppose nobody would know about them if they stay here at the spire. It's such a private place, after all. Everybody seems to agree to leave it alone for some reason. I must find out why that is. Listening to Jynheln might be the wiser choice. He knows far more than I do about these things. What would Henfylt do? She'd tell me to investigate.

The choice presented itself to her. She could either listen to the calm and wise Jynheln or do what her chaotic and curious partner in crime would.

Of course, she made a decision rather quickly, smiling to herself as she strolled through the door and allowed it to close behind her.

Made in the USA
Monee, IL
16 February 2025

12400617R00184